The world can't get enough of J.D. Robb

'Whether she writes as J.D. Robb or under
her own name, I love Nora Roberts. She is a woman
who **just doesn't know how to tell a bad story** ... an
authentic page turner, with Eve Dallas – tough
as nails and still sexy as hell ...'
Stephen King

'J.D. Robb's novels are **can't-miss pleasures**'
Harlan Coben

'Gut-searing **emotional drama**'
David Baldacci

'Anchored by **terrific characters, sudden twists** that
spin the whole narrative on a dime, and a
thrills-to-chills ratio that will raise hairs of even
the most jaded reader, the J.D. Robb books are the
epitome of **great popular fiction**'
Dennis Lehane

'This is **sheer entertainment**, a souped-up version of
Agatha Christie for the new millennium'
Guardian

'Truly fine entertainment . . . re
to leave you **hungering for more**'
Publishers Weekly

'Well written and **keeps you guessing** to the end'
Sun

'I hope Ms Roberts continues to write new
stories for this pair for a long time to come ...
Long live Eve and Roarke!'
Bella

'This is a series that gets **better and better**
as it continues'
Shots Magazine

'A **perfect balance** of suspense, futuristic police
procedure and steamy romance'
Publishers Weekly

'**Much loved**'
Daily Express

'A **fast-paced, superbly crafted story** that is an
amazing – and possibly unique – combination
of top-notch suspense, detection, and
intensely romantic sensuality'
Library Journal

'**Great fun**'
Cosmopolitan

J. D. ROBB

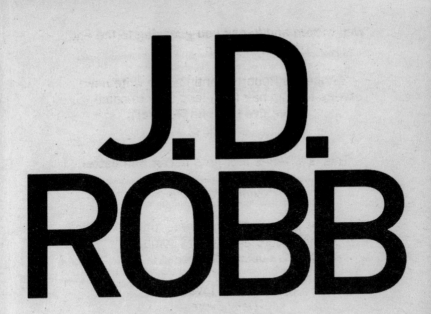

FESTIVE
IN DEATH

piatkus

PIATKUS

First published in the United States in 2014 by G.P. Putnam's Sons,
a division of Penguin Group (USA) Inc.
First published in Great Britain in 2014 by Piatkus
This paperback edition published in 2015 by Piatkus

1 3 5 7 9 10 8 6 4 2

A CIP catalogue record for this book
is available from the British Library.

ISBN 978-0-349-40370-0

Printed and bound in Great Britain by
CPI Group (UK) Ltd, Croydon, CR0 4YY

Papers used by Piatkus are from well-managed forests
and other responsible sources.

MIX
Paper from
responsible sources
FSC
www.fsc.org FSC® C104740

Piatkus
An imprint of
Little, Brown Book Group
100 Victoria Embankment
London EC4Y 0DY

An Hachette UK Company
www.hachette.co.uk

www.piatkus.co.uk

Sin has many tools, but a lie is the
handle which fits them all.

OLIVER WENDELL HOLMES

At Christmas play and make good cheer,
For Christmas comes but once a year.

THOMAS TUSSER

1

Men, Sima thought, can't live with them, can't beat them to death with a nine iron.

But a girl could exact some revenge, and she was a girl bent on just that.

Nobody deserved a good dose of revenge – or a beating with a nine iron as much as Trey Ziegler. The fuckball had booted her out of the apartment they'd shared, even though she had the same territorial rights to the place as he did.

In the seven and a half weeks of their unofficial cohabitation, she'd paid half the rent, half the expenses, including food and beverage. She'd done *all* the cleaning (lazy bastard), all the marketing. And in that seven and a half weeks had given him the best years of her life.

Plus sex.

After considerable thought, in-depth conversations with close friends and confidants, two ten-minute sessions of meditation and six tequila shots, she'd outlined precisely how, where, and when to exact her revenge.

The *how* involved that nine iron, an extensive collection

of cashmere socks, and itching powder. The *where* was that one-bedroom apartment over Little Mike's Tattoo and Piercing Parlor in the West Village.

The *when* was right fucking now.

He wouldn't have changed the locks – cheap bastard – and didn't know she'd given a copy of her swipe to one of those friends and confidants, who also happened to be her boss, right after they'd moved in together.

And if he had changed the lock, her friend said she knew people who knew people, would tag one up, and it would be done.

Sima wasn't sure she wanted to know the people who knew people or how they would gain access to the apartment. But she knew she wanted in.

So with her friend beside her for moral support, she pulled out her swipe key to open the main door to the apartments over the tat parlor.

Her tequila-fueled grin spread wider when the locks clicked open.

'I *knew* it! He'd never bother springing for the money to have me deactivated.'

'Maybe not on *this* door. We still have to see about the apartment.' Her friend gave her a long, hard look. 'You're abso-poso he's not in there?'

'Totally. His supervisor sprang for the weekend seminar, been in the works for weeks. No way he'd blow it off. Free hotel room, free food, and a chance to show off for two days.'

Sima turned toward the skinny elevator, started to take off her gloves.

'We'll walk up. Leave your gloves on, remember? No fingerprints.'

'Right, right. It's my first break-in.' With a nervous giggle Sima started up the stairs.

'It's not a break-in. You have a key, *and* you paid the rent.'

'Half.'

'*He* said it was half. Did you ever check for sure how much the rent was?'

'Well, no, but—'

'Sima, you've got to stop letting yourself get pushed around. What you were paying for the squeeze box up here probably covered the whole cha-cha.'

'I know. I know.'

'You're going to feel a lot better after you cut out the toes in his socks. Remember the plan – one sock from each pair, a little nip so it starts to unravel. You start on that while I put the itching powder in his moisturizer. Then we replace the golf club with the toy one, and we book. We don't touch anything else. In and out.'

'And he won't know what the hell. He's not going to golf until he gets somebody to pay the indoor fee, so that can't come back on me. The socks will make him crazy.'

'He'll figure it happened at the dry cleaners. He deserves it. A guy who has his socks dry-cleaned deserves it.'

'Yeah. And the itching powder? He'll go screaming to the doctor, figuring he's got a new allergy. Fuckball.'

'Fuckball,' her friend agreed, righteously, as they finally reached the fourth floor. 'Moment of truth, Sima.'

On a long breath, Sima steadied herself. Climbing three flights, dressed in her winter coat, scarf, boots, hat – December 2060 was as bitter as her heart – she had worked up a little sweat.

She pulled out the key again, crossed the fingers of her free hand, swiped.

Locks thumped open.

Sima gave a triumphant hoot, and was immediately shushed.

'You want the neighbors poking out?'

'No, but—' Before she could finish, Sima found herself pushed inside with the door quietly, firmly closed behind her.

'Turn on the lights, Sim.'

'Right.' She hit the switch, then hissed, 'Look at this mess! I haven't been gone a week, and he's already got crap tossed everywhere. Look in there!' She walked toward the kitchen bump as she pointed. 'Dirty dishes, takeout boxes. I bet there're bugs. Ew, I bet there're bugs in here.'

'What do you care? You don't live here, so you don't have to pick up his mess or worry about bugs.'

'But still. And look at the living room. Clothes tossed all over, shoes just – Hey!' She marched over, picked up a scarlet-red high heel, then scooped up a bra with yellow polka dots over purple lace.

4

'I never noticed any trany tendencies.'

'Because he doesn't have any!'

'I know, Sim. It's like we all told you. He only booted you because he sniffed up a new skirt. And jeez, it's been like a week since he did the booting, so you have to figure . . . Don't blubber,' she ordered as Sima started to do just that. 'Get even! Come on.'

Focused on the task at hand, she pulled the shoe, the bra away, tossed them down again, took Sima's arm. 'I'll get you started on the socks.'

'I sort of loved him.'

'Sort of is sort of. He treated you like crap, so you pay him back, then you can move on. Trust me.'

Sima's tears-and-tequila-blurred eyes tracked back to the bra. 'I want to bust something up.'

'You're not going to. You're going to be smart and hit him where it hurts. Vanity and wallet, then we're going to go do some more shots.'

'Lots of them.'

'Bunches of lots of them.'

Sima squared her shoulders and nodded. With her hand in her friend's – moral support – they started toward the bedroom she'd shared for seven and a half weeks with her cheap, cheating, callous boyfriend.

'He didn't even put up any Christmas decorations. He has a cold heart.'

She couldn't have been more right.

Trey Ziegler sat propped on the bed, the long chestnut-

and-gold-streaked hair he was so proud of matted with blood. His eyes — most recently tinted emerald green — staring.

The kitchen knife jammed in his cold heart pinned a cardboard sign to his well-toned chest. It read:

Santa Says You've Been Bad!!!
Ho. Ho. Ho!

As Sima peeled off screams, her friend slapped a hand over her mouth, dragged her away.

'Trey! Trey!'

'Shut it down, Sima. Just shut it down a minute. Jesus, what a mess.'

'He's dead. There's blood. He's dead.'

'I got that. Holy shit.'

'Whattawedo? Oh God! Whattawedo?'

Running away would be awesome but . . . Even buildings as lousy as this probably have some security. Or somebody might have seen them come in. Or heard them work out the plan over tequila shots. Or something.

'You've got to calm down some — and don't touch anything. Not anything. I've got to tag up somebody.'

'You're going to have somebody come get rid of the body?' Sima dragged her fingers down her throat as if she were being strangled. 'Oh my God!'

'Grip reality, Sima. I'm tagging a cop.'

*

Two in the morning, two in the freaking morning in the frozen bowels of December, and she had to roll out of a warm bed beside a hot husband and deal with what might be a dead body – or a drunken prank by a woman who drove her crazy on the best of days.

In moments like this, being a cop sucked.

But Lieutenant Eve Dallas was a cop, so she pulled up in front of the dingy box of a building in the West Village, grabbed her field kit – if there was an actual DB, it would save her coming back out for it – and stomped across the icy sidewalk.

She'd have used her master to swipe in, but the door clicked and buzzed as she reached for it.

She didn't much like the look of the elevator in the skinny, smelly lobby, but opted for it. The sooner to get this over.

She jammed her cold hands – she hadn't thought of gloves – in the pockets of her long leather coat and scowled with golden brown eyes at the numbers creeping from one to two to three, and finally to four on the dented panel.

When the doors opened, she strode out, a tall, lean, pretty pissed-off woman with a shaggy cap of hair nearly the same color as her eyes.

Before she could bang a fist on the door, it opened. There stood the woman who cut her hair – often whether Eve wanted the service or not. Who'd seen her naked – and that Eve *never* wanted.

'If you're fucking with me, I'm hauling your ass in for filing a false report.'

'Hand to God.' Trina shot up a hand – fingers tipped in swirls of holiday red and green – then used the other to yank Eve inside. 'His name's Trey Ziegler, and he's really dead in the bedroom.'

'Who's that?' Eve demanded, jerking a head toward the woman with an explosion of red curls smashed under a black watch cap who was currently holding some sort of red-and-blue plastic golf club and blubbering.

'That's Sima. His ex. She lived here.'

'You live here?' Eve asked Sima.

'Yes. No. I did, but he – then he … He's … he's … he's …'

When Sima dissolved, Eve turned back to Trina. 'Stay here, don't touch anything. Don't let her touch anything.'

She took the short five steps to the bedroom door, looked in.

Okay, that was a dead man.

She set down her field kit to pull out her 'link. She called it in, arranged for her partner to be notified.

'You.' She pointed at Sima. 'Sit over there. Don't touch anything.' Then she gestured Trina over to the kitchen bump. 'If she doesn't live here, how did you get in?'

'She still has her swipe. Or the copy she made for me when she hooked into the place with him. He only kicked her out a week ago.'

'Why did the two of you come here – and you're both lit. I can see it, hear it, smell it.'

'About half lit,' Trina corrected with the faintest smirk. Eve's flat, narrow gaze had her shifting side to side, giving her tower of hair – swirled in the same color and pattern as her nails – a little toss.

'Okay, look, full disclosure, right? Trey dumped her. She came home from work and he'd packed her stuff, said they were done and to get out.'

'They had a fight.'

'Hell no. She's got the spine of a worm – can't help it – so even though she's been paying the rent, he said half but I know what this dump should go for and it was plenty more than half. *And* she paid for December, so she paid *this* month's rent, and she has rights. Right?'

'Just keep going,' Eve ordered.

'Okay. So she just starts crying, takes her stuff and goes. Anyhow, she got a flop for about a week, doesn't tell me or any of us 'cause she said she was all embarrassed, then finally spills it. I have her at my place, on the pullout until she can get it together.'

'And?'

'And?'

'Let us wind around to tonight and the dead man.'

'Right. Well, tonight, a bunch of us were hanging after work, and there was tequila. And we got this idea about payback. He's supposed to be in Atlantic City for a couple days, so we bought the toy golf club and some itching powder. We were going to unravel the toes of his socks, put the powder in his face cream, replace one of his clubs with the toy, then book. That's it. We came in, headed back there, saw him. I pulled her out, tagged you.'

'Itching powder?'

'Serious shit.' Trina nodded wisely. 'He'd've wanted to scratch his face down to the bone. He deserved it. Look at her.'

Sima sat, head bowed, tears dripping.

'Jesus Christ. Did you know this guy?'

'Yeah, some. Massage therapist, personal trainer. He worked at Buff Bodies, the fitness place near my salon. Most of the staff there use my salon. Sima works for me. That's how they met.'

'Did you ever roll with him?'

'Shit no.' Trina's eyes – a bold Christmas green lidded with gold glitter – reflected both insult and disgust. 'Guy was a prick and a player. I can do better. Sim didn't think she could. Self-esteem issues, you know?'

'Whose red shoes, whose underwear?'

'No clue. Not Sim's.'

'Stay here.'

'Hey, Dallas, go easy on her. She's a real sweetie, and I talked her into this. I thought giving him a punch would make her feel, you know, empowered. Otherwise, somebody else would've found him, and she wouldn't have that in her head.'

'For all I know the two of you did him, and pulled me in to cover it up.'

10

Trina snorted out a laugh, sobered instantly at Eve's stony stare. 'Shit. Really? Come on!'

'Stay here.'

She walked back over to where Sima sat quietly hiccuping through tears.

'Tell me what happened.'

'Trey's dead. Somebody killed him.'

'Before that. How did you and Trina end up here?'

'Oh, well, after work we – me and Trina and Carlos and Vivi and Ace – we all went to Clooney's.'

'Clooney's?'

'It's a bar. We hang there sometimes. Their twisted onions are pretty good, so we got some and some cheesy bits and some margaritas. Then we did some shots because I was feeling bad about Trey dumping me. So Ace said – I think it was Ace, or maybe Vivi, how I should get some of my own back, then somebody said I should come over and toss his stuff out the window, but Trina said no. She said that was too obvious, and I could get in trouble. I should do something more subtle-like. Then we went and bought the trick club and the powder, and we came here, and – and – *Trey!*'

'Okay.' Eve held up a hand, hoping to ward off hysterics, then quickly wound Sima back, pulling out details.

Details, she thought, that lined up with Trina's statement.

'Did he ever knock you around, Sima?'

'What? Who? Trey?' Her tear-drenched eyes, outlined in

shimmering blue and silver, widened to horrified saucers. 'No! He'd never do that.'

'Not physically,' Trina said from across the room, and earned another stony stare. 'I'm just saying. He didn't tune her up, but he picked at her self-esteem. He knocked that around plenty. He wasn't good to you, Sim.'

'Sometimes he was. He used to be.'

'Did he cheat on you?' Eve asked her.

'I didn't think so, but . . . ' She pointed to the shoe and bra. 'Those aren't mine.'

'Was he in trouble with anybody? Women, work, illegals, gambling?'

'No . . . I don't think. He, I guess, was sort of distant lately, and spending more time at work or on his computer working on routines for clients and stuff. I asked him if something was up at work, since he was there late a lot, but he said no. And how I should mind my own business.'

'He was up to something.' When the comment got Trina another stare she tossed her hands in the air. 'I can hear you over here, and it's stupid to pretend I can't. He was up to something.'

'Such as?'

'I don't know such as, I just know something. A lot of my people – staff, clients – use BB, and some of them use Trey for personal training, or for massages. Word was going around he was acting weird – more than usual – the past couple months maybe. Put a second lock on his locker at the gym, spent a lot of after-hours time there when he

12

didn't have a client. A couple mutual clients told me he was talking about opening his own place, like a high-class spa deal, maybe on St Bart's or Nevis or some shit.'

'You never told me!'

Trina shrugged at Sima. 'I was going to, but then he dumped you. I didn't see the point since it was only the rumor chamber. And I figured if we did the deed here tonight, maybe we'd see something lying around. Like confirmation.'

'Did he have any valuables?' Eve asked Sima. 'Anything worth stealing?'

'Oh . . .'

'I see a mini-comp there – pretty high end, the entertainment screen, good-sized but portable. How about jewelry, art, cash?'

'He has a really good wrist unit for work – a sports model – and a really nice dress one. And, um, his collection of ear hoops, and a couple rings. One yellow gold, one white gold. He never wore them when he was working because they got in the way. He's got the golf clubs, and like golf accessories. He didn't keep any money around that I know of. We didn't really have any art, except a couple photographs he had taken and framed.'

She gestured to the photographs – of the dead guy in sports skinwear, posing to show off his biceps, his delts. They flanked a shelf that held several trophies topped with a figure dressed the same, doing the same.

'Hold on.' Eve turned to open the door at the knock,

then stepped out – leaving the door open – to instruct the two uniforms who'd reported to the scene.

'Okay, I need some information,' she said when she stepped back in, closing the door. 'The name of his employer or immediate supervisor, a list of friends and/or coworkers. Did he have a live-in or serious relationship prior to you, Sima?'

'Oh, well, I guess. Sure.'

'He bounced around on Alla Coburn right before Sim,' Trina said helpfully. 'Mutual client. She owns Natural Way, a health-food place near BB. And FYI, she was pretty ripped about their breakup. Put on the good-riddance face, but she didn't mean it. I know what's what with people who sit in my chair. Plus he banged a lot of his clients.'

'He stopped that when we got together,' Sim said, blinking at Trina's look of frustrated sympathy. 'He didn't? But – but he said . . .'

'We'll talk. Anyway, his supervisor's Lill Byers, and she'll talk to you straight. You'd do better with coworkers. He didn't hang with anybody for long outside of work.'

Sensing there was more, Eve only nodded as she noted down the names. 'An officer's going to drive you home.'

'We can just go?' Sima asked.

'Stay available. You're at Trina's for now?'

'Well, I—'

'She's with me until this all shakes out. You're with me, Sim, don't worry about it.'

That started fresh waterworks, so Eve opened the door.

14

'Go down with Officer Cho,' she told Sima. 'Trina will be right down.'

Once Eve got Sima out, she turned to Trina. 'Spill.'

'Okay, I wanted to be careful around her. He was an asshole. I'm sorry he's dead and all that, but that's mostly for her. Look, he'd barely rolled off Alla before he rolled onto Sima. Guy was a player, and a user. Some of the stuff in here? It's hers, but she didn't think of saying hey, my stuff. She did all the work around here, you know what I'm saying? Picking up after him, stocking the AutoChef, seeing about the laundry and the dry cleaning. Fucker dry-cleaned his freaking socks.'

'Get out.'

'Hand to God! You're going to find a lot of slick clothes in his closet, lots of top-drawer face, hair, body products. Asshole was a peacock. He looked good, I'll give him that, but he swept women up, then swept them out after he got what he was after – and not just sex.'

'What else?'

'You can bet he didn't buy those wrist units for himself, or half that slick wardrobe. He scouted out rich, older women. Clients, like I said. Or that's the word. Probably one of them jammed that knife in his heart, but it wasn't Sim. She didn't kill him.'

'I know that.'

'She couldn't – oh. Well, solid.'

'Do you know who belongs to the shoes and the polka dots?'

'No, but I could maybe find out.'

'Leave that to me. Go home. And next time you do a bunch of shots, go home.'

Emboldened, Trina ticked off points on her festively tipped nails. 'She paid the rent. She had a key. Some of her stuff's still here. She's got a right to come in.'

'Got that. But the itching powder could be considered assault, the socks destruction of property and the golf club theft. It's inventive payback, but it's not worth the legal fees.'

Trina shrugged it off. 'Anyway, thanks for handling it.' Trina narrowed her eyes, got the look in them that chilled Eve's blood. 'You could use a little shaping on the do, and a hydrating facial. Winter's a bitch on skin.'

'Push it, Trina, and I'll have you taken into Central, put in the box and make you go through all this again.'

'Just saying what I know. We'll give you the works before your big bash.' She stepped to the door, paused. 'Sim's a little naive and way trusting. Some people never get over that, even when they end up covered with bruises.'

True enough, Eve thought.

Eve walked back toward the bedroom, picked up her field kit. She'd gotten over any naivete and excessive trust long, long ago, she decided as she pulled out a can of Seal-It to coat her hands, her boots.

A cop did better cynical and suspicious. Considering herself armed with healthy portions of both, she went in to deal with death.

She took a slow scan to allow her lapel recorder to document the scene, including the blood spatter on the wall, the smears of it on the floor. And the gore clinging to the base of what appeared to be another trophy.

An open suitcase holding precisely folded clothes sat on the foot of the bed, opposite side from the body.

'It appears the vic was packing – nearly done with it – for a scheduled trip. Wits state a work-related seminar in Atlantic City. A lot of clothes for a couple days,' she commented. 'Which would coincide with wits' opinion of vic as a peacock. Nice threads, top line,' she said after a quick look. 'Also verifying wits' statements.'

She poked in a little more, came up with a small baggie filled with dried leaves.

'What have we here? It looks like . . . tea leaves.' She opened it, sniffed – and had a flash of the flowery tea Mira, the department shrink, swore by. 'Smells like tea. Doesn't look like any illegal substance I've come across. Bagging for analysis. Not a priority as we're not going to bust the dead guy for possession.'

She crossed back, crouched to examine the large trophy with the figure of a seriously ripped male, clad only in compression shorts, flexing both biceps. 'A couple trophies like this in the living room. The blood and gray matter on this one – Personal Trainer of the Year, 2059 – indicates it was used to strike the victim on the left side of the head.'

She lifted it, pursed her lips. 'Yeah, it's got some weight to it. A couple good whacks would do the trick.'

17

Setting it down again, she rose, walked back in the living room, lifted the other trophies.

Twin circles of clean under them. Dust skimmed the rest of the shelf.

'The murder weapon wasn't here with these two.' She walked back into the bedroom, found a similar circle on the dresser.

'The murder weapon sat right here. The killer and vic are in the vic's bedroom. No overt signs of break-in, so it's probable the vic knew his killer. No signs of a struggle – none from a vic who wins personal trainer trophies, so it doesn't look like a physical fight. No scuffle, but maybe an argument. The killer picks up the trophy, and bashes.

'But doesn't leave the body where it falls, and that's interesting. The killer drags the body to the bed – leaves some blood smears on the way, hefts it on there, props it up. Takes the time – and has the rage or coldness – to get the knife, write the message, and stab what I'm betting was a dead man in the chest just to ice the cookie.'

She took her Identi-pad, her gauges, out of her kit, rose to walk over to the body.

Victim is identified as Trey Arthur Ziegler, mixed race male, age thirty-one. Resided this apartment. Single. No marriages, no legal cohabs, no offspring on record.

She heard the door open, paused until she heard the clomp of her partner's boots.

18

'Back here,' Eve called out. 'Seal up.'

Detective Peabody came to the bedroom door. Pink cowboy boots, big puffy coat, a couple miles of rainbow-striped scarf and a bright blue hat with earflaps.

She looked, Eve thought, like an Eskimo running away to the circus.

'I saw Trina downstairs,' Peabody began, then looked at the body on the bed. 'Wow, ho, ho, humbug.'

'Yeah, he won't be going home for Christmas.'

'I got from Trina this was her pal's ex-boyfriend.'

'Who they found when they snuck in to put itching powder in his face gunk.'

'Fun.' Peabody pulled the cap off her dark hair, stuffed it in her pocket. 'You don't think Trina had anything to do with the dead guy.'

'I wish I did, then I could toss her in a cage.'

'Aw.' Peabody began unwinding her scarf.

'But according to my on-site,' Eve continued, removing the gauges, 'it looks like he bought it about eighteen-thirty hours. We'll check Trina and Sima's alibi, but it's going to hold up. Besides, Trina's too cagey to kill somebody this way, and the friend doesn't have the balls.'

Eve replaced her gauges, pulled out microgoggles. 'Check and see if there are any security cams, then go ahead and call in the ME and the sweepers. Let's get the uniforms started on a canvass of the building. Maybe somebody heard or saw something.'

'Oh boy, a bunch of pissed-off neighbors.'

'Not once they find out there's been a murder. People love finding out somebody's dead and they're not. Get that going, then we'll go through the place when I'm done with the body.'

Eve fit on the goggles, leaned over to peer at the shattered side of the skull. 'So, Trey,' she murmured, 'what have you got to tell me?'

2

Death killed any illusion of privacy. After she'd examined the body, Eve began a systematic search of the bedroom.

As Trina stated, Trey owned an extensive wardrobe. Slick, sexy workout gear, spiffy suits, stylish club wear.

'He coordinated his socks and underwear,' she commented when Peabody came back in. 'Colors and patterns. Who does that, and why?'

'I read this article about how what you wear under your clothes is all about what makes you feel empowered and in control. It's the Under You.'

'If wearing matching boxers and socks makes you feel empowered, you're a weenie. He's got standard over-the-counter male birth control, a few unimaginative sex toys, some porn discs in the bedside goodies drawer. Golf clubs, various golf paraphernalia in the closet with his clothes. No female clothes in here.'

'Did you check this?' Peabody held up a 'link sealed in an evidence bag.

'Yeah, some client checks, a couple guy conversations,

some out-goings to women, not yet answered. Nobody threatening to kill him.'

'There's a knife block in the kitchen with one missing,' Peabody said. 'The one sticking out of him looks like part of the set.'

'Bash with the trophy, it's handy. Then get a little creative with the kitchen knife, again handy.' Eve put her hands on her hips, then walked out to the living area.

She scanned the room – messy, sloppy, but nothing that indicated a fight. 'Okay, considering there's no sign of break-in, no sign of struggle out here, the vic let the killer in. He knows him – or her. He's wearing drawstring pants and a T-shirt – at-home clothes, so he's comfortable with the killer, enough that they went back to the bedroom together.'

'Maybe he was forced into the bedroom. Maybe the killer had a sticker.'

'If the killer had a sticker,' Eve argued, 'why bash the vic in the head with a trophy? Plus, the vic's extremely buff, so I've got to figure he'd put up a fight. But the vic was taken by surprise. They go back in the bedroom. For sex? The bed's messed up, so maybe there was sex.'

'Red-shoes lady?'

'Possibly.'

Eve studied the shoes, the bra, all out in plain sight.

'But if you have the cold blood to haul a dead guy onto the bed, go into the kitchen, rip off the top of a take-out pizza box, write up the message, take the knife, go *back* in the bedroom, stab the dead guy, wouldn't you have the brains to grab your shoes and underwear?

'You've got enough brains and cold blood to take the marker used to write the message – because I haven't found one on scene – to wipe off the knife handle and the trophy base so you don't leave prints, but you leave your polka-dot bra and red shoes?'

'Yeah, it'd be a pretty big oops.'

'Still . . . Maybe there's sex, or the start of it – he's fully dressed, so either they did and he put his clothes back on, or he never got them off. Either way, before, during, after, whoever came back here with him grabbed the trophy, swung. Vic goes down, but you bash again because we've got one wound on the side of the head, one on the back of the head. You don't panic, you don't keep bashing, so there's some control. But you've got a need to – ha ha – twist the knife, so you dig up some cardboard, write the note. You've got to haul him onto the bed, prop him up, then jam the knife, with note, into his chest.'

'That part's just mean. Yeah, murder's the ultimate mean,' Peabody said when Eve glanced at her. 'But the knife and note's salt in the wound. Seriously.'

'It's steel in the chest. He really pissed you off,' Eve continued. 'But you paid him back. There's satisfaction here. Quick violence – probable impulse – followed by a cold-blooded flourish.'

'Well, just for the sake of argument, say it's Red Shoes.'

Trying to visualize an alternate scenario, Peabody circled said shoes.

'Things get hot, they're moving along into the bedroom. She changes her mind, he gets pushy – bash. Or they do the deed, then he acts like a jerk. Says something about her weight, her technique, or whatever. Bash. She holds it together long enough to set him up like this – it's all fury and adrenaline. *Then* she panics, and runs.'

'Possible.' She'd put away people who'd done stupider, Eve considered. 'Let's have his comp taken in, go through it. And let's find Red Shoes.'

'They're really nice shoes. I wonder what size they are.'

'Jesus, Peabody.'

'Just wondering,' she said and hurried to the door to let in the sweepers – and avoid Eve's wrath.

By dawn, Ziegler lay on a slab at the morgue, the sweepers swarmed over his apartment, and the initial canvass of the building netted a not-unexpected 'nobody saw nothing.'

'I vote the classic crime of passion.' Peabody, once again wrapped up like a woman facing the Ice Age, walked out of the building with Eve. 'Jewelry, cash, credits, plastic, electronics, fancy sports equipment still on premises, no sign of break-in, obvious signs of hanky-panky.'

'How does hanky-panky translate to sex? Who comes up with words like that?'

'Probably people who don't have sex, which doesn't

include the dead guy. The lab should be able to give us the DNA on whoever he hanky-pankied with when the sweepers get the sheets in.

'I wish it would snow.'

'If the state of his apartment, and Trina's statement about him banging anything not already nailed are indicators, they'll probably find multiple DNA – What?' Her brain caught up with Peabody's last statement. 'Snow?'

'If it's going to be this cold, it should snow.' Peabody jumped into Eve's car, shivered. 'It's almost Christmas so we should have snow anyway. Snow's pretty.'

'Then we could creep behind the plows that shove it against the curbs where it turns to black sludge, wind our way through all the vehicles that spun out because people don't know how the hell to drive in the snow, or step over all the pedestrians who slip on the snowy sidewalks.'

'You need a good dose of holiday spirit.' Peabody wriggled down into her seat, grateful and happy with the automatic seat warmers. She thought, at that moment, a warm ass was a happy one. 'We should get some hot chocolate.'

Eve didn't spare Peabody a glance. 'We're going to the gym.'

'If we got hot chocolate first, we could work it off at the gym.' Peabody tried a winsome smile, gave it up with a shrug. 'I'll run the supervisor.'

'What a fine idea.'

Eve navigated the streets, still quiet in the weak winter dawn. Streetlights fizzed off, leaving the air cold and gray with puffs of steam rising intermittently through the subway vents. She passed one half-empty maxibus where the passengers all looked dazed and palely green in its flickering security lights.

Even at the early hour, she had to wrangle a parking spot in a loading zone, half a block from Buff Bodies.

She flipped on her On Duty light.

'Lill Byers,' Peabody began as they got out into the frigid swirl of wind. 'Age thirty-eight, divorced, one offspring, male, age seven. Employed with Buff Bodies for twelve years, currently as manager. Little bump here – arrested for destruction of property, disturbing the peace, six years back. She took a tire iron to her ex-husband's vehicle. I guess it wasn't an amicable divorce.'

'There's no such thing as an amicable divorce.'

The lights of the gym shone bright against the wide front windows. The glass rose high, to expose three spacious floors. Through the first level Eve saw several bodies – appropriately buff – running, lunging, lifting, climbing.

While the maxibus passengers had looked stunned and weary, the dawn workout brigade appeared terrifyingly alert.

'I hate them all,' Peabody muttered. 'Every one of them. Just look. All perfectly packed in frosty outfits designed to show off every cut, rip, and ripple. Smug looks on their faces, a sheen of sweat on their skin. And zero percent body fat among the whole buff bunch. How am I supposed to enjoy my frothy hot chocolate now?'

'You don't have a frothy hot chocolate.'

'In my mind I did. Now even its imaginary frothy goodness is spoiled.'

'Buck up,' Eve suggested, swiped her master over the members' entrance pad, and walked inside.

Straight into a wall of noise.

Screaming, pounding, throbbing music blasted out of the speakers and banged against her eardrums. She saw a woman on a cycle crouched over, face fierce as she sang along, presumably at the top of her lungs.

Her eyes looked just a little insane.

Machines whooshed and whirled, feet slapped on treads, weights clinked and thumped. The open three-story space boasted a juice bar – currently unoccupied – on the second level, and what looked to be classrooms, glassed in, on the third.

She could see more buff bodies performing graceful yoga sun salutations behind the glass of one of the rooms.

'Must have amazing soundproofing,' Eve decided.

The check-in desk – a semicircle of glossy white – was currently unmanned, but Eve spotted a woman in snug shorts and an equally snug tee sporting the gym's double B logo whipping a client through a series of punishing squats and lunges on a teeterboard while he curled twenty-pound free weights.

'Come on, Zeke! Quads of steel! Get low. Push off. *Squeeze!*'

'Excuse me,' Eve began.

'One sec. Dig for it, Zeke. Five more!'

'I hate you, Flora.'

She absolutely beamed at him. 'That's the spirit, that's what I want to hear. Four more.'

'Lill Byers?' Eve said.

'Should be here, should be in her office. Don't you quit on me, Zeke. Don't you quit. Three. Squeeze it, pump it, form, form, form. Two more. Just past check-in,' she added for Eve. 'You got it, you got it, last one. Finish strong.'

Eve heard the guy collapse, gasping, when Flora whistled her approval on the last set.

'Thirty-second water break,' Flora announced as Eve headed toward the office. 'Then it's time for crunches.'

'You're a monster, Flora.'

'That's what you love about me.'

'Maybe I should get a personal trainer,' Peabody speculated. 'If I had someone like that hammering at me, I'd have a perfect heart-shaped, drum-tight ass in no time.'

'You'd blast her with your stunner before the end of the first session.'

'Other than that.'

Through the narrow glass of the office door Eve saw a woman with a skullcap of orange hair and a body honed scalpel sharp sitting at a comp with two screens running.

One showed the CGI image of a woman carrying maybe twenty-five to thirty extra pounds struggling through a session of core work – crunches, leg lifts, crisscross – while the other ran a spreadsheet of names and figures in various columns.

Eve knocked briskly.

The woman tweaked one screen so the figure pushed through some single leg stretches.

Rather than bang on the glass again, Eve pushed in, said, 'Hey!'

'Let's add five full roll-ups,' the woman said, and the figure on the screen moaned and began them.

Eve tapped the woman on the shoulder. She squealed and jumped as if she'd been scalded, spun around to goggle, then to laugh. And finally removed earplugs.

'Sorry, so sorry, I didn't hear you come in. The first shift wants the music up to scream, so I use these. What can I do for you?'

'Lill Byers?'

'That's right. I'm the manager.'

Eve pulled out her badge. 'Lieutenant Dallas, Detective Peabody. Is there somewhere we can talk?'

The healthy color in Lill's face dropped to gray. 'My kid. Is my kid okay? Is Evan okay?'

'It's nothing to do with your son. It's one of your employees.'

'Oh Jesus.' She ran a hand over her bright cap of hair. 'Sorry. My kid's with his father for a few days – a pre-Christmas deal as the asshole's going to Belize with his current slut over the actual holiday, so too bad for his son.

29

Anyway.' She let out a long breath. 'Something's up with one of my gang?'

'Is there somewhere quieter we can talk?' Eve asked.

'Sure. Relaxation room, this way.' She led the way out of the office, across the workout area, passed a mini self-serve juice bar, up the curl of steps to the second level and into a room with soft gray walls, two long benches and a half dozen padded sleep chairs.

The door closed, brought silence.

'We offer clients a meditative space to balance things. Yin and yang. Somebody's in trouble?'

'Trey Ziegler.'

'Crap.' Lill dropped onto a bench, gestured for Eve and Peabody to have a seat. 'He swore he'd behave in AC. Do I have to post bond?'

'He never got to AC. I regret to inform you Trey Ziegler's dead.'

'Dead?' She didn't go gray again, but stiffened, toe to crown. 'What do you mean dead? Like *dead*?'

'Exactly like dead.'

'Oh my God.' She shoved up, holding her hands on either side of her head as she walked up and down the room. 'Oh my God. Was there an accident?'

'No. We're Homicide.'

'You're . . . ' Lill stopped, dropped down again. 'Homicide. Murder? Somebody killed him? How? When?'

'He was killed yesterday evening. When did you last see or speak with him?'

'Yesterday. About two – no, closer to one. I let him go early so he could finish getting his shit together and get to AC in time for the mixer, get familiar with the facilities. I sent Gwen, too. Is Gwen okay?'

'Gwen?'

'Gwen Rollins, one of our instructors.'

'Were they traveling together?'

'No, no.' She paused, nearly did an eye roll before she caught herself. 'No.'

'Didn't get along?'

'Didn't *not* get along. Jesus, what happened to Trey?'

'That's what we're going to find out. Did anyone have a problem with him?'

'Not a murder problem. Give me a sec, okay?'

She sat there, pressed her fingers to her eyes, took long slow breaths. 'He's somebody I worked with, saw every workday, and sometimes off days if he came in. You get to be part of each other's lives, you know, in a way. We weren't tight outside the work, but he was part of my life. Now he's dead.'

She lowered her hands, met Eve's gaze directly. 'He's – was – a good trainer. He tapped into the client really well, knew how to motivate. Better at the one-on-one than group – he couldn't spread his attention out to a group very well, so I didn't use him as a Group-X instructor unless I was squeezed. Damn good massage therapist. I used him a few times myself for that.'

She pushed her hands through her hair again, huffed out a breath. 'And he was kind of an asshole.'

31

'Which kind?'

'With women. He was a user. Didn't see any problem juggling them. Liked the attention, and he bragged about his sex life. I had to tell him to chill there more than once.'

'Did he hit on clients?'

'Sure, and vice versa. But he was careful there, I mean careful not to screw it up. Lose a client, lose money, and he liked money as much as sex. So he'd keep it light with the clients if it went in that direction. He'd been living with somebody for a few weeks, but that broke off. Sima Murtagh – but she wouldn't hurt anybody. Best thing that happened for her when he cut her loose. He'd been play-ing around on her the whole time.'

'Did she know?'

'I don't think so.' Lill sighed. 'She's a sweet kid. She works at the salon just down the block. Ultra You. I know he was tapping a couple clients when they were together. He leaned toward older women there with disposable scratch. The kind who'd book a hotel suite for a few hours or a night, buy him dinner or gifts and not get emotional about the whole thing. And, shit, he was rolling with Alla again, I'm pretty sure.'

'Alla Coburn?'

'Yeah, yeah. She owns Natural Way – it's local, too. They were a thing for a while, then he ditched her, or she ditched him depending on who's telling it, and he went for Sima. Alla's a member, and I walked in on her and Trey in a clutch just the other day. He got a big laugh out of it.'

She looked down at her hands, miserably. 'You've got to understand. The guy had the looks, the body, the charm when he wanted to use it, and from the reports, knew what to do in bed.'

'Did you ever test that one out for yourself?'

Lill's head came up again, and again her eyes were direct. 'No, and two reasons: I'm his supervisor, and I like my job. I've got a kid to think about – which actually makes it three reasons and Evan's number one. And the last? I was married to a Trey Ziegler–type for four years. I don't repeat myself.'

'But I bet you could put together a list of names who tried him out.'

'Yeah.' Lill huffed out a breath, pressed her fingers to her eyes again. 'Yeah, I could. You think it was a jealous thing or sex thing that did him? I get that. I wanted to drop-kick my ex out a twelve-story window plenty before we were done. Still do now and then.'

'But you took a tire iron to his car instead.'

Lill winced. 'Yeah, I did. Look, I come home sick one afternoon – crappy cold. Things weren't great, but we had a kid and I wanted to try to stick it out. He's supposed to be writing some freelance travel article, watching Evan, and I come home. Evan's in his crib, crying, soaking wet, and the asshole's in bed, banging our next-door neighbor. I took Evan straight to my mother's, got him changed, fed, settled, then I went back, gathered up all of Evan's stuff, my stuff, I could carry while the asshole's saying, Hey, don't get so wound up. She'd come on to him. I haven't been putting

33

out much anyway. He needed to relax, and he wasn't a fucking nursemaid.'

'He's lucky you didn't hit him with the tire iron,' Peabody commented.

'Oh yeah, he is. Me, too, I guess, but I had a kid to think of first. I was going to take the car – hell, it was half mine – and he's yelling out the window how if I'm going I'm going on foot with what's on my back. If I take the car, he's calling the cops saying it was stolen. So I lost it. I got out the tire iron, beat the living crap out of the car. Ended up getting arrested. It was worth it.'

'It's got to be irritating, having someone like your ex on staff.'

'God.' She rubbed her hands over her short crop of hair again. 'Okay. It makes me jittery, but I get where you're coming from so I'll tell you straight. The first couple of times I saw him playing one of the instructors, I gave them the word. You know, you want to be careful. And got told to mind my own. So I minded my own, even when I lost a few instructors. I laid it out to Trey. I lose another, I'm going to find a way to lose you. He didn't like it, but I'm the freaking manager, and I'd have gotten rid of him – professionally,' she added. 'He stopped hitting on coworkers because he knew I could and would cut him loose. What he did outside BB? It's not for me to say.'

'Rumor is he was thinking about starting his own place.'

Lill laughed. 'He wouldn't be the first to have the dream. Trey got pretty grand recently from what I heard. But it was just talk. Look, he targeted women like Sima and Alla because they were hard workers, because they'd pay the rent or the bulk of it. He could live off them and blow his pay on clothes and sports equipment. He'd never have put enough scratch together to finance a place like this.'

'I'm told he was doing some after-hours work around here.'

'I work days – I've got Evan – but yeah, he'd been coming in off-hours. Staff's allowed to use the facilities off their shift, or adjust their schedule to suit a client. We run six A.M. to ten P.M., and I noticed him swiping in pretty regularly after ten on the log. He said he was using the comps to program some new training sessions, getting a late workout in when the place was quiet. He brought in the clients, earned his pay and commission. I didn't make a thing of it.'

'Okay. He has a locker here.'

'All the staff have lockers.'

'We'd like to get into it. I can get a warrant.'

'No need for it. If he doesn't want the cops to have all the information they can get on finding out who killed him, he's too stupid to live anyway.'

Intrigued, Eve nodded. 'That's one way of looking at it.'

Lill took them down to the staff lockers – a tight little room with wall units, two narrow benches, a toilet stall and a skinny shower.

'We have another staff locker room on the third floor. Mostly the guys use this one, the women use that, but they're coed. He put a second lock on his a couple weeks ago. People do, sometimes – clients and staff. Which is why I have a universal master because half the time people forget their codes.'

Lill ran it under the first lock once, then twice. Frowned, ran it under the main lock.

'It's not reading.'

'Let me try mine.' Eve stepped in, repeated the process with the same results. 'He's gone to some trouble here. That's interesting.' She glanced at Peabody. 'McNab.'

'On it.'

'I'm calling in someone from our Electronics Detective Division. He'll access and confiscate anything in the locker. You can be present if you want.'

With her hands on her hips, Lill frowned at the locker. 'I kind of do just because I want to know what the hell he's got in there.'

'Meanwhile, why don't you give me a list of names. People, you know, who might have wanted to take a tire iron to his car.'

Lill laughed weakly, said, 'Crap.'

While they waited for McNab, Eve had Peabody do a run on Alla Coburn and the names Lill listed while Eve talked to the instructors and trainers on duty.

She broke off when she spotted McNab.

He stood out among the hard bodies, the six-packs, the oiled guns.

Then again, he stood out anywhere.

In his long red coat and bright green watch cap he looked like a skinny twig in a forest of sequoias. The long tail of his hair bounced sunnily at his back as he pranced in on gel boots the same color as the cap. A line of silver rings glittered on the curve of his ear.

She watched his pretty face light up, followed the direction of his gaze to Peabody.

Love, Eve thought, came in all colors, shapes, and sizes.

She cut across his path before the EDD ace and her partner did something embarrassing like lock lips on duty.

'Double locks,' she said without preamble. 'One factory installed, one add-on, both reprogrammed to block master access.'

'Got your bypass right here.' He patted one of the half dozen pockets of his coat. 'Some sweatbox,' he added with a glance around. 'Your DB work here?'

'He did.'

'Guess he died fit. Makes you think, doesn't it? Eat rabbit food, sweat daily, die anyhow. Hey, She-Body. You forgot your toe warmers this morning.' He pulled a pair of thin gels out of one of his pockets.

'Thanks. Aw, you activated them.'

'Can't have my girl's tootsies cold.'

'Don't say *aw* again,' Eve ordered, anticipating. 'And never say tootsies. You're wearing badges, for God's sake. This way.'

She knew damn well they did their little finger tap behind her back.

37

'Nothing stood out on the run, Lieutenant.' Peabody made up for the finger tap with a brisk report. 'A couple minor bumps, one with some outstanding traffic violations, but nothing that rang. Coburn's run her business out of its current location for nearly six years.'

'Okay. Nobody liked him. Most of the coworkers don't come right out and say so, but it's clear he won't be especially missed around here. Words like *arrogant*, *sneaky*, *ambitious*, and *asshole* are the most popular.'

She nodded to Lill.

'Lill Byers, the manager, will witness our access to the deceased's employee locker. I'd also like Detective McNab to take a look at any computer Ziegler would have used.'

'Oh, man.' Lill did the hand over hair scoop. 'Staff lounge on the third floor. We've got two minis up there. Mostly everybody brings their own pocket or tab, but we provide the two minis, full software. I don't know his passcode.'

'I can get it,' McNab assured her.

Inside the locker room he pulled a scanner out of his pocket, ran it over the first lock.

'Changed the factory default, upgraded. Wait.' Using his thumbs he keyed in some sort of code, ran the scanner again. 'Serious upgrade. Bank-vault quality on a gym locker. Huh.'

'How long is this going to take?' Eve demanded.

'He redid the works, and he's got a thirteen-digit code on there, layered. It's going to take a few minutes.'

Eve jammed her hands in her pockets, thought of

Roarke. Her husband, the former thief, would likely slip through the damn locks like smoke. But she could hardly ask him to put a pause on his day as emperor of the business world to open a damn gym locker.

'Why would he go to all this trouble?' Lill wondered. 'What the hell has he got in there?'

'That's what we're going to find out.'

'Why the hell not get a lockbox at home, or a bank box?'

Eve watched McNab painstakingly work through the code. 'Employee locker's free, right?'

'Yeah.' Lill sighed, shook her head. 'Cheap bastard. Shit, shit! That's horrible. He's dead. I didn't mean—'

'Don't worry about it,' Eve advised.

'Maybe I could get you all something. Some juice, a smoothie. We have some really nice teas. Why don't—'

'Got it!'

The last number clicked, disengaging the primary lock.

'Okay, he put two layers of twelve on this one,' McNab muttered, more to himself than the room. 'Total overkill, total waste 'cause all I have to do is . . . Yeah, yeah, yeah.'

Numbers popped up on his scanner, glowing red as he tapped his thumbs, jiggled his hips, tapped his foot in the dance so many e-men choreographed while working.

Seconds ticked to minutes until Eve had to pace away and back again a few times to keep from nagging him to get the damn thing open.

'Nearly there, Dallas. Not such a tricky one. Just tedious.

He spent a lot of time on the layers, but no pizzazz. Just takes some time.' He glanced over at her, grinned. 'Watch it be empty after all this! Wouldn't that be a bitch?'

'Don't make me kick your ass, McNab.'

'Last sequence coming up, locking in, and ... bam! Overridden. It's all yours, Lieutenant.'

'Okay, let's see what was so fricking important.'

It wasn't empty.

Wrapped packs of bills formed neat stacks and rows. Low denomination, Eve noted, banded in thousand-dollar packs.

'Holy shit!' Lill clamped a hand on Eve's shoulder as she leaned in, goggled. 'Holy shit, where did Trey get all that money? Cash money. Who has that kind of real money anywhere?'

'Good question. Peabody, let's get an accurate count with Ms Byers as witness, then seal and log. He put the second lock on when?'

'Ah. God. Maybe a month ago,' Lill managed. 'Maybe more like six weeks. Yeah, more like six weeks ago.'

Just what kind of side business had Ziegler launched in the past few weeks? Eve wondered. Whatever it had been, it had proven lucrative and deadly.

'A hundred and sixty-five thousand, Dallas. A hundred and sixty-five thousand-dollar stacks, and one broken stack with five thousand. Crisp new twenty-dollar bills,' Peabody added. 'Rubber-banded. Not bank-banded.'

'Seal it up. McNab, go through the staff comps here,

then take his home unit, his 'link. Do the works. We appreciate your time and cooperation,' she told Lill.

'Will you kind of keep me up on things? I can't believe Trey had all that money in there. I can't believe he's dead. None of this is really getting through, you know?'

'Will let you know what we can when we can.'

'Okay. Oh, listen, let me get you a bag. A complimentary Buff Bodies gym bag. You can't carry all that money out of here in those clear bags.'

'Good thought.'

Once it was loaded up in the bold red bag with the glittery double B logo, Eve glanced at her wrist unit. 'We're going to take a good, hard look at his financials. We need to get this into evidence, then double back here, talk to Coburn, check in with Morris, and start working down Ziegler's client list.'

'I know but, Dallas? I'm carrying a hundred and sixty-five *thousand* dollars in a gym bag.' Peabody slung it over her shoulder like Santa Claus as they walked back out into the cold. 'I mean, jeez! Ho, ho, freaking ho!'

3

'I've never held this much money at one time in my life. I thought it would be heavier,' Peabody said as they walked into Cop Central.

'What kind of asshole keeps that much cash in a staff locker at a gym? Cheap bastard's right. Wanted the cash,' Eve speculated. 'No record of it that way, you can wash cash easy enough.'

'I'll start on the financials, but no way that was saved up or legit. It was all new money. New money smells really good.'

'No sniffing the evidence.' Eve hopped off the glide.

She wanted to swing into Homicide, check a few things, start her murder book and board while Peabody dug into the vic's financials. Then they'd circle back around for interviews.

Plus her office at Central offered the one thing she hadn't had access to since she'd been rudely called out of a warm bed in the middle of the night.

Real coffee.

She turned into the bullpen and the noise of comps,

voices, 'links. Someone had dug out a tatty and tawdry length of silver garland, strung it over the side windows. An even tattier sign announcing HAPPY HOLIDAYS hung crookedly from it.

Perhaps the same determined elf had dragged in the pitiful, spindly fake tree, propped it in a corner. ID shots of detectives and uniforms decorated the branches with Eve's stuck on the stubby top.

'Seriously?'

The slick-suited Detective Baxter stepped over to study it with her. 'Santiago pulled it out of the recycler.'

'Waste not, want not,' Santiago said from his desk. 'Carmichael did the decorations.'

'We're the spirit of Homicide Christmas,' Carmichael claimed. 'If murder cops can't be festive this time of year, who can?'

'What? "Happy holidays, fucker, you're under arrest"?'

Carmichael grinned. 'Works for me.'

'It's not bad. Peabody, financials.' She turned, started toward her office, and got the next surprise when Roarke walked out.

He looked perfect – as if the gods had gotten together over drinks one night and decided to join together to create something extraordinary. So they'd carved the face of a wicked angel, added eyes of wild blue, then sculpted a mouth designed to make a woman yearn to have it pressed to hers.

Those eyes warmed now, the mouth curved.

Love, she thought again, came in all colors, shapes, and sizes.

She'd hit the jackpot with hers.

'There you are, Lieutenant.' The Ireland of his birth wound smoothly through his words. 'I just left you a memo cube.'

'Did I forget my toe warmers?'

His eyebrows, the same inky-black as the hair that spilled nearly to his shoulders, raised. 'Your what now?'

'Nothing. Come on back if you've got a minute.'

'I do now.'

He brushed a hand down her arm as they started back. His version, she supposed, of the Peabody/McNab finger-tip tap.

'Your men weren't sure when to expect you back. I had a quick meeting down this way, so I stopped in.'

They stepped into her tiny office.

Roarke cupped her face in his hands, kissed her before she could object. 'Good morning.' Then he flicked a finger down the shallow dent in her chin. 'You've put in a long day already.'

'Dead guy,' she said simply.

'And what does the dead guy have to do with Trina?'

'Ex of a friend. I need coffee.' She turned to the AutoChef, programmed two, hot and black. 'I was ready to strangle her with her own hair for getting me up and out at that hour, but – Oh, thank fat Santa and all the pointed-nosed elves,' she said at the first sip of coffee.

She took another hit, then shrugged out of her coat, tossed it aside. 'She and her pal got juiced up, went to the ex's place to do some mischief – itching powder level. Jesus, are they twelve? Instead they find the ex dead. Bashed in the head, then stabbed. Killer left a festive note.'

He followed it, and her, easily enough as he sipped his coffee. 'You've eliminated Trina and the friend?'

'Yeah, yeah. Guy was an asshole. Worked over at Buff Bodies. We've just come from there. I had to send for McNab to access his employee locker. The vic doubled the lock, programmed it to block masters.'

'A pity you didn't tag me as I was close.'

'Didn't know or I might have.'

'And what was he hiding?'

'A hundred sixty-five thousand in cash. All twenties, all new bills.'

'Interesting. Now, that's very interesting indeed.'

'Not a huge haul in the grand scheme – a Roarke grand scheme anyway – but a nice pile for a guy who lived in a cramped little apartment in a dicey neighborhood and liked really nice clothes.'

'It's considerable,' Roarke corrected, 'in any scheme, when tucked away in a gym locker.'

'Yeah, it is. The way it looks, he got the windfall in the last few weeks and dumped Trina's friend shortly thereafter. He was already banging somebody else. And he was up to something at work. Don't know what, but something. McNab's on his electronics. Peabody's on the financials. I'm going to write up the report, open the book, then go talk to the ex before his last ex.'

'Busy, busy. What did he do at Buff Bodies?'

'Personal training and massage work.'

'Hmm. The sort of intimacy that leads people to talk about personal business. Blackmail?'

'My first pick.' She could appreciate he'd lean there first, too. 'I've got to figure whatever he was into, it was a new enterprise. He made noises about starting his own place in the tropics.'

'It would take more than under two hundred K to start up a tropical fitness business.'

'Yeah, but he was an asshole.'

'Perhaps one who planned to add to that windfall. I'll let you get back to it. I can fit a quick bit of shopping in before my next meeting.'

'Don't say shopping.'

He grinned at her. 'Haven't finished yet, have you?'

'There's time. Plenty of time.'

'Mmm. Barely started then.' He kissed her between the eyebrows. 'Best of luck there. I'll see you at home.'

'I started,' she called out, heard him chuckle as he walked away. 'Sort of.'

Frowning, she picked up the memo cube he'd left on her desk. Activated.

I was in the neighborhood, so I stopped in. Charming holiday decor in your bullpen, Lieutenant. As I didn't give you your daily reminder this morning, consider this that. You've two days until our holiday party. Meanwhile, take care of my cop.

'Two days? How did it get to be two days?'

She dropped down at her desk. Okay, she admitted, shopping had now bumped up to the urgent area on her to-do list.

But first things first.

She began setting up her murder board.

Blackmail, she thought. Extortion. A scam.

No way she'd buy Ziegler came into more than a hundred fifty large by legal means.

So who had he blackmailed, extorted, scammed?

Whoever it was would top her list of suspects. She just had to get there.

RED SHOES, she wrote on her notes, then grabbed her coat, headed out.

'Peabody, with me.'

'Nothing hinky in his financials I can find,' Peabody said, scurrying to keep up. 'He lived close, but not because he spent a lot on food and lodging. It's all clothes, skin care, body and hair services, that sort of thing. He spent on himself, his appearance. No major deposits or withdrawals. A lot of charges, but in the areas I said. He ends up with a lot of late fees, but he eventually pays.'

'So, it's all show and self-indulgence. And sex.'

'Sort of like a licensed companion without the license.'

'Not bad, Peabody.'

Eve risked the elevator, wondered who had had the bright idea to pump in holiday music in a cop shop. And how she could punish them.

'He could've started charging for sex on the side, but I don't care how good he was, nobody's worth that kind of scratch inside a few weeks. A client could get a good, experienced, safe LC for a reasonable rate. But blackmail's another thing. Threaten to tell a spouse, maybe.'

'Shortsighted,' Peabody commented as they reached garage level. 'You'd for sure lose the client if you blackmailed her, then you lose the commission and any chance for more.'

'Some people only see the right now, and end up killing the golden duck.'

'Goose. The golden goose.'

'Duck, goose, what's the difference? They're both weird-looking birds.'

'Did you ever play Duck, Duck, Goose?'

Eve pulled out of the garage, into traffic. 'Did I ever play with ducks and goose – geese? Why the hell would I?'

'No, the kids' game, where you sit around in a circle, then one kid walks around, tapping the other kids on the head. She says, "Duck, duck," until she taps one and says, "Goose." Then that one, the goose, chases her around the circle, tries to catch her before she gets to where the goose one was sitting. If she doesn't catch her, she goes around the circle.'

Eve stared out the windshield. 'That has to be the dumb-est-ass game of all dumb-ass games.'

'It's kind of fun when you're six. We had roast goose when we went to Scotland to visit McNab's family over Christmas,' Peabody continued, obviously caught in a theme. 'It was really good. We're doing the quick in and out shuttle this year to see my family. It'll be soy and tofu and lots of veg, which doesn't compare. But my granny will bake, a lot – and that makes up for everything. She makes the most incredible mincemeat pie.'

'I thought your guys didn't eat meat.'

'Mostly they don't. Mincemeat isn't meat.'

'Then why do they call it meat?'

Peabody sat a moment, baffled. 'I don't know. Maybe it used to have meat, but my granny doesn't make it like that. It's all kind of fruit and spices and I think some whiskey or something. I have to ask for the recipe now. I like making pies.'

Holiday shopping had infected downtown. With all the shops open, hyping gifts everyone had to have, parking became more challenging. Eve beat out a mini for a second-level space by punching vertical and zipping up and in with a couple of coats of paint to spare.

'Jesus, Dallas, warn me next time. Look there's a bakery. Bakeries sometimes have hot chocolate, and always have pastries. I had a simulated egg pocket from Vending. It was worse than it sounds. A lot worse.'

'Later,' Eve said and arrowed straight to Natural Way.

It was a quiet little place, homey, with what Eve thought of as Free-Agey, foresty fairy music playing softly.

It smelled of cranberries, and a little pine, a hint of cinnamon. And, indeed, she saw the daily special drink was some sort of cranberry-cinnamon tea.

A few people sat at tiny tables drinking out of mugs the color of stone or eating what looked to Eve like grass and berries, or in one case a muffin that resembled tree bark.

The countergirl offered a dreamy smile. 'Welcome to the Natural Way. What can we do for your body, mind, and spirit?'

'You can get the owner.' Eve held up her badge.

'Oh, you'd like to see Alla? She's busy in the kitchen. We've already run out of our yamberry muffins, and we're low on our nipnanna pie.'

'That's a problem. You need to get her.'

'I do?'

'Yes, for the good of your body, mind, and spirit.'

'Oh, okay.'

'What the hell is nipnanna?' Eve wondered.

'Turnip and banana pie.'

Eve turned her head, looked hard into Peabody's face. 'You've got to be lying.'

'Not. My aunt makes it. It's not quite as bad as it sounds, but almost. Yamberry muffins, now – that's yams and cranberries – that's pretty good stuff.'

'Please.'

'It's no apple Danish, but it's pretty good.'

Alla stepped out. Her chestnut hair was bundled under a squat chef's cap, leaving her fresh, pretty face unframed. She wore a long, flowered dress over a willowy form, and a gray bib apron over the dress.

'Is there a problem?' she began.

'Could be.' Eve showed her the badge. 'We need to talk.'

'I don't understand. I'm up to date on everything. Business license, health department.'

'It's not about that. Is there a place we can talk?'

'We're really busy in the back.' She glanced behind her. 'We're running holiday specials, and they're paying off. We can grab that table over there. Dora, let's have three-drink specials. I could use a little break.'

'Right away, Alla.'

She pulled off her cap as she walked around the counter. A long, sleek tail of hair tumbled out.

'What's this about?'

'Trey Ziegler.'

Irritation flickered in Alla's large brown eyes. 'What about him?' she demanded as she sat. 'If he's in trouble and looking for me to bail him out, he can forget it.'

'He's dead.'

'What?' She jerked back as if punched. 'What do you mean?'

'His body was found early this morning. When did you last see him?'

'That's not right. That's a mistake.'

51

No tears, Eve noted, but if she was faking the shock and denial, she was damn good at it.

'You've made a mistake,' Alla said, the words slow, careful. 'Trey's not dead.'

'Trey Ziegler,' Eve said, keeping her tone flat and brisk as she brought his ID shot up on her PPC. 'This Trey Ziegler.'

'This can't be right. This can't be true.'

Still no tears, but trembles in the voice, in the hands.

'You and the victim were involved.'

'Vic – victim? Victim?'

'Here you are, Alla. Would you like to split a yamberry muffin? A fresh batch just came out.'

'We're fine,' Eve said when Alla only stared straight ahead. 'Go away.'

'How . . . what happened? How?'

'When did you last see or speak with Trey Ziegler?'

'I . . .'

'Are you missing a pair of red shoes, Alla?'

'Oh God. Oh God.' She covered her face with her hands. 'I was going to lie. I don't even know why. I can't take it in. I saw him yesterday, just yesterday. He was fine.'

'Tell me about yesterday.'

'I'd seen him that morning, early, at the gym. Buff Bodies. I was there for my early yoga class and . . . we'd started thinking about seeing each other again. He'd broken things off with the woman he'd been living with, and he said he missed me. It was stupid. I was stupid, but he asked me to

52

come to his place. I took off for a couple hours, even dressed up for it. Stupid, stupid. And I jumped right back in bed with him.

'I missed the sex,' she admitted. 'He's good in bed, and he's got a way of making you feel you matter, for as long as he wants to make you feel that way. Afterward, he started talking about going to Aruba or St Bart's, starting up a fitness spa. At first I thought he was asking me to go with him, how we could start up this whole thing together. It was fantasy, but it was nice. But that wasn't it.'

She pressed her hand to her mouth, rocked herself a moment. 'That wasn't it at all. We had a second round of sex, and I really needed to get back, but I would've stayed if he'd asked. That's how stupid he could make me. Instead he said I was one of the best bangs, that I could make a living at it. Like I should be flattered. Then he asked if I'd be interested in doing a threesome, that he had this client, and she was looking for a little adventure. He . . . He said he'd pay me.'

Tears shimmered now. 'He'd *pay* me.'

'That must've pissed you off.'

'I couldn't believe how stupid I'd been. How stupid, and all for an orgasm. I told him to go to hell. I started grabbing my clothes, and he's lying there laughing, saying, Oh, come on, baby, it'll be fun. How he'd make it worth my while, how I was the first woman he'd thought of when it came up.'

53

The tears flowed out now, but not from grief. Eve read the shame clearly.

'That's what he thought of me. I *allowed* him to think that of me. I got out, I got out, and I said . . . Oh my God, I said I wished he was dead. Now he is.'

'You left in December, with no shoes.'

'I had my work shoes in my bag.' She showed Eve the navy blue recycled-material clogs. 'I didn't even think about the damn red shoes. I never want to see them again. I wore them for him. I let myself think he cared about me, but he didn't.'

'What time did you leave the apartment?'

'Um, about three in the afternoon. I went home, took a shower, and I came right back here. I needed to work. I think I was back here before four. You can check with any of the staff.'

'And what time did you leave here yesterday – for the day?'

'Six-fifteen, six-thirty. I went home. I live right upstairs. I went home, and I had a good cry. Then I ate my entire secret stash of cookie dough ice cream – the real stuff. I drank a half bottle of wine and watched cheesy vids.'

'Did you talk to anyone, see anyone?'

'No. I turned off my 'link. I wanted to wallow, so I wallowed. I didn't kill him. I said I wished he was dead, but I didn't kill him.'

Back outside, Eve gauged the distance from the health-food store to the crime scene.

'She could have walked out of here at six-fifteen, gone back to his place, bashed him on the head. Plenty of time to get from here to there by TOD.'

'Yeah, but her statement really rings,' Peabody argued. 'Eating ice cream, drinking wine, watching sad vids. It's what a lot of women do after a bad breakup or an emotional jolt.'

'Which is why she'd run that route for us, wouldn't she? It may ring, but she had motive and she's got no alibi.'

'It feels more like she'd have bashed him, if she's inclined to bashing, when he brought up the threesome and paying her for it.'

Though she agreed, Eve shrugged. 'Maybe she's a slow burn. Let's go check in with Morris, then we can start working on the clients. Maybe we can find out who he had in mind for the third member of his threesome.'

The white tunnel of the morgue smelled of a recent cleaning. Something that brushed lemons over death and left an undertone of industrial antiseptic.

Eve wondered if those who spent their days and nights working in its warrens even noticed.

She passed Vending's bright and colorful lights, felt a low-level craving for more caffeine, nodded to one of the crew pushing a body bag on a gurney.

Not all the dead were hers, she thought, but in an odd way, they all belonged to Morris.

She found the chief medical examiner standing over her dead, a clear protective cape over Morris's sharply elegant suit of forest green.

Two more bodies waited on steel slabs.

'You've got a backup,' she commented.

'Holidays. Some deck the halls, others opt to haunt them. An apparent suicide pact, but we'll see.' He lowered his microgoggles, smiled. 'A long day for you already. Can we offer you some refreshment? I have orange fizzies in the friggie.'

Peabody brightened. 'Yeah?'

'I know my cops. Pepsi's cold, Dallas.'

'Thanks. You look . . . cheerful.'

'I had a couple of days off, visited some old friends. It was good for me.'

'Nice.' And it was good to see him wearing color again, looking relaxed. In the months since he'd lost the woman he loved, the grief and strain had weighed visibly on him.

She cracked the tube Peabody brought her, took a swig of cold caffeine. 'So. Ziegler, Trey. He won't be decking any halls, either.'

'Blunt force trauma, tried and true.'

'Personal trainer of the year trophy.'

'Ah, the irony. Your vic was rather fiercely fit. Exceptional muscle tone, low body fat, no signs whatsoever he paid for body work. And I must say his skin's wonderfully taut and smooth.'

'He loved himself, a lot.'

'He had a bunch of high-end products,' Peabody added. 'Hair, body, skin. Some of it wasn't even opened yet.' Her wistful sigh earned a hard stare from Eve. 'It just seems like a waste, that's all.'

'And it doesn't seem ghoulish to covet a dead guy's face gunk? Face-to-face, the first blow?' Eve asked Morris.

'Yes. Striking here, on the left forehead, and the second on the back of the skull.'

He turned to his screen, brought up the view of the second wound, now cleaned. 'While the first blow would have incapacitated – severe concussion, considerable bleeding, leaving the jagged gash you see here, the second, a down-blow of considerable force, fractured the skull, driving bone fragments into the brain. Death within minutes. The trophy had some weight, I'd say.'

'Yeah, it's hefty. A good six, seven pounds. About eighteen inches high.'

'We'll just add that in.' He turned to his comp, keyed in some data.

'It had a figure on top,' Peabody added. 'Ripped body.' She held out her arms, flexed.

'Of course,' Morris murmured, his exotic eyes amused as he added more data. 'From the angles, the depth of the head wounds, the attack would have gone – probability ninety-six-point-eight percent – like this.'

On screen two figures faced. One gripped the trophy in both hands swung right to left, striking the other figure on the temple. Ziegler's figure staggered back, then pitched forward. As it fell, the attacker swung again – now left to right – striking the back of the skull.

'Double-handed blows.'

'Considering the weight of the weapon, and the angles, the force, that's my conclusion. Like swinging for the fences on the first, then rounding back, striking down – almost a chop – for the second.'

'Ziegler was six-one. You have the killer about the same height.'

'Yes, from the angles, near to the same. An inch or two either way, but I wouldn't say more. And I'd also conclude the killer had excellent upper-body strength. These were not glancing blows.'

'Yeah, I get that. Then you've got a hundred-eighty pounds of dead weight – all muscle – to haul off the floor and onto the bed.'

'Our killer isn't a ninety-pound weakling. An old cliché,' Morris said at Eve's blank look. 'As for the knife wound, the vic was dead before that was inflicted – and still there was considerable force used, enough to break the tip of the knife.' He gestured to a small sample bowl, and the tiny piece of metal it held.

'Somebody was really pissed off,' Eve acknowledged. 'Did the vic have sex before death?'

'I can't think of anyone who wouldn't like to, but I can't tell you. He'd showered or bathed – and thoroughly. He sports what's called a Continental.'

Eve looked down at the razor thin, sharply edged zigzag of hair at the crotch. 'Yeah, I noticed that. Weird.'

'But tidy. His genitals and what pubic hair he has were thoroughly washed and groomed. He died clean. He'd consumed about eight ounces of red wine less than an hour prior to death, a field green salad and an energy drink about two hours prior.'

'He had a little bag of dried leaves in his suitcase. Looked and smelled like tea to me, but ...'

'The tox isn't back yet – they're backed up as usual – but from the condition of his body, his organs, I'd doubt he had any habitual illegals use. I see no signs he took any sort of drugs on a regular basis. This was a very healthy man in peak physical condition.'

'Personal trainer of the year.'

'In life and in death.'

'Thanks.' She rolled up her empty Pepsi tube, two-pointed it into his recycler. 'That helped.'

'Anytime. I'm looking forward to your party. It's the bash of the season.'

'Yeah? I'd guess Ziegler probably feels his big trophy was the bash of the season.'

'Ha,' Morris said.

With Peabody, Eve worked down Ziegler's client list, giving priority to women of means.

She hit the managing partner of a SoHo art gallery, the CFO of a real-estate company, the owner of a small chain of boutique day spas, and a couple of women who'd married well and spent most of their time spending money.

'The last one was skinny as a snake and barely five-foot-four.'

'And her current husband is six-foot, also has a BB membership, and plays lacrosse. Jealous husbands qualify, Peabody. We run him.'

'Got it.'

Eve walked toward the elegant three-story brownstone drenched in holiday glamour. 'We'll take this one – Natasha Quigley, spouse John Jake Copley – both clients. Then we'll call it for the day.'

'Yay. My butt's dragging.'

'Well, hike it up.' She rang the buzzer.

Good afternoon.

The computerized voice intoned polite reserve.

Please state your name and your business.

'Lieutenant Dallas, Detective Peabody. NYPSD.' Eve held up her badge to be scanned. 'Our business is with Ms Quigley and Mr Copley.'

Your identification has been verified. One moment please.

'People ought to answer their own doors once in a while,' Eve said, 'just to see what it feels like.'

'You have Summerset,' Peabody pointed out. 'And a really big gate.'

Before Eve could respond, the door opened. A woman – no a droid, Eve realized quickly – in a smart gray uniform smiled with the same reserved politeness as the security comp. 'Please come in. Ms Quigley will see you.'

The house opened up to a soaring three-story foyer. Free-form silver chandeliers dripped down, showering light over what Eve thought might be the original wood floors.

That space flowed into a living area where a fire snapped inside a black marble hearth, a tree draped in crystals and red ribbon glittered, and two women sat on a massive circular sofa drinking clear liquid out of martini glasses.

They were both blond, both lookers, with enough similarities in sharp features and coloring for Eve to surmise family connection.

One – the oldest by maybe five years in Eve's estimation – tapped the cushion beside her. A sleek, narrow arm glided up. She set her drink on it, rose.

'I'm Natasha Quigley. This must be about Trey. Martella just told me he was murdered. My sister. We're both clients. Actually, we're *all* clients. My husband and hers. How can we help?'

'When did you last see or speak with Mr Ziegler?'

'I – oh, I'm sorry, this has been a shock. Please, sit down. Can I offer you anything?'

'We're fine, thanks.' Eve took a chair with a low, semi-circular back. Everything in the room seemed to follow the round theme.

'Sorry.' Natasha sat again. 'I think this is the first time we've had police in the house – officially. I had my usual Tuesday morning session with Trey. I work with him twice a week. Tuesdays and Thursdays, ten A.M. Thursdays I follow the workout with a massage. We didn't have a session scheduled today as he was going out of town to a conference.'

'And you, Mrs Schubert? Since you're here.'

'Oh.' Martella took a quick sip of her drink, bit her lip. 'It would've been Wednesday morning. I was Wednesday mornings and Friday afternoons. So, um, yesterday morning. Tilly said he died yesterday, but I saw him, and he was fine.'

'Tilly?' Eve prompted.

'Tilly Burke. She heard from Lola. You went to see Lola, and she talked to Tilly. Tilly didn't work with Trey, she worked with Flora because she wanted a female trainer, but she knew Trey. Everyone knew Trey.'

She paused, drank again. 'I'm talking too much.'

'Yes, you are.' Natasha patted her on the leg. 'It's upsetting.'

'It feels awful.'

'How long were you clients, specifically of Mr Ziegler's?'

'It must be six months now. A little longer for you, Tella.'

'I switched to BB. Tilly and I used to go to Sensible Fitness but they just got really boring, and BB had just remodeled, done a whole vamp of their locker rooms. It has such a good feel, so we joined, then Tash joined when I told her how much more I liked it. Then I started working with Trey. He really upped my game. I bought Trey for Lance for his last birthday.'

'She means she bought her husband weekly personal training sessions,' Natasha explained. 'Tella raved so, I took a two-week trial with him myself and I was hooked.'

'Did you socialize with him?'

'Socialize?' Natasha lifted an eyebrow as if the question baffled her. 'You mean personally? I had lunch with him a few times in the juice bar to discuss fitness options and strategies.'

'And outside the gym.'

'Not really. Though JJ and I invited him to our club once or twice. We felt he'd vastly improved our tennis game. Speed and endurance,' she added with a smile. 'And his focus on upper-body work seriously strengthened my backhand. He and JJ played golf now and then,' she added. 'They're both fanatics about golf.'

'Did you ever go to his apartment?'

'Why no. Why would I?'

Eve shifted her attention to the sister. Martella gave all hers to her drink. 'Mrs Schubert?'

'Yes? What?'

'Did you ever see Mr Ziegler outside of the fitness center?'

'Oh, well ... He came to the club. Tash, I'm going to ask Hester for another drink.'

'Mrs Schubert?' Eve said, voice firm and flat.

'Yes?'

'How long were you sexually involved with Mr Ziegler?'

'That's a ridiculous question,' Natasha snapped out. 'That's incredibly rude. Tella, you don't have to dignify that with a ... ' She trailed off after a look at her sister's face. 'Oh God. Martella!'

'It wasn't like that! It wasn't like that at all! I was going to tell you, Tash, I was just about to tell you, but then they came in. It was just one time. Well, two times, but on the same day. And it was weeks ago. Weeks and weeks.'

'I don't think you should say any more.' Natasha put a restraining hand on her sister's arm. 'I don't think my sister should say any more without legal representation.'

'That's her choice. We'll need you to come with us, Mrs Schubert, into Central for further questioning. You're free to call in your lawyer or legal representative.'

'But I don't want to go with you.' Her voice cracked and her big blue eyes pleaded. 'I don't want that. Lance would find out. Tash, it was just that one time. Lance and I had that big fight. You remember. And he just *left* on that business trip even when I was so upset. Listen. Just listen.'

She took her sister's drink, tossed back the contents.

'I told Trey all about it, about the fight, about how

Lance just left while we were mad at each other. And he could see I was really upset. He said he'd come over to the house, give me a massage, help me relax and detox. So he did.'

'And sex was part of the service?' Eve asked.

'No! I never – It wasn't supposed to be. I was upset and he was sympathetic, and caring. He even made me tea, started with some Reiki just to help me find my center, then he started the body massage and . . . it just sort of happened.'

'Twice?' Natasha said crisply.

'Yes. It was just . . . I was so relaxed, just drifting. I never felt so loose, and it was all so warm, and smelled so good with the incense.'

'Incense,' Eve murmured.

'And the tea was so nice.'

'What kind of tea?' Eve asked.

'Herbal tea. A special blend.'

'I bet. Mrs Schubert. Martella. Look at me. Did you intend to sleep with Trey? Was it your intention or did you consider having sex with him before that incident?'

'No. No. I mean, he's really great-looking, and that body is amazing. But no, I swear. I never even thought about it. I love my husband, I really, really do. It's just I was so tense and upset, and he – Trey – didn't have any openings for a massage or detox during working hours. He was doing me a favor by coming over, making a personal visit.'

'For how much?'

'Two thousand, but it was an in-home, personal treatment. Afterward, I got upset again. I'd cheated on my husband, but Trey said it wasn't like that. It was just finding my balance, opening up and letting out the negative feelings, embracing the positive. Being all clear again, I could understand how much I loved Lance. And he was right. But Lance, he wouldn't understand.'

'How much did you give him to be . . . discreet.'

'I added a thousand dollars as a personal thank-you, and we agreed we'd never think about it or speak about it. And I really didn't, speak about it.'

'Did he ever offer you the tea again? Before or after that incident?'

'No. I don't get massages from him anymore. It didn't seem right. I didn't want to − I just didn't want him to touch me again, remind me. I get massages from Trudy at the club now. And I . . . ' She flicked away a tear. 'I was going to switch to Gwen for training. I just hadn't figured out how to do it without making everyone upset.'

'Who initiated the sex?' Eve asked.

'God. I did. I'm so ashamed. It was my fault. All my fault.'

'You initiated − after you drank the tea? After you were on the table, and he'd lit the incense?'

'Yes. I just felt so drifty, and so . . . needy. It's terrible.'

'What are you implying. Do you think he gave her something?' Natasha gripped her sister's hand. 'Do you think he gave Tella some sort of drug?'

'He'd never do that. He was only trying to help me. He did help me. Please.' She held out both hands to Eve. 'Please, I don't want Lance to know. He wouldn't understand.'

'What you tell your husband's up to you,' Eve said. 'Where were you between five and seven last night?'

'I was with Tilly. We were at the salon. We were at Ultra You. We had the works done. Hair, nails, facials, body treatments. All for Tash's and JJ's big party last night. I was at the salon with Tilly from one until seven. We had the full-bliss package.'

Six hours in a salon sounded like the full-torture package to Eve. 'I need your friend's full name and contact, and the name of your technicians.'

4

The streetlights had flickered on while they'd been inside the Quigley brownstone. She'd started the day in the dark, Eve thought, and would end it the same way.

'You think he slipped her something.' As she opened the car door, Peabody glanced back toward the house. 'So do I.'

'I'm leaning that way, and leaning toward whatever it was he'd packed in the suitcase. Tea.' Eve got in the car, drummed her fingers on the wheel. 'Something in the tea, and he decides to take a supply with him to the seminar. Either he had a target there, or he'd pick one that struck his fucking fancy.'

'And he targeted Martella Schubert because she was rich, attractive, vulnerable. And she trusted him,' Peabody added. 'She felt safe with him.'

'Easier to roofie the trusting. She just blurted it all out,' Eve added. 'If it went the way she says, he went to her home a couple weeks ago. The odds of us finding that out were slim, but she blurted it out.'

'I'd say she's lousy at keeping secrets, but she kept this one from her husband.'

Eve edged out into the street. 'Maybe she did, or maybe he found out, went over to Trey's, and bashed him in the head with a trophy. If she kept it zipped, it's because she convinced herself it was some Zen thing instead of cheating. I need to get a better sense of who she is, but my initial take is not so much dumb as gullible. She's led a privileged lifestyle – the Quigleys come from money – and she married money. She took her husband's name. That's a bit old-fashioned, so I'm gauging her a romantic. Again, if it went as she said, Ziegler opened her up. He played the sympathetic ear, offered her a service – not sex. A service. And he comes with tea and incense.'

'It changes things – adds additional motive, and maybe suspects. With some luck the lab can analyze the hair strands you talked her into giving us.'

'If her timing's true, and it's only been a couple weeks, they can find Rohypnol or one of the compounds in the hair. Either way, we'll know more when we get the results of the stuff in the baggie, the stuff in the locker. I should've put a rush on that.'

'It looked like tea in the baggie and it looks like incense cones in the locker. Fussy, but not especially weird for somebody to take their own tea on a trip. Not weird to find incense cones in a locker at a fitness club with massage services.'

'Maybe not.' Still she regretted tagging them low priority.

69

'But why would he do it?' Peabody wondered. 'He had a girlfriend, another one ready to jump, and from what we're hearing plenty of action from clients anyway. Why dose one to get some? She'd've paid him the money for the straight massage and sympathy.'

'Conquest. Ego. Practice – bigger pay when you add the "please be discreet" money. Who the hell knows what goes on in the head of somebody so in love with his own dick? I'm betting he figured he was doing her a favor.'

Considering, Eve took a corner. 'I'll drop you home.'

'You will?'

'It's on the way, basically.' And, she remembered, Peabody began and ended her day in the dark, too. 'Check the alibi. It's going to hold, but check it through.'

'It's Trina's salon. I can tag her, get the full skinny.'

'Yeah, you do that.'

'It's a wonder he didn't tap the sister. She's just his type, right? Just into her forties, plenty of money, really attractive.'

'Who says he didn't?'

'Well, she did.' But now Peabody's eyebrows drew together. 'But yeah, she strikes as a better liar than little sister.'

'We'll see. And we'll run through the rest of the client list tomorrow. Martella Schubert's not going to be the only one he dosed, if he dosed her. We can start working that angle.'

'He's our dead guy,' Peabody said, 'but I really hate when they're fuckheads.'

'Being a fuckhead's a good reason to punch somebody in the face, not to cave in their skull.'

'Still, I wish he'd been a nice guy. On the other hand, then he'd be a dead nice guy, and you'd have to feel bad. So maybe being a fuckhead's better.'

'Just check the alibi, Peabody.' Eve pulled over to the curb.

'On it. Thanks for the lift. Hey, look at that hoodie!'

She pointed to a sidewalk stall and the virulent orange hooded sweatshirt with an animated hula dancer plastered over the front.

'That's just perfect for McNab. A little from-Santa present.'

'Does he know Santa doesn't exist?'

'Santa exists in the hearts of all true believers.' Face aglow, Peabody patted her own. 'Can I borrow fifty bucks?'

'What?'

'I'm short until payday.'

'You're short every day.'

'Ho, ho, ho. Financially, in this case. Please? He'd really love that hoodie.'

'Christ. Santa Claus and hula dancers,' Eve muttered as she dug into her pockets.

'Oh, there's one with a gyrating Elvis in a Santa hat! How much fun is that!'

'Elvis has been dead a hundred years. How is it fun to have a dead man gyrating on your chest?'

'Elvis never dies, just like Santa. No, it's the hula girl. Except—'

Eve shoved money at Peabody. 'Go, buy McNab a ridiculous hoodie. Get out of my car.'

'Fun! Shopping! Bye!'

Eve pulled out, flicked a glance in the rearview. And saw Peabody doing a happy little bounce in front of dancing, gyrating hoodies.

Merry Christmas.

But it got her thinking, made her curse and check the time. If she only had two days, and today was practically over, when the hell was she supposed to buy stuff for people the rules somehow dictated she had to buy stuff for?

She headed uptown, took a detour. It was a little late in the day, but there was a chance she'd find a source who could wrap it all up for her – or at least some of it – quick and easy.

She drove by first, spotted the kid on his corner, manning his stall, then dealt with the insanity of parking.

She had to hoof it two blocks, through the raging sea of tourists, of shoppers, of semi-sane New Yorkers just trying to get the hell home after the workday.

She studied the stall as she approached. Scarves, capes, socks, gloves, mittens, caps, hats – the kid had expanded since their last encounter.

She watched him make change, fold three scarves into a clear bag. 'Have a good one.'

Then his dark eyes shifted over, met hers. His grin spread. 'Yo, Dallas. What you say?'

'Yo, Tiko. Business is good.'

'Business is tight.'

He was a squirt of a thing, a kid who probably should've been home playing video games or sweating over math homework. But at heart, Tiko was a businessman.

'You catch any bad guys?'

'Not today, but the day's not over. Late for you out here, isn't it?'

'Holiday business. I got till seven-thirty. My granny's good with that. Deke! Help that lady there. One of my employees,' Tiko told her, nodded toward a skinny kid wearing fingerless gloves and an earflap cap. 'I got two.'

'Employees now?'

His eyes did an amused dance under the bright stripes of the watch cap he wore pulled low. 'For the Christmas rush, sure. Got some nice scarves here. Got cotton, got wool, got cash*mere*, got silk blends. You can match 'em up with gloves and a cap, make a gift set.'

'Yeah. Yeah.' She stuffed her hands in her pockets. 'I've got some girl types I need to get stuff for.'

'What kind of girl types? Friends, relations, coworkers?'

Eve huffed out a breath. 'Friends, I guess. Friends.'

'Good ones? Or the kind you just gotta come up with shit for?'

73

She had to laugh. He knew the score.

'Good ones.'

'I'm gonna take you to my associate.'

'Your associate?'

'Yeah. Deke, Manny! You mind the store now, and don't screw around. You come on with me.' He took Eve's hand, marched her to the corner. 'You remember that shop you busted last time? I told you about how they were bad guys, and you came and took them down?'

'Yeah. Street thieves, identify theft racket.'

'Got a new business in that shop now. Mom-and-pop deal. They're good people. They're going to fix you right up.'

'Are they?' Willing to try if it finished this shopping crap once and for all, she crossed the street with him.

'True. Give you a good deal, too, since you're with me.'

He zigged, he zagged his way through the crowds, then zipped into the long, narrow store.

'Hey, Pop!'

The man, probably no more than thirty-five, used a long hook to reach the strap of one of what looked like a half million bags. He snagged it off the wall, lowered it, offered it to the waiting customer.

Then smiled at Tiko. 'Hey, Tiko!'

'Hey, Mom.'

The woman, back at the counter, folded and fluffed tissue into a shopping bag. 'Tiko!'

Young for the mom-and-pop label, Eve thought. They

looked entirely too relaxed and happy to be New York City merchants. And neither wore black.

'Happy holidays,' the woman said as she gave her customer the shopping bag. 'You come back and see us.'

Tiko dragged Eve straight back. 'This is Dallas. She's the cop who cleared this place out so you could rent it.'

'Oh, Lieutenant Dallas. Tiko's told us all about you. I'm Astrid.' She offered a hand. 'It's great to finally meet you.'

'Dallas, she needs presents for some girlfriends. How many friends you got?'

'Crap. I need something for . . . I guess there's five I need to take care of.'

'Let me just . . . Ben, this is Tiko's Lieutenant Dallas.'

'No kidding? Great to meet you. If you'll excuse me a minute, I'll be right with you.'

'Do you see anything you like?' Astrid asked Eve.

'I don't know.' There were bags, with straps, without straps, satchels and cases, tiny little purses that would be absolutely useless, enormous ones that could hold a room of furniture. 'I don't get this stuff.'

'Ladies like bags. Don't you got bags?' Tiko demanded.

'I have pockets. I have a field kit. I've got a file bag when I need it.' And she had the dozens of girlie bags that found their way into her closet along with the dozens of shoes, the forest of clothes.

Her husband definitely got that stuff.

'Why don't you pick one of the five,' Astrid suggested. 'Tell me a little about her.'

75

'Ah. Okay, elegant, classy, not rigid or stuffy, but classy. Mostly goes for soft colors, but can surprise you. Everything always goes together like she worked it out on a program first. Professional, smart. Kind.'

'I like her already. I've got something in the back that just came in. I think it might work.'

'Told you they'd take care of you,' Tiko said when Astrid hurried off.

'The stuff in the back isn't hot, is it?'

Insult covered his face. 'What you think? These are good guys.'

'Okay, okay. Shopping makes me twitchy. Why is there so much of everything?'

'So not everybody has the same.'

Astrid came back with a box, slipped out the long, narrow bag. 'I only ordered a few of these, just to see how we did. They're hand-painted. Really special, I thought.'

'Ah.' Eve studied it. Smooth, a little silky, with a pastel garden of flowers and a jeweled butterfly as a clasp.

'Since they're hand-painted, they're one of a kind.'

'I guess she is, too,' Eve said, thinking of Mira. 'I think she'd go for it.'

'I got a nice silk scarf that color pink.' Tiko tapped one of the flowers. 'You fluff it up inside the purse, and you got class, like you want.'

Eve eyed him. 'Sold. Moving on. Now I've got one who's out there. Nothing's too much, too wild, too anything.

Color, bright, changeable, bouncy. Oh, and she's got a kid. A girl kid, not quite a year old.'

'Oh, I've got it.' Astrid clapped her hands together. 'We have these great mother–daughter bags. Just so much fun. Practical, too, as they'll convert from shoulder bags to handbags to backpacks.'

Astrid pointed up.

Eve spotted an explosion of bright colors, big bag, small bag, hooked together. And a pair with a sparkly unicorn dancing over each.

'Oh yeah, that's Mavis and Bella. The unicorn set.'

'Let me get the hook.'

While Astrid did just that, Eve looked down at Tiko. 'I bet you've got a scarf that'll go with it.'

'I got a scarf for the mama be perfect, and I got a baby girl cap, a pink one shaped like that horse with the horn.'

'Jesus, Tiko, you're killing me. Sold.'

Forty minutes after she'd parked, Eve loaded shopping bags in her car, then got behind the wheel.

Then just sat there until her head stopped spinning.

God, she wanted a drink. Two drinks.

Telling herself to be grateful Christmas only hit once a year, she pulled back into traffic and fought the holiday rage of it all the way to the gates of home.

Diamond white lights twinkled in the trees along the drive, lending a fanciful air to the grounds. And the house rose, all gorgeous gray stone and shining glass, a fancy itself with its towers and turrets.

Lights glimmered, gleamed, outlining home against the night sky. Greenery draped and dripped, adding warmth to elegance. Candles glowed in every window, and that was welcome.

She, the lost child, had grown used to its beauty – that was love. But she would never take a single inch of it for granted. That was gratitude.

At the moment, some eighteen hours after she'd walked out its doors, the prospect of walking in again mainly brought relief.

She got out of the car, into the cold where the wind kicked at her like a bad-tempered child. She dragged the shopping bags out of the back. How had she bought so damn much? The entire event seemed like some kind of fever dream now, leaving her exhausted and with a low-level headache.

She dragged, pulled, lifted. How did she even know so many people in the first damn place? How had it happened?

Tissue flicked, threatened to fly, boxes clunked. She told herself if the bags ripped she'd leave the whole stupid lot wherever it fell.

With bags thumping against her legs she hauled everything to the door, fought it open, staggered in.

He was there, of course, lurking – the scarecrow in a black suit that was Summerset. Roarke's majordomo stood in the brilliantly lit foyer, a smirk on his pale, bony face, and the fat cat Galahad squatting like a furry Buddha at his feet.

'Is this the Ghost of Christmas Present?' Summerset wondered aloud.

Eve narrowed her eyes. She wanted to fling something back, some sharp-edged retort about cadavers on holiday, but . . .

She dumped everything where she stood. 'I'll pay you a thousand dollars to wrap everything in here.'

His stone-gray eyebrows winged up. 'I can't be bought. However,' he said as the cat padded over to sniff at bags and tissue. 'I could be persuaded.'

'What do you want?'

'You're hosting a party night after next.'

'I know that. Of course I know that.' Night after next took it down to one day, didn't it? She didn't want to think about it.

'Preparations for welcoming two hundred and fifty-six people into your home begin at eight a.m.'

She thought: *Two hundred and fifty-six people? Jesus Christ. Why?* But she said, 'Okay.'

'Participate.'

'But what if . . .' She looked down at the pile of bags, at the ass-end of the cat as he tried to burrow into one. Surrendered. 'Done.'

She shed her coat, tossed it over the newel post – a small defiance.

There was no shame in retreat, Eve told herself as she bolted up the stairs. There would be other battles, other wars. She aimed straight for the bedroom, and on a moan flung herself on the glorious blue lake of the bed.

Ten minutes, she vowed. She'd take ten minutes to

79

recover from shopping trauma and Summerset negotiations. Then she'd go to her office, set up her board there. Clear her head and start working on who killed Trey Ziegler.

Asshole or not, he deserved the best she had.

Ten minutes, she thought again, and dropped into sleep like an anchor into the sea.

She drifted out again. There was a weight on her ass she recognized as the cat. Fingers twined with hers – Roarke's.

She opened her eyes, looked into the impossible blue of his.

The bedroom tree twinkled. He'd lit the fire, so the flames simmered low and red. All things being equal, she'd have curled up against him and gone right under again.

But all things were rarely equal for a cop.

'I shopped,' she said.

'Dear God! Are you all right? Should I call for the MTs?'

'Smart-ass. I hooked the kid – you remember the kid. Tiko.'

'Ah, yeah, the young entrepreneur. I remember, fondly, the pie his grandmother baked us.'

'He's got two other kids working for him for the holidays. Expanded his stock, too. He dragged me over to this place I busted. New tenants. They sort of look like they could be related to Peabody. Free-Agey. And then ... it was like I'd walked through some portal into an alternate universe.'

'The alternate universe of a retail establishment, without crime.'

'That,' she agreed. 'So there was all this stuff, and some-body was like this would be good for this person, and I'm okay fine. Then it's this would be good for that other person, and fine. Jesus, okay, fine. But it kept going and going. And the kid started hauling in stuff from his stall, saying you put this scarf or whatever with that thing, and this thing with the other. I just kept saying okay, fine, okay, because I wanted it to be over.

'I might have post-traumatic stress.'

He kissed her lightly. 'Poor baby.'

'You don't mean that. You think it's funny. You think it's funny because you'd have actually enjoyed all of it. But it gets worse.'

'How is that possible?'

'I was weakened by the experience. I made a bargain with Summerset.'

He pressed lips to her brow as if checking for fever. 'It may be too late for the MTs.'

'Ha ha. Now because he's going to wrap all that stuff, I have to *participate* in preparations for the party. Why are there two hundred and fifty-six people coming?'

'I believe it'll be closer to two-seventy, and we welcome your participation. You're a boss, remember? You'll assign, delegate, decide, order. You might even enjoy it, a little.'

'I don't think so, but a deal's a deal.' She shifted a little, studied him. She thought of her reaction that morning when he'd walked out of her office unexpectedly.

So perfect, so pretty. All hers.

'You're not wearing your suit.' She ran a hand down the cloud softness of his stone-gray tee.

'I've been home a bit longer than you. Actually got a quick swim in.'

'Huh. That doesn't seem fair. You get a refreshing swim, relaxing clothes, and I get murder and shopping mayhem. Plus I'm still wearing my boots.'

'It doesn't seem just, does it? Let's see what I can do to even it all out.'

He levered up, lifted one of her legs, worked off the boot. Repeated the process. 'Better?'

'It's a start.'

'We might both be more relaxed if you weren't armed.' He released her weapon harness, peeled it off. Laid it on the floor with her boots. 'Now?'

'Murder and mayhem,' she reminded him. 'You had money and meetings.'

'Quite a bit of both, actually.' He straddled her, drew off the navy V-neck she'd pulled on in the middle of the night. 'How would you feel about owning a little town in Tuscany?'

'A town? Come on.'

'A village, actually, and quite charming.' Smiling down at her he unhooked her belt. 'An old ramshackle villa that could be a showpiece with the right touches. Lovely views, narrow cobbled streets, the remains of a medieval wall.'

'You bought a town.'

'Tomorrow I will.' He drew her trousers down, down, off. 'My wife has such long, amazing legs.'

'They help me get from point A to point B.'

He ran his hands up them, calf to thigh. 'You're not going anywhere at the moment.'

The diamond he'd given her when she'd accepted he loved her hung around her neck, resting on her simple white tank. He lifted it, rubbed his fingers over the tear-drop shape of it, remembering how shocked she'd been by the gift – the diamond, and the love.

'More relaxed now?'

'I'm getting there. When I drove home I thought what I need is a really big glass of wine. Then I got here and I thought, No, what I need is to fall on my face for ten minutes. But that wasn't quite it, either.'

'What was?'

'What I needed – what I need—' She pushed up, wrapped her arms around him. 'Is you.'

Those long, amazing legs hooked around his waist. Her hands slid up, gripped his hair. Holding on, he thought, to him, to them, to what they made.

All warmth and welcome, all strong and real.

He could shed his day as she shed hers, mouth to mouth, heart to heart.

They swayed there on the big bed, holding on, sliding into what was for both of them home.

He pressed his lips to her throat, to the pulse that beat for him. 'I missed our time this morning, just that bit of time over coffee and breakfast.'

'I know. Me, too.'

'It makes it all the more precious.' His lips brushed her cheekbone, her temple. 'Those times, these times.'

She burrowed into him. 'Every time.'

She lay with him, gentle strokes and long, soft kisses that washed away the hours between. Just him, just them for this little space outside the world with all its noise and harsh lights, mean shadows.

She slipped his shirt up and away, gave herself the pleasure of the warm flesh, the lean muscle, arched like a purring cat under the skill of his hands. Her heart began to kick, its beat spurred by his lips, his tongue, his teeth.

Need spread, simmering low like the fire in the hearth, then snapping into flame.

He took her over, he always could, so need and pleasure knotted together, tight, tight, driving her up, holding her on that single pinpoint of glory, then over to release.

She could have wept from the simple joy of it.

Cupping his face in her hands, she found his mouth with hers again. Sank with him, sank deep. Murmuring, she eased him onto his back. Now she straddled him, now she took him in. Slowly, slowly, slowly, her eyes on his face, she took his hands, pressed them to her heart as she began to move.

Fluid as water, building on the pleasure, drawing it out and out while her heart thudded under his hands.

He let her take, let her give while the beauty of it burned in his blood. Firelight shimmered gold on her skin, caught in her eyes. Gauzy layers of sensation thickened until he wondered he could breathe through them.

She pressed a hand to his heart, leaned over to take his mouth with hers.

'Eve.'

'I know, I know, I know.' Rising up again, she let her head fall back, let her eyes close, and rode them both into the perfect dark.

5

Now in comfortable at-home clothes, a glass of wine in her hand, and slices of some sort of savory chicken along with little golden potatoes and some unidentifiable leafy green on her plate, Eve figured the long day had rewards.

She felt loose and relaxed now instead of tired and traumatized. And though they'd missed their morning ritual, at least they'd preserved the evening's.

She'd set up her board – or started to – and now she could roll through the day over dinner at the little table in her home office.

'First,' Roarke began, 'what did you buy?'

'A lot of stuff. Heavy on bags.'

'A lot of stuff makes for a heavy bag.'

'Exactly.' She pointed at him with her fork, then stabbed some chicken. 'If people didn't cart around so much stuff, they wouldn't need bags to hold it all. Handbags, shoulder bags, tote bags. People carry their life around with them, like refugees. I don't get it.'

'But you bought them anyway, as gifts, which is what giving is all about, isn't it?'

'There were socks, too. Fuzzy socks,' she remembered, dimly. It was like the fog of war, she realized. 'And caps, and things to put other things in that go in the bags. They make fancy little cases just for lip dye. It's crazy.'

'You can't be serious!' He widened his eyes, got a narrowed stare from hers. 'Astonishing.'

'Funny. And I got roped into buying a talking unicorn.'

'Excuse me, a what?'

There, at least, she'd surprised him, she decided – and wasn't sure why she found it satisfying.

'A talking unicorn that goes in the unicorn bag for Bella that matches the big-ass unicorn bag for Mavis. It's pink – the unicorn – with a silver horn thing, and it says stuff. And it dances. It's probably going to scare the shit out of her.'

'I wager she'll love it.'

'It kind of scared me. But Tiko kept zipping out, then zipping back with more stuff. He had to tag his grandmother, get a little extra time due to all the zipping out and back. I think he put the whammy on me.'

'Yet here you are, with your shopping done.' He toasted her. 'Kudos.'

'I'd rather go hand-to-hand with a couple of Zeused-up chemi-heads than go through that again. What is this green stuff?'

Roarke only smiled. 'Any progress on your investigation?'

'I'm learning the vic was probably a bigger asshole than I already thought. I'll verify tomorrow when I go by the lab, but I think he roofied one woman, and probably more.'

Roarke's smile faded. 'That makes him more than an asshole.'

'Yeah, it does. And if I'm right, it's a damn shame he won't get his ass kicked for it. But since he got himself murdered, I've got to do the job.'

'A woman who found out what he did to her? I'd be inclined to take her side of it.'

'He deserved a cage, not a slab. Maybe a woman who found out he'd given her a boost, maybe a husband or boyfriend who found out. Maybe a woman who didn't like him juggling her with others, or a guy who didn't like being cheated on. A lot of variables. Then you add in the money, so maybe blackmail, which never ends well.'

'And yet remains a classic,' Roarke commented.

'Secrets plus greed generally equals a slab for somebody.'

'Cop math.' Roarke lifted his wine. 'And usually accurate.'

'His client list skews heavily female, though he's got men on it. It also skews heavily monied.'

'And somewhere along the line he tapped the wrong well.'

'Yeah, I'm thinking. I think, too, this new area of business – the money for sex and/or blackmail – was fairly new. Not that he didn't cheat and reap some reward, but going into it heavier. He kept Trina's friend around until a couple weeks ago, but he added the locks two or three weeks earlier.'

'Hedging his bets, perhaps,' Roarke suggested.

'Making sure he had a nice stockpile, working on sniffing up the ex before this ex. It could be. And yeah, tapped the wrong well.'

She glanced over at her board, at the IDs she'd started putting up. 'He had a lot to choose from. I'm going to have to talk to Sima again, and that means I have to talk to Trina again.'

'Did you buy her a gift?'

'No.' Appalled, she gaped at him. 'Why would I – I don't have to – Do I? I'm not going back there, Roarke. They were decent, the bag people, but I'm not going back.'

'Why don't I take care of that for you? She is your hair, face, body consultant – whether you want her to be or not. A small token would be appropriate.'

'This is way, way out of hand.' She poured more wine. 'It's completely out of hand.' In her shock, she ate the leafy green stuff. 'You've got her coming over here, don't you, to jump all over my hair, face and body before the party?'

'It's the price you pay, darling Eve, for hosting what many consider an important holiday event.'

'I'm finding those chemi-heads,' she muttered. 'I'm going out and hunting out a couple of Zeused-up chemi-heads.'

'Won't that be fun? Would you like me to check your asshole vic's financials? See if he had any more tucked away.'

'I don't think he did, but it wouldn't hurt if you've got time for it.'

She looked back toward the board. 'If he wanted to trade sex for money, why not get a license? Potentially, he could've made more, and made it legit.'

'Some, including you, still see licensed companions as prostitutes.'

'Well, sex for money.'

Roarke shook his head, offered her a roll. 'Licensed, regulated, taxed, safe. People pay for therapy, for physical training,' he added, nodding at the board. 'For spiritual guidance, and so on and so on. People pay for all manner of basic needs, and others train to provide those needs. Sex is a basic need.'

'It's legal so I've got no beef with it. But you've got a point.' She considered her board while she ate. 'He didn't see it as a business transaction – or didn't want to. Didn't want to see himself as selling a service. He was doing them a favor, allowing them to bask in the wonder of his looks, his body, his skill. The money, the money he justified as it allowed him to keep up his looks.'

She sipped at her wine. 'Yeah, yeah, yeah. It starts off for fun, for the conquest – and you get to have sex in a nice hotel suite maybe, have some champagne, a good meal – maybe she buys you a token or two. She had a good time, didn't she? Then maybe you decide to work it so she understands a little token or some under-the-table cash would really be appreciated. You gave her a good time, she gives you a little bonus. What's the harm? You're not selling yourself; she's just showing her gratitude. Just a friend, just a client, giving you something extra because you gave her something extra.'

'It sounds like you're getting to know him.'

'Maybe. The one I talked to today, the one I think he roofied? He charged her two grand for an in-home massage – that was always going to be sex for him. So he could call it a massage, a service, something special for a client, and he could set a rate. I bet he's done a lot of in-homes recently. Massages, personal training. A couple, three thousand a shot. It adds up. Add in the pillow talk, and yeah, you could work some blackmail into it. Fucker.'

'But he's your dead fucker.'

'Yeah. Yeah, he is.'

So she gave Ziegler her time, her attention, the best she had.

She wrote up her notes, put together a progress report, including all the interviews conducted.

She created a chart listing the clients who had so far admitted to having any kind of sexual relationship with Ziegler, and how much each had admitted to paying in cash, gifts, hotel expenses.

Beside each name she added marital status, or cohab status, added how many of those husbands, cohabs, were also on Ziegler's client list.

She ran each one, digging in for any instance of violent behavior or criminal offenses.

She cross-checked with the names Trina had provided, did a pass on coworkers.

And considered.

When Roarke walked in, she had her feet up on the desk. 'Another angle,' she began.

'It's not the financial one. Unless he's a great deal more clever than I give him credit for, he doesn't have any accounts other than what you have on record.'

'Didn't figure on it, but it's good to have an expert opinion on it. A competitor. I've been narrowly focused on clients and sex. But he was bashed with a trophy. He gets and keeps a lot of wealthy female clients not only because – by all accounts – he's good at his work, but because he offers them some hard-bodied sex. He makes solid commissions, the extra from sex, and he gets recognition. The trophy – I checked – also comes with a cash prize of a grand. He's won the last three years running, and was favored to win this year. But instead of going to AC for the conference, and campaigning for the competition, he's in the morgue.'

'You think another trainer killed him for a thousand dollars and a trophy?'

'Prestige, potentially more clients, bragging rights. He didn't have friends at Buff Bodies. I bet he didn't have any at other centers, either. Somebody he knew – it was a face-to-face, close-in attack. So, yeah, maybe a competitor, an associate, a peer who'd had enough of him.'

'An associate,' Roarke repeated, 'a competitor or a peer.

You could add the sex in – because you can never have too much of it – and speculate that this competitor was also used for sex, or cheated on.'

'That's a good one. That's a thought. I'd say Peabody and I are going back to the gym tomorrow.'

'With that in mind.' He took her hand, pulled her up. 'Let's go to bed.'

'Didn't we do that already?'

'And sleep. It's nearly midnight. If you keep at this much longer you'll have been up for twenty-four hours.'

'I feel like I want to push it, and it's because I don't like him.'

'You won't like him any better tomorrow. You can push then.'

'It looks like I will. Whatever else you can say about Ziegler, he wasn't lazy. Between work and sex, the guy kept revved every damn day.'

'As you do.' He tugged her along. 'Time to shut down the engines.'

She woke to the scent of coffee, and really, it didn't get better than that.

And yet it did.

When she slit open her eyes, she saw Roarke. Fully dressed in one of his ruler-of-the-business-world suits – the cat sprawled over his lap. He sat on the sofa in the bedroom sitting area, working on a tablet. Financial numbers, data, codes, scrolled by on the screen he'd switched to mute.

The faint blue wash from tablet and screen provided the only light, making him look both mysterious and fascinating.

She had no idea of the time, was too lazy to look. Instead she watched him work while she ticked off the order of what she needed to do that morning.

She needed to tag Peabody, tell her partner they'd meet at Buff Bodies, pursue the angle of competitor killer. Swing by the lab, browbeat or bribe Dickhead – Chief Tech Dick Berenski – on the tea and incense. Talk to Trina and Sima again. And she thought another pass through the crime scene was in order, this time looking specifically for tea and incense.

Do that, she decided, before the lab. Have the samples right there in hand – if she found more.

And onto more interviews with the vic's clients.

Someone who knew him. Someone he'd let in the apartment, let into the bedroom while he packed for his business trip.

Client. Coworker. Blackmail mark. Lover.

Would he have been confident or arrogant enough to let a mark or a seriously pissed-off client, lover, associate into the bedroom?

She suspected not, but it wouldn't hurt to get an expert opinion.

Add a quick session with Mira to the list.

'Lights on, twenty percent,' Roarke said, looking over into her eyes. 'You might as well have some light since you're thinking so loud.'

'I was thinking very quietly. You have bat ears.'

'When it comes to you, apparently.'

She pushed up to sit. 'What're you working on? I can take an interest,' she added when he cocked an eyebrow. 'At . . . shit, five-thirty-eight in the morning.'

'Actually, you might be interested. We've made a few changes to the design of An Didean, and have added a memorial roof garden.'

The old building in Hell's Kitchen, she thought, he'd bought with the plan to rehab and turn it into a safe house for troubled kids. And where the bones of twelve young girls had been discovered behind the walls.

'That's nice.'

'We'll have a dome so it can be used year-round, and those we house there can learn something of horticulture. The architect's wondering if we should use stones or benches with the names of the girls who died there.'

Eve rose, saying nothing as she crossed to the AutoChef for coffee. The cat deserted Roarke to sprint over to her, winding slyly between her legs, ever hopeful, she knew, that food was involved.

'I think, I guess you're asking what I think.'

'I am,' he told her.

'I think creating a garden shows respect. And I think the kids you'd shelter there, educate there, don't need to be reminded of cruelty and death, but of life. Of the, well, garden of possibilities of life.'

'I think you're exactly right. Thank you.'

'Anytime. I'm going to grab thirty in the gym before I get ready.'

Coffee in hand, she took the elevator down, got in a good run along a simulated shoreline with blue waves breaking.

After a blistering hot shower with the multi-jets on full, she stepped into the drying tube.

'It's too bad the rest of the world can't be heated up like a shower,' she commented as she headed for her closet.

'Since it can't you'll want to dress for it. Not as windy today, though, according to the questionably reliable forecast.'

She grabbed a sweater she knew to be warm despite being thin and soft as a tissue, straight-legged pants and a vest that would add warmth and cover her weapon harness.

After pulling on clothes, she grabbed a pair of boots.

'Not those boots,' Roarke said with barely a glance when she came out to sit and pull them on.

'What's wrong with these boots?'

'Not a thing, but the gray with the mock laces will pick up the color of that sweater, polish things off.'

'I don't need to polish ... Fine, fine, fine.' Easier, she figured, to change the damn boots than get into a fashion debate she'd certainly lose.

Plus she wanted to see what was under the silver domes on the table. If she changed the boots, maybe it wouldn't be oatmeal.

He poured her coffee as she sat down again. 'Good morning, Lieutenant.'

'We'll see about that.' She lifted the dome. 'Oh hell yeah, it's a good morning.'

'I thought, considering yesterday, you'd earned pancakes.'

She immediately drowned them in syrup.

'They're all apple and cinnamonny.'

'And deserve better than being a vehicle for syrup, but ah well.'

In any case, he loved watching her appreciation of food, especially since she so often forgot to eat it.

'I might need a bribe for Dickhead,' she said between bites. 'Considering he's had twenty-four hours, my wrath should be enough, but just in case.'

'Take him a bottle of unblended scotch,' Roarke suggested. 'We've several already in gift bags. It'll throw him off-balance straightaway if you offer him a holiday token.'

'It would, wouldn't it? I really hate to go bearing gifts and all, but any lack of cooperation after that would make him an even bigger Dickhead than he is. It's kind of win-win for me.'

'It's the old catching more flies with sugar than vinegar.'

'Why would anyone want to catch flies? What you want is to make them go the hell away.'

'That's a point, and now another classic adage bites the dust.' He patted her leg. 'Breakfast with you is a continuing education.'

'I do what I can. If it turns out the vic's blend of tea included a date-rape drug, I can use that to pry open more of his clients. Outrage tends to turn off filters.'

'You've never mentioned next of kin.'

'Only child, parents divorced when he was ten. Both remarried. He bounced between the mother in Tucson and the father in Atlanta until he was of age. Neither of them have seen him for more than six years. They were both shaken, but I didn't get any sense of close family ties.'

'So no friends or family.'

'Not really. And from what I can tell, by his own choice. Friends and family take work.'

She thought of her forty-minute battle for sanity with Tiko and the bag people. Fucking A, it took work.

'All his work was focused on himself,' she added. 'Speaking of family, I guess you got all the gifts off to Ireland.'

'I did, yes. You did some work there.'

'I didn't shop.'

'You helped me decide on several things, and the *Cops and Robbers* comp game for young Sean was your idea.'

'He was an easy one. Peabody and McNab are doing an in-and-out shuttle for Christmas to her family. You don't want to do something like that, do you?'

'We had Thanksgiving, and that worked well for me, having them all here. I like having our Christmas, you and I.'

'I do, too. And since I'd really like to get this case closed before that, I'd better get going. Good pancakes,' she said, leaned over and kissed him.

'I'll see you tonight. We might talk about strategy for the deal you've made with Summerset.'

'I'm trying not to think about that.' She shoved up. 'Where's the hooch – for Dickhead?'

'Fourth-floor gift room.'

She stared at him for ten silent seconds. 'We have a gift room?'

On a half laugh, he shook his head. 'One day, darling Eve, you really should go through the entire house. East wing, fourth-floor tower.'

'Okay.' Since she wasn't completely sure where that was, she walked to the elevator. Ordered it.

'Don't bother shaking boxes,' he called out. 'None of yours are in that location.'

'I don't snoop,' she said as the doors shut.

But, of course, now she wanted to.

Gift rooms, she thought. Who gave so many gifts they had to have an actual dedicated room to hold them?

The doors opened; she stepped out. Her jaw dropped.

Apparently they did.

Shelves and counters held a colorful array of wrapped gifts with shiny, elaborate bows. Gift bags in silver or gold or red or green stood like uniformed soldiers.

She opened one of the doors along the wall, discovered more shelves with rigorously organized gifts not wrapped.

Fancy candle sets or fancy bath sets — male, female, or unisex varieties.

Boxed wineglasses, elegant picture frames, electronics, even some toys.

Why the hell did she have to go shopping when she could just come up here?

She found more ruthless — to the point of scary — organization with gift boxes, wrapping paper, tissue paper, ribbons and bows.

Everything as pristine as some high-end gift boutique and all in the tall tower room complete with a wall screen and a comp. She just bet the comp held a complete catalog of the contents of the room, down to the last inch of shiny ribbon.

She grabbed one of the silver gift bags, checked the contents.

Bourbon.

Checked a gold one, found the scotch, then, out of curiosity, checked one of the red bags. Cognac. She found Irish whiskey in the green bags — figured.

Both impressed and intimidated, she got back in the elevator, ordered the main floor.

She grabbed her coat off the newel post, and decided a man who owned half the world anyway might as well have a room loaded with stuff he prepared to give away.

At least she knew just where to go the next time she needed a bribe.

She'd left early enough that traffic stayed light and gave

her the opportunity to bypass Mira's admin who'd give her grief for asking for a quick session. Instead she shot a v-mail straight to Mira's 'link.

'I'd like a quick consult today if you can fit me in. I'm sending you the Ziegler file. Mostly I want to be sure I've got the right handle on him. If you can't squeeze in a consult, maybe an overview profile, vic and killer. Appreciate it.'

The first ad blimp lumbered across the sky as she hit the edges of the West Village. It announced a last-minute SALE SALE SALE at the SkyMall running until ten p.m. Christmas Eve.

Jesus, even she wasn't so lame she waited until Christmas Eve to grab a gift.

Then, amazing to her, it announced a door-buster SALE SALE SALE at the SkyMall beginning at one a.m. on December twenty-sixth.

Why would people do that? What could they possibly need to buy the day after Christmas, in the middle of the night the day after? Her second thought was she believed she would self-terminate if she had to make a living in retail.

She parked, noted she was about ten minutes early. Rather than wait for Peabody, she opted to go in, get started.

Ear-splitting music greeted her again, but this time with some amusement as she recognized Mavis's voice wailing about having fun now that love was done.

She spotted Lill crouched beside a puny guy who struggled sweatily through some push-ups.

Eve crossed over, heard the man wheezing even over Mavis and the *thump, thump* of feet racing nowhere on treads.

'Need a minute.'

Lill nodded. 'Come on, Scott, just two more. Don't you quit on me. All right!' she shouted when he collapsed in a heap. 'Thirty-second breather, then I want you to do ten minutes on the tread. Level five, Scott. Don't wimp out.'

'Okay.' He got shakily to his feet. 'Okay, Lill.' And staggered toward the tread.

'I've got to keep an eye on him,' Lill says. 'He's really coming along.'

'Did he start out at a crawl?'

'Just about. It's clients like Scott make this job worthwhile. He really tries, he really works. Do you have news about Trey?'

'I've got some follow-up questions. This trainer of the year thing, how competitive?'

'Very, or else what's the point? I submit progress reports for all my trainers, showing the improvements of their clients. And each trainer submits three separate original programs they've put together. The trainer's fitness and established routines are also factored in. It's a process. Why?'

'Who was his main competition?'

'Hard to say for certain, but in the BB franchise, I'd go

with Juice – Jacob Maddow. But then he's one of mine, so I'm biased. And there's Selene, she's right up there. She's out of our Morningside Heights location. Outside BB, I'd lean toward Rock. He has his own gym – bare-bones place in Midtown – West Side. Rock Hard it's called – and he is. But I have to say I figured Trey would grab the prize again this year. He'd worked up some fierce programs.'

'Did they all know each other?'

'Sure, you tend to. Rock and Juice hang together, have for years. I'd've lost Juice to Rock Hard, but most of Juice's clients wouldn't have gone with him. They like the perks here.'

'Any trouble between any of them and Ziegler?'

'Crap.' Sighing, she rubbed her orange hair. 'Juice is a go-along guy, a family man. He sure wasn't a fan of Trey's, and maybe they had a few words now and again. But Juice isn't one to start trouble. I don't know Selene all that well, but I heard Trey hit on her. Didn't matter to him she's gay – she has tits, and that was enough for Trey to give it a shot. Rock hated his ever-fucking guts, but they didn't run in the same circles.'

'Then why the hate?'

'Some time back – maybe close to a year – Trey banged Rock's sister. They were both at some club, and she was pretty wasted. He took her home and banged her, then bragged about it. He *knew* she was Rock's sister. Juice warned him to shut up, and finally I had to tell him to shut up, at least around here. I heard he and Rock squared off about it, and Trey backed down. But I don't have the details. I didn't want them. The truth is Trey was a personal pain in my ass. But professionally, he was an asset, and it's my job to hold on to the assets around here.'

'Okay.'

'About Rock. I didn't think of him yesterday because it was close to a year ago, and as far as I know those two never see each other except maybe at the AC conference or the competition we have in New York every spring. That's it.'

'I still need to talk to him. To the three of them. Where would I find Juice?'

'See the guy over there bench-pressing about one-fifty? That's Juice.'

'Okay, thanks.'

'He's a nice guy. He's got a wife, a kid, and another kid coming.'

'I'll keep that in mind.'

Eve moved over to the weight area, and the man currently bench-pressing more than she weighed.

'Jacob Maddow?'

'Juice, yeah.' He continued to press, sweat slicked on his pleasant face, on his very impressive biceps. But he gave her a quick smile. 'What can I do for you?'

'Lieutenant Dallas, NYPSD.' She showed him her badge. 'I'd like to talk to you.'

'About Ziegler? I heard yesterday, when I came in.' He set the bar in the safety, slid out from under.

He hit about six feet, Eve gauged, and most of it muscle. He wore his streaked brown hair in a stub of a tail.

'We can take it in the private classroom. Nobody's in there right now, and we won't have to yell at each other.'

'Works for me.' She spotted Peabody. 'One minute, that's my partner.'

'Mind if I get a drink?' He gestured toward the juice machine in the corner.

'Go ahead.'

'Get you something?'

'No, thanks.' She signaled to Peabody, then motioned her over to the machine. 'Detective Peabody, Jacob Maddow. Goes by Juice. We're going to talk in private.'

'It's just through here.'

He led them into a room with frosted glass walls where the noise level dropped to a backbeat murmur.

'I want to say I'm sorry about what happened to Ziegler, but I'm not going to lie. We weren't friends.'

'Why don't you tell us where you were the evening before last, from say five p.m. to seven.'

'Home. My day off, so we don't get a sitter. I had my kid while my wife was at work. She got home about five. We ate about six, I guess, and then she took Mimi up for a bath. I spent the next two hours putting this tricycle thing together for Mimi for Christmas. It comes cheaper unassembled, but let me tell you, it ain't worth it.'

'You didn't get sent to AC?'

'Lill would've sprung for it, but this close to Christmas,

I want to be home with my family. Plus, my wife's pregnant. Seven months along.'

'I heard you're one of the top competitors for the next trainer of the year award.'

'I got a shot.' He chugged down juice. 'It'd be nice – the cash prize – with another kid coming along. Another girl,' he said with a quick smile. 'I'm surrounded by girls.'

'I also heard you had some words with Ziegler over your friend Rock's sister.'

'Okay, sure – that was a while back, but sure. Look, I've known Kyria since she was a kid. When this happened, she was barely legal, and, okay, sowing some wild – but he didn't have any business touching that. But that was Ziegler. I know damn well he messed with her because she was Rock's. I didn't like hearing him brag about it, so I told him to knock it off, and I warned him he didn't want the shit he was spreading to get back to Rock.'

'And when it did?'

'Rock did what any brother would do. He got in his face about it. And as soon as he did, as *soon* as he did, Ziegler backed off.'

After a look of disgust for the cowardice, Juice guzzled some of his drink. 'He shut up,' Juice continued, 'and he slunk off. He wasn't going to risk a pounding. I know he spread some shit about Rock's place, but that didn't matter. Rock Hard doesn't cater to the same kind of clients we do here, so that wasn't any skin off Rock. But that was the only way Ziegler could try to get his own back, smearing Rock's rep.'

'If somebody smears my rep, I'm going to want to get up in their face,' Eve commented.

'It didn't matter. The guy was like a gnat buzzing. You just ignore it. The way I figured, either me or Rock would take that award next spring, and that would pay Ziegler back.'

'He was favored.'

'Not anymore.' Juice shook his head. 'I know how that sounds, but I said I wasn't going to lie. I hated the son of a bitch.'

Outside, Eve headed for her car. 'A competitor may just be a good angle here. I'll fill you in on the three top candidates I got from Lill on the way to Ziegler's apartment.'

'Did you see the arms on that guy? And the pecs?' Peabody bundled herself in the car. 'I wonder what he charges for personal training.'

'You've got access to a gym right at Central,' Eve reminded her.

'I don't have access to those arms.' Peabody glanced back as Eve pulled into traffic. 'Or those pecs.'

6

Eve broke the seal on the apartment door, stepped inside.

It smelled of death and sweeper dust.

'Logical place for tea's the kitchen, right? Where do people keep incense?'

'There wasn't any in the bedroom, not that I remember,' Peabody began. 'If he uses it on off-the-book or in-home massages, maybe he has some with his gear.'

'Check the gear, I'll check the kitchen.'

Eve moved into the small U-shaped kitchen, gave it a quick overview. Standard AutoChef, friggie, compact oven, three-burner range, mini dishwasher.

Not that Ziegler made much use of it, she noted. Dishes, glassware piled in the sink, empty or near-empty takeout boxes scattered the counter. The sweepers had taken the lidless pizza box, but she couldn't imagine what that might tell them.

In any case, the obvious conclusion was, Ziegler had been too lazy for the recycler.

Out of curiosity, she opened the friggie. Energy drinks,

lite beer, box wine, a jug of one of those mixed fruit and veggie juices, a small container of soy milk.

She checked the menu on the AutoChef. A couple of whole wheat bagels, a veggie pizza, coffee, veggie hash, and tofu turkey.

No tea, she noted, and turned to the short line of cupboards.

Soy chips, dry cereal that looked like bark and twigs, some dehydrated berries, several bottles of vitamins and supplements. And three small containers of leafy substances labeled as tea: Relaxation Tea, Digestive Tea, Energy Tea.

She bagged them all.

'Cone incense – a variety pack.' Peabody came in with a clear case holding about a dozen colorful little pyramids. 'In his massage bag. It's a smart way to transport and store, kind of like a small fishing tackle box. They're all labeled by scent. None of them say sex-inducing. You've got patchouli, vanilla, lavender and so on.'

'I don't think he'd label it sex-inducing. I've got three teas – the loose leaf stuff like in the baggie.' Eve stepped out of the kitchen bump. 'We'll take another pass through the place. The sweepers wouldn't have been looking for anything like this. Then we'll talk to Sima again before we get these to the lab.'

'If any of this contains some sort of date-rape drug, he probably used it on her, too. I mean, why wouldn't he?'

'Yeah. I'm counting on it.'

*

Music played at Trina's salon, but not at the head-throbbing volume of the gym. Here it provided a bouncy bit of background. The place smelled a little too much like a meadow for Eve's taste – with a faint underpinning of chemicals. God knew what they mixed up here to slather on your hair, your face, and other parts of the anatomy.

People sat in brightly colored chairs sipping fizzy drinks, babbling away with each other or focused on provided discs – fashion mags, beauty mags, music – while techs slathered or snipped or painted. Products lined the walls.

Farther back, thin partitions offered some privacy for whatever the hell went on behind them. The place buzzed with voices, little tools that clipped or hummed or buffed, and chairs being lifted or lowered or reclined.

A woman with a fountain of red-tipped white hair talked cheerfully on an ear-link while she tapped a tattooed finger at a calendar on her screen.

'I squeezed you in, Lorinda. Two-fifteen, New Year's Eve, with Marcus. You've got his last block. Oh, don't I know it! We'll see you then. Have a wonderful Christmas!'

She tapped her earpiece, beamed at Eve and Peabody. 'Good morning! How can I help you today?'

'We're looking for Sima Murtagh.'

'Sima's with a client, but she's got an opening at . . . ' *Tap, tap* with the finger tattooed with a red butterfly. 'One-thirty.'

'We're not here for a service.' Eve drew out her badge.

The woman's lime-green eyes went wide. 'Oh! Oh.

You're here about ... ' Her voice dropped to a whisper. 'Trey. It's awful,' she said in the same hissy whisper. 'Just tragic! Let me just run back and check where she is on her service.'

She hopped off the stool and clicked her way to the back on the towering heels of thigh-high red boots.

Eve started to speak, then noticed Peabody wasn't beside her but had edged over to a counter to play with samples.

'Stop it,' Eve ordered.

'It's just sitting here.' Hurriedly Peabody rubbed some cream over her hands. 'And it smells really good.'

'Try for some dignity,' Eve muttered as Trina swept in from the back.

Unlike her receptionist, Trina wore flat-soled shoes – but Eve found it hard to deem them practical as red-nosed reindeers cavorted over them.

'Sima needs a couple minutes. She's at a critical point of the service. She can take five when she finishes applying the full mask. You should come back. I've got one treatment room open – we're slammed with holiday party prep – but we can use it for a few.'

'Fine.' Eve started back with her, grabbed Peabody by the arm to make sure her partner didn't go back to playing with samples. 'You didn't mention Ziegler used persuaders on women.'

'Do what?'

'You know, a little something in the tea to make a woman more ... agreeable to having sex.'

111

Trina stopped dead in front of a line of cushy chairs where some women had their feet in bubbly blue water, others had them covered with green goo, and still others had techs painting their toes.

'I knew it. I *knew* it! Fucker.'

'You knew, but didn't think it worth mentioning?'

'I didn't *know* know it, but I knew it. Fucker,' she repeated, angry color rising up in her high-planed cheeks as she stomped off toward a door in her reindeer booties.

Inside she paced around a padded table, passed shiny silver counters holding what looked to Eve like devices of torture.

'You can't say shit like that if you don't absolutely know. But I *knew*. In my gut.'

She threw up her hands, still pacing so the red lab-style coat she wore over a black skin suit flapped.

'I told you I've had some women in my chair who'd slept with him, and some of them said how they didn't plan on it, but how they just got the urge during a session – always a home session. Massage or personal training.'

'Names.'

Now Trina stopped in her tracks. 'Come on, Dallas, my clients have to know I won't mouth off about their personal business. They have to trust me.'

'It's murder, Trina, and getting dosed is a hell of a motive for it.'

'Christ! None of my clients killed the slimy bastard.' She kicked a cabinet, a sentiment and temper reliever Eve understood. 'Fine, fine. Fuck. I'll give you the names, but you gotta let me contact them first, give them a heads-up. I need to make it right with them.'

'No details, Trina. You can tell them the cops forced you to give their names as part of the investigation, but that's it.'

'Damn it. Damn it. I wish he wasn't dead so I could peel the skin off his balls. Sima. Motherfucker! He probably used something on her, too.'

Even as she spoke Sima poked her head in the door. 'I'm really sorry. I couldn't leave my client until I'd finished the application.' She came in, closed the door behind her, then twisted her hands together. 'Do you know who killed Trey?'

'The investigation's ongoing. Sima, do you know where Trey got his tea?'

'Tea? Oh, you mean the herbals. Gosh, I really don't. He bought it loose, and it came in little bags. First time I thought they were illegals, maybe Zoner or something – and I was really surprised because he's so careful about what goes into his body, you know? But he said they were specialty herbals, just a nice little perk for clients before a massage or after a workout. He didn't even charge extra.'

'And the incense?'

'I don't know. He hardly ever burned it at home. It was for clients again. You know, aromatherapy.'

'He used at home, with you?'

'A few times.'

'Did he ever make you tea?'

113

'Sure, a few times. To help me relax after a tough day. The tea and incense, and a shoulder massage.' Tears shimmered. 'He could be so sweet that way when he wanted to.'

Out of the corner of her eye, Eve saw Trina set her teeth, turn away – and saw Peabody give her arm a rub.

'Let me ask you, Sima, and I need you to be square with me. When he made the tea, lit the incense, did you have sex with him?'

'Well … I guess.' She frowned a little, flushed a little. 'Yeah, I guess. I'd get relaxed, you know.'

'After a hard day,' Eve continued. 'So you maybe weren't feeling much like having sex … until you got relaxed.'

'Sometimes you're on your feet for like eight hours, hardly a break. It just can go that way, and that's good because it means people ask for you especially. But when you get home, maybe you just want to sit down, watch some screen, maybe go to bed – to sleep I mean – a little early.'

'Sure, I know how it goes.'

'Everybody does, right? Well, mostly. Trey, I swear, he could want to do it twice a day every day.'

'So you maybe just wanted to kick back, watch some screen, and he wanted sex.'

'He wasn't pushy about it. If I told him I was really tired or whatever, he was okay with it.'

'He'd make you some tea, to relax you.'

'Yeah. And it did, and I'd start getting in the mood after all.'

114

'Sima, I've taken a statement from one of his clients, one who wasn't in the mood, either, until he made her tea.' Eve waited a moment to let it sink in – saw it didn't. 'It's pretty clear there are going to be more.'

'I don't understand.'

'We're taking the tea into the lab for testing, and I believe they'll find some form of date-rape drug in the mix.'

'No, no, he wouldn't do that. Holy God! You're wrong. Trina.'

'You think about it, Sim. Think,' Trina insisted. 'Did he ever make you the damn tea when you already wanted to have sex, or after you had sex? Or in the morning before you both left for work, or any goddamn time you didn't have sex after drinking it?'

'I . . . He . . .' Her eyes filled. 'No. But – why would he do that? Why would he do that to me? He didn't have to do that to me. I mean sometimes you just want to sleep or just cuddle. Don't you?'

'Sure you do, honey. Sure.' Trina went over, hugged Sima close. 'It's not on you, and don't you think that. It's not on you, and it's not about sex.'

'But—'

'It's about him wanting to make you do something you didn't want to, so he could feel like a big man. Anybody who does that is small.'

'I cared about him. I thought he cared about me.'

'He never cared about anybody but himself.' Over Sima's

head, Trina's eyes met Eve's fiercely. 'And that's not on you, either.'

'Run the names Trina gave us,' Eve said as they started back to the car.

'On it. It really flattened her.' Peabody pulled out her PPC to begin the runs when she got into the car. 'Imagine it. Imagine finding out someone you thought cared about you, someone you lived with, slept with, slipped you a sex drug. If he did. We're not a hundred percent sure.'

'I'm sure enough. Profile it, Peabody. Everything we know about the vic. Is he the kind of guy who makes tea for his girlfriend when she's too tired for sex?'

'Probably not, no.'

'And then, coincidentally, once she drinks the tea, she's, bang, in the mood to do it after all? If that's straight tea, I'll eat the leaves dry.'

'It's rape.' Peabody scowled at her PPC as she worked. 'If we're right, and I think we are, it's rape. It's no different than holding a knife to her throat. It takes choice away.'

'That's exactly right.'

'It was bad enough when he was just an asshole.'

'Whatever he was, he's dead. We do the job. We can think it's too damn bad Trina didn't get a chance to skin his balls, but we do the job.'

She answered the in-dash 'link when it signaled, watched Mira come on screen.

She's done something different with her hair, Eve thought. What did they call that sleek sort of curve. A bob? Why did they call it a bob? What kind of name was *bob* for hair?

'Eve. I've read the report you sent. I actually have a fairly light morning, so I can certainly meet with you.'

'Great. I've got another stop to make, but I'm not sure how long it's going to take.'

'If you can be here in an hour, I have time. If not, I have time, a bit, later this afternoon.'

'I'll make it in an hour, thanks.'

'Hey, Dr Mira.' Peabody angled over. 'I really like your hair.'

'Oh, thanks.' As women did, Mira fluffed at it. 'Not too severe?'

'Totally no.'

'I wanted a change, so I'll live with it a few days. I'll see you in an hour, Eve. I have a session about to start.'

'I'll be there. Thanks.'

Eve signed off as she hunted for parking. 'Why do women always want to change their hair? If they liked it one way, why change it to another way?'

'For fun. Or just to mix things up. You change your shoes or your jacket or whatever all the time.'

'They're not attached to me.'

'So changing your hair makes it even more about you, the way I see it.' Peabody twisted a lock of hair that poked out from her cap. 'I think I'm going to try

117

something different for the holidays. I should've talked to Trina.'

'I shouldn't have brought it up,' Eve decided, pulling into a slot. 'We'll take Schubert's hair to Harvo.'

'The Queen of Hair and Fiber.'

'Yeah, her. Just give it to her, ask her to get us the results as soon as she can, then we'll get Dickhead to make some tea.'

Holiday fever had infected the lab with colored lights and a tree — twice the size of the puny reject in Homicide — decorated with evidence bags, brushes, tweezers, and other sweeper tools.

But the centerpiece was a fat Santa dressed like a sweeper toting a banner that read:

CSI SANTA KNOWS WHEN YOU'VE BEEN BAD!

It kind of gave Eve the creeps.

But then, so did Dick Berenski.

Still, she carted her gift bag toward his long counter where he sat on his rolling stool. His spidery fingers switched between two computers. He sported a half-assed goatee — that was new. The pointy triangle on his chin, the sparce hair above his upper lip made her think of graffiti drawn inexpertly on an egg.

She set the gift bag on his counter. 'Merry Christmas.'

He paused in his work, gave her then Peabody a wary look before reaching into the bag.

Surprise flooded his face, then delight – demonstrated by the shift in the poor excuse for a mustache when his skinny lips curved.

Then with eyes darting left, right, he shoved the bottle back into the bag, shoved the bag into one of the drawers of his workstation.

'Thanks.'

Eve wiggled fingers at Peabody, who lined up evidence bags on the counter.

'What's this?' Berenski demanded.

'That's what I need you to tell me. Now.'

'You want me to do an analysis on all this, right now?' He swept his arm over his workstation. 'Can't you see I got work going here?'

'This is work, too. We had samples sent in already.'

'Low priority.'

'Now it's high priority. Start with this.' She pushed the tea labeled Relaxation toward him. 'That might be enough for right now. If you're so busy, delegate. How long does it take to analyze some tea leaves?'

'Get in line. We'll get to it when we get to it.'

Saying nothing, Eve tapped the drawer where he'd hidden the scotch.

He radiated insult. 'That was a gift.'

'Yeah, and if you ever want another *gift*, you'll analyze this evidence.'

Maybe Summerset couldn't be bought, she thought, but she knew damn well Dickhead could.

119

'I'm doing you a favor.' He pointed one of his long, skinny fingers at her.

'Okay.'

He snatched up the tea, did a fast roll to the other end of his counter, muttering all the way.

Satisfied, Eve said nothing, leaned on her side of the counter. She watched him pull on thin gloves, open the evidence bag, unstop the container.

He took a sniff of it, frowned. 'Chamomile and lavender shit.'

He took tweezers out of a tray, transferred some of the leaves into a tube, put the tube in a slot of a small machine on the counter. He repeated the process, this time adding liquid to the tube with an eye-dropper.

'Why are you doing that?'

'Do I tell you how to do your job?'

Eve only shrugged as he gave her the evil eye, then went back to work.

He lowered a clear lid over the tubes, ran those skinny fingers over a control panel. The machine began to hum, and Eve, still leaning on the counter, felt it vibrate.

Curious, she pushed off the counter, intending to walk down for a closer look.

'Lieutenant Dallas, Detective Peabody.'

Dr Garnet DeWinter, the new forensic anthropologist, swept up. She wore a hot pink lab coat over a pink and green striped dress that molded her tall, curvy body. She'd slicked her hair back into some sort of sleek twist that made her exotic eyes dominate the sharp-featured face.

Her green, ice-pick heels sported tiny pink bows at the ankle straps.

'Dr DeWinter.'

'Someone must be dead.'

'Someone always is.'

'That's true, isn't it? Oh, well, it keeps us busy. Richard, I just wanted to come down and thank you for getting that report to me so quickly this morning.'

Richard? Eve thought, and watched Berenski preen.

'No problem, Doc. We're on the same team.'

'Yes, we are.' She moved down, laid a hand on his shoulder, studied the computer screen along with him. 'Chamomile, lavender, valerian. Tea? A soother?'

'So far.'

Stuffing her hands in her pockets — no way she was touching Dickhead — Eve moved down the counter to read the screen herself.

'What's that?' she demanded with a long, unpronounceable element scrolled on.

'Hold on,' Berenski murmured, then nodded as a second, then a third element popped up.

'Those sure as hell aren't herbs. That's a Rohypnol-bremelanotide compound. Erotica with a twist. It's a sex drug.'

DeWinter glanced over at Eve. 'The combination would stimulate the sexual drive, yes, and potentially lower

121

inhibitions. The tea is a relaxation blend, and would mask the chemicals, add to the lack of inhibition and certainly increase sex drive.'

'Your vic didn't have any of this in him,' Berenski told her. 'I saw his tox screen, and it was clean.'

'No, he didn't drink it. He used it on women.'

'What you've got here is like a super soother, and it's laced with illegals. Sort of a mild date-rape drug.'

Eve scorched him with a look. 'Nothing's mild about rape.'

'Don't get twisted. I ain't saying that. I'm saying the product's on the mild side. It's not like whore or rabbit, and the user's likely to feel relaxed instead of jumpy after the job's done. It don't make it legal, and it sure don't make it right. Your vic was an asshole if he used this without telling the women what it was.'

'No memory loss with this,' DeWinter added. 'No wild up and downs or desperation. But compliance and escalated sexual desire. His victims, as that's just what they were, would likely have thought themselves agreeable, even pleased. Afterward, again depending on the circumstances, there may have been some regret or embarrassment.'

'He used these, too.' Eve gestured for Peabody to put the incense case on the counter. 'In combination.'

'I'll check them out. You want the other teas analyzed?'

'Yeah, do the whole lot, but I think we hit the mother lode. Appreciate the quick work,' she added, and turned to go.

DeWinter fell into step beside her. Eve spared her a look. 'Richard?'

'It makes him feel special, and by making him feel special I often get my samples and specimens moved to the head of his list. Is he a bit of a dick?' DeWinter said with a hint of a smile. 'Absolutely. But he's also excellent at his work.'

'I just bribe him.'

'Also a viable option. I wanted to say I'm looking forward to your party. Li's bringing me.'

'Morris? You and Morris?'

'Yes – and no, so don't look so appalled. We have the dead, an appreciation of music, and absolutely no interest in a relationship in common. So it's nice for both of us to have a date for your party. So, I'll see both of you then.'

'It is nice,' Peabody said as they headed out. 'It's nice that Morris has someone to hang out with. He's a sociable guy.'

'Maybe.' Eve had yet to make up her mind about DeWinter.

Eve pushed through the door. 'I want you to start on Trina's list, start talking to these women. Any one of them admits to drinking Ziegler's tea, give her the details, and get a full statement. Press the money angle, too. Let's find out who gave him cash and why. Get a feel for them, Peabody.'

'Because one of them might've killed him.'

'Get started. I've got to get to Central, meet with Mira. I'll tag you as soon as I'm done, catch up with you.'

'I've got this, Dallas. I'll be the sympathetic cop – because I do sympathize. I can usually get more that way than going in tough.'

'Is that the fly, sugar, vinegar deal?'

'Yeah, I guess it is.'

'I still don't get it,' Eve said and strode to her car.

7

Mira's admin offered silence and a frosty stare when Eve walked into Mira's outer office. Eve wondered if she should've grabbed another one of those handy gift bags, but the woman with the icy eyes tapped her interoffice 'link.

'Lieutenant Dallas is here. Of course.' She tapped it again. 'You can go in.'

'Thanks.' Eve opened the door, walked in. 'Your admin's pissed I went around her.'

Mira glanced up from the work on her desk, smiled a little. 'She's protective. But I do have some free time this morning, and I do enjoy consulting on your cases.' She rose. 'Tea?'

'Definitely not, but that's something I want to discuss with you.'

'Tea?' Mira said again as she turned to her AutoChef.

'Yeah. Turns out Ziegler mixed a low-grade date-rape drug with loose tea, brewed it up when he got the urge.'

Eve flipped out her notebook. 'A Rohypnol-bremelanotide combo mixed with chamomile, lavender, and valerian. Dick-head called it Erotica with a twist.'

'I see.' Mira programmed one cup of the flower-smelling tea she liked. 'I'm not surprised to learn that.'

'Because?'

'Sit,' Mira invited, bringing her tea over to one of her pretty blue scoop chairs.

They suited her – elegant and functional. As the soft coral of her dress, the slightly bolder color of her ankle-breaking heels, the understated but excellent jewelry suited the department's top shrink and profiler.

'He was a narcissist,' Mira began. 'Extremely self-focused. His choice of career, and apparent skill at it, provided a service to others, but put him in control of them, physically and emotionally. Even spiritually for some who consider their physical regimen a kind of religion. It also put him in the spotlight.'

'Yeah, I get that. Add the photos – of himself – in the apartment, the mirrors, the clothes, the really extensive collection of hair and body products. He could've opened his own store there. I also get some people can self-focus, can indulge themselves without being narcissists. Or rapists.'

'Rapists.' Mira sipped her tea. 'Tell me about that.'

'One of the women who slept with him – married, a client – described the experience.'

She laid out Martella Schubert's statement, her suspicions, and the discovery of the tea.

'He laced tea to gain this woman's – and you believe other women's – acquiescence for sex. Tea he served them as if a kind of romantic gesture.'

'Exactly. He even used it on his former live-in girlfriend when she wasn't in the mood.'

'He wouldn't have seen it as rape.'

'That doesn't change the fact.'

'No, but he would've seen it as a kind of seduction. Setting the scene. And it again, put him in control, physically and emotionally. To this man sex was another act of being admired, a validation of his prowess, his physical appearance, his body. He gave them a service, he'd think. He gifted them with his skill. And as with his other skills, why shouldn't he be paid for it? A narcissist, a sex addict with sociopathic tendencies.'

'No friends,' Eve added. 'Coworkers who could respect his skill, but only tolerated him at best. All that money in his locker.'

'His secret. Banking or investing money is so ordinary, isn't it? He was extraordinary. And why should he make an effort to be friendly with coworkers when he was so obviously superior?'

'Too special, too superior to go through training and channels and get a license for sex.'

'Why train for something he excelled at? Be screened by some bureaucracy? A license? Far too regimented.'

'And it costs. Word is – and it's bearing out – he was cheap with everything but himself. He dealt in cash, cash only. Unreported cash. And I think greedy enough to resort to blackmail.'

'Oh, absolutely, though again he wouldn't have

considered it blackmail. The exchange of pay for a service.'

Mira sipped her tea, recrossed her very fine legs. 'In his mind, he deserved it all, and more. I believe he'd have escalated – sex and money – as he went on. The use of the illegals certainly demonstrates his driving need to have exactly what he wanted, to control the women he selected. They not only succumbed to his allure – in his mind – but paid for the privilege. Every success would reinforce his self-belief, and he would have wanted more.'

'The awards – the trophies – they played in.'

'Reinforcing again he was special, above the rest. You're approaching this from a different angle,' Mira commented. 'A profile of your victim rather than the killer.'

'The more I learn about him, the more it's clear pretty much anyone who knew him could've done it. Temper, payback, an argument over sex, blackmail, a competitor, a client. I think the murder itself was a moment of fury, impulse, but the rest . . .'

'Cold, calculated. Still angry. How could you drive a knife into a dead man unless there was anger? The message left? An insult. A brutal sort of sarcasm.'

'A definite fuck-you.'

'Precisely. The anger was personal and intense, but controlled. Absolute rage? You'd expect more violence. And I agree with your conclusion in your report that he knew his killer, had no fear, no time to defend. He was a very strong and fit individual. But there were no signs of struggle, no offensive or defensive wounds on the body, just the killing blows and the postmortem stab wound. And nothing taken?'

'Not that the ex-girlfriend knew. Plenty of easy money in electronics and jewelry, so not robbery, no. I can't know if the killer gave him something the ex didn't know about, then took it. Jewelry again or more cash. But he was packing to go out of town, and let this person in the apartment, and by the evidence at the scene, let this person into the bedroom.'

'He was fully dressed when killed.'

'Dressed, yeah. The blood spatter on the sweater from the head wound. I don't think the killer came for sex, or Ziegler was looking for sex. He should have left for AC about thirty minutes after TOD, and he wasn't fully packed.'

'Are you thinking one of the women he raped learned what he'd done?'

'I've got Peabody talking to a short list right now. Could be that. Could be a husband, a boyfriend, especially since you say he wouldn't have considered it rape, wouldn't see the wrong in it.'

'More, the wrong in it wouldn't have mattered to him.'

'Right. Or it could've been a competitor,' Eve added. 'I've got one guy I need to talk to. One of the top competitors for the stupid award – and Ziegler had sex with his barely of age, impaired at the time, sister.'

'Again, I'm going to agree with you. Any one of those types could have killed him in this way, at this time. That isn't a great deal of help.'

'It helps that I don't lean too heavy on it being a woman. The bedroom as the killing field. It leaned woman to me. The killer was about the same height, but even a shorter woman in heels would fill the bill. But the way you've profiled him, I can see him letting some annoyed guy back there while he packed. It's like another slap, isn't it? I'm busy, got places to go. You can have a couple minutes of my valuable time.'

'He must have been an infuriating individual. Yet he accumulated clients, and short-term girlfriends. He knew how to be charming and attentive. Most narcissists can be, particularly if it gains them admiration and attention.'

'He got plenty of both. The murder weapon. It's probably an impulse – something right at hand – but you can't miss the irony.

'Thanks for squeezing me in. I'd better go catch up with Peabody.'

'Dennis and I are really looking forward to tomorrow night. It's one of the highlights of our holiday season.'

'Really?'

'You and Roarke throw a marvelous party, Eve, in your gorgeous home. And there are always so many people there we enjoy. I also know that while at least part of you would be thrilled never to host or attend another party in your lifetime, you'll enjoy it, too.'

'I had to make a deal with the devil and agree to help with the prep.'

Mira laughed. 'Not Roarke – Summerset.'

'That's why you're the head shrink around here. Yeah.' She pushed to her feet. 'As if they need me to tell somebody where to put a pot of flowers or whatever.'

'I'm sure Summerset could run the preparations seamlessly. But, Eve, your participation is valued.'

'Yeah? Let's hear him say that after I screw it up.'

Eve caught up with Peabody on the corner of West Twelfth and Broadway after squeezing her car into a skinny, overpriced lot a couple blocks north. The walk through the brisk winter air gave her a little more time to think.

'How many did you talk to?' Eve asked.

'The first three, so only one more on Trina's hot list. But there's still more on the overall client list.'

'We'll talk to the last on Trina's, then hunt up Rock Britton. He's probably at his gym, and it's not that far.'

'Okay. Oh, look, there's a cart. We could grab a couple of dogs, and I could fill you in before we talk to the last woman. Kira Robbins.'

'You're thinking about filling your stomach more than filling me in.'

'Two birds, one dog. Each.'

Amused, Eve headed for the cart. 'Still short, right?'

'Just till payday. We started this savings program – McNab

and me. We've almost got enough put away to give to Roarke.'

Eve stopped at the cart. 'Why would you give money to Roarke? He already has almost all the money in all the known universe.'

'To invest for us. He said he would, and who would you trust more to do that than Roarke, who has almost all the money in all the known universe?'

'Good point.' She held up two fingers at the cart operator. 'Loaded,' she added. 'And smart,' she added for Peabody.

'We figured, in a couple years maybe we could buy a place. That's a kind of investment from an investment, so we put some away each payday, and it's like gone.' She swiped her palms together. 'I mean it's something we agreed not to dig out except for emergencies. Not for Christmas presents and going to the vids and stuff like that.'

'That's pretty . . . adult.'

'I know! It's a little scary.'

'Tube of Pepsi,' Eve told the vendor, glanced at Peabody.

'I already had a fizzy. Damn. Make mine a Diet Pepsi.'

'Okay.' With the dogs in hand, Eve turned back to Peabody. 'Report,' she said and took her first bite.

'Louanne Parsons,' Peabody began as they started to walk. 'I tapped her at work. She and a friend own a gift boutique in SoHo, not that I could afford anything in there. Anyway, she denied, initially, any sort of sexual encounter with the vic. She's in a long-term monogamous relationship. But with a little prodding, she admitted to it. One time, she said. Just one time. She'd hurt her shoulder, and Ziegler came over to do a massage.'

'With tea.'

'You got it. Long and short, when I filled her in, she didn't get mad, she started to cry. Just sat there, tears streaming. She didn't strike me, Dallas. I didn't get the tini- est buzz from her.'

'Alibi?'

'At the boutique until five, both her partner and a clerk verified. Says she went home, boyfriend got home from work around five-thirty, and they stayed home until eight. Went out, met friends for dinner. She said she was going to tell her boyfriend, all of it, and didn't know what he'd think or do. They've been together six years. She asked if I'd give her time to do that before we told him.'

'We'll toggle her down for now, and take a pass at the boyfriend. Maybe he found out, took care of Ziegler him- self. Next?'

'Teera Blankhead. On her second marriage, money on both sides. Big converted loft in Greenwich Village. Three kids. One from his first, one from her first, one together. She admitted it, was pissy. What the hell business was it of mine? She went out of orbit when I told her the details. Cried, too, but she was raging while she cried.'

Peabody took another bite of her soy dog. 'Man, why are street dogs so good? Anyway, Blankhead has a pretty sweet gym in her house, though she goes to the fitness

133

center twice a week. She had Ziegler come over, twice a month for a personal session. He had the tea iced, called it an energy/detox blend. They ended up finishing the session by doing it on her yoga mat. Said she was pissed at herself after, that she and her first husband had both cheated, and she'd gone into this second marriage promising herself she wouldn't, no matter what. She stopped the personal sessions after that, and kept it to the fitness center.'

Peabody sucked down soda. 'She has a temper, and she's tall – about your height – strong. She was believable, but I could see her picking up a blunt object and bashing Ziegler in a rage.'

'Whereabouts?'

'Charity lunch deal until about three. She says she opted to walk home, did some window-shopping. Older two kids had after-school activities, husband dinner and a basketball game with a couple friends, and the nanny had the youngest at a holiday party. She was alone at home until after seven, when the kids started coming in.'

'Then we keep her high on the list for now.'

Peabody stopped in front of a trim, whitewashed building. 'Robbins lives here. Forty-two, currently single. Two previous cohabs, no marriages. She's a writer. Fashion blogs and books. She has the entire fifth – top – floor of the building. I found an article on her,' Peabody explained as they walked to the entrance.

The building didn't boast a doorman, but it did include

door and lobby security. At the swipe of Eve's master, a computerized voice requested her badge number for verification. Once she'd given it, the same tinny voice asked the nature of her business.

'It shouldn't be any of yours,' Eve shot back. 'Police business. We're here to speak with Kira Robbins.'

Thank you for your cooperation. Ms Robbins will be notified of your visit. Please wait.

'It just pisses me off on principle,' Eve said, moving across the polished concrete floor to the polished silver of the elevator. 'Having a bunch of chips and circuits tell me what to do.'

She jammed the up button, scowled when the voice said:

One moment please. Ms Robbins requests the nature of your business.

'You can tell Ms Robbins that if she doesn't engage this elevator, we'll come back with a warrant and a lot more cops.'

Thank you. Your message will be relayed.

'Fucking A,' Eve replied, but seconds later, the elevator door opened. Inside, before she could order the fifth floor, the voice spoke again.

This car will now take you directly to Ms Robbins's residence, where she is expecting you. Please enjoy your visit and the rest of your day.

'Good God, do they ever shut up?' Eve wondered as the elevator smoothly rose. 'I don't get why people tell you to enjoy your day, much less machines. If they don't know you, what the hell do they care?'

'No man is an island?' Peabody suggested.

'Why would anybody say that? An island's a scoop of land floating around on a bunch of water.'

'I think it means – never mind,' Peabody decided as the doors opened onto a wide foyer with a bunch of tall potted trees.

Kira Robbins stood between two flowering trees, a waterfall of blond hair spilling over the shoulders of a short, snug red dress. She wore matching heels and lips and a curious look in slanted blue eyes.

'I honestly thought it was a joke, but you *are* the cops. I know you,' she said, pointing a finger with a glossy red nail at Eve. 'Eve Dallas. Roarke's inamorata, and top cop of Icove fame. And Delia Peabody. My God,' she continued, moving toward Eve, 'that's a *fabulous* coat. Just fabulous. Italian leather, slightly masculine cut, which only makes it more female on you. And powerful. And I love the boots. Would you mind if I got a picture? "Lieutenant Dallas, Fashionable Cop". A great article for tomorrow's blog.'

'Yes. I'd mind. We're here on official business. We have some questions.'

'I'm always on official business. And speaking of boots.' She smiled down at Peabody's. 'Those are adorable. Well, come in. We can have a drink and get down to business, whatever it might be.'

She turned into a large open area with windows overlooking downtown – and a tall holiday pine decorated in gold and silver in the center.

A low-profile sofa in a buff color was mounted with bold, floral pillows. It faced a small arched fireplace. Glossy black tables topped with bright white lamps with blue shades flanked floral-print chairs – with buff-colored pillows.

'So what will it be?'

'Answers,' Eve told her.

'I meant to drink.' Robbins headed toward a high-gloss black bar. 'I feel like some fizzy lemon.'

'We're fine. You're acquainted with Trey Ziegler?'

'Trey, of course.' Robbins opened the small, built-in friggie, took out a tall bottle. 'I heard about what happened to him last night, and more when I went to the gym this morning. It's terrible, of course. He was a terrific trainer but I didn't expect to have the cops come to my door about it.'

She plopped ice in a long, slim glass, poured the lemon drink over it. 'Sure?'

Eve only shook her head. 'You don't seem too broken up about it.'

'Why would I be? He was a terrific trainer, but there are

others. And he was kind of a shit otherwise.' She carried her drink to the sofa, sat down, leaned back. 'Have a seat.'

'You didn't like him?'

'Personally? Not really. He was great to look at. I mean that body was a killer. And he knew how to work me so I kept mine in shape. But he was smug, arrogant, and not terribly smart.'

'But you slept with him anyway.'

Robbins lowered the glass she'd started to bring to her lips. Her voice went as cold as the ice in her glass. 'What does that have to do with anything?'

'Sex can often lead to murder.'

'Is that so? I hadn't thought of it. For me, it generally leads to release, or what's the point. Am I actually a suspect? Seriously? Because I slept with him once, against my better judgment, I'll add. I don't know what the hell I was thinking.'

'Day before yesterday, between five p.m. and seven. Where were you?'

'Here, working. I'm nearly finished with a new book, and I have the blog. I've been putting in a lot of day hours on both as I spend most evenings out. Holiday parties, events – they're my fodder.'

'Alone?'

'Yes, alone.' She gestured. 'I prefer to work alone, without distractions. I have an assistant, but I've got her out most days right now, scouting the stores and boutiques, sending me pictures.'

She drank now. 'God. I'm supposed to have an alibi. I have a January one deadline on the book I want to meet, then I'm going to Milan and Paris, doing coverage of spring trends. I didn't kill a man because I was stupid enough to have sex with him. It was good sex, for that matter. Even though he's not my type. He was an asshole – on a personal scale, I mean.'

'How much did you pay him?'

Robbins hissed through her teeth. 'What the hell? I gave him five thousand. He didn't come out and say – exactly – that some of the competition in my field might find it amusing that I'd slept with my trainer, but why take the chance? It wouldn't make that much difference, I know how to spin it. I could probably do a series of blogs on it, but . . . the asshole factor.'

She sighed, drank. 'I was embarrassed,' she admitted. 'Embarrassed I had sex with a man I didn't like, on a personal level. So I gave him five thousand, said this was nice, but let's keep it between us, and that was that. I figured next spring when my membership's up, I'd switch gyms.'

'He hinted at blackmail?'

'I guess that's the term for it, yeah.'

'When did this happen?'

'A couple of months ago. No, more like six weeks, I guess. Not my finest moment.'

'He came here? An at-home massage? Training session?'

'A combo. We'd done that – not the sex – a couple times

before. My assistant, too. I gave him extra to work with her a couple times. It was fun.'

'Was your assistant here for this one?'

'No.'

Her right leg, crossed over the left, began to swing. Eve read irritation and nerves in the movement.

'Look, do we have to go over every damn detail? I had sex with him, I paid him. It's humiliating. But I didn't kill him.'

'What did you have to drink?'

'Jesus Christ.' Robbins shoved up, threw her hands in the air. 'I was doing a workout. I wasn't drinking. Some tea. Just some herbal tea he made. I iced it, and it was nice enough.'

'Did he light incense?'

'So what?' But Robbins's eyebrows drew together, and she sat again. 'Yes. Right before the massage. The massage that wasn't a massage because I decided I'd rather have sex. How do you know about the incense, what do you care about the tea?'

Color dropped out of her face. 'Jesus, Jesus, did he drug me? Oh God, did he give me something?'

'We believe Ziegler routinely gave at-home clients, potentially others, a date-rape drug in the guise of tea, and accentuated it with incense that was also laced.'

'I see.' She pressed her lips together, looked away. 'That explains it. I wasn't attracted to him that way, simply wasn't, but that evening . . . I initiated it.' Her voice trembled a little. She picked up her glass again, drank slowly. 'I initiated it almost as soon as I was on the massage table.'

'No, you didn't,' Eve said. 'He initiated and took your choice away when he gave you the drug without your knowledge.'

'I don't know how to feel about this.' She pressed the cold glass to her forehead. 'I don't know how to feel. I was raped when I was sixteen by a boy I thought liked me. He slipped me something, too. Not enough, because I didn't really drink much, just enough I felt weird and off. Not enough, so I said no. And when I said no, he held me down. He hurt me, and he forced me. And I didn't tell anyone, I was so ashamed. It was years before I told anyone, and came to terms with it. Now this.'

She closed her eyes again. 'Trey didn't force me. He didn't hurt me.'

'Yes, he did.' Eve's flat tone had Robbins opening her eyes again. 'He didn't hold you down or put bruises on you, but he forced you. He raped you.'

'You're right. You're right.'

Her eyes filled. Eve watched her wage a fight against them. Win it.

'Now I have to come to terms with it again. I will. Well, back to therapy.' She lifted her glass in toast. 'What fun.'

'I can give you a contact for a rape center,' Peabody told her.

'That's okay. I have a shrink on tap. I don't have an alibi, and it looks like I had a motive. I didn't kill him, but I'm sure as hell glad he's dead. What happens now?'

Eve rose. 'We talk to other people in your situation. And

if we find out you're lying and you did kill him, we'll be back to arrest you.'

'Great. Terrific.' Robbins managed a weak smile. 'That's still a fabulous coat.'

On the way down to the lobby, Peabody brooded.

'Don't sulk over it,' Eve ordered. 'Spill it.'

'I'm not sulking. I'm considering. Her statement makes it unquestionable our vic used date-rape drugs on numerous women, at least over the last couple months. And it also confirms he extorted money from at least some of them. Either one of those acts equals motive. Combine them, and it becomes a really strong motive. I know she doesn't have an alibi, but I don't think she did it.'

'Because you liked her. And because you felt sympathy after her claim she'd been date-raped in the past.'

'Well, yeah. In part anyway. Didn't you?'

'I didn't not like her. As for the claim of previous date rape, she also indicated she never reported it. We can't confirm it ever happened.'

'No, we can't, and, yeah, it could've been a bid for sympathy. But I believed her.' Still brooding, Peabody stepped out of the elevator, crossed the lobby with Eve. 'I guess you didn't.'

'Actually, I did. Going through that humiliation and trauma a second time? Adds to the motive.'

'I didn't think of it that way.' Peabody glanced up at Robbins's windows as they walked to the car. 'Damn it.'

'We've got an asshole, fuckhead, serial date rapist as a vic, Peabody. We're going to feel sorry for pretty much all the suspects. The women he used, the spouses, boyfriends, fathers, brothers, friends who learned about it. And now we veer off to yet another angle.'

'Another angle?'

'Competitors.' She slid behind the wheel. 'David "Rock" Britton also has a personal motive. The vic banged his baby sister – and maybe, who knows, he slipped her something to get her between the sheets.'

'Well, hell.' Peabody pulled the address of the gym off her PPC, plugged it into the dash comp. 'I hope I don't like him.'

8

Eve liked him, or more accurately liked his gym. A lot.

She saw Rock Hard as a bare-bones, sweat-and-grunt facility. Clean, well-lit, and without a single frill. Top-of-the-line equipment – including heavy bags, speed bags, and a sparring ring that took center stage appealed to those who came in to put in their time, shower off the sweat, and move on with their day.

No music played, so the sound of fists striking bags, of jump ropes whizzing through the air, and feet slapping the floor played all the tunes necessary. Lyrics? Grunts, curses, insults, and orders not to drop your guard, don't be such a pussy, sang out.

She liked the industrial beige walls, the no-nonsense gray floor, the filmy windows that blocked out the street and sidewalk. This wasn't a place to preen. It was a place to work.

She made Rock from his ID photo, watched him holding a heavy bag, spitting out hard-line encouragement to the woman – stripped down to sports bra, shorts, and sweat – who pummeled it.

'From the shoulder, Angie, fer chrissakes. Use your hip. Switch it up. Right cross! Left cross! Right cross! Jab, jab, jab!'

Though she hated to break it up – the woman was game – Eve crossed over. She palmed her badge behind the woman's back, waited for Rock's dark brown eyes to skim over it, lift to her face.

'Finish him off, Ang. Pepper him. Pepper him. Go, go, go! Okay, okay, take a breather.'

'Thank Jesus and his loving mother,' Angie said in a Brooklyn accent thick as a brick. She hugged the bag, swayed with it while she caught her breath.

'I want ten minutes with the rope,' Rock told her.

'You're a freaking sadist, Rock.'

'You're damn straight.' He tossed her a towel, jerked his head to Eve and started back toward what she saw was an office even smaller than her own.

He grabbed a power drink off a skinny shelf, the contents of which too closely resembled infected urine for her taste. But he glugged it down.

'Ziegler?' he said in a voice that suited his name. Hard, with rough edges.

'That's right.'

He shrugged, wiggled a thumb toward a ratty-looking folding chair.

'We're fine,' she told him. 'You and Ziegler were top contenders for the personal trainer award coming up this spring.'

145

'Maybe.' He shrugged excellent shoulders, naked but for the straps of a black tank. A tattoo of a dragon, breathing fire, coiled around his impressive biceps. 'There's a long winter between now and spring. Things change. I guess things have seeing the fucker's dead. I got no problem with him being dead. Didn't make him that way, but I got no problem with it.'

'You had an altercation with him.'

'We weren't buds.' His smile hinted toward a sneer before he guzzled down some more urine-colored liquid. 'I hated his ever-fucking guts, but he wasn't somebody I thought about much.'

'The altercation was due to his sexual relationship with your sister.'

Now those dark eyes fired. 'Tricking a drunk girl into bed, then booting her out when she's half sick and con-fused, *then* bragging on it, ain't no relationship. He knew she was my sister. He did it to rile me. He riled me.'

'In your place, I'd've wanted to kick his ass.'

'Considered it. Maybe I would've, but you can add coward to his other sins. In the end I got in his face, I told him if he ever touched her again, ever said her name again, and I heard about it, I'd break that pretty face he was so proud of.'

'Maybe he did . . . mention her name again.'

'Not that I ever heard.' Rock rested a hip on the corner of his dented metal desk.

He was a big man with strong, defined arms, a broad

146

chest, a face that sported a couple of scars and a nose that listed to the left. Attractive, she thought, in a rough, hard-edged way.

'You box?' Eve asked.

'Used to do some. I liked it okay, but I got tired of punching people, so I switched it up. Ziegler, he had that sweet gig at Buff Bodies, but he liked to give me the zing over my place here. Juice — he's the one told me you'd be coming — said how Ziegler was jealous because he wanted his own place. No reason for him to go after my baby sister. Did it for spite. Did it because he could.'

'He beat you out of the top award the last couple years,' Eve pointed out.

'Yeah. Don't give a shit about the trophy, but the prize money would've been handy. BB, places like that, they've got a strong rep, so their trainers get one, and that weighs on the competition. BB's got — what do you call it?'

'Cachet?' Peabody ventured, and he pointed a finger at her.

'Yeah, that. I've been building up my place. Cachet, maybe not, but I'm solid, and I've got a strong following now. My time was coming. I don't kill somebody over a contest and a grand.'

'Add in your sister,' Eve said.

'I don't kill somebody over what's done. It doesn't change what's done.'

'Where were you the day he was killed?'

'Here till about four. Got in at four-thirty — a.m. — that

147

day to work with a guy – welterweight trying to make a comeback. So I left about four. Went home, had a beer, a shower, turned on some sports, did some paperwork. It's hard to get any paperwork done here, work on programs for clients. Then I went to my mama's for dinner. Got there about seven, I'm guessing. Maybe a little after. I didn't clock it. Went home about nine, stayed in.'

'Did you speak or see anyone between the hours of five and seven?'

'No. You going to arrest me?'

'Not yet.'

'Where does your mother live?'

'Same apartment building, two floors down. I moved there to help her out. She thinks it's the other way around. We're probably both right on that.'

He'd smiled, a real one, when he spoke, but now his face hardened again. 'She doesn't know about Kyria. I don't want her to know. You got no reason to bring that up, if you talk to her.'

'No, we don't. We appreciate your time.'

'That's it?'

'Have you got anything else to tell us?'

'It's going to sound like spite.'

'Why would I care?'

'Okay. I'm just going to say, he had more money than he should have, seems to me. More than he should've had from the work. I don't know how he came by it.'

'But you have your suspicions,' Eve finished.

'I do. Kyria was pretty upset when I found out, when I pushed her about what happened. She finally told me how he kicked her out right after she did it with him. She said how she wanted to stay, she didn't feel good, didn't feel like she could get home on her own. And he said women didn't stay in his place unless they paid for it. Said maybe he'd let her stay till morning for a thousand. Girl didn't have that kind of money on her, so he tossed her out.'

He stared down into his power drink. 'I figure he got women to pay. Everybody knew he banged clients – that's up to the client, to my way of thinking. Not my business. But when you charge money, that's not legal without a license. Maybe he had one.'

Rock shrugged again, drank again. 'But I don't think so.'

'We appreciate the information, and the time.'

'Are you going to have to talk to Kyria?'

'We may.'

He let out a long breath, stared down at what was left of his drink. 'Go easy, will you? She's embarrassed it happened. Put it behind her the way you should with mistakes. But she's embarrassed.'

'Understood.' Eve walked to the office door, opened it, turned back. 'I like your place.'

His grin spread, quick, bright, added unexpected charm to his face. 'You box?'

'I fight.' Eve smiled back. 'There's a difference.'

Peabody waited until they were outside, then poked a

finger in Eve's biceps. 'You liked him. You don't think he did it because you like him.'

'I liked him. I know he didn't do it because he'd have used his fists. I know he didn't do it because the vic would never have opened the door to him much less taken him back into the bedroom. There would've been signs of struggle, of a fight. Alternately, *if* Britton had grabbed the trophy on impulse, rage would have jumped right in with it. He wouldn't have settled for two blows. He'd have beaten Ziegler's head in, and he'd have gone for the face, too. The "pretty face" Ziegler was so proud of.'

'Oh, well, when you put it that way. But you still liked him.'

'He said right out he hated Ziegler and wasn't sorry he was dead. That takes balls. He resisted caving in Ziegler's face and/or skull months ago when the sister thing happened. That takes control. I like balls. I respect control.'

'Are we going to talk to the sister, the mom?'

'I don't see any reason to rush that.' Time, to Eve's mind, to circle back around. 'We're going back to do a follow-up with Natasha Quigley.'

'Okay. Why?'

'Because she's lying. She slept with Ziegler. I figured it for a lie yesterday. I'm more sure of it now. She's good-looking, wealthy, a client. Married. She's a prime target. We'll go shake it out of her.'

'Okay. Why would she lie, especially when she could've jumped right on the he-gave-me-tea-too gambit?'

'First, because we didn't know for certain the tea was laced, and that possibility came out after she'd already – pretty vehemently – denied having sex with the vic.'

'That's right.' Peabody pulled her earflaps down more securely. 'We've got so many women either saying they paid him for sex, or saying they paid him to keep it quiet after tea-induced sex, we're going to need a spreadsheet. Or a chart.' She brightened a little. 'I like making charts. Anyway, if that's first, what's second?'

'Second, because it's just easier to say no, not me.'

'It is. And it's knee-jerk, too, at least from the women I've interviewed.'

'And third, I bet she was weirded knowing she and her sister had slept with the same guy.'

'That would be weird.' Peabody piled in the car. 'My sister – the one closest to my age – and I had a serious thing for the same guy when we were teenagers. So we took an oath that neither of us would move on it. We fought about it first, but we took an oath.'

Peabody settled back. 'It turned out he'd have rather our brother moved on him, but we didn't catch that until we'd taken the oath. Zeke didn't move on him because he's not into guys that way, but he'd've sworn an oath otherwise.

'It's going to be great seeing them all on Christmas. I wonder what ever happened to ... What the hell was his name? Stanley, I think. Yeah, Stanley Physter. But he wanted everyone to call him Stefano.'

'And you didn't get the gay?'

'Huh. Good point.'

They went back to the brownstone, were admitted by the same domestic droid. As they sat in the living area, Eve pulled out her PPC. 'Look stern,' she said to Peabody.

'Okay.'

'Not constipated, stern.'

Peabody relaxed the look fractionally as Quigley came clipping in.

'I'm sorry. I'm just back from a committee meeting, and was on the 'link. Can I order up anything for you?'

'We're fine.'

'Do you have more questions about Trey?' she asked as she took a seat. 'I don't know what more I can tell you.'

Eve looked up from her PPC, deliberately turned the screen away, but kept it in her hand. 'You can start by telling us why you denied having sex with Trey Ziegler.'

'Because I didn't have sex with him.'

'Peabody, what happens when an individual lies to the police during an investigation?'

'Charges are forthcoming. Obstruction of justice is generally first, but we can follow that with—'

'We'll just start there,' Eve interrupted. 'And here: You have the right to remain silent.'

'Wait. For God's sake. This is ridiculous.'

'You're going to want to listen to your rights and obligations, Ms Quigley,' Eve advised, then recited the rest of the Revised Miranda. 'Do you understand your rights and obligations in this matter?'

'I'm not an idiot. Of course I do. And I resent being treated like a criminal.'

'You're going to have cause for even more resentment then when we take this interview down to Central.' Eve rose.

'I'm not going anywhere. You can't force me to go anywhere.'

'Peabody?'

'The suspect can voluntarily be questioned. Or we can get a warrant compelling her to submit to questioning. She is, of course, entitled to a legal rep either way, but the second option could include restraints.'

'This is ridiculous.' Color rode high on her cheeks; her hands balled into fists. 'It's outrageous. I'm contacting my lawyer.'

'Please do. He can meet us here, if you speak voluntarily. Or my partner will get the warrant, and your representative can meet us at Central. Your choice.'

'I tell you I didn't have sex with Trey Ziegler.'

Eve looked down at her PPC, back at Quigley. 'You're lying.'

'What do you have on there? What are you looking at?'

'Peabody, get the warrant.'

'Wait, wait. Just . . . wait.' Quigley dropped down again. 'All this, all this insanity over sex. All right, I slept with him. I didn't want Tella to know. I don't want JJ – my husband – to know. I don't see it's any of your business.'

'Your bedmate was murdered.'

'Well, I didn't kill him. Why would I? Over sex?' She waved that away with a flash of the emerald on her finger. 'It was stupid – no one likes to broadcast stupidity. It's humiliating to talk about to strangers, to police. My marriage has been a bit fraught for the last few months.'

'Fraught?'

'We've been in a rough patch, and we're working through it. Marriages have rough patches.' She crossed her arms over her chest defensively. 'In fact, things are getting better. But, well, I have needs like anyone, and Trey made it obvious he was attracted, that he was interested. He was sympathetic when I told him things weren't good between me and JJ, and that, well, and that we were sleeping in separate rooms. He suggested he come here, when JJ was away, and give me a private massage.'

Rising, she walked to a cabinet, took out a decanter, poured herself amber liquid in a short glass. 'I knew what he meant. It wasn't a secret he offered separate and private services.'

She stared down at the glass. 'Intimate services. I wasn't going to have him come here, in my home. I wouldn't . . . not in the same bed I slept in with my husband. So – as I also know other clients had – I suggested a hotel. I booked a suite, ordered up champagne. He met me there. We went through the pretense – or the foreplay – of the massage. Then we had sex. He's good at it, and JJ hadn't been attentive in some time.'

'How much did you pay him?'

Color stained her cheeks again before she drank. 'Three thousand extra, then I booked another private session. We had two a week for three weeks before ... he died. We were booked for one right after Christmas. I was going to cancel that as JJ and I ... things are better. We're talking about taking a holiday after the first of the year, JJ's idea. We're trying to find the magic again.'

'Did Ziegler threaten to tell your husband?'

'Why would he? We had a mutually beneficial arrangement. If he told JJ, it couldn't continue. I hadn't canceled the last session as yet.'

'Why, if you're coming out of that rough patch?'

'God.' She rubbed her temple. 'I'd thought I'd see him once more – not for sex – but to tell him we had to end it. I'd planned to give him a little extra, a thank-you. And then ... Not only did I learn he'd been killed, but that my own sister slept with him. He shouldn't have slept with Tella – it's just unseemly. And believe me, it was awkward when she told me.'

'"Unseemly,"' Eve repeated. '"Awkward."'

'Yes. A woman might share a hairdresser, for instance, with her sister. A designer, a decorator. But not a lover. It was a business transaction, basically. I knew that going in. But ... a woman in my position can't hire a professional. An affair – and I could let myself think of it as an affair – it had more ... romance.'

'Were you in love with him?' Peabody asked. Quigley laughed.

155

'Please. I said before, I'm not an idiot. He provided a service, I paid. But he was someone I knew, someone who understood my body and my needs. It was good for me. It may have helped my marriage, though JJ would never see it that way. I'd like to salvage my marriage if I can. I'm realistic enough to know that may not be possible, but I'd like to give it some time, and try.'

'You set the time and place, a clear understanding what was to transpire on both sides of this arrangement with Ziegler.'

'Yes. My marriage may have been in that rough patch, but I have enough respect for JJ not to carry on an affair in the home we share.'

'You're so sure your husband doesn't know?'

'If he did, even if he suspected? The way things have been the last few weeks, he'd never have suggested we take a trip, spend a week in Tahiti rekindling our marriage. No.' She set her jaw. 'He'd have thrown it in my face, and called a divorce attorney.'

'Would he have thrown it in Ziegler's face? Wasn't he also a client?'

'Confront Trey? No, no, he'd blame me, and he'd never let me forget it. He wouldn't have confronted Trey.' But she wet her lips, drank again. 'JJ's excitable, and he's been angry with me — and I with him — but he's not really a violent man. He'd never have . . . he wouldn't.'

'You don't sound convinced,' Eve pointed out.

'Because you're throwing all this at me.' Her voice rose,

flirting with hysteria. 'Because it's all so upsetting. I had an affair, and I paid for it. Literally and emotionally.'

She took another drink, breathed in and out. 'My husband doesn't know, and I want to keep it that way. I'd like to mend the frays in my marriage. If I can't, I'd prefer to end that marriage as cleanly as possible.'

'Do you love your husband?' Peabody asked her.

'I want a chance to find out, that's all. I'd like the chance to find out the answer.'

'Where were you when Ziegler was killed? Your sister gave us her whereabouts.'

'I was here, preparing for the party that night. You can question the domestics, the decorating team – they, and I, were here all day. I had catering staff arrive at seven-fifteen, and was here to speak with them. I was here all day, supervising the preparations.'

'And your husband?'

'I'm honestly not sure, and it's ridiculous. I was working with the staff, the caterers, so I'm not sure when he arrived. But I know he was here by seven-thirty, as he was dressing when I ran up to change for the first arrivals.'

'Where's your husband now?' Eve asked her.

'I – at his office, I suppose. Please.' She sat again, leaned toward Eve. 'Lieutenant, Detective, please don't take away my chance to save my marriage. If you tell JJ I had an affair with Trey, it's over. He won't forgive me for it. I only want the chance to fix things, to try to hold on to my marriage. I made a mistake – a stupid, selfish mistake – but right now

157

what I did hurts no one but myself. If you tell JJ, it hurts him, and destroys the future we want to make together. Please.'

'I can't make you any promises, but we won't share that information unless we find it necessary to the investigation. While your marriage is your priority, Ms Quigley, finding the person responsible for taking Trey Ziegler's life is ours.'

Eve got to her feet. 'Did Ziegler ever push you for more money, ever indicate he might use your relationship with him against you?'

'No. It was, as I said, mutually beneficial. We enjoyed each other for a brief time. No more, no less.'

'Okay. Thanks for your time.'

'What would you do?' Quigley rose, clasped her hands together. 'In my place, what would you do?'

'I can't tell you. I'm not in your place.'

Peabody bundled up her coat again as they stepped outside. 'What would you do? Would you confess the cheating, or bury it like she's trying to do?'

'I wouldn't have cheated in the first place.'

'Well, yeah, but—'

'There's no "but".' Eve pulled open the car door, slid in. 'You go into marriage, you plow a road. You're going to hit rough patches, and some may be rougher and last longer than others, but you've got choices to make. You work to smooth them out, you hold until they do, or they don't. You stick with the road, or you get off. But you don't do something to make it worse, don't do something that maybe makes you feel better for the short term while it sucker punches the person you're married to.

'Plug in Copley's office. We'll talk to him next.'

Peabody keyed the address into the in-dash. 'Some people cheat because they can't see a way out.'

'Bullshit. There's always a way out. You just have to pay the price, whether it's money, status, the emotional hit, or all of that and more. Cheating's cheap and it's lazy.' Pausing at a light, she drummed her fingers on the steering wheel. 'It's not just about sex,' she said. 'Marriage is a series of promises.' When she'd realized that – marriage equaled promises – she hadn't feared it. As much.

'Maybe you can't keep them all. The whole till-death-do-us-part business. Maybe you can't keep that one. Life can be long, and people change, circumstances change, so okay. You realize you don't really want this life or this person, or the person you made the promises to isn't who you thought, or they've changed in a way you can't accept or support. Whatever. You make a choice. Stick and try to work it through, or don't. But don't give me the boo-hoo, I'm not happy so I'm getting naked with somebody else on the side. It insults everybody.

'Walk or work,' she concluded. 'But don't make excuses.'

'I can feel that way personally – and philosophically. But ... people are flawed.'

'People aren't flawed, Peabody. People are deeply fucked up.'

159

'So, considering that, didn't you feel a little sorry for her? For Quigley?'

'I might if she grew a pair and went to her husband, told him she'd fucked up, been stupid and selfish and so on. She cheated, now she's lying. How's that going to fix anything if she's serious about fixing things? Added to it, I don't feel sorry for either of them at this point because one of them may have killed Ziegler. Since she's a known cheater and liar, she may be lying about Ziegler not pushing for more. And if he did, bash, bash. Or the illusion of romance she claims was more real, and she finds out he's playing her like he played the rest.'

'Bash, bash,' Peabody said as Eve hunted for parking.

'Or, Copley did find out, confronted Ziegler. Bash, bash from his side. So let's stay objective here.'

Peabody climbed out of the car, pulled on her gloves. 'Pretty much everyone we've interviewed had motive to bash, bash. Our vic's the guy people loved to hate. They used him – as a trainer, as an employee, as a massage therapist, as a bedmate, but any one of them could've picked up that trophy and given him a couple solid whacks.'

'And murder trumps cheating, lying, blackmail, and being a general asshole. So let's see where John Jake Copley falls on the map.'

Inside the steel-gray lobby of the office building, Eve badged the security guard at the sign-in station. 'John Jake Copley. ImageWorks Public Relations.'

He scanned her badge, nodded. 'That's your thirty-ninth floor, elevator bank B.'

Peabody pulled her gloves off as they joined a small pack of sharp suits for the elevator. Half of them nattered away on earbuds, others frowned importantly at their 'links or PPCs as they scrolled through data.

One of them, a six-foot blonde in a dark purple coat with lips dyed to match, did both.

'The Simpson meeting ran over,' she barked as they all piled on the car. 'Shift my three-thirty to three-forty-five, and my four to four-thirty. I know I have a four-thirty, Simon, you're going to reschedule that for five – drinks at Maison Rouge. I'll follow up with the five-thirty, same place. Keep these meetings on schedule, Simon. There'll be hell to pay if I miss Chichi's holiday pageant tonight. I'm on my way up now. Get it together.'

As the woman marched off on the twenty-second floor, Eve decided she'd hold her own stunner to her own throat – on full – if she had to live by meetings scheduled minute by minute.

She'd much rather screw those meetings up by flipping out her badge.

Which she did at the glossy gold reception counter of ImageWorks.

A trio worked the counter, all in dark suits, all with perfect grooming and toothy, professional smiles.

The sleek brunette's smile didn't waver a fraction. 'What can I do for you, Officer?'

'Lieutenant.' Eve tapped the badge. 'Dallas. With Detective Peabody. We need to speak with John Jake Copley.'

'Mr Copley, of course.' She tapped nails painted cold, hard blue on her screen. 'I'm showing Mr Copley in the executive lounge for a strategy meeting. But he does have a few minutes free later this afternoon where I can schedule you in.'

'Do you see this?' Eve held up the badge again. 'This is my strategy meeting. Where's the executive lounge?'

'It's through the double doors to your right, down to the end of the hall, to the left, through the double doors, and—'

'I'll find it,' Eve said.

'But ... It's for executives,' the brunette said as Eve turned away.

Eve merely held up her badge again, kept walking.

'I really love that part,' Peabody said. 'I'm a little ashamed, but I can't help it.'

They passed doors, both opened and closed, busy hives of cubes, turned the corner, passed a staff lounge with Vending and a couple sofas, a wall screen scrolling through ads.

Things quieted through the next set of doors.

Eve nodded at yet one more set. 'Odds are,' she said, and strode to them, pulled them open.

Laughter poured out.

On the wall screen a golfer teed off on the eleventh hole under sunny skies on a course green as Ireland. Around the room men – but for a lone woman who looked bored and annoyed – sat or stood with drinks in hand.

JJ Copley stood in front of the screen, teeing up just as his CGI counterpart. Handsome and fit in shirtsleeves and loosened tie, he swung. On screen, his avatar perfectly mirrored the move – and sent the little white ball soaring – over a sand trap, over a sparkling blue pond, and onto the edge of the eleventh green.

Raucous applause ensued.

'And *that's* how it's done.' Grinning, he turned toward another fit and handsome man holding a club, then spotted Eve.

'Ladies? Can I redirect you?'

'Copley, John Jake?'

'Guilty.'

'Well, that makes it easy.' Eve took out her badge again. 'You have the right to remain silent—'

'Whoa, whoa!' He laughed, but this time a little nervous around the edges. 'What's all this about?'

'Murder,' Eve said flatly. 'Trey Ziegler.'

'Oh, right, right. Damn shame. I'd be happy to sit down with you in, say, thirty? We're in a strategy session.'

'Yeah, I can see that. Now works for me. Does now work for you, Detective Peabody?'

'Yes, sir, it does. This room works, too, but then so does Central.'

'Yeah.' Eve stared into Copley's eyes. 'Either way.'

'Fine, then, fine. Never let it be said I didn't cooperate

with the boys – or girls – in blue. Fellas, give me the room for a few minutes. Guys – oh, and Marta – I need the room. We'll take this up as soon as I'm finished.'

Eve watched the lone woman shoot Copley a look of cool dislike before she filed out with the rest.

'Have a seat. What can I get you?'

'Answers.'

'No problem there.' He dropped down onto a black sofa. 'It looked like we were goofing off, but the fact is we represent the company – and the spokesman – for the games. A new set of interactive sports games and training vids they hoped to launch next spring. We're working in tandem with the ad company on a smooth launch. You gotta know the product to rep the product.'

'Sure. Tell me about your relationship with Trey Ziegler.'

'He's – he *was* – my personal trainer. Damn good one, too. I worked with him at my gym. Buff Bodies.'

'And outside of the gym?'

'We played golf a couple of times. He loved the game. He and my brother-in-law and I played a few times. Treated him to a round, some drinks, that sort of thing.'

'When was the last time you were in his apartment?'

'I . . . Why would I go to his apartment?'

'You tell me.'

'I never went there. No reason to. He was a damned good trainer, worked you until you wanted to cry like a girl. Gave a good massage, too. Pretty good golfer. But we weren't buddies, if that's what you mean.'

He rose, walked to the wet bar, poured himself a tall glass of water, squeezed a lemon slice into it. 'Sure?' He tipped the glass right and left.

'Yes. When was the last time you saw or spoke to him?'

'I guess it would've been Monday morning, regular session with him at the gym. I actually had one scheduled yesterday, but they tagged me, told me he'd been killed. That was a shocker,' Copley added, drank deep.

'Did he ever ask you for money? Hit you for a loan?'

'Money?' Copley drank again, slid one hand into his pocket, jiggled whatever he carried in there. 'No. I always slipped him some extra after a massage, but he never had his hand out. Look, I liked the guy. He was a good trainer, so I liked working with him. I gave him a couple perks – golf at the club, like that. We had some laughs on the course. That's it.'

'Did he ever contact you at home, at your office?'

'What for?'

'I'm asking you.'

'I don't remember anything like that. I'd see him a couple times a week at the gym. A couple times at the club when either I or Lance – my sister-in-law's husband – set it up. Maybe once a week I'd get a massage from him. That's it.'

'Are you nervous, Mr Copley?'

'The cops are talking to me about a guy I knew that was killed. So, yeah, some. Plus I've got work waiting. I can't tell you anything about what happened to Ziegler, so . . . if

165

there's more you should go through my lawyer. We'll keep it smooth that way. Is that it?'

'For now.' Eve started for the door. 'Oh, you mentioned your brother-in-law. But you didn't mention your wife also used the deceased as a trainer and a massage therapist.'

'So what?'

'Interesting.' Leaving it at that, Eve started out.

She walked down the wide hallway again, through the doors, glanced at Peabody.

'He's lying.'

'Oh yeah, he is.'

9

She wanted Copley in the box, Eve thought, but knowing in her gut he was lying didn't equal proof. The minute she tapped him, he'd lawyer up. She didn't begrudge him legal representation – rules were rules for reasons – but a lawyer was bound to block and dodge her questions, see she was on a fishing expedition.

But Copley was lying, and there was damn well a reason for that, too.

'We dig,' she told Peabody as they took the elevator up from the garage at Central. 'We dig on Copley until we find enough to stand on, then we bring him in. He's not going to talk to us again without a lawyer, so we find some holes.'

She checked her wrist unit for time as a couple of uniforms pulled in a heroically drunk Santa who looked – and smelled – like he'd spent some time rolling around in reindeer dung.

'Really? You couldn't take that up the stairs a couple flights to the drunk tank?'

'Gotta take him up to Sex Crimes, Lieutenant. He—'

'Hey, little girl!' Drunk Santa sent Eve a bleary smile. 'I got whatcha want for Christmas right here!'

He grabbed his crotch, pumped his hips, then spread open a slit in the dirty red pants to reveal an unfortunately grimy penis.

'That,' the uniform finished.

'I like 'em naughty!' Santa exclaimed, then broke fantastic wind.

'Oh, for Christ's sake.'

'Somebody crack a window!' Santa suggested, and added, 'Ho, ho, ho!'

Eve did better. She leaped off the elevator on the next floor, one short step in front of Peabody. As the doors shut, she heard Santa bellow, 'Merry Christmas to all!' right before the gagging noises.

'I think that was alive.' Cautiously Peabody sniffed at her own sleeve. 'We may need detox. Uniforms don't get paid enough.'

'Nobody gets paid enough around here. Send a departmental memo. Nobody rides in that car for a month. That should be about long enough. I'm not kidding,' she added when Peabody laughed.

'On it.'

'Meanwhile, back to murder. We dig on Copley. His business, his marriage, his finances, any priors no matter how minor. His politics, his religion, his favorite fucking color. Everything.'

'You think maybe Ziegler was blackmailing him.'

'It's possible,' Eve said as she and Peabody stepped onto a glide. 'It's just as possible his wife's fling with Ziegler wasn't as discreet as she thinks. Let's get a couple of uniforms over to Ziegler's building with a shot of Copley. Maybe we'll find somebody who saw him visit Ziegler's apartment. We just need to find one lie to deepen the hole.'

'He struck me as too weenie. Shit! I wish I hadn't said weenie because it makes me think of that sick pervert's weenie. Do we smell like Drunk Santa fart?'

'If we did, people would be diving off this glide like lemmings.'

'You're right.' Still, Peabody took another cautious sniff of her sleeve. 'We escaped in time. I need a replacement for the *W* word. Copley struck me as too wussy. There, a *W* for a *W*.'

'Wussies kill, too.' Eve stepped off the glide, headed for Homicide. 'He finds out his wife's been doing the trainer. He thinks: That asshole's fucking my wife, laughing at me behind my back. I'm paying him, and he's doing my wife. I took him golfing at my club, for Christ's sake. Who the fuck does he think he is?'

'He'd be pissed,' Peabody agreed. 'Anybody'd be pissed.'

'He goes to Ziegler's place to confront him – or maybe if he really is a wuss, he goes to plead with Ziegler to break it off. Either way, why wouldn't Ziegler let him in? "Hey, man, I'm packing, but come on back. What's up?"'

'Copley says, "You've been banging my wife. It has to stop."'

'Maybe. And maybe Ziegler starts off denying, maybe not,' Eve speculated. 'Maybe he pushes for money. "Just providing a service. I can stop the service, but you have to make up the fee." Simple business transaction. Ziegler's not worried about this guy. Hell, he's the *trainer*. "Your wife was happy to pay, so if you don't want me providing the service, cough it up."'

'And Copley snaps. Bash, bash.'

'Maybe,' Eve said as they turned into the bullpen.

Someone had added a dented menorah to the decor. It stood on a bed of virulent greenery she suspected was supposed to be pine boughs. Beside it stood a sickly gray figure in a Santa suit, grinning viciously.

'What the hell is that?' she demanded.

Santiago glanced up from his work. 'It's Zombie Santa. We're trying to be inclusive.'

'They make Zombie Santas? Who thinks of things like that?' Shaking her head at all mankind, she strode to her office.

It surprised her to find Feeney studying her board.

The EDD captain, her former trainer and partner, wore a rumpled suit the color of . . . reindeer dung, Eve decided. Wiry silver strands poked through his explosion of ginger hair like carelessly tossed tinsel.

Like the suit, his face had a rumpled, lived-in look. His eyes might have resembled a basset hound's, but they were cop sharp as he scanned her photos, timelines, data.

'Your vic was an asshole.'

'Completely,' she agreed, walking straight to her Auto-Chef to program two coffees, strong and black. 'Lead suspect, as of now, is this guy.'

She brought up Copley's ID shot after passing Feeney coffee. 'One of the vic's regular clients. Turns out the vic was banging his wife twice a week for the last few weeks – for a side fee. She claims the husband didn't know.'

Feeney gave the coffee a surface blow, drank. 'It's hard to hide regular banging.'

'Damn right.' Pleased to have him to bounce around the speculations, she eased a hip onto the corner of her desk. 'Rough patch, the wife claims. Separate bedrooms for a while.'

'No sex for a while's a rough patch. Separate bedrooms is a crater.'

'Yeah?'

He eyed her. 'How long you been married now?'

'Couple years.'

'Take my word. You can climb out of a crater, but it's harder than riding out a rough patch.'

'She claims they climbed out, mostly, and are working on the rest of the way. But if he finds out she got naked with their mutual trainer, it's off the cliff for the marriage.'

'You didn't tell him.'

'Not yet. We ran the basics with him, and he was nervous. And he was lying. Something more there, something with the vic he's hiding. So he's top of my list right now.'

'Smashed his head in, hauled the body onto the bed, then put a knife in the chest. With a ho, ho, ho.'

Like Feeney, she studied the crime scene shot, drank coffee.

'The last's a kind of rage, isn't it?' she said. 'A cold one. The smash, bash, that strikes me as hot. But the flourish? It takes cold blood. Copley could fit.'

'A liar's one thing. A nervous one's another. You could shake it out.'

'Yeah, but he's already brought up the *L* word. I'm going to do some digging on him, let him settle. His business is a boys' club.'

Feeney's shaggy eyebrows rose. 'He works with kids?'

'No – big public relations firm, but he runs it like a boys' club – on the exec level, at least. One woman in the meeting I broke up today, and she didn't look real happy with him. I think he's an asshole, but I have to ask myself if I'd just like to find an asshole killer for my asshole vic.'

She shrugged, sipped coffee, studied her board. 'He had a lot of clients, used a lot of women. The killing field's a big one.'

'Somebody who needed to put a sticker in a dead guy's going to break at some point.'

'That's what I think, too. I need to be there when it happens.'

He nodded, and for a moment or two they drank their coffee, studied death in companionable silence.

'The wife's all over me to wear a monkey suit tomorrow.'

Eve frowned, shifted her thought process. 'Why?'

'How the hell do I know? You're female. Why do women like men dressed up in monkey suits?'

'I don't, especially.'

'Tell me this.' He pointed at her. 'Is Roarke putting on a monkey suit for this shindig tomorrow?'

'No. I don't know.' For unexplained reasons, she had a moment of panic. 'How would I know?'

'You live with him.'

'I live with me, too, and I don't even know what I'm wearing tomorrow.' But Roarke would, she thought. Jesus, was she supposed to know what he was wearing? Was that another damn marriage rule?

'Did he wear one last year?'

How was she supposed to remember? But she tried. 'I don't think so. I can ask him not to if that helps you out.'

'Do that. You do that.' With a righteous nod, Feeney smoothed a hand down his wrinkled jacket. 'Bad enough to have to get all fancied up without that.'

'Tell me,' she said, with feeling. 'I'm the one who'll have to have glop all over my face while I walk around on stilts.'

'What you get for being female.'

'It's not right.'

'The wife likes the fancy, and the stilts. Looks good on her, too. Anyway.' He scratched at his ear. 'Anyway, I'm going to tell you she made you guys a bowl in her pottery class. It's not bad – doesn't even wobble. Much.'

'Ah . . . that was nice of her,' Eve said cautiously.

'I figure how many bowls can somebody use, but that's not something you say when you're married to somebody who keeps making them. Unless you want to hit a rough patch.'

'I get it.'

'So I got this.' He reached into the inside pocket of his ugly jacket, took out a small, slim square wrapped in shiny red paper.

'Oh,' Eve said when he shoved it at her.

She was lousy at giving gifts; she was worse at getting them.

'I didn't want to give it over tomorrow, with the party and the people and all that.'

'Okay. Thanks.' After an awkward pause, she deduced she was meant to open it on the spot.

She pulled off the paper, crumpled it, shot it into her recycler. She lifted the lid, just stared.

Small reproductions of the medals she and Roarke had been awarded the month before floated inside clear glass. Etched beneath each were their names, the award, and the date presented.

'This is . . . ' Her throat closed up on her. 'A lot,' she managed. 'This is a lot.'

'I figured you could put it somewhere you could take a look at when the job gets heavy. Maybe not here. It's a little like bragging if you put it in here.'

'Yeah. It should be at home. It's Roarke's, too.'

'The highest honor given a cop.' There was a light in his voice that had her throat clogging on her. 'The highest given a civilian. I was real proud of both of you.'

She struggled for composure before she risked looking up at him. 'That's a lot, too.'

'Can't get a little sentimental at Christmas, when can you? Well.' He gave her a light punch on the arm, settled them both. 'I gotta get back. No monkey suit,' he reminded her.

'I'll tell him. Thanks, Feeney.'

She stayed where she was when he walked out, ran her fingertip over her name, over Roarke's.

She looked up at her board, at the image of Trey Ziegler propped in bed, that mocking note pinned to his chest with a kitchen knife.

'You were an asshole, Ziegler. A user, a whore, a rapist. I wish you were alive so I could toss you in a cage. But since you're dead, you're going to get the best I've got.'

Carefully she put the lid back on the box, set it aside.

She sat down with what was left of her coffee, and went to work.

Nearly two hours later, she programmed another cup of coffee, drank it standing at her skinny window looking out at the hustle-bustle of New York.

She heard the clomp of Peabody's boots, didn't bother to turn. 'It gets dark so damn early.'

'We just passed the solstice, so the days are starting to get longer.'

'It takes too damn long. Copley looks ordinary. Parents divorced, half sib on the father's side. Average student. Little ding on possession right out of college, that would probably have gone away if he hadn't mouthed off to the cops. Traffic tickets, and I dug into those a little. He went to court on every one of them, and in two cases ended up paying an extra fine for mouthing off to the judge. So, some temper there, some righteousness, some assholey behavior. Nothing violent.'

'I didn't find anything there, either,' Peabody said. 'First marriage lasted four years – no record of domestic disputes, but he sure filed a lot of papers on the ex. The split probably cost him three times what it would have if he hadn't kept pushing the buttons. Still, she had more money than he did, and no prenup, so he fought his way to a bigger chunk than he might've gotten.'

Intrigued, Eve turned. 'I hadn't looked at marriage one yet, but Quigley's rolling in it. His income's a fraction of hers. There's a prenup, bet your ass. Second marriage for both, yeah, she covered herself. It might be interesting to get a peek at the terms of that one.'

'She's the admitted cheater. It seems to me he'd make out bigger, considering.'

'It doesn't mean she's the only one who cheated.'

Peabody pursed her lips. 'Hmm. Hadn't gone there. I did take a first pass at his financials. I didn't see anything out of line, nothing to indicate he's stepping out. Unless he's doing it on the cheap. No hotel bills in the city, no second rent going out, no personal travel that doesn't jibe with the wife's. And no withdrawals that say blackmail.'

'He'd have an expense account. That's worth a look. And maybe, having married a second time to a woman with money, he learned something about socking money away.'

She'd see if Roarke wanted to play with that.

'From what I can see, he's good at his job,' Eve continued. 'Maybe a righteous asshole when it comes to being caught doing something wrong, or with an estranged wife, but he's worked his way up at ImageWorks to partner.'

'I couldn't find anything that said other than he can be a jerk, but he's pretty much a law-abiding professional with some skill in his chosen field.' Peabody lifted her shoulder. 'I couldn't find any real dings.'

'It doesn't mean they're not there. Pack it in for the night.'

'Are you?'

'Pretty much. I think I'll swing by the Schuberts on the way home, poke at the husband a little. I might get another angle.'

She tilted her head when she heard the oncoming prancing she recognized as McNab.

He bopped into her doorway. 'Hey, Dallas. Peabody, you off or on?'

'Just going off.'

'Me, too. We can go home together. I got some data from your vic's home mini, LT. I'd've had it earlier, but I got pulled off on a hot one. Just got back to this a couple hours ago.'

He offered Eve a disc.

'Report?'

'What's interesting is the accounting program I dug out. It doesn't list names – just initials – but I did a quick cross with his client list, and there's plenty that match. Some repeats, some one-offs. And he lists amounts. It would look up-and-up if I didn't know what Peabody told me about how he took some clients for a ride between the sheets – at a cost. He's listed them as private massage or trainer or consults. Initials, dates, fees, and what I'm thinking is a rating system.'

'Rating?' Eve repeated.

'Hey, some guys are shits. He qualifies. He's got some rated with stars. One to three. I figure he rated the clients on, you know, performance.'

'Scumfuck,' Peabody muttered.

'Wouldn't say otherwise.' Then he leaned in, whispered something in Peabody's ear that made her flush and giggle.

'You just said some crap about there not being enough stars, or something equally full of it.'

McNab only grinned. 'What can I say? I'm a romantic, not a scumfuck.'

'Go home, get out, scram. Both of you.'

'See you tomorrow. Party!' Peabody did a quick jig in her pink boots, then dashed.

178

Alone, Eve turned the disc in her hand. It would wait, she thought, until home.

It wasn't much of a detour, and Eve wanted to tie off, or at least shorten, as many loose ends as she could manage before the party, the weekend, the whole crazy Christmas extravaganza sucked up any time for work and reality.

Once she parked, she joined the sidewalk traffic – those headed home, those headed out, those hauling shopping bags and likely on a self-imposed forced march to another retail outlet where they could accumulate more shopping bags.

Thank tiny birthday Jesus she was done with that part.

The Schubert townhouse sat within spitting distance of Martella's sister's brownstone. Still, the relatively short distance put it in a more active section where Eve imagined street artists set up during the day, and the snug outdoor spaces a few restaurants boasted likely did yeoman's duty in good weather.

An actual human voice responded to Eve when she buzzed at the door.

'May I help you?'

'Lieutenant Eve Dallas, NYPSD, to speak with Martella or Lance Schubert.'

'One moment please, Lieutenant.'

It took hardly more before a woman with toffee-colored skin and icy blue eyes opened the door. She wore her golden brown hair in dozens of thin braids all gathered into a tail, and made simple black pants and white shirt look glamorous.

'Please come in, Lieutenant. I'm Catiana Dubois, Mrs Schubert's social secretary. May I take your coat?'

'I've got it.'

'If you'll come with me.' She led the way left through the foyer – everything bright and fresh with those tall-stemmed red flowers Eve couldn't remember the name of grouped together in abundance on a long table – into a spacious sitting room with more bright and fresh in bold colors, silvery trim, and a tiny fireplace simmering in the wall.

The tree centered in the window. Angels flew on its branches and shimmered in its tiny white lights. Under it, elegantly wrapped gifts, artistically arranged, added more color.

'The Schuberts will be right down. Can I offer you something? Coffee or tea – or hot cider?'

The cider sounded tempting, but she hoped to make it quick. 'No, thanks.'

'Please sit, be comfortable. It's a lovely picture, isn't it?' Catiana said as she noticed Eve studying the image of Martella in miles of frothy bridal white caught in the arms of a striking man in formal black.

'Great-looking couple.'

'They are. And still very much like the newlyweds you see there. Lieutenant, I don't know if it's appropriate or necessary, but I'd like to tell you I knew Trey Ziegler. Not well,' she added quickly when Eve turned to her. 'Part of my benefits is a membership to Buff Bodies. I didn't work with Mr Ziegler. I don't use a trainer, but I attend some classes when I can juggle them in, and I often use the facilities in the early morning or after work. So I knew him, a little.'

'Did you ever sleep with him?'

Catiana winced. 'You're direct. But I suppose that's best. No. He didn't appeal to me in that way, which from what I sensed was the exception rather than the rule. I didn't like him, and I didn't like that he hit on me – subtly, but unmistakably. Maybe someone else would have taken his offer of a free trial as a trainer as a courtesy, or a way to drum up business, but to me, it felt too . . . suggestive. I can't say he crossed any lines, but he brushed awfully close to them – for me. And when he brushed too close for my personal comfort, I told him to piss off.'

'You're direct.'

Catiana smiled. 'I can be. I tried to be both firm and discreet, but I thought I should tell you in case I wasn't as discreet as I assumed. He didn't like my reaction, and when one of the women I often took a class with asked me out – and my reaction was surprise, she was embarrassed, and told me the word was I preferred women. It happens I don't, and it was easy to trace the rumor's source.'

'To Ziegler.'

'Yes. I let it go. It didn't matter to me. I wasn't looking to start any sort of romantic or sexual relationship at my gym, so it didn't matter. And he left me alone. I assume he believed the only reason I turned him down was because I was inclined toward women. But then ...'

She trailed off as Martella and her husband came in.

'I don't want to hold you up. Can I get you anything before I go?' she asked Martella.

'Why don't you finish it off?' Eve looked at Catiana, then her employers. 'Any problem with that?'

'You're telling her?' Martella asked. 'You should tell her all of it. Tell her, Cate.'

'All right, thanks. I'd rather finish it off. I wouldn't have thought anything – or not much of anything of it, Lieutenant, but after ... In brief, a couple weeks ago the man I've been seeing for a while stopped by the gym. I was meeting him for breakfast between class and work, but he came in just as I was coming out of the locker room. I guess it was obvious we're involved as several people asked me about him the next time I went in.'

'They're still at the glow stage,' Martella said. 'It's sweet.'

'It's still new,' Catiana said. 'I had a massage booked that week, end of the day, with my usual therapist. But when they called me out of the relaxation room into the massage room, Ziegler was there. He said Lola – my usual – wasn't available, so he was doing my massage. He offered me some tea. I declined, and I said I'd reschedule.'

'Why?'

'Bottom line?' She moved her shoulders in an elegant sort of shrug. 'I didn't want his hands on me, it was as simple as that. So I walked out, got dressed, went home. That was a couple days before he was killed. I wouldn't have thought anything of it, just an annoyance, but . . .'

'I told her everything.' Martella groped for her husband's hand. 'I told Catiana and Lance everything about what happened, about what you found out. About . . . He was going to do it to her. You said when you contacted me this morning, he'd put something in the tea.'

Lance Schubert, just as striking as his wedding photo, drew his wife close to his side. His eyes, hard as stone, held Eve's. 'That's rape. It's no different from sexual assault.'

'No, it's not,' Eve said.

'If he hadn't made my skin crawl – and it was as simple and as visceral as that – I'd have gone ahead with the massage.'

Catiana rubbed her arms, then sighed, leaned in a little when Lance put an arm around her in turn.

'I'd have tried the tea. When Martella told me, I realized he wasn't just annoying, wasn't just someone who made me feel uncomfortable. He was a predator. I don't want to get in the way of what you're here to talk about, but I thought I should tell you.'

'I appreciate that you did. It was his pattern, and your instincts were good. Walking out kept you from being another victim.'

'I didn't walk out. I let him in. I'm so sorry, Lance.'

'Stop.' He angled to press his lips to Martella's hair. 'Stop.'

'I'll leave you to talk,' Catiana began.

'Stay, please. Can she stay?' Martella asked Eve. 'I've told her all of it, then she told me. It helps a little.'

'It's up to you.'

'Why don't we sit? Let's all sit down.' Lance led his wife to the sofa, kept her hand in his.

'Mr Schubert, you're aware that the deceased, Trey Ziegler, administered an illegal substance to your wife, without her knowledge, and while she was under the influence of same, raped her.'

Schubert's smooth, handsome face hardened. 'Yes.'

'And when did you become aware of these circumstances?'

'This afternoon. Catiana contacted me, told me I needed to come home as soon as possible. I came home – by one-thirty – and Tella told me what had happened.'

'I thought I'd cheated.' Tears swirled in Martella's eyes. 'I thought I'd cheated on Lance, and I couldn't understand how I could have. I tried to tell myself it was just an awful mistake, just sex, and at a weak moment, but it made me sick inside. Then you contacted me, and told me there'd been something in the tea, that he'd put something in the tea he'd given me, and . . . '

'She fell apart,' Catiana said. 'I was here, and when she got off the 'link, she went to pieces. She told me everything, and when she was calm enough, I told her what had happened with me. I gave her a soother and got in touch with Lance.'

184

'You also worked with Ziegler,' Eve said to Schubert. 'You had no indication prior to today of this incident with your wife?'

'None. I wouldn't have thought of it, considered it. I knew something was wrong. You've been trying too hard,' he murmured to Martella. 'I knew there was something, but I never considered ... If I had, if I'd known what he did, I'd have killed him.'

'Lance!'

'I'd have killed him,' he repeated, his voice stone cold, a mirror of his eyes. 'I'd have beaten him to pulp with my own hands. I wish I could. She's naive, kind, trusting,' he said to Eve. 'He took advantage of all of that, and the fact that we'd had a stupid fight, and I went out of town on business before we'd resolved it. He raped my wife. I'd have gone after him, and I'd have beaten him into the ground for it.'

'Did you go to his apartment?'

'I don't even know where it is. But I'd have found out. No,' he corrected, fury alive in every word. 'No, I'd have gone to where he works, where he's so proud of himself, where he preens and struts, and I'd have taken him apart, in public. Humiliated and hurt him, the way he humiliated and hurt my wife. He raped her, then he extorted money from her. I didn't kill him, more's the pity. But I'd shake the hand of the person who did.'

'I should never have let him come here. I shouldn't have—'

185

'You're not to blame.' Schubert turned his wife toward him, took her shoulders gently. 'You're not to blame for this, for any of it.' He drew Martella in, looked at Eve. 'She's not to blame.'

'No,' Eve agreed, 'she's not. There were others, Martella. We're finding a lot of others. They're not to blame, either.'

10

She let it all circle in her mind on the drive home, hoping she'd find a solid place for a theory to land. But the ground remained too soft.

Too many people, she thought, with too many motives. Alibis that she imagined could be toppled or at least shaken with enough of a push.

Maybe it was the season of goodwill toward men – not that she'd found that ever held fast – but with Ziegler ill will seemed the primary emotion.

And damn it, she felt some ill will of her own. She wanted to shut the door on the investigation – and the killer – tie it all up so she could enjoy the festivities, the holiday, the lights, the tree, the time with Roarke.

Throughout her childhood Christmas had been empty or painful or just lacking. A day other kids rushed out of bed to tear off paper and ribbon and find shiny dreams realized.

Until she'd been eight, her best gift had been if her father had been too drunk to knock her around. Or worse.

And after she'd killed Richard Troy – to save herself from the 'or worse' – she'd been no one's child. A foster, an add-on, a token. Part of that was probably her own attitude, she admitted as she drove through the gates. But she'd had pretty bad luck in the system. State school had been bland and gray, but easier.

But now, she had home – as bright and shiny as it got. She had Roarke, the epitome of all gifts. And for reasons that often baffled her, she had friends. More than she sometimes – most times – knew what to do with, but they'd added dimension to her life while she wasn't looking.

Thinking of her victim, of what he'd done to fill his own life, she found herself grateful for what she had.

Even – when she walked in and saw him – Summerset. Sort of.

The cat pranced over to her, jingling all the way. She supposed it had been Summerset who'd added the bow and bell to Galahad's collar.

She'd have said something snarky, but the cat appeared to enjoy the adornment.

'The first team of decorators will be here at eight a.m. sharp,' Summerset informed her. 'They'll begin in the ball-room. A second team will arrive by ten to complete work on the terraces. Catering arrives at four in the afternoon, and waitstaff at six for a run-through. Other auxiliary staff will arrive by six-thirty.'

'Okay.'

'Your stylist will arrive by six, giving her ninety minutes to deal with you. You'll be finished, prepared to greet guests at seven-fifty-five.'

'I don't want ninety minutes, for God's sake, with Trina. Who needs ninety minutes to get ready for a party?'

Eyebrows raised, Summerset looked down his nose.

'The arrangements have been made. The schedule is set. The gifts you brought home are wrapped, labeled, and under the tree in the master suite. What you've had wrapped or are in the process of inexpertly wrapping for Roarke remain in the Blue Room.'

Her eyes narrowed. 'What were you doing in there?'

'My duties. Do you want the rest of those gifts wrapped and brought down to the tree in the main parlor.'

'I'll do it.' Her back stiffened. 'I know the rules. I'm supposed to do it. There's still time. Just . . . stay out of there until I'm finished.'

Flustered, she shot up the stairs with the belled cat jing-a-linging after her.

She hadn't forgotten Roarke's gifts – God knew she'd squeezed her brain to putty to come up with things the richest man in the free world wouldn't have and might want – but she'd mostly pushed aside the reality of wrapping them up.

Now she had to do that, order decorators around, deal with Trina, make nice with a houseful of guests, and, oh yeah, close a murder case.

Maybe she could hire someone (not Summerset) to

finish wrapping Roarke's stuff. It wasn't really cheating if she paid. People did it all the time, didn't they?

In fact, how did she know Roarke personally, physically wrapped up whatever he got her?

Stewing over it, she marched into the bedroom where Roarke stood pulling on a steel-gray sweater.

'Do you wrap my gifts yourself?'

He finished pulling on the sweater, shook back his hair, eyed her. 'Isn't that what elves are for? Why would I put good, enterprising elves out of work?'

'That's right.' She jabbed a finger at him. 'That's fucking A right!'

'I'm glad we agree.'

'Where do you get the elves?'

'Each must find one's own.' He walked over, caught her face in his hands, kissed her. 'Hello, Lieutenant.'

'Yeah, hey. Let me ask you something else.'

'I'm here to serve.'

'What's the first thing you'd do if you found out I'd cheated on you with . . . an elf. A sexy, buff elf.'

'The first thing?'

'Yeah, go with the gut.'

'I'd toss you out on your ear, naked as I'd have burned all your clothes along with the rest of your belongings.'

Reasonable, she thought.

'What if things were reversed, financially, and the big bulk of the dough was mine.'

He flicked a finger over the dent in her chin. 'What

190

difference does that make? You'd be naked on the street, weeping as you begged for forgiveness that would never come.'

'Harsh, but fair.'

Amusement lived in those wild blue eyes, but she seriously wanted that gut instinct.

'Okay. What if you found out I'd been duped, slipped an illegal so the elf could bang me without my consent, but without my objection as I was under the influence?'

'I would beat the elf into elfin ooze immediately and mercilessly, then . . . acid, I believe,' he said after a moment's thought. 'Acid would be the final touch, poured liberally over the ooze.'

'Nice. With your fists – the beating into ooze part?'

'Do I love you?'

'Yeah, you do.' She gave his chest a light punch. 'Sap.'

'Then it has to be my fists. He put his hands on you. Mine have to be on him.'

'Yeah. Yeah.' She sat, pulled off her boots. 'Yeah. They love each other.'

'Who are they?'

'The Schuberts – Martella and Lance. The vic dosed her, and he's on my list. But he's down the bottom because, yeah, I think he'd have confronted Ziegler if he'd known. I think he'd have hunted him down like a sick dog, and I think he'd have gotten physical. But not the grab-a-blunt-object physical. If he'd known she'd rolled with Ziegler, whether or not he'd known about the date-rape drug –

191

he'd have used his fists. That's how he strikes me. Still, I have to consider.'

She got up to dig out thick socks. 'She's the sister of another of Ziegler's marks – though the sister – Natasha Quigley – was willing, and paid for sex. I don't like the husband – Quigley's. He's got a wussy, entitled thing that rubs me wrong. I can't tell if it's just that or if he's sending off bells. But I want a good dig on his financials.'

'Ah. Playtime for me.'

'It would help me out, if you've got time for it.'

'Why don't we have a drink, some food, and you can tell me more about it?'

Her first thought was to get everything down, write it out, then she realized she might have it more concise after rolling it around with him.

'Works for me. Oh, I nearly forgot. We got a Christmas present.'

She dug into her coat pocket, took out the box. 'From Feeney. He warned me his wife's made us a bowl, but this is from him to both of us.'

'I find his wife's pottery charming.'

'Yeah, I know, since you actually find places for it instead of accidently breaking it or hiding it in some dark closet. Go figure. But I think you're really going to like this.'

He opened the box, took out the glass, and simply stared at it.

'I had the same reaction. He said he wanted us to have it, to remember, to be able to see it when things got heavy.

He said he was really proud of us. And like that. I didn't really know what to say.'

'It means a great deal,' Roarke murmured. 'A very great deal that he'd do this, think of doing it.'

'I know. And he got that. He said he thought we should keep it at home, because if I put it in my office, it was sort of like bragging.'

Roarke's lips curved. 'Trust Feeney.'

'I figure he's right, that it should stay here. And I thought, not my office, not yours, because it's ours together. I thought maybe it should stay in here because this is our space. Especially ours, I mean.'

'Yes. Especially ours.' After a glance, Roarke moved over to a table in the sitting area, set the gift down. 'How's that?'

'It's good.'

She joined hands with him, started out. The cat raced ahead, ringing cheerfully. 'Did Summerset put that stupid bell on him?'

'I put that stupid bell on him.'

'You?' She shot him a stunned glance. 'Seriously?'

'It was a weak moment,' Roarke admitted. 'Give him a bit of the festive, I thought. And now he's ringing like a mad thing, most of it on purpose to my mind. He's enjoy-ing it.'

'The bow, too?'

'I said it was a weak moment. I had to put in several short appearances at a number of office parties today. Obviously, it lowered my resistance.'

'How much did you drink?' she wondered.

'Not at all, but I will now.' In her office he opened the wall slot, chose a bottle of wine. 'A good, hearty red. How about a steak? All the mingling between meetings meant I missed lunch altogether. I'm starving.'

'I could go for steak. It's the first thing I ever ate in this house. Why did I remember that now?'

'Holiday sentiment.'

'I love you.'

He set the bottle aside, stepped over to gather her in. 'It's always lovely to hear you say it.'

'I thought of it today when I was listening to, watching the Schuberts. They love each other. I could see it, clear as water, because I can feel it, all the way through me. So I don't think they're involved with Ziegler's murder. Which is stupid because loving each other doesn't mean one of them didn't bash Ziegler then shove a knife in him.'

'But you don't think so.'

'I don't. But I'm a little worried about that holiday sentiment. I never used to have it.'

'A by-product of having love, and home.' He drew her back. 'And life.'

'I guess so. I'll get dinner.'

'No, you deal with the wine and I'll get dinner, or else there'll be nothing on the plates but steak and potatoes.'

'Why does there have to be anything else?'

'Because I love you.'

194

'Yeah, yeah.' But she opened the wine, poured for both of them.

'Let me tell you about Martella's social secretary.'

As they sat, she went over it from the start.

'I believed her,' Eve said. 'There was something so upfront and clear-eyed about it. And still, it's so damned convenient. No way I can prove or disprove what she told me, and it lays on the pattern, gives Martella, even the husband, some cover.'

'And still you believe her.'

'Do I just want to? Maybe I'm losing my cynical edge.'

'Never.' Laughing, he toasted her. 'You're a cop through and through, Lieutenant. Your cynicism and your instincts remain solid. To me, the story sounds plausible, and slides right into the pattern of your victim's behavior. She's attractive, this Catiana?'

'A stunner. More a stunner than her employer, and I got no vibe – not even a sniff of one – of interest between her and the husband.'

'But you're going to run her.'

'Sure.'

'There's my point.' He tapped his glass to hers. 'Your cynicism remains intact.'

'Whew. So the sister.' Eve cut more steak, considered it another miracle she could indulge in actual cow meat on any sort of regular basis. 'Yesterday she says nothing went on between her and Ziegler. I let it go because we got information from Martella, but it didn't jibe, not altogether.

And it fit less when we confirmed Ziegler used the drug on several women, did the extracurricular with several more for pay. And the straight sex for pay? He exploited female clients with money, and looks, and with about ten to fifteen years on him. Rich older women with time and money to spend. Natasha Quigley fit that criteria, but she wants to say nothing happened?'

'Not all rich, married, somewhat older women fall in bed with a gigolo.'

'*Gigolo.*' Experimentally, she let it roll over her tongue. 'That word's too fun and fancy for Ziegler.'

'You prefer?'

'Scumfuck, but back to the point. Sure, not all rich, married, somewhat older women fall, but she fit his pattern of mark right down the line. So if she'd said, yeah, he made the moves, but she doesn't pay for sex, or she gets so much sex at home she can't handle more, or anything that rang true, okay. A dozen ways she could have played it, but she played it wrong, so I knew damn well she'd done it with him.'

She ate, lifted her glass, then grinned. 'Hey, you're right. Cynicism intact.'

'And instincts correct, I take it.'

'Yeah, she spilled it once I popped the cork. Rough patch in the marriage. That's par for the course, right? I don't get using that as an excuse to play around.'

Playfully, he walked his fingers up the back of her hand. 'Which is why you're not naked on the street, my darling Eve.'

'Two can say that. Anyway, made a mistake, blah blah. Trying to fix the marriage, please don't tell my clueless spouse or he'll leave me and so on. Tells me he never dosed her, but she willingly accepted, booked a hotel suite, paid him for services rendered. But she was done with it when she and her husband decided to try to patch things up, and how they're taking a trip after the holidays.'

'She thinks lying to him, deceiving him about this, will improve things?'

Pleased he had the same reaction, the same question, she scooped up a bite of some sort of creamy potato. 'A lot of people think that way. When I nudged her on what would he do if he knew, she claimed he's not violent. But there was a little hesitation. And with some checking I found he's got a quick fuse. Nothing really physical, but a lot of mouth that's gotten him in trouble.'

'And he's an asshole.'

'What sort? There are so many kinds,' Roarke pointed out.

'That's so true. *Misogyny*, which is just a fancy word for a man who treats women like props or lesser conveniences. He was nervous when we talked to him, but snotty, too. I don't think he cared for being interrogated by a couple of "girls".'

'Well now, he'll rue the day.'

'Which is fancy talk for I'll kick his ass in the box if I can get him there. Which leads me to looking for money. Most of it's the wife's. So a guy like that has a rich wife, I just bet he's got some hidden away so he never ends up naked in the street. And if he's got some hidden away, just maybe we can find withdrawals that may indicate he was paying Ziegler to be quiet about something. Or that he has a skirt or skirts on the side for those rough patches. Hotel rooms or gifts, or a little love nest. Something.'

'Well now. You didn't like him at all.'

'Not even a little.'

'I'm happy to look. What did you say he did?'

'Public relations. Something he's apparently pretty good at. So he's high on my list. Along with him, I have a female writer type who was one of the vic's clients, who he slipped the drug to, who has no alibi for the time in question. And a former boxer, current gym owner and trainer who hated the vic, and had good reason to want some payback.

'There are others,' she added, 'which is the problem. We have no shortage of people who might have given Ziegler a good whack, with what could be argued as cause.'

'You could give me an early Christmas gift,' Roarke suggested. 'Provide me a list, and I'll comb over all the financials.'

'You really would consider that a gift.'

'Stealing was such bloody fun.' He leaned back, gesturing with his glass before savoring more wine. 'The thrill of sliding through the dark, into places meant to be locked and barred to me. Places with such beauty – the sort a Dublin street rat could never hope to see, much less touch.

And never hold, never keep. Beyond the need for survival that started it with lifting locks or pinching purses, it became a world of possibility, as much an art as the paintings or jewelry I might have nicked.'

'Did nick,' she corrected.

'Did indeed,' he said with the wistful affection of memory. 'And beyond the light fingers and slipping into the dark, there was the technology that so appealed to me.'

'A geek thief.'

'As you like. More slipping, more sliding, more lifting. More worlds of possibilities. Now the stealing's off the table, isn't it?'

'It is – you took it off yourself.'

'Without a single regret from where I'm sitting now, looking at the only world of possibilities I need for a lifetime.'

'Is that like saying there aren't enough stars?'

Curious, he smiled at her. 'It could be. But the point is, darling Eve, survival through possibilities, and those possibilities became a kind of game or indulgence as I'd learned to make my own through business. Legitimately. A man can put aside games and indulgences for bigger prizes.'

He lifted her hand, kissed her fingers. 'It doesn't mean he can't enjoy a bit of the slipping and sliding, if the lifting is in a good and righteous cause. You give me that, by trusting me, and sharing what you are with me. I've a medal that sits beside yours, floating in glass, given me by a man who stands as your father. A man I respect more than most. I have that as well because you gave me other possibilities, opened other worlds to me that were once barred and locked.'

'You opened them yourself. You earned them yourself.'

'I'd never have looked toward them at all without you. It doesn't mean I can't enjoy poking my fingers into bits of business some would say I have no business in.

'I'll find the accounts,' he promised her, 'as I agree they're there to be found. And consider the time well spent.'

She brought her hand to his cheek. 'Then Merry Christmas. Oh, wait. Shit. Don't wear a tux.'

'I had thought to change into black tie for a bit of cyber stealth, but I can stay as I am if you like.'

'No, tomorrow. Feeney's wife's been on him about wearing one, and he's standing firm – but if you wear one, she'll dog him on it. So don't.'

'I wasn't planning on it.'

'Good. Then it's simple. What am I wearing?'

'Not a tux.'

'Again good, because she'd probably dog him for that, too. You aren't going to tell me,' she decided after a moment.

'If you don't like what Leonardo designed for the occasion, you can choose something else. I hope you won't.' He kissed her hand again. 'I've seen the holographic image, and you'll look amazing.'

'If I'm going to look so amazing after I put it on, why do I need an hour and a half with Trina slathering stuff all over me first?'

He gave her hand a squeeze, then a quick pat. 'I stay out of such matters – for my own well-being.'

'I'm not going to think about it. That's tomorrow, and this is now, and who knows anyway?'

'Succinctly put.'

'Shut up. Money for you, murder for me.' She rose, bent over, kissed him. 'And, I guess, for us it doesn't get much better.'

She sat at her desk, coffee at the ready, her board in full view. And went back to the beginning.

She brought the crime scene reconstruction on screen, studied the two figures, the angles, the arc of the first blow, the second.

To be thorough, she checked her notes, found Sima's statement, rechecked Alla Coburn's. The two women known to have had access to the bedroom both stated the vic's latest trophy stood prominently on the bureau.

So the reconstruction held from her point of view. As did the probability – 97.4 percent – the murder was the impulse and passion of the moment.

A man, approximately six feet in height – or a woman of that height or in heels that lifted her to it.

Unless Sima had been standing on a box, that left her out. And however Eve felt personally about Trina, she couldn't see the hair-and-skin monster beating a guy's head in because he'd dissed a friend.

Coburn. Possible if she'd worn five-inch heels, which strangely women did. But then why leave so much evidence tying her to the scene? Panic? Possible. But writing a note, getting a knife from the kitchen, jamming that knife into a dead body, didn't speak of panic.

If a woman had the cold blood for that, she had enough control to grab her bra and her shoes.

Still ... Eve played with her notes. Would that same woman be clever enough to leave incriminating evidence behind as a kind of cover? A stretch, Eve thought. Something to weigh in, but she just hadn't gotten shrewd calculation from Alla Coburn.

Lill Byers, the vic's supervisor. Absolutely no evidence she'd had anything but a professional relationship with the victim. Physically, she'd fit. Height, strength, and she'd have known the vic's address. She'd known at least some of what he did on the side.

Possible kickback? Vic pays her a percentage of his side business in order to run it smoothly out of the facility. She wants more, they argue over it, she loses it.

Weak, Eve thought, just weak. And the computer agreed with her at a 53.6 probability.

David 'Rock' Britton. About the right height, certainly strong enough. Motive and potential opportunity with the lack of an alibi.

The computer liked him, she noted, with a probability of

nearly ninety percent. But the computer hadn't looked in his eyes. If he'd gone after Ziegler, he'd have used his fists.

The fashion blogger. Tall enough, fit enough. And if her previous experience with date rape held true, more than enough motive. Somebody got away with it once, by Christ, this fucker wasn't getting away with it.

So motive, no alibi, physically able.

Eve rose, walked around her board, rearranged some photos, some data.

She sat again, studied it again.

Of that group, the blogger went to the top. The flourish of the note, the knife? Yeah, she could see it. Insult to injury.

Martella Schubert. Delicate — but that was personality more than physicality. She *seemed* delicate, a little on the fragile side. Monied, pampered — and there was always power in money. Taken at face value, her statement indicated she hadn't known she'd been dosed, felt guilty for betraying her marriage.

And, taken at face value, her statement could indicate she felt guilty enough to confront the vic, argue with him. He wants more money to keep their tryst a secret. She loses it.

It could play, Eve mused. She could see that playing out. But she couldn't see the delicate Martella adding the flourish.

But who was she with the first time Eve had interviewed her?

The sister. Big sister.

Impulse, rage, violence, panic.

What if she'd called on the sister.

Tash, I'm in trouble. Oh God, he's dead! I killed him. What should I do?

What would big sister do? Would she run to the rescue, assess the situation? And with the knowledge the vic had slept with her *and* the sister, lead with a little of her own rage?

The note, the knife, then unity. Each keeping the big secret while dribbling out bits of the rest.

Maybe.

Or Natasha Quigley alone. She claimed the arrangement with Ziegler was over, ended with her hopes of mending her marriage. Maybe Ziegler didn't want it over – wanted her to keep paying. Or maybe she'd found out about her sister, confronted Ziegler.

Alibi reasonably tight, Eve mused. But all from staff of one kind or another, and staff often said or did what they were told to say and do.

And physically she fit the bill.

As for the husbands, she couldn't see Schubert. Like Rock, he'd have used his hands, his fists.

Now JJ Copley didn't strike her as a guy who led with his fists. A blunt object seemed more his style. And the flourish, well, that fit, too. Payback without any chance of confrontation.

She could see him stabbing a dead man. Yeah, she could see it.

But maybe she could see it because she just didn't like him.

Regardless, he topped the list of this next group, with his wife running a close second.

And still, not enough, Eve thought.

So she got more coffee, sat again, put her feet up on the desk and let the entire business begin again inside her head.

11

Roarke glanced up, distracted, by the jingle bells. Galahad slunk into his office just ahead of Eve.

'I have some data for you,' he told her, 'but I'm not altogether finished.'

'Okay.'

She set a fresh glass of wine beside him, knowing he cut off the caffeine intake a hell of a lot earlier than she did.

'Thanks. And this is for?'

'Interrupting. Go ahead and finish. I'm just taking my brain into a new space.'

The cat gathered himself, leaped onto Roarke's lap with a ringing of bells, kneaded and circled while Eve wandered to the wide window.

His home office space was sleeker and snappier than hers, she thought – by design. He'd created hers to mirror her old apartment, and to lure her in with the familiar.

Clever.

Wasn't it interesting how that single room was indeed just about as large as her former living space altogether? She hadn't given that much thought before, had just found herself – initially – baffled and touched that he would go to the trouble, that he would understand her so well so quickly.

She looked out the window, over the grounds, the holiday fantasy of them shining against the dark. He'd thought of that, too, built that, too. For both of them now.

She glanced over her shoulder at the painting she'd given him on their first anniversary, one of the two of them under the blooming arbor on that summer day. Their wedding day.

He'd placed it there, where he could see it from his workstation. She'd come to know him, too, hadn't she? Enough to know he'd cherish that image of them in that moment of promise.

He could see that when he worked, when he wheeled and dealed from this spot. When he bought and sold, ordered and cajoled, and did all the things she didn't fully comprehend.

He sat now, hair tied back in work mode, the sleeves of his sweater shoved up to the elbows, the cat curled in his lap, and his eyes – so brilliantly blue – focused on one of the three screens he utilized to do the slipping and sliding he'd talked about.

'You have something inside the brain you brought in here,' Roarke said as he continued to work. 'You might as well let it out. I'm tying things up here.'

'I have three people hovering at the top of my suspect

list. The computer doesn't completely agree, probability-wise, but they're my three.'

'Copley being one.'

'Definitely. And his wife – Natasha Quigley. I've got a couple of theories that could put her in the mix.'

'She developed actual feelings for Ziegler, no longer wanted to share. Killed him rather than watch him bed other women for fun and profit?'

'Huh. That wasn't one of them, but I'll toss it in, roll it around.'

'Who's your third?'

'Kira Robbins, the fashion writer.'

Roarke's brows lifted as he looked away from the screens. 'Really?'

'No alibi. Physically she fits the reconstruction. Add in former rape victim. I can't positively confirm that, but it rang true. You . . . you get an ear for it when you've been through it.'

He picked up his wine, sipped, said nothing.

'There's a part of me, I can admit, that hopes it's not her because of that. But I have to consider it. If she was raped as she said, as a teenager, it left a mark. No amount of healing erases the mark, and what I didn't pull in when I talked to her? If it had been done to her before, wouldn't she have wondered, suspected it had been done again? For the second time in her life she experiences date rape, but could she, did she, just pass this one off as bad judgment, as personal weakness? The more I ask myself that, the more I call it bullshit.'

'You believe she knew what had happened, what he'd done.'

'I believe she had to wonder, and I know I have to talk to her again, and push that. And I'm sorry for it. If it turns out she's the killer, I'm going to be sorrier.'

He sat back. 'There was a time I'd have questioned you on this. There's a part of me that still does, even though I know the answer. Even though I understand it, and almost fully accept it.'

'Can't change what was,' she said with a shrug. 'So you deal with what is.'

'It leaves a mark.' Eyes on hers, he repeated her words. 'No amount of healing fully erases it. She was a victim, and if she killed him she had reason. A reason you and I both understand far too well. He was an ugly sort, a vicious user of people, a rapist. But you'll stand for him even over a woman he used so meanly. You have to. You have to.'

He repeated it because that single reality lived in both of them now.

'More than the job, it's a duty, and your sense of right. Your line.'

'My line and yours run only so far together before they fork off. Sometimes that's a balance. Sometimes it's a problem.'

Considering, she ran a finger around the lip of one of the wobbly bowls Feeney's wife had given them.

He'd put that here, too, she thought – like the painting –

in his space. Because he understood, he valued, connections, symbols of family – far better than she.

'So. If it turns out to be her, I'll push for Mira to evaluate her, the circumstances, her state of mind, the PTSD angle. Mira's evals have weight.'

'They do. As do yours.'

'But that's jumping forward, and jumping far. Where it is now, I'll lean on her, push buttons, even knowing how it feels to have them pushed.'

'You'll stand for her, too, if she's killed. Because it's always more than the job, more than duty.'

'It's not about me.'

'Bollocks.' He said it mildly, even smiled a little when she frowned, though her words stirred up memories of what he knew she'd survived. 'Investigating objectively doesn't remove you. Your experiences, your understanding of victimology from the viewpoint of the victim is as much a part of what you do, who you are, as your training and your instincts. You are, forever, all points of the triad, Lieutenant: victim, killer, cop. And you know each section intimately.'

'Because I've not only been a victim, I'm not only a cop, but I've killed.'

'Yes. To save your own life, to save the lives of others, you've taken lives. It weighs on you every bit as much as what happened to you when you were a defenseless and innocent child. And it makes you who you are.'

'Maybe it's bollocks because I don't want it to be her.'

Because that weighed on her, too, she stuck her hands in her pockets, wandered his space. 'Because, objectivity aside for the right here and now, I want it to be Copley because it would go down easier.'

'I may be able to help you there.'

'Yeah?' She stopped, turned back to him. 'I'll take it.'

Roarke lifted the cat, giving him an apologetic stroke as he set him on the floor. Then he swiveled his chair toward Eve, smiled, and patted his knee.

'Get serious. I'm not playing office whoopee.'

'The price, and a fair one, for the data.' He patted his knee again.

She rolled her eyes, but walked over, sat on his lap. 'Satisfied?'

'I hope to be, eventually. But for now.'

He danced his fingers over keys, put data on the wall screen.

'As you can see the Quigley money – and here Natasha Quigley's share of it, which is quite comfortable.'

'Ha. A paltry quarter billion?' She angled her face toward his, grinned. 'Chump change from where I'm – literally – sitting.'

'Be that as it may.'

'Yeah, be it or may it, this part I knew. The sister's got about the same. Investments, trusts, and whatnot, all down the same road until each hit twenty-five. Some divergence there, choices – different investments, expenses, big sister purchased the New York brownstone and a second home

211

in Aruba, a flat in Paris – all in her own name. Little sis and her husband, who also has an even paltrier hundred and seventy-five-ish mil of his own. They bought the New York townhouse together. She also has a Paris flat – same building as big sis, bought on her own a couple years prior to her marriage. And as a couple they own a place on St Lucia. Copley, on the other hand, has a pathetic six million in his own name.'

'All but begging on the street.'

'Comparatively.' Shifting, she hooked an arm around Roarke's neck, studied the numbers. 'He gets credit for earning it, a mil at a time, but it's going to sting, isn't it, to have his whole shot be what his wife would think of as pocket change?'

'Does it?'

This time she rested her head against his. 'Not as long as you keep the coffee coming. But for him? He strikes me as a showboater, just the way he came across today.'

'He has a taste for the finer things, I can't quibble with that. Wardrobe, vehicles – though the wife appears to be reasonably generous there. His expense account at the firm is consistently at the max. He travels very well, profession-ally and personally.'

'This is all on the up-and-up?'

'This part, yes. He does, however, have two other accounts, both set up offshore – since the marriage – and both under very thin fronts. He went to some trouble to hide them, and they'd likely stay tucked away from any surface search his spouse or her money people might engage. Unless it got serious.'

'Or it got serious in a murder investigation with an exceptional civilian consultant poking into it.'

'Or that.'

He switched screens manually. 'Twelve million here, eight there.'

'Where'd he get it?'

'Those were some of the ends I was tying up. I'll want to dig a bit deeper, but again on the surface, from skimming. Personal and business expenses, carefully and craftily – and the personal would be from his wife.'

'He's stealing from his wife.'

'A bit at a time, and those bits, I've found, go back to the early days of their marriage. Not particularly greedy in it, but consistent. Some of it's earned right enough, just separated out into these other areas – out of the family coffers you might say. Solo investments, some tax wrangling – all close to the line but not really over it.'

'What's that one? The monthly direct pay deal. Six thousand, the first of every month.'

'Ah, you've a sharp eye. That would be the management fee, which includes thrice-weekly cleaning, all maintenance and so forth on a condo. Upper East Side. Bought with one of his shells about six months back. As there's no coordinating income from the property, I wouldn't call it an investment.'

'A place of his own – opposite end of the city from the

family house.' Eve shifted again, angling her head as she followed the numbers. 'Smells like a love nest to me.'

'It has that cachet. You'll also see some outlay – hotels, restaurants, boutiques. Go back about four months, there's considerable to design vendors, furniture.'

'Feathering the nest. What does that mean? Do birds use feathers to make their nest? Why would they? How would they? I don't get it.'

'I couldn't say, but I agree with the idiom. He bought it, furnished it, and as some of the outlets he paid out of these accounts are ladies' boutiques, I'd say he also outfitted the bird he's nesting with.'

'He's got a side piece.'

When she started to rise, Roarke simply wrapped his arms around her. 'I'm not done. Keep looking.'

She'd have looked better if she could get up, move, but she settled back. After all, he'd done the work.

'Cash withdrawals, three weeks running – back six weeks – for five thousand each. Paying somebody off? Has to be the vic. Wait, wait – it doubles at that three-week mark. Weekly again, but for ten thousand each. That's not walking-around money.'

'Perhaps he walks in very rarified areas.'

'I'm calling bullshit there. That's payoff, and it jibes with the accounting McNab pulled off Ziegler's comp.'

'Why didn't I know about this?' Roarke complained.

'Lost in the details, sorry. I just went over it before I came in. McNab pulled a kind of ledger from the vic's home comp. Amounts, initials, he had them listed as legit services. Training, consults, massages – but that's your bollocks.'

'Not mine.'

'Anybody's. He also rated some – which have to be the sex scales – with a star system. He gave Kira Robbins two and a half out of three.'

'Your victim truly was more than a bit of a pig.'

'Yeah, but my pig. I've got these amounts corresponding to the initials JJ – listed as private training sessions. Didn't figure they were. Can't prove they weren't. But seeing he withdrew the amounts, in cash, from hidden accounts? That says payoff loud and clear. It says, to me, Ziegler found out about the side piece, Copley paid him to keep it shut, then Ziegler got greedy. Doubled the payoff. Could start to piss you off. Maybe he wanted more yet.'

'I need the side piece. I need to talk to her.'

'That I can't get you.'

'Yeah, you can – have. You got hotels, restaurants, boutiques, the love nest. Somebody at those places knows her. I can find her. I will find her, and Copley will have told her something. Who can he bitch to about Ziegler hosing him, or his wife? His sex buddy.'

She circled around. 'His wife claims they were mending things, that he suggested they take a trip. Maybe he's broken it off with the side piece. That would piss her off, wouldn't it? Nest just got feathered, and now he's doing what a cheating husband usually does, runs back to his wife. His rich wife. Too much pressure from Ziegler,' she speculated. 'And he caved.'

'You're putting another suspect on your board. The mistress.'

'"Mistress" is too nice a word for a woman who lets some cheating bastard buy her shoes. I prefer "lazy, greedy bitch".'

'Harsh, without knowing circumstances. Perhaps she loves the cheating bastard.'

'Nobody loves a cheating bastard. He has hidden accounts, he has a separate address, a side piece, and very likely he's been paying his personal trainer blackmail. He definitely tops the list, with the wife and the greedy, lazy bitch right up there.

'Maybe she knew.'

'I'm going to assume you mean the wife.'

'Yeah.' Eve nodded, lining it up in her head. 'She knows he's got something going on the side. They mostly know even if they don't know exactly. It causes tension in the marriage. Separate bedrooms.'

'Separate bedrooms is more than tension,' Roarke commented. 'It's a fracture in the foundation.'

'Yeah, Feeney said the same. So you've got your crater, or your fractured foundation,' she continued. 'But Copley's happy screwing the side piece so he's fine not having to screw his wife. Except now he's getting pressure. From the wife who retaliates by having sex with their mutual trainer, and is maybe thinking fuck this marriage. Maybe from the side piece who wants him to leave the wife, and he doesn't want that because, lots and lots of money, and the prestige of the Quigley name and social status. He wouldn't want to give that up. Then there's Ziegler adding more pressure. Doubled the amount . . .'

'Copley ends it, or tries to, with the side piece,' Roarke suggested, 'and that ups the ante. It's more important now that little interlude be kept quiet.'

'Good thinking.'

'All in all, a sordid bit of business. I'm surprised the morgue's not littered with bodies of the participants.'

'It's not over yet. I still need to talk with Robbins. She fits fairly neatly. But Copley, he's just tailor-made.'

Considering, Eve shifted, slid an arm around Roarke's neck again, toyed with his hair. 'I need two hours.'

'I have all the time in the world,' he assured her as his fingers danced up her thigh.

'Not for that. Jeez, sit on a guy's lap and he goes straight into sex mode.'

'We're weak and predictable creatures.'

'I need two hours tomorrow, first thing in the morning, to see if I can get a line on the side piece, talk to the blogger. If I find the side piece, I may need a little more time to work on Copley, but I could maybe do it in two.'

'You're telling me this, while tacitly alluding to sex, because . . . ?'

'Just a couple hours.' She gave him a light, teasing kiss. 'I can be back by ten. Noon latest. And I'll dive right into party prep and all that. Total focus on it.'

'I've no problem with that. But,' he added when she smiled and leaned in for another kiss, 'you didn't make the deal with me. You made it with Summerset.'

'It's our party, right? You could talk to him.'

'It's your deal. You talk to him.'

'Damn it.'

'Meanwhile . . .' He scooped her up, stood, started out of the room with her.

'I'm not finished yet.'

'You've enough to chew on until morning. And you did sit in my lap.'

'Maybe I don't want sex.'

'You should've thought of that before you tried to use it to wiggle out of your deal.'

'I didn't make the deal with you.'

'Exactly.'

'Damn it.' Eve plotted how she could get out and back before Summerset knew the difference.

Then with the bed under her, her man on top of her, she decided to worry about it in the morning.

Somewhere in the dark, the dream formed. She didn't fight it, didn't try to struggle out of its grip, but gave over to it.

Through the dark came the bright, bright lights, the pounding music. She saw them on the treads, on the mats, on the other machines, decked in colorful gymwear, as their faces, their bodies, gleamed with sweat.

Trey Ziegler stood in the center, atop a kind of dais that

slowly revolved to give him a three-sixty perspective of the space. He wore black – snug black to show off every cut and ripple.

He looked, she realized, like the trophy that had killed him.

'They have to do what I tell them,' he told Eve. 'I'm the trainer.'

'At least one of them didn't.' She gestured at the knife hilt protruding from his chest, and the note with its large red letters and its single line of blood.

'I'm the trainer,' he insisted. 'I'm the best. I have trophies to prove it. Why shouldn't they pay more, plenty more, for the best? You think they'd look like that if it wasn't for me? Shit. Desk jockeys, socialites, rich bitches, and lazy bastards.'

'In other words,' Eve said, 'clients.'

'That's right. They've got good bodies because of *me*. They'd pay some sculptor to carve the fat off for twice what I get. I keep 'em honest, so I deserve more.'

'You didn't settle for that, Ziegler. You didn't settle for what you deserved.'

'Why settle? All that gets you is a dump of an apartment, crappy shoes, and some dumb-ass bimbo whining for more. No pain, no gain.' Smirking, he tapped his chest, either side of the knife, with his thumbs. 'I got gain.'

'You're a rapist.'

'Hell no! You!' He shouted over the music, jabbed a finger in the air at Martella. 'Bump up those weights! *Squeeze*

219

those biceps. Let me see some sweat! I never raped anybody in my life,' he said to Eve.

'You drugged them.'

'All natural product,' he insisted. 'Just to help them relax, ease those inhibitions. Some women, they tell themselves they don't want it, but they do. I just gave them a little help relaxing. And every one of them got off.' He grinned, cupped his cock. 'I'm the trainer.'

'You're an asshole. You raped them. And those women who were willing, though God knows why, you sold yourself to. Illegally.'

'It's not selling to take a nice tip for exceptional service. They got off, didn't they? So what if they gave me a few bucks?'

'Others you blackmailed.'

'So you say. Somebody offers me a few bucks to keep my mouth shut, why shouldn't I take it? I'm better than this place. I'm going to have my own place. You take money for what you do,' he pointed out. 'You're no different from me. Jesus, JJ, I want real push-ups, not those wussy girl excuses for push-ups. Burn it up a little.

'They keep coming back,' Ziegler told Eve, 'because I'm the best.'

They kept coming back, she thought. Copley, Quigley, the Schuberts, Robbins, Sima, Alla Coburn. All of them lifting, running in place, lunging, sweating.

And all of them watching Ziegler with hate in their eyes.

'They come back, but they hate you.'

'I ain't in it for love.'

'For money, for sex, for what you see as power? It got you killed.'

'That's not my fault. You're supposed to fix it, so fix it.' He reached out, grabbed her arm, squeezed. 'You need to build more muscle. I can help you with that. I can help you with a lot of things.'

'Keep your hands off me.' She yanked away, but he only grinned. Grinned as the blood from the shattered skull began to drip.

'What're you going to do about it?' He grabbed her again. 'Are you going to try to stop me like you stopped your old man?'

Her hand closed over the hilt of the knife. She felt the warm, wet blood in her hand, remembered, remembered how it sprayed and poured when she'd hacked and hacked.

He grinned at her while the blood slid between her fingers.

'If you had a chance to kill him now, you'd do it. You'd cut him to pieces if you had a chance to do it all over again.'

'No.' And God, dear God, that was a relief. 'No, I wouldn't. I'm not helpless now, not afraid for my life now. I'm a fucking cop.'

She shoved him back.

'I'm a cop,' she repeated. 'And I'll do my best by you.'

'I'm the best!' he shouted as she stepped down, walked toward the doors.

'You're nothing. You're worse than nothing. But you're mine.'

She walked out, into the night. She looked down at her hands, found them clean.

She woke in the soft gray light of morning in the warmth of her own bed.

'It's all right,' Roarke murmured, drawing her closer. 'You're all right.'

'I'm all right,' she repeated. 'My hands are clean.' She held one up, turned it in the quiet light. 'My hands are clean.'

On a half laugh, she shifted, found his eyes open and on hers. 'What are you doing here?'

'I live here.'

'That's right. Me, too. But what are you doing *here* when the sun's up? Why aren't you conferencing with Zurich or buying a solar system?'

'I'm sleeping with my wife on a Saturday morning.'

'The day of the week doesn't mean squat in your endless quest for world domination. Could be you're slipping, pal. Then where will I get my coffee?'

'I can always buy a solar system this afternoon if it makes you feel more confident in my ability to supply coffee.'

'Shake my confidence there, I could go hunt for another supplier. He might not be as pretty, but I have my priorities.'

'Feeling playful this morning, are you then?'

'Maybe. My hands are clean.'

'So you keep saying.'

'It's important. And since they are . . . ' She ran a hand down his chest, and down, then closed her fingers around him. 'Look what I found.'

'And now that you have?'

'I can probably think of something constructive to do with it.'

But first she simply rolled on top of him, her face buried in the curve of his throat, her heart beating lightly on his.

Warm, she thought, everything so warm and smooth and easy.

'We lose too many Saturday mornings.'

He ran a hand up and down her back. 'The day of the week doesn't mean squat.'

She laughed, pressed her lips to that curve, then lifted her head. 'You're right.' She kissed him, light as their heartbeats. 'But since solar systems are for later . . . '

She touched her lips to his again, then took hers sliding down the line of his throat, over his chest. Whatever the day, it was lovely to have the time to just be with him, to feel as she felt now. Warm and smooth and easy.

As she rose up to straddle him, bells rang and there was an unmistakable sound of irritation just before the thump of the cat deserting the bed for the floor.

'We've annoyed the cat,' Roarke commented.

'Well, three's a crowd anyway. Except it's really not. One too many people in a given circumstances doesn't make a crowd. Why are sayings so stupid?'

'Like the solar system, perhaps we can consider that later.'

'Good idea.'

She leaned down, and this time the kiss was long, slow, deep. Stirring them both so the hands sliding down her back fisted in the thin material of the shirt she wore.

Not too many people here, she thought, just the exact right amount. Just him. Just her. She felt his need for her, wakened so quickly, the strength of it, the depth of it. It was always a wonder to her. She hoped it always would be as the wonder added a layer of beauty over desire.

His heart beat a little quicker against hers. She swore she felt the vibration of it as she rose up again.

Those eyes, still watching her, madly blue and beautiful, as she crossed her arms, drew her shirt up and off. As she shifted. As she lowered. As she took him in.

The morning light bathed her in silver, the long torso, the lean sculpted arms. And in the morning hush there was no sound but her breath and his, and the soft slide of the sheets as she moved over him. Slowly, almost gently rocking to bring the pleasure in long, quiet waves.

The heat of her trapped him, gloriously, brought him light as surely as the sun slipping through the sky window overhead.

She gave them the morning, a reminder of what they were together no matter what the day might bring.

As her rhythm quickened, so did his heart, his blood, his need.

She arched back, a strong and slender bow, with a moaning sigh as she gave herself to that heat, to that light.

Then once again she bent to him, bracing herself as she captured his mouth. And moving, rocking, giving, took them both over that final wave.

She lay on him again, heart to heart, beats fast and thick now. This time her sigh was long and lazy and replete.

'They should make a law.'

Eyes closed, body loose, he stroked her back again. 'There are so many already, aren't there?'

'A law that every day has to start with an orgasm.'

'I believe I could adhere to that law without complaint.'

'You should run for office so you could make it the law.'

'If I ran for office I'd have myself committed as I would have, unquestionably, lost my mind.'

'Yeah, there's that.' She snuggled in. 'I had a dream.'

'I know. It disturbed you.'

'Some of it. Everybody was in this enormous gym. Like Buff Bodies, but bigger. Just as loud, but bigger. All my suspects and players pumping and sweating, with Ziegler on this platform running the show. Even in the dream he was a fuckhead. "I'm the trainer," he kept saying.'

She lifted her head. 'That's the thing, was the thing for him. Without him, the way he figured, they'd all be fat, lazy slobs. He *made* them. He's the trainer, and they did what he told them to do. The sex – willing or coerced – was just another aspect of it. Same with the money. All just his due because he – in his mind – was the one in charge.

225

His whole existence, really, was one big power trip. The people who came to him for training had more money, more prestige, more whatever, but *he* called the shots, and they fell in line.'

'Does that help you?'

'Mostly it's just reaffirming what I already knew, maybe kicking it up a little. Stay on a power trip long enough without real power? Somebody's going to kick your ass. He put his hands on me.'

'So you kicked his ass, dream-wise speaking?'

'No. I could have. I could have done worse. He baited me. He said we were the same, taking money for service. That's too stupid to get the rise, so he put his hands on me and asked what I was going to do about it? Was I going to carve him up like I had Richard Troy.'

'Ah, Eve.' He shifted to wrap around her.

'No, that's the thing. Maybe part of me wanted to. And I closed my hand around the hilt of the knife – he had the knife in him, like he did when I found him. But I didn't use it, didn't even consider using it. Because I'm a cop. Because even though I can see he shared some traits with Troy – the power trip, the utter contempt for others – I'm a cop and he's a victim. He's mine, and that's that. I walked out, and my hands were clean.'

'Darling Eve, they always have been.'

She pressed into him again, into comfort. 'I wasn't sure, I don't know why, but I wasn't a hundred percent until that moment in the stupid dream when I put my hand on the hilt of that knife if I'd kill him – if I hadn't killed Troy back then and he walked up to me now, would I, could I, kill him for what he'd done to me?'

She let out a breath. 'No. I'd do whatever it took to lock him up, to put him away, to make him pay even though payment never balances the scales. I killed him then because I was powerless and terrified. I'm not either of those anymore. I'm a cop, and my hands are clean.'

He took her hands, kissed them.

'Maybe it's not all the way behind me,' she said. 'I keep thinking it is – when the worst of the nightmares stopped, when I went back to Dallas, when I got through my mother, McQueen. But there's always some other angle to deal with. I'm okay with it. It happened, all of it happened, and it leaves a mark, like I said. But I'm okay with it.'

She curled in close. 'And I've got you on a Saturday morning.' They stayed as they were, taking just a little more time.

12

Over breakfast in the bedroom sitting area, she outlined her strategy for the day.

'I thought about tagging Reo, trying to wrangle a warrant to search Copley's love nest.' Eve bit into some bacon – honestly, good sex, a hot shower, then bacon? Did a morning get any better? 'Reo's a smart APA, and she'll follow the dots I lay out. But even so, it's a long, skinny stretch for probable cause.'

'I could get you in.'

'Yeah.' She slid a glance his way. 'It's tempting to go the clever-fingers and lock-pick route, but no.'

'I own the building,' he said and ate some eggs.

'I should've figured. But even with that, there's no legal peg to hang an entry and search on.'

'General maintenance, possible gas leak, suspicious sounds, smells, behavior. I imagine there are pegs.'

'Weak ones.'

'So your plan is?'

'To lie, if and when necessary. I'll get through building security, I've got a badge. If nothing else, I'll knock on doors, see if I can get a name and/or description of the side piece from neighbors, track her from that. I want a conversation.'

'It may be she lives there.'

'Yeah, that's the hope, but I'm not counting on that much good luck. Either way, it won't take long. Unless . . . '

'Unless?'

'Say I track her down, have a conversation and she says: JJ went to see that awful man, and there was a terrible accident. It wasn't Sugar Daddy's fault.'

'Sugar Daddy.'

'He qualifies. And she says how Copley tried to reason with Ziegler, but Ziegler got physical and then one thing led to another. Boo-hoo.'

'But you're not counting on much good luck.'

'I'm just pointing out the − very slim − possibility I might be more than a couple hours, considering if I find her, if she blabs, I'd have to go arrest Copley and try to grill him before he screams, "Get me a lawyer." Like that.'

'All very reasonable, but you don't have to explain to me. I'm bound to be fairly well occupied myself. I've some work to tidy up, then some preparation to oversee.'

'Right, but . . . ' She topped off his coffee, sent him a calculatedly innocent look. 'If you should happen to run into Summerset while I'm gone, you could—'

'No.'

'Come on.'

'Absolutely no. Your deal.'

She sulked over her eggs. Even bacon lost some appeal with the prospect of wrangling with Summerset.

'Isn't it bad enough I have to face hours of swarming decorators, then end that small nightmare by having Trina pour gunk all over me? Now I have to face the smirking disapproval of our resident corpse?'

'You run an entire division of murder cops firmly, cleverly, and efficiently. You'd step in front of a stunner to save an innocent bystander. You would, and have, faced off with vicious murderers. I think you can handle Summerset, decorators in our employ, and a hair-and-skin consultant.'

He topped off her coffee in turn. 'Buck up, Lieutenant.'

'Bite me.'

'I'll schedule that in.'

She downed the coffee, rose. 'Fine, but it's not my fault I don't know where the hell he is, and it's a really big house, so . . .'

She broke off, had to hold back a snarl when Roarke simply lifted his eyebrows.

'Okay, *fine!*' The battle lost, she stalked over to the house comp. 'Where's goddamn Summerset?'

Good morning, darling Eve. Summerset is currently in the Park View guest room.

'Great. Where the hell is that?'

Before Roarke could answer, the computer continued in smooth tones.

The Park View is located here.

The little screen displayed a floor plan with a red dot pulsing in one of the rooms.

'The elevator would take you directly there if you request it,' Roarke pointed out.

There was more chance Summerset would have moved on if she hoofed it. So she stalled. 'Do all the guest rooms have names?'

'It's a simple way to organize them. Would you like a list?'

'No. How many are there?'

'More than enough.'

'Ha!' She pointed at him. 'Even you don't know.'

'The number can vary as some of the salons, the sitting rooms, even entertainment areas can be utilized as guest rooms, if needed. Shouldn't you be on your way?'

'I'm going.' She shoved her hands in her pockets. 'I'll be back in plenty of time to do whatever.'

'I'm sure you will. And I'll wish you luck even though with it you might be longer.'

'Right.' She hesitated, but couldn't find another reasonable excuse to stall. 'If it's longer, I'll let you know.'

When he only smiled, she walked out. She detoured to her office, fiddled for a few minutes, grabbed the coat she'd left there, then followed the route from the screen map.

Everything smelled faintly of pine and cranberries – how was that even possible? Floors gleamed, art shone.

She found the bedroom, started to knock. Stopped herself. It was her house, too, she reminded herself, and opened the door.

Easy to see how it got its name as windows framed with shimmering drapes opened to a view of the great park.

The bed struck her as sort of regal with a lot of deep carving on dark wood, and more shimmering stuff flowing over it under a bold garden of pillows.

Galahad sprawled over the foot of the bed as if he lived there.

Summerset, in his habitual funereal black, set a large painted vase filled with bloodred lilies on a table, turned to her.

'Is there something you need, Lieutenant?'

'No. What are you doing in here? Are those flowers for the cat or what?'

'I'm sure he appreciates them, but no. You're entertaining this evening, and there would be the possibility a guest might overindulge and be best served by staying the night.'

'That's what Sober-Up's for.'

'Regardless, hospitality decrees guest rooms are prepared for any eventuality. It's called courtesy.'

'I'd say courtesy is not getting shit-faced drunk when you come to someone's house to a party, but that's just me. I have to go out for about an hour. I'll be back to do the stuff.'

He arched one skinny eyebrow, made her teeth want to grind. 'It's police business. I'm the police. I'm not welshing on the deal. I'll be back.'

'As you say.'

'That's right, as I say. So . . . go fuss with other bedrooms for potential drunks.'

She walked out. She would *not* feel guilty for doing her job. She had a possible lead, and she had to follow up while it was hot, didn't she? Damn right.

But she checked the time, quickened her steps.

She considered pulling Peabody in, but didn't see the point. If she pulled a name out of the fishing expedition, she could toss it to her partner, have Peabody do a run.

While she herself told people, who knew better than she did anyway, where to put flowers and lights and shiny balls.

And maybe, if she got through that fast, and Peabody came up with some solid information, she could squeeze out another hour to tug that line.

She'd honor the deal, she'd contribute, but she wasn't going to spend an entire day playing lady of the manor. It made her feel stupid.

She headed east, zipping through traffic – blissfully light as the shops hadn't opened yet. It didn't stop the ad blimps blasting out with a kind of frenetic desperation about how many days, hours, minutes shopping time were left.

The carts were open, smoking with offerings of egg

pockets and seasonal chestnuts, doing early business for the poor saps who'd open those shops and deal with the Saturday-before-Christmas insanity.

A SkyMall blimp announced the first two hundred paying customers would receive a FREE GIFT! She decided working security at the SkyMall ranked high on her list of worst ten jobs, right up there with shark tank cleaners – somebody had to do it – and proctologists.

Considering the motivations of obtaining a medical degree to poke into assholes kept her entertained until she pulled up in front of the shiny glass-and-steel building overlooking the East River.

She expected the doorman in his black-and-gold livery to hustle over and bitch about her substandard vehicle, and was prepared to snarl at him.

He was quick on his feet, actually opened the car door before she could.

'Lieutenant.' He offered her a hand and a dignified smile. 'I'll keep an eye on your vehicle.'

She narrowed her eyes. 'Roarke contacted you.'

'Moments ago. I'm Brent if there's anything I can help you with. I did check our records, as Roarke requested. I'm afraid we have no John Jake Copley listed.'

Eve pulled out her PPC, scrolled through to Copley's ID shot.

'Do you recognize him?'

'Yes, of course. That's Mr Jakes.' Brent's eyes widened. 'Oh, I see! Mr Jakes – or Mr Copley – has number 37-A.

The northeast corner unit on thirty-seven. He shares the unit with Ms Prinze.'

'Full name?'

'One minute.' He took out his own handheld. 'Mr John Jakes and Ms Felicity Prinze.'

'Okay. Give me a sense.'

'They're relatively new to the building. I don't see Mr Jakes – Copley,' he corrected, 'often. I'm pretty sure he works downtown as I chatted once or twice with his driver. Ms Prinze is very nice, ah, considerably younger. She's a … performer.'

'I bet. What sort?'

'From what I've heard, she was a dancer. She's taking acting classes, dance classes, and I believe voice lessons.'

'Okay. Is she up there?'

'I'd say yes. She's not what you'd call an early riser. Has she done something wrong, Lieutenant?'

'I'm going to find out.'

'I hope not,' he said as he opened the door of the building for her. 'She's a very nice young woman. Should I call up for you?'

'No, thanks. Do you know if Copley's up there?'

'I can't be sure as I came on this morning at eight. He hasn't gone in or out since I've been on the door.'

'If you see him – come in or go out – tag me. This number.'

She passed Brent a card, walked to the elevator. 'I appreciate the help, Brent.'

'Anything I can do, Lieutenant.'

She stepped into the elevator, texted Peabody the name of the side piece, the address, the bare bones, with instructions to do a full run.

The elevator rode smooth, but then Roarke knew how to bring smooth into a building. The hallway on thirty-seven was wide, quiet and tastefully painted, with carpets of classy black swirls on elegant gray.

Good security – and she'd have expected nothing less there in a Roarke's property. Discreet cams worked into the crown molding, and each apartment outfitted with top-grade palm screens, cams, and alarms.

She stopped at 37-A. Double doors, she noted, to add that more powerful, important touch. She pressed the buzzer, waited.

She gave it three tries – increasing the length of the buzz – before the intercom clicked.

'Is that you, baby?'

'I don't know, sweetie.'

'Huh?'

'Dallas, Lieutenant Eve.' Eve held up her badge. 'I'd like to speak with you, Ms Prinze.'

'You're really not supposed to try to sell stuff in the building. You could get in trouble.'

'I'm not selling anything. I'm the police.'

'The police?'

'NYPSD. Dallas, Lieutenant Eve.'

'Oh … But … How can I be sure you're the police, Officer Eve?'

'*Lieutenant.*' For the second time that morning Eve struggled not to grind her teeth. 'Lieutenant Dallas. Look at the badge, Ms Prinze. You can scan it.'

'I don't think I know how to do that. This whole security thingy is so complicated.'

Since she had some sympathy for technology fumblers, Eve dug for patience. 'Okay. Do you know Brent – the doorman?'

'Oh, sure. He's just a sweetheart.'

'You can call down, verify with him. I can wait.'

'Oh, well, shoot, that's okay.' Locks clicked and snicked before the doors opened to frame a serious bombshell.

She couldn't have been more than twenty-one or twenty-two. Curvy as a country road, she stood maybe five-two in her bare feet with their glittery red toes. Each big toe sported a painted snowflake in bright white.

She wore what Eve supposed would be called a peignoir – white as the snowflakes – a duet of a long silky gown, cut low on very healthy breasts, and an unbelted robe with fluffy white feathers decking the collar.

She had a heart-shaped face, all rose and cream, with a deeply bowed mouth – accented with a tiny beauty mark at the corner. Sleepy eyes in china-doll blue smiled out of a thick fringe of dark lashes.

'I'm not supposed to let just anybody in, you know? But since you're the police ... *OH!* I just *love* your coat. It's so totally mag! I couldn't carry it, but – *OH!* Is it real leather?'

Before Eve could respond or evade, Felicity reached out

237

to stroke the sleeve. '*OH!* It *is!* It's just gooshy-smooshy. I love real leather, don't you? I wonder if they make it in red. I love red, and I could have it cut down to knee-length maybe. Where'd you get it?'

'It was a gift.'

The china-doll eyes sparkled. 'I just love gifts, don't you?'

'Can I come in and speak with you, Ms Prinze?'

'Oh, sure, sorry. You can call me Felicity. I'm sort of thinking of dropping the last name – professionally, you know? It's more fun, and sexier. Just one name. You know, like Roarke.'

'Huh' was the best Eve could think of.

'You know: Roarke. The abso-ult rich guy. And completely iced. He actually owns this building. I would *die* to meet him, wouldn't you?'

'Well.' She decided it was best not to mention she'd just recently banged said abso-ult iced Roarke into a mutual puddle.

'Hey, sorry! You maybe want some coffee? I have a stash of real. Police probably don't get real very much. I have a friend whose brother is a policeman back in Shipshewana. He's a sweetheart, but they sure don't make much money.'

'What ship?'

'Shipshewana,' Felicity said with a bubbly giggle. 'Indiana. That's where I'm from, but I've been in New York almost a whole year now. I just got up, so I could sure use some coffee. I'll get us some, okay?'

'Great.'

It gave Eve a chance to think. She watched Felicity walk away – who knew an ass could move in so many directions – then took stock.

As love nests went, Eve considered it upscale. A good-sized living area with a stellar view of the river through a wall of glass. The holiday tree stood front and center, rising from floor to ceiling, topped by a white angel and covered with red and gold balls.

She suspected Copley had let Felicity have her way with the decor as it ran to bright and fussy, feathers and beads. Like a cheerful bordello, Eve decided, all plush and girlie.

She wandered, noted the dining alcove – large enough for dinner parties with a red lacquer table holding a center Santa easily three feet tall.

She moved quietly, took a quick scan of a powder room – red accents, fussy soaps, frilly towels – a room with a ballet bar, a keyboard, a wall screen, rolled yoga mats, a glass-fronted friggie stocked with bottled water. One wall held a screen, another was completely mirrored.

She took a quick glance in the master bedroom – golds and reds, more feathers and beads, a huge mirrored bed, a bureau topped with a half dozen fancy perfume bottles, a masculine chest of drawers. A chaise piled with stuffed animals and dolls.

Gauging the time, Eve slipped back into the living area just before Felicity came out carrying a red tray holding two flowery cups with a matching creamer and sugar bowl.

'I didn't ask how you take your coffee.'

239

'Just black's good.'

'Ugh! I like *lots* of cream and sugar.' She set the tray on a low table, sat. When she leaned over to doctor her coffee – and she did mean 'lots' – Eve expected the impressive breasts to tumble right out of the peignoir.

'So.' Felicity sat back, holding her cup with her pinkie curled out. 'Are you all ready for Christmas?'

'Pretty much. Listen.' How to begin? With a standard side piece, she'd have known her approach. But bombshell or not, this one was green as grass. 'You live here with John Jake Copley?'

'You know JJ!' Delight pinkened her cheeks. 'Why didn't you say so! Isn't he a dream? He's the sweetest man, and so good to me. I'm not really supposed to talk about him too much because, well, you know, he has to get his divorce and all.'

'How did you meet him?'

'Oh, he didn't tell you?'

'We didn't get into that.'

'It was so cute! I'm a dancer. I'm going to be a triple threat – that's what my voice coach says. I'm taking lessons, and acting lessons, and more dance lessons. JJ's paying for all of it. I'm an investment.'

She flushed prettily.

'Anyway, I just couldn't stay in Shipshewana my whole life, could I?'

Eve got a strange picture of a pirate ship sailing through fields of corn and cows. 'I don't see how.'

240

'I *know*. Even though I miss everybody like crazy, you have to, you know, *try* to like fulfill your destiny. My theater teacher back home said I had real talent. A natural talent. So I came to New York. I want to work on Broadway, but it's really hard. They can be so mean at the auditions. And I didn't have as much money as maybe I should have. Things are really expensive here. I got a job as a waitress, but it gets really confusing. Then I got a dancing job. In one of *those* places, you know.'

She winced a little.

'Yeah, I know.'

'It was embarrassing at first, but like Sadie said, everybody's got a body, so big deal. And if you have a nice one, you can make some real money. I didn't like it a whole lot, but I was willing to sacrifice until I got my big break. You've got to pay your dues.'

She took a sip of her coffee-flavored cream and sugar.

'So,' Eve speculated, 'you met JJ at the place where you danced.'

'Oh yeah, right. One night JJ came in, and he got a lap dance. And then he got another one, and he bought me a drink. He wanted to, you know, but I don't do that. I'm not licensed, plus I don't want to, you know? For like money.'

Eve considered the fancy apartment, the feathery peignoir – reserved judgment. 'Okay.'

'So JJ was with some, what do you call it, colleagues, and some of them got a little pushy. But not JJ. Anyway, he came back the next night and bought me another drink, and he was nice to talk to. Then he asked me out.'

She pinked up again. 'A real date. Dinner and everything. He took me out a few times – twice to a Broadway show, which was the *ult*. Then we, you know, but it wasn't like he was a customer. We were dating. I didn't know he was married, then he told me, and I was going to break it off because, you know, that's just not right.'

'He didn't tell you he was married before . . . you know?' Eve qualified.

'No, but he explained how his wife's so awful, and controlling, and he's trying to get a divorce, and they don't even have sex.'

'She doesn't understand him, appreciate him,' Eve said.

'I know!' Irony wafted over Felicity's blond curls. 'Then he bought this place so I'd have a nice, safe place to live. And he got me the lessons. And I have charge accounts and everything. I just have to be patient. It gets lonely sometimes because he has to travel so much for work, and he's trying to convince his terrible wife to agree to a civilized divorce. He's so sweet to me, and after he gets his divorce we're getting married. See.'

She held out her hand – fingernails painted like her toes – to show off the rock on her ring finger.

Eve thought back to the hidden accounts, calculated what the rock would go for, if real. No charges or withdrawals corresponding, to her memory.

It struck her Felicity got the clichéd line and the fake diamond, and was naive enough to believe both.

'We're just crazy about each other. We'd spend every minute we could together if it wasn't for his awful wife, and if he didn't have to travel for work, like he is now.'

Eve wondered if they grew them all this naive and gullible in Shipshewana.

'He's away on business now?' she asked.

'Yeah, he had to leave a couple days ago to give a big presentation way out in New L.A. He's really important, but you know that, so the client people wanted him especially. But he's going to be back for Christmas. He maybe has to spend most of it with his wife, because of how people gossip and stuff, but we're going to have our own Christmas here. Isn't the tree pretty?'

'Yeah, it's pretty. Do you know a Trey Ziegler?'

'Uh-uh. Is he a friend of JJ's? I haven't been able to meet his friends because of gossip and how his awful wife would use it to ruin him in the divorce. It's nice to meet you, so I can have somebody to talk with. Sadie, my friend from where I used to dance, says men never divorce their wives like they say, but JJ's not like that. We're crazy about each other.'

'So you haven't seen JJ for a couple days?'

'Uh-uh. He had to go out of town, like I said, kind of all of a sudden. But he tags me every day, and he sent the flowers over there just yesterday.'

Her extraordinary breasts swelled over the silk and feathers as she sighed.

'He's such a sweetheart. He's under a lot of stress what with work and his wife so we don't go out so much anymore. He needs the quiet. She's, what do you call it, vindictive. So I try to be really understanding, and make things nice for him when he's here.'

'I'm sure you do. When did he leave town?'

'Um. Wednesday maybe. Was it?' She caught her pouty bottom lip between her teeth as she taxed her memory. 'I get mixed up. He had to do the party with his wife – you know, for appearances – that night. Did you go?'

'I couldn't make it.'

'Oh, too bad. I love parties. JJ was going to come over here afterward. And we were going to go have a big, fancy brunch at the caviar place for a treat. I just love caviar, don't you? But he had to go out of town.'

'And he's never mentioned Ziegler?'

'I don't think so. Is he a client? JJ takes really good care of his clients. That's why he's so successful.'

'I bet.'

'Do you want to go out for breakfast maybe? My treat. I don't have dance or acting lessons today, and my voice coach doesn't come until two.'

'I'm sorry. I can't.'

'Oh, do you have to go already?' Felicity asked when Eve rose.

'I do, but maybe I'll come back. When JJ's here.'

'That would be mag! We can have a little party.'

'Why don't you get in touch with me when you

expect him?' Eve pulled out a card. 'We'll have that little party.'

'Sure! This is, well, it's just magolicious. I can't wait.'

'Neither can I.' She opened the door, glanced back at the bombshell. 'You know, Felicity, your friend Sadie sounds pretty smart.'

'Oh, she's really smart. She's a really good friend, but she worries about me, and doesn't have to. She thinks I should go back to Shipshewana.'

Eve decided Sadie might be the only person in New York dealing Felicity the truth.

'Have you talked to her recently?'

'I talk to her most every day. JJ doesn't want her to come here because, well, people don't always understand about the dancing, but . . . you've got to have girlfriends, right?'

'Yeah. What did she say about JJ having to go out of town, all of a sudden?'

'Oh, well, Sadie doesn't trust most guys. She's had some bad experiences. She never thinks JJ's telling me the truth.'

'Like I said, she sounds pretty smart. Maybe you should listen to her. You ought to tag her up. And, Felicity? Maybe you should ask yourself why an important, successful man's doing out-of-town business over a weekend instead of grabbing a shuttle back to take you out for caviar.'

Leaving it at that – the best she could do – Eve made her way out, nodded to Brent.

She hated feeling sorry for the woman – no, she corrected, girl. No more than a girl really. But it balanced out, she supposed. The sorrier she felt for Felicity, the more contempt she felt for Copley.

First chance, she promised herself, the two of them were going to have a long, fascinating conversation.

And it wasn't going to be much of a party.

13

Kira Robbins let Eve in herself. She looked heavy-eyed, strained, and wore baggy flowered pajama pants and a gray NYC sweatshirt. A far cry, Eve thought, from the smart red dress and heels of the day before.

'You want to go over it all again.' She didn't ask Eve to sit, didn't offer her a drink, just flopped down on the sofa. 'That's how this works. Just going over and over it again.'

'You said you were alone, no outside contact, during the time Ziegler was murdered.'

'Yeah. Damn book. I haven't written a word since I talked to you yesterday. I'm not going to make deadline. I just want to sleep, but . . . '

'How many times did Ziegler come here for a private session?'

'Four – no, five. Twice with me and my assistant, three times just me. I think.'

'How much extra did you give him for adding in the assistant?'

'Ah . . . five hundred.' Robbins rubbed the spot between her eyebrows with two fingers. 'Yeah, five.'

It jibed with Ziegler's accounting.

'How many times were you intimate with him?'

'It wasn't intimacy. There's nothing intimate about having your choice taken away. He had sex with me – once. He raped me. Once.' Something fired in her eyes. 'It wasn't intimacy.'

'You're right.'

'You're wondering – I'm wondering – did I ask for it? Did I open the damn door to it? I had him in here, I paid him to come here. I knew he was a user. I heard the talk, but I kept going to him, I had him come to me.'

'Why?'

'He was a really good trainer.' She pressed her fingers to her eyes. 'Oh God. He was tough on me, and charming about it. He helped keep me in shape. Fashion blogger,' she said with a bitter half laugh. 'You have to look good. You're not competing with the people you're writing about – the stars and butterflies and trust-fund babies – but you absolutely are. I didn't want to go to a body sculptor – wanted to do it myself. That's something to feel smug about when you know who's getting work done, and how often. So I stuck with him. I stuck with Trey.'

She let her head fall back. 'So I'm asking myself did I ask for it. When it happened before, I was in love with the bastard. Just a kid, and in love the way you are at sixteen. After, he said I'd wanted it. I'd teased him. So he'd given me a little something to relax me, so he'd held me down when I said no, when I said stop. But I'd wanted it, and if I made a big deal about it, everybody would know I'd asked for it.'

'No one asks to be raped, Kira.'

'No, and I *know* better. I just can't get to it yet. I thought I could handle Ziegler – no problem. I'm smart, I'm strong, I learned how to take what happened before and get smarter, get stronger. But knowing's one thing, feeling's another.'

Her eyes filled; she pressed her fingers to them as if to push the tears back in. 'Sorry, rough night.'

'You'd been dosed and raped before, but you didn't wonder – you didn't ask yourself – if it had happened again. You just got the urge, had sex with a man you've stated you weren't attracted to, didn't even really like. And after, didn't wonder?'

'I never thought of it. It never so much as floated over my head. I'd put it behind me. I wasn't that girl anymore. I was too smart, too strong, too careful. It could never happen to me again.'

She squeezed her eyes tight for a moment, balled her fists until the knuckles whitened. 'But it did. It did happen again, and I feel just like that sixteen-year-old girl. Maybe even worse, because I really believed it couldn't happen again.'

She loosened her hands, took a couple slow, deep breaths. 'I didn't kill him, that's the best I can give you. I wouldn't have if I'd known before someone else did. But I wouldn't have made the same mistake I did at sixteen. I'd have gone straight to the cops. And if some people wanted to think I'd asked for it, fuck them. Fuck them.'

On a half laugh she scrubbed her hands over her face. 'Yeah, rough night. But I've got an appointment with my therapist in a couple hours.'

'Good. You meant nothing to him.'

'What?'

'Understand that,' Eve said. 'You meant nothing. You were just another notch to him, another body, another way for him to feel important and powerful. You didn't ask for it, you didn't open the door to it. You were just another opportunity for him, another income source, and that's it.'

'That's supposed to make me feel better?'

'Up to you, but it's truth. It's fact.'

Kira breathed out again. 'It's harsh, and maybe because it's harsh, it makes me feel better.'

'I appreciate the time.' Eve started for the door, stopped. 'I figure you'll make that deadline.'

'Oh yeah?'

'Yeah. You won't let him screw you over again.'

She mulled over the conversation, her impressions, what she'd seen, heard and felt on the drive home. All she needed was maybe a half hour more – that wasn't much – to write it all up, shoot it off to Peabody, Mira.

And, okay, maybe another ten or fifteen to update her

board, review the data Peabody would have accumulated by now.

Forty-five minutes, another hour tops, then she'd switch gears, go into full party-prep mode.

It was fair.

Satisfied with the bargain, she drove through the gates. And stopped the car in the middle of the long drive to gape. Appalled.

Trucks and vans and *people* crowded and swarmed at the entrance of the house. Those people carted trees – how could they possibly need more trees – plants, flowers, crates and boxes and God only knew.

She watched as some of the vehicles drove around the sprawling house to, she assumed, go around the side or the back where undoubtedly they'd unload more trees, plants, flowers, crates and boxes and God only knew.

They comprised an army of workmen, decorators, gofers. And she imagined this first wave didn't include the second force that would deal with food and beverage.

You didn't need armies for a party. You needed armies for a war.

Apparently, this was war.

And where the hell was she supposed to dump her car?

Seeing little choice, and hoping to avoid the various battalions for as long as possible, she drove around to the garage.

She sat in the car a moment, drumming her fingers, trying

to remember how to gain access. Damn place was as big as a house. Normally she just parked out front. She knew Summerset – in his anal, everything in its stupid proper place way – remoted whatever vehicle she dumped there into the garage, and had it remoted back out front in the morning.

So she didn't hassle with the garage as a rule. She considered leaving it where it was, but that felt stupid. Instead, she tapped the in-dash, tagged Roarke.

'Lieutenant.'

'Yeah, hey. Thought I should tell you I'm back.'

'And in a timely fashion.'

'Yeah. There's a bunch of everybody out front. A parking lot of vehicles so I'm going to pull into the garage.'

'Well, all right then.'

'But, the thing is, I can't remember the code.'

On the dash screen, he smiled at her. 'Eve, have you still not read the bloody manual for your vehicle?'

'I find stuff when I need it.'

'In that case, you'll find you've only to access your in-dash comp, request accessories, order the garage doors open by remote. It has your voiceprint. You'd close them the same way, or by the garage comp once you've parked.'

'Right. Got it. Thanks.'

'I could point out, that if you'd read the manual, you could have parked out front and sent the car to the garage by remote, but that would be rubbing it in, wouldn't it?'

Rather than respond, she cut him off, snarled after the screen went blank. 'Smart-ass. Computer engage.'

Engaged, Dallas, Lieutenant Eve.

'Accessories.'

Accessories confirmed. Would you like a listing by alpha order or by category?

'Just open the damn garage door.'

Do you wish to open the garage door at your current location, which is residence, or an alternate location?

'Why the hell would I want to open a door where I'm not? Never mind. Open the door, current location.'

Garage door, residence. Would you like to open the main door, the rear door, the second level—

'Main door, for God's sake. Open the main garage door, residence.'

Garage, residence, main door opening.

She waited while it rose, slow and silent, then drove in.
She wouldn't bother to roll her eyes at the number of vehicles housed inside. Or just a minor eye roll. All-terrains, sedans, sports cars, muscular trucks, sexy motorcycles.
Some flashy, some classy, some sinewy, some sleek.

She was pretty sure there had been some refinements since she'd last been inside – she knew there hadn't been a slot labeled DLE, the make of her car, the last time she'd been in here. No question there'd been some additions because the man purchased vehicles the way others might buy socks.

She pulled into the slot as the computer asked politely,

Do you wish to close the main garage doors, residence, at this time?

'Yeah, yeah, do that.'

She got out, glanced around at Roarke's shiny toys, and spotted a pristine work counter – who else had a pristine garage? – with a computer, an AutoChef and a friggie.

'A garage you could live in. Who else?'

Inspired, she crossed to the counter, narrowed her eyes at the computer.

'Computer on.'

It sprang immediately to life.

Good morning, Dallas, Lieutenant, Eve.

'Yeah, yeah. Can you interface with my home office computer?'

Affirmative. Would you like to do so at this time?

'Yeah, I'd like to do so. Open files on Ziegler, Trey, subset Interviews. Create new doc on Prinze, Felicity, crossed with Copley, John Jake.'

Working ...

'Pull up any incoming communication or data from Peabody, Detective Delia.'

Secondary command in progress. Initial command complete.

'Why doesn't my office comp work this fast?'

Would you like a scan and diagnosis of this specific computer?

'What's the point? Negative.'

Acknowledged. Secondary command complete.

'Give me Peabody's data first. On screen.'

Data on screen.

She'd been right on Felicity's age. Barely twenty-one. Born Shipshewana, Indiana, one of three offsprings – all female – of Jonas and Zoe Prinze, with Felicity being the youngest. No criminal, not even a little dent, unless she counted two minor traffic violations during the teenage years.

And she didn't.

Graduated high school, and Peabody had added the shiny bits. Homecoming queen, captain of the cheerleaders, the lead in the school musical two years running, president of the theater club.

Two years community college, majoring in theater.

Employed, part-time, for three years at Go-Hop as a server.

Relocated to New York, resided for seven months in Alphabet City – a flop, Eve noted, reading Peabody's research on the address – that rented by the hour, day, or week.

Employed as a dancer, Starshine Club, for three months. Current residence, the big, shiny apartment overlooking the river.

No marriages, no cohabs, no current employment.

A corn-fed, naive kid, potentially with some talent, with big dreams, who got herself scooped up by some guy twice her age. Who was potentially a killer.

Eve added her notes, compiling them into a report.

As she read it over, refined it, the side door opened.

Roarke walked in.

'Did you get lost?' He cocked an eyebrow. 'You're working in the garage?'

'It was here, and it's quiet, and I only needed a few minutes.' She glanced at her wrist unit, winced. 'Or so.'

She'd refine later, if necessary, but shot the report to Peabody, to Mira, and as an update to her commander.

'That's it. I'm going in. Why are there more trees?'

'Than what?'

'Than we already had. Guys were hauling in more trees when I drove up. Why?'

'Because it's Christmas.' He took her hand. 'If you need more time, you don't have to take it in the garage.'

'It's nice in here. A vehicle palace with technology and snacks. But that's it for now.'

She could always slip away later, squeeze in a little more.

'All right then. Want a lift back?'

He gestured to a short line of motorized carts.

'I've got legs.'

'Which I admire as often as possible.'

Still holding her hand, he led her out the side door. 'We'll stroll back then, and you can tell me about the side piece.'

'She's pitiful. No, that's not fair.' She stuck her free hand in her pocket to warm it. 'She's a kid, Roarke, twenty-one and painfully naive. From someplace out in corn land. Shipshewana, Indiana.'

'Shipshewana? Are you winding me up?'

'It's an actual town, I looked it up. If you consider a place about one square mile a town. Barely six hundred people live there. A lot of them farm. They probably have more cows than people there.'

The thought of which gave her the serious creeps.

'So our young side piece bid farewell to Shipshewana, came to the bright lights, big city, and ended up in a river-view apartment, being kept by a married man.'

'That's the short of it,' she agreed. 'The long's got more gray areas. She's desperate to be a Broadway star. Came to New York for those bright lights, and ended up working at a strip joint.'

'All too common, isn't it?'

'Says she just danced – no sex – and you have to believe her. Not just that open face, the way she just babbles out reams of information because she's lonely, but her background data finishes the picture. Copley's set her up there with the usual bullshit. His wife doesn't understand him, treats him bad, he's working on a divorce, then they'll get married.'

'You're saying they grow them green in Shipshewana.'

'If Felicity's an example, they don't grow them greener. And, meanwhile, Copley will invest in her future by paying for dance and voice and acting classes. And she sleeps with him whenever he's available, fawns over him, makes him feel desirable and important. She thinks he's out of town right now, on important business.'

'Did you tell her otherwise?'

'Not directly. She wouldn't have bought it from me anyway. I sort of put a couple thoughts out there, and steered her toward talking to her stripper friend who seems to know the score. She took me for a pal of his, was pitifully grateful to meet what she took as a pal of his, to spend time, to talk about him because – she says – she's not really supposed to talk about him or them. Fucker. She's going to have a few scars from this. Still, maybe they'll be good for her in the long run.'

'And Ziegler?'

'She didn't recognize the name. She doesn't know anything on that. Copley tells her what works for him, and that's it. But what it told me? She's young, sexy, and built like every straight man's wet dream.'

'Is that so. Have you a photo?'

'Pervert,' she said mildly.

'Perhaps, but as a straight man I could verify your findings.'

'My findings tell me he wants to keep his sexy toy as long as he can. He gets sex, adoration, and devotion, and since he's paying for it out of money he's skimmed from his wife, it's a full win for him. One he might have killed for if Ziegler found out, threatened to clue in the wife.'

'So you managed to cross a name off your suspect list with the young Broadway hopeful, and gain another area of motive for one of the top on your list. Not a bad bit of work in a short time.'

'I had Peabody do the run on her, so that saved me time. Data indicates the kid came from a solid, two-parent household, has two older sisters, played well in school. Why do they call it "homecoming"?' she wondered.

'Who calls what "homecoming"?'

'People – the thing in high school.'

'Ah.' He paused by a side door of the house. 'That's an American thing, isn't it?'

'You live here,' she reminded him.

'I do, yes. I think it's something to do with football. American football, and a particular game that gets specifically celebrated with a dance, perhaps a parade as well. And they choose students to be king and queen.'

'That's just weird. But she was one of those, and head cheerleader, leads in plays, part-time work at some fast-food joint until she came here. A few months working in a strip club should've scraped some of the green off. It didn't. I think it goes down to the bone.'

'You liked her quite a lot,' he said as they went inside.

'I don't know if it was like, but I hope somebody can cushion the fall when she finds out the truth about Copley.'

'A solid family, older sisters. That could provide the cushion.'

'I guess it could. Either way, my job is to drill Copley. She's going to tell him I was there.' Considering it, Eve stepped into the elevator with Roarke. 'The next time he tags her up, she'll tell him. That's going to chap his ass. How did I find out about her – was it something Ziegler had documented, which reminds me to check Ziegler's spreadsheet on his side businesses. He's going to want to know exactly what Felicity told me, and if he's not smart and careful how he does that, he's going to have even ridiculously gullible her wondering what the hell. Unless her stripper pal does that first.'

She stepped out with him into her home office. 'What are we doing in here?'

'You won't need your coat, nor I mine.' He took hers, then his own to a small closet she never thought about much less used. 'And you'll want a bit more time to update your board, check that spreadsheet.'

'It won't take long.'

'Again, you don't answer to me on this.'

Her shoulders hunched. 'I'm not talking to Summerset again. I'm back. I'll be up there, on the battlefield in like fifteen minutes.'

'I'm sure I'll see you at some point during the fray.' He took her shoulders, yanked her in for a hard, quick kiss. 'Secure your weapon, would you, Lieutenant, before you join in? Otherwise you may be tempted to use it before we're done.'

'I'd keep it on low stun.'

'Regardless.' He kissed her again. 'If you run much over the fifteen,' he said as he started out, 'Summerset will have something to hold over your head for years.'

'Crap.' That was so true.

She went straight to her board. She added Felicity's photo, some basic data, crossed it with Copley's. Then after a moment's thought, with Natasha Quigley's, with a question mark.

She couldn't be sure the wife didn't know about the side piece.

Stepping back, she studied it.

Of all the players, Felicity and Sima struck her as the most naive and vulnerable. Though Sima not as much as Felicity. Then again, Eve figured no one over the age of four could equal Felicity's level of naivete.

Still, wasn't it interesting that Ziegler and Copley – victim and potential killer – both hit on the naive and trusting? Copley paid the freight – or more accurately his wife (whether or not she knew of the arrangement) paid the freight for living quarters, expenses. Ziegler had exploited Sima's desire for a hot boyfriend so she paid most of the freight.

But they'd both manipulated women to get what they wanted.

Ziegler made a habit out of manipulating and exploiting, she thought as she circled the board.

Had Copley?

Maybe another pass at his financials would tell her, but for that she'd have a smoother path with Roarke. Plus, she just didn't have the time right now.

But she could squeak out a little for the spreadsheet.

At her desk, she brought it up, scrolled through looking for Copley's initials.

She highlighted them, transferred the payments and dates to her board.

She found other sets of initials with different amounts, but nothing else as consistent over the past six weeks – which corresponded to the new locks on the vic's employee locker.

Records and payments for *NQ* (Natasha Quigley), *MQS* (Martella), *KR* (Kira Robbins), all jibed with their statements. These, too, she added to her board.

There were plenty of others, he'd had a hell of a sideline. Those she could cross with clients already interviewed also jibed. Extortion in some cases, or straight money for sex in most of the others.

Sex and money, two of the top motives for murder. She could ascribe both to Copley, add in fear of exposure, which would likely lead to loss of money when the wife booted him.

And wouldn't she?

Going through a rough patch, trying to save the marriage. Quigley had all but begged her not to tell Copley about the sexual arrangement she'd had with Ziegler.

She backtracked to her notes on that interview, refreshed her memory.

Quigley stated if Copley knew she'd been sexually involved with Ziegler he would end the marriage. Because he wouldn't tolerate the cheating, Eve assumed.

But what if Quigley had copped to Copley's arrangement with the sexy young thing, had used that knowledge to pressure Copley into fixing the marriage – or losing the big house, the big income, the status? It wouldn't do for him to get wind she'd been playing around on the side right along with him. She'd lose her leverage.

She gives Copley the ultimatum. He decides Ziegler

263

double-crossed him. Kills Ziegler. Fit of passion and temper, followed by the flourish. Merry Christmas, fucker.

Goes home, parties, tells the wife he'll break it off, they'll go on a trip. Has to tell sexy young thing he's been called out of town, give it all a chance to cool down.

He'd have to break it off with Felicity, or convince Quigley he had. With Ziegler out of the picture, he'd have a better chance of keeping things status quo if he played penitent with the wife.

Another round with Quigley, Eve decided. Drop Felicity's name, get a reaction. Ruin a marriage, most likely, she thought, but one that was built on a pile of lies and betrayals anyway. Likely topple it on that shaky pile, but potentially bag a murderer.

Something to think about.

'But not now, damn it.'

Seeing her time was more than up, she shut down, hurried from the room.

Hurried back, muttering curses as she stripped off her weapon harness. She secured it in her desk drawer, secured the office doors for good measure. Then bolted in the direction of the ballroom to face the music.

It was a war, she realized when she pulled up at the open ballroom doors. Just as chaotic, just as fraught, just as noisy.

Some shouted or snapped out orders or directions like commanders to the foot soldiers who hauled, carried or clashed. Some stood on towering ladders that made her stomach jitter.

People of all sizes, shapes, colors swarmed the enormous room, trudged or scurried in and out of the open terrace doors where more of them swarmed.

The trees recently brought in stood in each corner, celebrational giants now outfitted or being outfitted with lights, gold beads, red berries, and long drops of crystal. Under one, someone arranged boxes wrapped in red paper with gold bows, gold paper with red bows, as meticulously as if placing explosives.

She saw what appeared to be miles of tiny white lights, acres of greenery, pounds of berries, and enough crystals to blind the sun.

That didn't count wreaths, filmy drapery, plants, or flowers.

She thought about running away, dealing with Summerset's righteous wrath. It could be worth it.

She actually took one testing step in retreat.

'Mrs Roarke!'

A woman burst through the swarm. She waved a tablet, streaked across the crowded floor on glittery airboots. What looked like a couple sets of painted chopsticks stuck out and up from her messily bundled hair.

No retreat, Eve ordered herself. No surrender.

'Dallas. Lieutenant Dallas.'

'Yes, yes, of course. Pardon me, I'm just a little frantic. Ha. Ha. Ha.'

She actually laughed like that. In three, distinct *Ha*'s.

'We worked with each other before.' She stuck out her hand, gave Eve's a solid pump. 'I'm Omega.'

'That's a name?'

'Ha ha ha. Yes, indeed. I'm the head designer. I realize you and I didn't have a chance to go over the decor and details for this evening's event, but Roarke did sign off on the design.'

'Okay.'

'Naturally there are always a few tweaks on-site, particularly when coordinating with other vendors. And while the florist has done an amazing job . . .'

She turned, aimed a look at another woman jabbing fingers in the air while a couple of guys hauled around a big gold urn with enormous red and white flowers. The look didn't speak of admiration.

'An amazing job,' she continued, 'there are some adjustments we need to make.'

'Okay.'

'I just need to go over a few points with you, and address a few questions. All of us, of course, want tonight's event to be absolutely perfect.'

'Right. Okay.' Eve braced herself, thought: Ready. Aim. 'Fire away.'

Within ten minutes, with her head throbbing, she admitted Roarke had been right to tell her to leave her weapon in her office.

266

Really, she would have done a service for all mankind to stun the decorator and the florist.

Within thirty, she considered going back, getting the weapon and taking them both out.

They complimented each other with icy smiles and words like *brilliant*, *beautiful*, *bountiful*. Then jabbed at each other with sharp little insults.

The urns were too gold a gold. The tulle was too fussy.

The florist claimed her measurements were precise. The designer disagreed – hers were. And as far as Eve could tell there were bare inches between.

'I need that space for my poinsettia snowflakes,' the florist, who introduced herself as Bower (seriously), insisted. 'They've been created specifically and exclusively for this event.'

'As you can clearly see on *my* design, that space is required for the gift table, and you are to provide for that table – per my notes – gold mini trees, red amaryllis, and white flameless candles.'

'We discussed this design change, Omega.'

'I don't recall that, Bower.'

'We absolutely—'

'What gift table?' Eve demanded, and stopped both women from snarling.

'The holiday gifts for your guests,' Omega told her. 'A gold bag for the ladies will contain a limited edition bottle of the new fragrance, Snow Queen – not on the market until February. A red bag for the gentlemen will contain a portable bar set in a custom-made case. At last count, the number of guests—'

'I don't want to know.' Eve waved that away. 'We can put the gift bags in one of the other rooms out there.'

'But ... Well, I don't want to insult your guests, of course, but if the gifts are placed elsewhere some might, mistakenly, of course, take more than their share. Or some of the staff might help themselves.'

'If we're giving stuff away, what do we care? There's that salon place out there – we get spillover in there when we have these deals. Just set up the gifts in there, do the snowflake thing in here. Problem solved. Next?'

'I'd have to see the salon area,' Omega insisted. 'In order to display the gifts to the best advantage I may need to make further adjustments, add some decorations to that space.'

'Help yourself. That way.' Eve pointed. 'Hang a left. You want to add tinsel or lights or whatever, fine by me.'

'We'll need to be sure there are complementary floral arrangements,' Bower put in.

'Great. Make it happen.'

Both women, elated with the idea of having another space to haggle over, rushed off. Eve let out a single grateful breath.

'Well done.' Roarke stepped up to her, offered her a tube of Pepsi.

'Thanks.' She cracked it, guzzled. 'Why do you have gifts for everybody? They get to come, get to eat, get to drink, get live music. I see the stage over there.'

268

'They're guests, it's Christmas. It's a token.'

'They didn't sound like tokens. But it's your dough.'

He slid an arm around her waist, kissed her temple. 'Our party.'

'Yeah.' Cleared of florist and decorator, she took a fresh look around.

All the trees up and dressed, and, okay, they looked pretty terrific. She watched a guy in a watch cap and combat boots fiddle with some sort of handheld – then grin as lights, pale gold, spread tiny stars over the ceiling.

'Fucking A, I'm just that good!' he called out, and someone laughed.

Tables, she assumed for food, ranged against the two side walls. Little hightops clustered here and there, all draped in that pale gold again. She noted some of them already held a low display of red flowers, tiny gold pinecones, white candles.

She began to see how it would be.

'Pretty snazzy.'

'One hopes.' He took the tube, had a sip for himself.

'But friendly. And – I get the crystals, the snowflakes. It's Christmas, it's winter. But it's warm. It's welcoming, I guess.'

'Then we've hit the mark, haven't we?'

'Hey!' She called across the room, grabbed the tube back from Roarke and strode over to two workmen wheeling in another tower of flowers. 'Don't bring that in here.'

'Bower said—'

'It's too much for in here. It'll look better on the terrace.'

'But Bower said—'

'I don't give a rat's ass what Bower said. This is my party. I'm in charge. Take it out. I'll show you where.'

Slipping his hands into his pockets, Roarke watched her point the workmen out again.

Yes, indeed, he thought. They'd hit the mark.

14

Eve wouldn't say she enjoyed a couple of hours ordering around decorators and florists and the people who – apparently – feared them. But she couldn't deny a certain satisfaction in it. And a deeper satisfaction from making sure everyone involved feared her more.

Still it was with huge relief she snuck away, confident everything was under as much control as possible, to grab twenty minutes – okay, maybe an hour – in her office.

She checked her incomings first, surprised and grateful to find one from Mira.

She opened it, scanned it, then homed in on one section.

Victim Ziegler and Suspect Copley both demonstrate a skill in recognizing the needs and desires, strengths and weaknesses of others, and forged careers which utilized that skill. Ziegler in personal training, i.e. the desire of a client to appear more attractive or become more fit, what will motivate them to succeed or appear to succeed. His instinct for culling through those clients, and others, for

women who would be amenable to exchanging money for sex and his exploitation of same. His success in these areas encouraged him to expand his limits, exploiting other clients for gain, using illegals to 'persuade' other women to engage in sex, then exploiting them for financial gain.

In Suspect Copley's case, his skills guided him to public relations where he could read clients, using words or images to create campaigns to influence opinion. His secret accounts, financed primarily with money taken from his wife, demonstrate a need to control and, again, for gain. While his career benefits make him financially secure in his own right, he requires more, and feels he deserves more.

He, like Ziegler, has – at least for the short term – successfully lived two lives. With money taken from his wife, money he would feel rightfully his, Copley has established a second residence where he has placed a woman for his own sexual gratification and ego. His choice – a young, naive woman – demonstrates a need for dominance. His wife has more – maturity, experience, and money – therefore he cannot dominate in that relationship. He exploits a younger, financially inferior, and inexperienced woman, using his skills to identify her needs, desires, strengths, weaknesses, and using deception, fabricating facts, ensures her devotion while he continues to benefit from his wife's financial and social positions.

Both individuals demonstrate narcissistic tendencies, predatory sexual behavior, a need to prove their self-worth and desirability through sex, show, and money.

If, as you believe, Ziegler blackmailed Copley, the benefit to Ziegler would have been money and a demonstration that though Copley appeared superior in social status and financial holdings, Ziegler 'won'. The cost of said blackmail to Copley was, in addition to the dollars and cents, a loss of face and ego.

Considering the unplanned, impulsive nature of the murder, as per evidence, followed by the deliberate physical and personal insult, Copley's profile and personality make him a strong suspect. The stress and fear of discovery by his wife and by the woman he has established in a second residence, along with the shame of being bested by someone he would consider an underling, increases his probability in this incident.

If and when he is brought in for formal interview, I would like to observe.

'Yeah, we'll make sure of it.'

Sex and money – and ego – for both of them. And both working overtime to appear superior to others, better than others.

She recalled the woman in Copley's staff meeting – ignored, knowing it, both pissed and resigned by Eve's take. Included in the meeting, Eve thought, but not treated like the rest. Just a little less than the rest.

It made her think of country clubs and golf, and treating a man who provided a service to a fancy round and manly drinks.

Following a hunch, she did some digging. In ten minutes, she had the golf pro at Copley's club on the 'link. In five more, with some pushing, she had Copley's regular caddy.

In about seven more, with some persuasion, she had a very clear image of how that initial round of golf went down.

She added to her notes – anecdotal evidence maybe, but it was adding up.

Forgetting the time, she went back to her incomings, opened one from Peabody.

Had a brainstorm during my pedicure so did some surfing. Got some skinny on Copley – couple articles attached. Gist is: First wife came from money. Not Quigley money, but pretty shiny. Five years in, divorce. Accusations of cheating on both sides. Word is, he ended up with a nice if not princely settlement.

Was next-to-engaged to another highflier a couple years later. Accusations of cheating – and one of the cheatees was – wait for it – Natasha Quigley, also married at that time. He and Quigley got married twenty-two months later.

Romantic story is he whisked her off to Hawaii, where her family has a home on Maui – proposed. He'd already

274

applied for the license, done the paperwork, even bought
her a dress, the flowers – then sprang it on her. They got
married the next day on the beach. Some rumors at the
time – he was stepping out with his former almost-
fiancée, and there was trouble in the Quigley-Copley
paradise – quashed with the elopement.

I really like the romance stuff, but it sounds like he got
caught cheating or was suspected of same by Quigley,
and handled it with a quickie wedding. Sewed up the bird
in the hand, right?

This is all Gossip Channel stuff, so needs lots of salt.
But he's coming off a son of a bitch, I think.

Can't wait to dance on my sparkly
    new toes! See you soon.
    P,DD

'Good work,' Eve murmured. She saved the incoming –
she'd read the articles later.

For now, she pulled up his financials again, emphasis on
his hidden accounts. Side pieces, even when you didn't buy
a fancy apartment to keep them in, cost money.

Dinner, gifts, little getaways.

She began combing through, brought up Quigley's as
well to try to coordinate.

Her eyes, aching from studying figures, lifted to Roarke
when he came in.

'I did everything. I was just taking a break from it. I've

only been in here . . . forty-six minutes,' she calculated after a quick check.

'I'll say again, I'm not in charge of all that. I will say I just did a walk-through. It looks very well, and the adjustments you made here and there work nicely. Also, first wave of catering's just arrived. The head there is nose to nose with the head decorator. There may be blood.'

'If so, I'll make the arrest. I'm just going to let that play out for a bit.'

'How about a glass of wine?'

'Oh yeah, how about that? I got a report from Mira and I really wanted to read it. It adds weight to Copley as my prime suspect. Then I talked to his caddy.'

'As in golf?' Roarke asked as he poured wine.

'Yeah. Her report and analysis got me thinking about how he and Ziegler both had this ego that needed stroking – sex, status, money. So how would the golf game go? I played it with the caddy that I was digging for info on Ziegler seeing as he's dead, then tickled out what I wanted about Copley. Copley played benefactor – and made sure Ziegler knew it, felt it. His club, his course, his caddy, his *treat*.'

'For some a gift is only a symbol of their own superior position, which makes it not a gift at all.'

'I'd just say the gift came with sharp, sticky ribbons – which is pretty much the same.'

'And more visual. Ziegler's reaction to Copley's largess?'

'The caddy said Ziegler expressed gratitude but didn't

mean it, not if you paid attention. The caddy said he thought Copley was a little ungracious, but probably because Ziegler trounced him four holes in a row, and Copley gets a little testy when he's losing, which he told me means he – the caddy – gets blamed and gets stiffed on the tip at the end of the round.'

'So we add poor sportsmanship to Copley's sins.'

'The caddy confided – we bonded – that Copley's known for hurling his clubs into the trees after a bad – what is it – slice. And once after a bad lie – lay?'

'Don't ask me.' Roarke only shrugged. 'I'm no fan of the game.'

'After whatever it was, Copley and the guy he was playing against got into a shouting match that went into a pushy-shovey match. The other guy ended up in the water trap thing.'

'Extremely poor sportsmanship.'

'Wet guy threatens to kick Copley's ass, sue off what's left of it. He's pulling himself out of the drink,' Eve continued. 'People are starting to zip up in those cart things, and Copley backs down, lots of apologies. Buys the guy a high-class putter. And according to the caddy, bad-mouths the wet guy every chance he gets.'

'We have poor sport who has a poor temper to match, and is also a cowardly backbiter.'

'That's what I see. So back to Ziegler and that golf game. Ziegler's clearly winning by the sixth hole.' She paused to drink. 'Who decided how many holes there had to be?'

'Again, I only play when I can't avoid it. Ask someone else.'

'Maybe I will. Meanwhile, Ziegler's ahead, Copley's bitching. But then Copley ordered up drinks – prime brew. He stuck to water and power drinks while Ziegler got half cut and, being half cut, lost his focus and his form.'

'And Copley won the round?'

'Yeah, rubbed it in some, but took Ziegler to the nineteenth hole for more drinks. I get why they call the bar the nineteenth hole, but why are there eighteen to begin with?'

'It's as good a number as any,' Roarke supposed. 'Why four bases in baseball?'

'Because they make a diamond.'

'One might ask what a diamond has to do with baseball, but I won't or we'll be at this half the night. Let's just finish off the golf.'

'Right. Copley had him back a couple times, but with the brother-in-law along, and that's about it for the golf portion. Then Peabody came up with more weight, but of the gossip variety. Tales of cheating, divorce, cheating, elopements.'

'I may need more wine,' Roarke considered.

'Quick version. Copley cheated on first wife, cheated on almost-fiancée *with* current wife, and may have cheated on current wife before elopement with almost-fiancée.'

'He keeps busy.'

'Yeah, and for both of them it's all about sex and money.

Not for pleasure, but for ego and power. They had a lot in common only Ziegler was blackmailing and sleeping his way up, Copley married his way up.'

'Yet the side piece – this would be Felicity?' He tapped the photo on the board.

'Yeah, Shipshewana Felicity.'

'She's lovely and very young. Shipshewana Felicity doesn't have money or social status.'

'She provides the sex and the adoration, and makes Copley feel superior.'

'If there aren't any feelings, genuine ones, involved, why not find that sex and adoration with money?'

'He wouldn't be the first who lost it over big eyes and tits. Maybe this time out he wants to be the one with the big bucks, comparatively. But if his wife cuts him off, he can't afford his current lifestyle. He can afford a good one, one a lot of people would be happy with, but not what he's gotten used to. So Ziegler held that threat.'

Eve studied her wine. 'I have to go up there, don't I? I have to go back up there with the crazy people in the ball-room.'

'That's up to you.'

'Which means I have to go up there and step between caterers and decorators. I'm not wrong for preferring murderers.'

'I'd never say so. But before you go face the worst, I have an early Christmas gift for you.'

'We're almost there, why does it have to be early?'

'It's for tonight, and as Trina will be here within the hour—'

'Why! Why did you have to say the name!' She gripped her hair in her fists, turned a fast circle. 'I was mellowing.'

'You'll muddle through it. In any case, she'll need this.'

He held out a small, wrapped box. Eve eyed it suspiciously.

'Is it something she's going to slather on me?'

'I wouldn't think so. Open it, find out for yourself.'

She dealt with the fussy ribbon, tore at the shiny paper.

The classy box had the name of the jewelry embossed on the lid.

Ursa.

The generational family-run shop which had provided her with a solid lead on another killer. She remembered Ursa – the dignified older man who'd been so appalled he'd purchased antique watches stolen from dead parents by their ungrateful and murderous son.

'You pay attention.'

'To you? Always.'

'I don't know what it is, but it means a lot you went there.'

'It's a good place, as you said. Run by good people. They asked that I give you their best.'

She shook the box, heard the soft rattle. 'This probably is.'

He laughed. 'We all agreed it suited you.'

She opened it. It was some sort of comb. From its jewel-encrusted peak fell a rich medley of diamonds and rubies.

'Trina will know how to work it into your hair.'

'You always figure out another way to hang shiny things on me.' She shook it lightly, watched the stones dance. 'It moves. It's really beautiful. It looks old – in a good, classy way.'

'Early twentieth century, reputedly a wedding gift from groom to bride. A few generations later, the fortune was squandered, and this, among other things, was sold. Mr Ursa acquired it in an estate sale a couple years ago, and – he tells me – kept it in the vault, waiting for the right person. He thought you were, and so did I.'

'Since you're giving it to me now, I bet it goes with whatever I'm wearing later.'

'I believe it does. You can judge for yourself, but I hope you'll wear it.'

'I'll wear it.' She stepped up, kissed him. 'Even though I'll have to suffer through Trina sticking it in my hair.'

'That's love.'

'Looks like. And so we're even . . .'

She went to her desk, opened a drawer, took out a small box with the same wrapping and ribbon. 'One for you, early.'

The flicker of surprise, the half smile told her she'd caught him off guard. 'Really?'

'You're not the only one who can think about stuff.'

'Apparently not. And it seems Ursa knows how to be discreet. He never mentioned he'd seen you.'

'Maybe you got there first – but in that case, same goes.'

Like Eve, he shook the box, then unwrapped it. He couldn't begin to guess as buying jewelry of any kind wasn't on her radar. But inside a small white flower made of mother-of-pearl and platinum nestled.

'You don't go for the shiny stuff – nothing but a wrist unit for you. But two can play. It's a lapel thing. A white petunia.'

'Yes, I see. Your wedding flower.'

When he looked up, when those fabulous blue eyes met hers, she saw she'd hit the mark.

'He made it. Mr Ursa. I can't take much credit. I just asked him if he could make up this little thing, and he did the rest. Small because you don't go for the flash, but personal, I figured. And it holds on to the lapel with this little super magnet, so no pins or holes. His idea.'

'You had it made for me?'

'He did the work.'

'It couldn't mean more to me. The thought, or the symbol. The day you carried these flowers is one of the best days of my life.'

She gave him a smirk. 'One of?'

He drew a gray button out of his pocket. 'The day I met you, the day this dropped off that hideous suit you wore, is another.'

'Sap.'

'Guilty.'

'Me, too.' She moved in, held him close. 'I'm feeling pretty lucky. Even decorators, florists, caterers, and Trinas can't take that away.' She tipped her head up. 'It almost makes me want to have a party.'

Laughing again, he kissed her.

'Aw, look how sweet you look!'

Eve glanced over, watched Mavis Freestone bounce in. She wore red tights with boots of the same color that slicked up toward the crotch a sparkling white top barely managed to cover. Her hair was a tumbling mass of silver-streaked blue.

'It can't be that late,' Eve said.

'I'm early. Way early. I came with Trina. She wanted plenty of time to set up. Leonardo's hanging with Bella until later, and he'll zip uptown after the sitter comes. I figured I could get dressed here, surprise him, because my outfit is fan-mega-tastic. And even if he did design it, he hasn't seen me in it yet.'

She danced over to them, fairy-like, even on the skinny heels of her boots, wrapped arms around them both. 'Merry-squared! I so totally love Christmas and you guys and everybody else.'

'How do you feel about caterers?'

'I've got goodwill pumping out of my pores. Extreme.'

'Then come with me.'

*

283

When Mavis stepped into the ballroom she gasped. Then she squealed. Then she bounced.

'This is ultramazing! Holy wow, Dallas, it's like a vid set or a fairyland. It's like both and with *elegante* tossed in.'

Eve took a long look. The massive trees, the lights, the flowers – the plantings that looked as if they grew out of pristine mounds of snow. All the pale gold, shimmering over tables and chairs, the bold red, the bright white, the arbor of greenery and crystals around the fireplace, combined to just that. Ultramazing.

A woman in sharp black marched in, gave Eve the eye. 'Why isn't the terrace bar set up? We don't have time to stand around doing nothing.'

Mavis patted the woman's arm. 'She's so totally not one of you. She's the boss. Hey, you guys are going to pass drinks, too, right? The bubbly for sure. And little nibbly food. I so abso-poso love the bubbly and little nibbly food. If you need to practice, I'm all in for volunteer. Hey, Dallas, maybe you should have nibbly trays in that other room, you know the one. People hang in there sometimes, and nibbly trays would be mag.'

'Nibbly trays,' Eve directed the woman in black, 'in the salon where the gifts are displayed.'

'Of course. We'll set that up.'

'Great.' Eve turned to Mavis. 'Anything else?'

'Oh . . . let's see.'

For the next few minutes, Eve entertained herself watching Mavis send the head caterer scrambling to comply with suggestions, wishes, additions. Because it was Christmas, she opted for mercy, and pulled Mavis away.

'That was fun,' Mavis commented.

'Not for her, but yeah. Best, everything's under control, I kept my part of the deal, and Summerset can polish it all off.'

'Now we get to groom. My favorite pre-party activity.'

'Why?'

Mavis hooked her arm through Eve's. 'Because it feels good, it smells good, and when it's all done, you look good. But we're not going to look good.'

'We're not?'

'Hell no. We're going to look ultramazing. Take it easy on Trina, okay?'

'Again, I say why?'

'She's still a little whacked about finding the dead guy. Sima's dead guy. She's been putting on the brave since she's looking out for Sima, but she let it drop with me. So I know she's still pretty whacked about it. Most people don't find dead bodies unless they're you. Finding them, I mean, not being them.'

'She wouldn't have found a dead body if she hadn't been where she shouldn't have been. Okay, okay,' Eve muttered when Mavis just looked at her.

'It's worse maybe because she knew him and really didn't like him.'

'Nobody really liked him.'

'Sima did. Mostly.'

'Did you know him?'

'Nope. I don't use Buff Bodies. I started using Fit Plus. It's "plus" because they have all these parent/kid classes, or kid classes. We all go, my honey bear, our Bellisima and me, when we can. Or one of us goes with Bella. Completely family friendly, so we like it. But I know Sima a little, and Trina gave me the whole lowdown on the dead guy before he was dead, and more LD after he was. She's a little bit freaked you're going to arrest her for something, but you're not. Right?'

'I would if I could just to keep her out of my hair. Literally.'

With Mavis, Eve turned into her bedroom.

Trina stood, quietly arranging what Eve thought of as her instruments of torture on some sort of table beside some sort of salon chair. Another table – a massage table, Eve recognized – stood in front of the simmering fire.

'Hey!' Her voice bright, Mavis bounced to Trina. 'Dallas is all done, and early! We can get this part of the party started. How about we have a drink?'

'I want a shower,' Eve said. 'But go ahead.'

'When you're done, if you'd come out in just a robe,' Trina said, voice subdued, eyes on her tools. 'We'll start with the massage and body glo.'

'What the hell's a body glo?'

'It's a hydrator with a light sheen. We can test it on your arm to make sure you approve. I also brought the no-sheen if you decide against it.'

Eve narrowed her eyes. She didn't like the real Trina, with her brisk bossiness and sneaky ways. But she liked this fake, mealymouthed Trina even less.

'Whatever.' Eve spotted the gift bag on her dresser, poked at it, noted Trina's name on the tag. Roarke had, as promised, seen to it.

'This is yours.' Eve picked up the bag, pushed it at Trina.

'What?'

'A thing. A Christmas thing.'

Eve turned away, started toward the bath, spun back when she heard the blubbering sobs.

Trina, with her tower of swirly hair, wept into her hands while Mavis cooed and stroked.

'Shit. Shit! Why is she doing that? Stop doing that. I mean it.'

'It's my fault. Sima's a wreck, and it wouldn't be so bad if she hadn't seen him. He'd still be dead, the fucker, but she wouldn't have seen him so she wouldn't be so bad. It's my fault. And you gave me a present.'

'I'll take it back if you stop that. I don't even know what the hell it is. Roarke did it. Go find Roarke if you're going to do that.'

'I thought, what if I'd talked her into going and whoever killed him was there, and killed *her*. I thought—'

'Snap out of it!' Eve slapped out the order, causing Mavis's mouth to drop open in shock, and Trina's head to jerk up.

'What-if's aren't dick. It didn't happen. It's not your fault

287

she went there. Did you drag her kicking and screaming? And even then, he'd've been dead anyway. He was a shit. An asshole. A rapist. A blackmailer and a cheat. I'll find who killed him because that's my job, but if she's wasting tears over him, somebody needs to tell her she's just stupid. And if you're blubbering over what can't be changed anyway, you're stupid.'

'Dallas,' Mavis began.

'Shut up a minute. You want what-if? What if she'd gone back in there to get her things or to confront him, and found him herself? Alone. Without you there to hold it together? She didn't have the first clue what to do. You did. You tagged me. The fucker deserved more than toe-less socks and itching powder – not that it was your place to give that to him – but he didn't deserve dead. He deserved a couple decades in a cage, but am I blubbering because I don't get to give him what he deserved? So snap out of it.'

There was a moment of absolute silence. Then Trina sniffed. 'You're right. You're fucking A right. And when I'm done here I'm going back and having a come-to-Jesus with Sima, even if I have to get her drunk first.'

'Great. Now that it's settled, I want a shower.' She remembered, pulled the box from her pocket. 'Roarke wants this in my hair.'

Trina opened it. Both she and Mavis *oooohed*. Both she and Mavis swiped tears from their cheeks, looked back at Eve.

'It's a total winner,' Trina decreed. 'I'm going to do something different with your hair.'

'What? No. No, you're not.'

'Not with the cut or color. For Christ's sake, have I fucked up your hair yet?'

'No, but—'

'You get a piece of art like this to wear in your hair, your hair should earn it. I'm going to think about it. Get the shower, but don't use any scent. I'm going to take care of that.'

'I don't want to have—'

'You don't know what you want. I'll take care of it. You'd better get in there and wash up. Unless you want me to take care of that, too.'

'Keep out of the bathroom.' Eve stalked off.

Real Trina was back. Maybe, if she'd given it time, she'd have liked fake Trina. Now she'd probably never know.

15

It could have been worse, Eve supposed. She could have been attacked by flesh-eating cows. No one would ever convince her cows didn't occasionally enjoy a meaty snack.

So it could've been worse.

She told herself so while Trina slathered stuff on her – the mostly naked her – and Mavis cheerfully babbled. To take her mind off what was going on, Eve knew very well, especially when Trina shifted gears, shifted her, and layered some sort of toxic-looking green goo all over her face.

Then told her to relax for ten minutes.

Who could relax with toxic-looking green goo all over their face, that was possibly literally toxic?

But Mavis stuck a glass of champagne in her hand, and eagerly sat while Trina started painting Mavis's face with the arsenal of paints, brushes, powders, and God knew what else she armed herself with.

Apparently, from the conversation Eve tried to ignore, Mavis had been through the green goo stage – self-inflicted – that morning.

The goo came off, and as far as Eve could tell didn't take her skin with it. More gunk went on, with Mavis chattering as she stripped down naked. It always puzzled Eve how some people could be naked without a single qualm.

Fortunately, Mavis dressed again in a teeny-tiny sparkle of a dress that made Eve think of a prettily wrapped present, right down to the shiny bow on Mavis's ass. She slid on high, thin-heeled shoes with skinny straps that wound around her ankle, hung a trio of glittery balls on each ear, an army of glittery bracelets on one arm halfway to the elbow, all while chattering away.

It was sort of fascinating, Eve decided, even admirable in a way, and God knew it was hard not to be amused and happy with Mavis shining up the room.

'Oh, that's just the right lip dye,' Mavis decreed. 'Subtle, barely there. Just slicking them up, highlighting their shape.'

'It's all about the eyes,' Trina said wisely.

Eve studied the sparkling gold and silver glitter on Mavis's eyelids. Felt her entire being clutch.

'I don't want my eyes all glittered up like that. No offense, Mavis.'

'Totally none taken. Glittery eyelids are so not Dallas.' She did a little spin, studied herself in the mirror. 'And so completely me. Abso-mag on me, Trina. Party perfect. Yours, too,' she added, turning back to Eve. 'In a Dallas way. Promise.'

She crossed her finger over her heart. 'Hey, Treen, if you have time, can you do a temp boob tat for me? I'm thinking a little Christmas tree with two presents under it. Bella on one, Leonardo on the other.'

'Sweet. Yeah, no prob. Soon as I'm done.' She stepped back, gave Eve the long, beady eye. 'Yeah, yeah, that's going to work.'

She moved behind the chair. Out of the corner of her eye, Eve saw her pick up a tube, squirt some of the gunk that looked distressingly like cum in her hand.

'Do you have to do that?'

'It's a good product, especially good for your hair.'

She pulled, tugged, scrubbed, then picked up a tool that looked – distressingly again – like a very skinny dildo.

'What is that? What does that do?'

'Magic,' Trina said, and went back to tugging.

'What are you spraying on it?' Eve demanded. 'Why are you spraying stuff on it?'

'Because it's my job.'

'Chill,' Mavis advised, circling the chair. 'Ooooh, I get it. Oh yeah, way uptown, Trina. Soft and sexy, right?'

'That's the plan.'

'Define sexy? My commander's going to be here, and probably the chief. With spouses. I don't need sexy hair.'

'Chill.' Trina echoed Mavis's word, but her tone was a lot more forceful.

'It's the center deal,' Mavis began. 'She doesn't like it.'

'What center? My hair has a center?'

'I mean you. I'm explaining to Trina how you don't like the center spot when it's not cop stuff. It wigs you a little.

292

But, you know, it's your party and hello, Roarke, so it just is.'

She picked up Eve's glass, put it back in Eve's hand. 'Drink your champagne. You'll toggle around some.'

'I don't want to toggle around. I want to be finished with this part.'

'Nearly are. Mave? Hand me the comb, will you?'

'A-plus class,' Mavis commented as she passed the comb to Trina. 'Okay!' she added as Trina placed the comb. 'Trina, you're the bestest of the bestest.'

'Solid,' Trina agreed, but to Eve's consternation, did more spraying.

'My hair's what's going to be solid if you keep that up.'

'Done. Take a look.' She swiveled Eve's chair around to face the mirror.

It was a shock but not a jolt, which was something anyway. Her face mostly looked like her face. Her lips were kind of red, but the dye was sheer and pretty subtle. And no glittery stuff on her eyes, so that was a big plus. Instead she looked more defined, she supposed, and fussier with the pale gold on the lids, and all the darker stuff blended in wherever.

But she could recognize herself.

The hair wasn't like her hair. Was it? Scooped back, higher on the top, fussier again with a little bit of curl.

'You've got to see the back,' Mavis told her, and grabbed a big hand mirror. 'It's all about the back.'

Mavis held up the mirror; Trina angled the chair.

'Eve saw now the higher top and little bit of curl held up with the comb. A few more little curls dangled down with the rubies and diamonds.

'It's . . . girlie.'

'Be a girl tonight. It won't kill you. The do fits the comb and the dress.'

'How do you know it fits the dress? I don't even know what the dress is.'

'How am I supposed to do you up if I don't know what you're wearing? I saw the dress. The do and the rest of you are designed for the outfit.'

'And it's fabulolicious,' Mavis assured her.

'Why don't you get it, Mavis? Roarke said it would be front and center of her closet, shoes and accessories with it.'

'I'm all over that!'

'You look good.' Trina began packing up her tools. 'My work always looks good. I'd leave you the lip shine, but you wouldn't remember to slick it up anyway, so I'll leave it with Mavis. She'll remind you. Your man's going to look strip-me-naked good 'cause he was born that way. You need to look good.'

'I don't want people to strip naked when they look at me.'

On a bray of laughter, Trina continued to pack up. 'They're going to look at you and think: That's one frosty bitch cop. Maybe you were born the bitch cop, I added the frosty. It's what I do.'

'I can live with that. For a party.'

'This is the max,' Mavis cooed as she came back out of the closet. 'The maximum mag. It looks like somebody melted old gold coins and made a dress. That's my Leonardo.'

Eve studied as Mavis held it up. A pale, luminous, somehow watery gold with what looked like a very low-scooped neckline and long thin sleeves. She wouldn't have called it – quite – teeny-tiny like Mavis's dress. But it definitely earned tiny.

'Is that all of it?'

'You've got the body for it. Runway model but with muscle tone.' Trina closed two satchels, the size of the Dakotas – North and South. 'The fabric's why I used the Gold Dust shade of body glo.'

'You're going to look awesomillion,' Mavis declared. 'Want help getting into it?'

'I can get myself dressed.'

'Step into it, pull it up,' Trina ordered. 'Don't put it on over your head. Come on, Mavis. We'll find a spot and I'll do your temp.' She shouldered each enormous satchel, picked up the small gift bag. 'Thanks for the candles. I really like burning the fragrance, like there's one for each season.'

'No problem. I didn't really—'

'Thanks.' Trina cut her off. 'We'll have the chair and table out of the way after I do this temp.'

'Right behind you, Trina.' But Mavis scurried over to Eve as Trina walked out. 'You helped her.' She kissed Eve's cheek lightly.

'I didn't do it on purpose.'

'Maybe not, maybe that's even better. See you at Party Central at Party Time! And we'll all woo to the hoo!'

Alone — at last — Eve took her glass of champagne, drank. Breathed for a minute or two. All that female energy in one place tended to make her jittery. And, yeah, Mavis had it right. All that energy focused a little too closely on her made her jittery.

She looked at the dress again, then the shoes Mavis had set down by the bed. Gold again, with high red heels, red piping around the edges, even around the open toes. But, thankfully, no fussy straps. Still, she wasn't putting them on until zero hour, she promised herself, and glanced down at her feet.

Her toenails were painted gold. When had that happened?

She'd live with it, that was all. It was one night. She could live with gold toenails for one stupid night.

She saw the incredibly tiny thong-type deal with the dress, sighed and wiggled into it. Happily, Leonardo had built in the tit support, so now she wiggled into the dress — as ordered — from bottom up.

It fit like it had been made for her because it had been. So there was comfort, at least, and it was really nice fabric, soft, sleek, with a gleam rather than a glitter. She could live with gleam.

She opened the jewelry case. Long, twisty diamond and ruby drops for the ears, another ruby in a star-shaped setting dangling from three thin chains twinkling with tiny diamonds. Her dressy wrist unit, and a trio of thin bangles – one ruby, two diamonds.

She had some small relief she'd, at least, seen all the pieces before. So he hadn't gone out and bought her more.

She put on the earrings, the necklace, was fighting with the last bangle when Roarke came in.

Trina was right, she thought. He did look strip-me-naked good in his dark suit and his perfectly knotted tie of gold and red. He wore the little petunia on his lapel.

'When did you get dressed?'

'I used alternate quarters. You look wonderful. Absolutely wonderful.'

'The word's *ultramazing*.'

'It certainly fits.' He circled his finger in the air, smiled when she huffed at him. 'Indulge me, would you?'

She did the turn.

'Once more?' he asked as he approached her. Then he caught her shoulders from the back. 'Well now, that's adorable.'

'What? What?' She struggled to see her own back, caught sight of something painted just above the low, nearly ass-brushing, back of the dress. 'Shit. Shit! What the hell is that? What did she paint on me? Get it off!'

'I believe it's a sprig of mistletoe, and I wouldn't remove it for the world.'

'Why would she do that?' Aggrieved, Eve kept twisting to try to get a full look. 'I was actually nice to her. Sort of.'

'That may be why. Mistletoe, Eve. And what is the tradition for under mistletoe?'

'How the hell do I know – that kissing thing? That's the kissing deal, right?'

'So it is. And it appears to me she's just given you a celebrational way of saying kiss my ass. It's you, darling. Absolutely you.'

'She's not supposed to – wait.' She twisted herself around again, narrowed her eyes in the mirror. 'Kiss my ass? Huh. Maybe I won't kick hers for doing it.' She untwisted, looked at him.

'You dressed me to match the decorations.'

'Precisely the opposite. The decorations were chosen to spotlight your dress. You.' He flicked a finger down the dent in her chin. 'We should go up to the ballroom, be ready to greet guests – or we'll both suffer Summerset's wrath.'

'Okay.' Ordering her feet to suck it up, she put on the shoes. 'If men had to wear heels, they'd be outlawed across the land.'

But she took his hand, walked with him.

It did look pretty great, Eve admitted, and looked even better really when people began to arrive. When they began to mingle around or gather in clutches. Servers wove through with offerings from the spectacular display of food or sparkling drinks from one of the bars.

Speaking of colorful, she spotted Peabody and McNab

come in. He wore Christmas red tails with a silver shirt, a reindeer tie, and short silver boots. To complement, Eve supposed, Peabody's frothy dress of holly green picked through with glittery silver. Since her partner's hair was a mass of tiny curls with silver banding woven through, Eve felt less self-conscious about the hint of curls in her own.

'Peabody.' Roarke kissed her hand, then her cheek, then her lips. 'You're gorgeous.'

'Oh boy. I really worked on it.'

'You're a vision. Ian, you're a lucky man.'

'You got it. Here you go, She-Body.' He plucked two glasses of champagne from a tray. 'This is the iciest party of the year. We're ready to cut the rug, kick the heels, shake the booty.'

'Look at the food. It's so pretty. We have to dance asses off so I can eat the food. Is that a sugarplum tree? It's a sugarplum tree. Oh my God.'

'Before you pick sugarplums,' Eve interrupted, 'I need you a minute.'

Wanting to get this part over with, Eve started out – got waylaid twice by people who wanted to be sociable – and finally managed to get into the salon, shut the door behind Peabody.

'It's going to be hours of that,' Eve realized. 'Hours of people wanting to talk to me.'

'Here, you need this more than I do.' Peabody started to hand Eve the glass. 'Wait, there's more.' Instead, she walked over to the ice bucket, poured champagne into a glass on the tray nearby.

'Great. Good. Thanks. Listen.'

'I'm going to keep digging on Felicity Prinze tomorrow. I think she's clear, like you do, but I can dig deeper, see if there's anything there.'

'This isn't about that.' She picked up a box from the table where Summerset had arranged her wrapped gifts. 'It's for you. Roarke has something for McNab.'

'Oh! We put yours under the tree downstairs. I can go get it.'

'No, we'll get to it. Thanks in advance. I'm just – I'm giving these out tonight when I can, that's all.'

'So I can open it now? I love when I can open it now. The paper's so pretty.'

She picked at it delicately, carefully breaking seals.

'Jesus, Peabody, rip the damn thing open. I don't have all night.'

'I can use it again. I haven't wrapped everything yet.'

She slid the box free, carefully folded the paper, preserved the ribbon and bow. And finally opened the box.

'Oh!' She pulled out the gift, stared at it, eyes and mouth wide. 'It's a magic coat. It's my own magic coat. It's pink! It's a pink magic coat. Holy shit! Holy pink magic shit, Dallas.'

'The pink was Roarke's doing. You can't hang that on me. I said brown.'

300

'I have to sit down. No, I have to try it on, then I have to sit down. Holy shit, you got me a pink magic coat.'

'Don't blubber! Why is there so much blubbering today?'

'Thank God I used all waterproof, sweatproof, smudge-proof face enhancers, because I'm going to blubber. Dallas, wow. Just wow, it's *leather*. It's pink leather.'

'The pink's not on me. Ever.'

'Holy, holy, *holy* shit. I can't stop saying it.' She swung the coat on over the frothy dress. It looked silly with it, Eve thought, the military style of it over the party dress. But apparently Peabody didn't think so. She twirled in it so the knee-length pink leather billowed and swirled.

'Oh my God, it's beyond. Just beyond. It feels like leather. It *is* leather. It has pockets and pretty buttons. And it's magic. and it's pink.'

'I can't go around wearing coats with internal body armor when my partner's not.'

Peabody stopped twirling. She didn't blubber, but a couple tears trickled down. 'It means so much to me, that you'd have it made for me. For my safety. That all by itself means everything. But the rest? It didn't have to be leather, it didn't have to be pink. But you did that because you knew it would make me happy.'

'You get stunned or stuck or blasted, it's pretty damned inconvenient for me.' On Peabody's watery laugh, Eve sighed. 'You're . . . . family. That's it.'

Peabody grabbed her, squeezed. 'Okay, okay.' Eve tapped her on the back. 'Okay, okay.'

301

'I love you. People don't say that to people enough, so I'm saying it. I really love you, and I'm going to let go in a second because I know it weirds you. But thanks. Thank you so much.'

'Okay.'

'I have to go thank Roarke.' Peabody pulled back. 'And show McNab. Then I need to put it away safe. Is there someplace I can put it?'

'Give it to Summerset. He'll stow it.'

'Right. Oh, wow. Just wow. I'm thanking you again right now by not hugging you again and kissing you on the lips.'

'And I'm saying you're welcome by not putting a boot up your ass.'

Still wearing the coat, Peabody bolted out.

Eve took another minute. She really hadn't signed off on the pink, but that was okay. In the big picture way, the color had been the icing on the Peabody cake, so it was okay.

Eve opened the door just as Charles Monroe and Louise walked up. 'Hey.'

Charles did kiss her on the lips. 'Merry Christmas, Lieutenant Sugar.'

'Merry Christmas. Hey, if I give you a present,' she said to Louise, 'can I have a couple minutes to talk to Charles?'

'What kind of present?' Smiling, looking elegant and sleek in a shimmer of winter white, Dr Louise DiMatto winked at her husband. 'He's a pretty special present himself.'

Eve stepped back, gestured them in. She found the gift bag for Louise. 'This kind.'

'I was kidding, but I'll take it.' Louise pulled out froth after froth of sparkly tissue paper, unearthed the handbag.

It borrowed its shape from the old-fashioned doctor's bag, changed it up with the color of smoky lavender, the silver buckles.

The inestimable Tiko had polished it off with one of his scarves – deep purple, metallic silver, tied artistically on the handles.

'Oh, I love it! Dallas, it's fabulous. It's gorgeous – and the scarf is just lovely. Thank you.'

Eve got another hug, a buss on the cheek.

'Good, welcome. Now give me a couple minutes with Charles. If you see Summerset, he'll stow that for you.'

'I can build an outfit around this bag and scarf.'

When she left them alone, Charles gestured to the ice bucket. 'Mind?'

'No, go ahead. It's a party. I just wanted a couple minutes to pick your brain – exploit your two careers, if it's okay?'

'It's always okay. So you're picking for sex?'

'You could say. When you were an LC – and I guess now, too, in your sex therapist job, did/do you run into many people who trade sex for money? Unlicensed. Who just make a sideline out of it?'

'Sure. Not always money, but compensation. Clothes, jewelry, a favor, a trip. Some live their lives trading sex for money or things. You'd know that.'

'Yeah.' But this was different, she thought. 'I mean someone who pursues it as a serious sideline, even keeps books.'

'Well, that would be less common.' He sat, a vid-star handsome man who might have been born with a flute of champagne in his hand. 'I haven't worked with anyone in therapy who has that issue, but I knew a few in my LC days.'

'And what sort of clientele are we talking? What drives the bargain, on both sides?'

'For the provider? Sex is a commodity or a power or so confused with their self-worth they can't separate the two. For the receiver, it's most usually romantic confusion. They can tell themselves it's not business, which in this case it is, just not legal business or structured business. Or, often if there's an age or monetary gap, the receiver feels they're simply taking care of the giver. Simply providing them with little gifts or advantages. This gives them the power, or at least the illusion of it, in the relationship.'

'Why not just go to an LC, keep it . . .'

'Inside the lines? For some it might be more exciting, or more intimate, or it could be the relationship devolved into pay for play. Who was killed?' he asked. 'The provider or the receiver?'

'Provider. I also suspect him of blackmail. And I know

in several cases it wasn't a receiver in the sense they agreed. He dosed them.'

His eyes changed, hardened. 'That changes quite a bit. Do you know if he'd attempted to get a license?'

'Not as far as I can tell. He kept a spreadsheet, kept his money off the books, but kept a personal record. Women only for the sex. And some were fine with paying him. Others, generally younger than the willing ones, some of them married, he lured in, dosed, raped, then blackmailed.'

'He'd never have gotten through the training or the psych tests to get a license, not in New York. Not even street level if he'd been screened. What you're describing, to me, is someone who felt no real connection to the receiver. It's a business transaction, of course, but an intimate one that requires, at least on the higher levels, some finesse, some care and considerable training to handle various needs and situations. Above all, there has to be trust in the provider. A man like this would never have been able to gain real trust. You've spoken with Mira?'

'Yeah, and this is all running along her lines and my own. But you've been in the life, and now you treat people for sex stuff.'

Nodding, Charles sipped the frothy wine. 'Do you suspect one of the women he used?'

'Maybe. Maybe. It feels like, if that's the case, okay, you bash him in the head a couple times on impulse. That's how he bought it. But then if you're going to add a flourish, and the killer added one, wouldn't you cut off his balls, or jab the knife in his groin – something that relates?'

'First, let me say: Ouch. They stabbed him after – so you're thinking it might have been a jealous partner of one of the women, or one of the people – male or female – he blackmailed?'

'Maybe. Likely. I'm gathering information.'

'What sort of flourish, if you can tell me?'

'Stabbed. His own kitchen knife.'

'I meant where was he stabbed?'

'In the chest.'

'The heart?'

'Not exactly. It was more … oh. The heart? Symbolically, you're thinking.'

'Some receivers fall in love. It's a good LC's job to walk the line between trust and affection, even a touch of infatuation, and love. A client who falls in love is dangerous, to the LC, to themselves. A knife through the heart?'

He drank again, shook his head. 'I'm no cop, so I can't say, and imagine you see plenty who've been stabbed in that area without any love gained or lost, but …'

'Yeah, but. Something else to think about. I appreciate it.'

'Absolutely anytime.' He rose, took her hand to walk out with her.

'You and Louise still look pretty shiny.'

'I feel pretty shiny. Marriage is an adventure. And a comfort.'

For some, Eve thought. For others? She thought of Quigley and Copley. For others, maybe a competition.

The music rolled now, and the ballroom throbbed with it, and with people. So many, Eve realized, had arrived in the time she'd been in the salon.

She spotted Feeney – wearing not a monkey suit but a black one she knew he kept for memorials and funerals – by one of the bars chewing the fat with Jenkinson. And Nadine, wearing ice-pick silver, dancing with the damn-near seven-foot Crack. The ace reporter and the sex-club owner looked to be having a hell of a good time.

She'd have to get Nadine in the salon, give out that gift.

And there was Mira and the truly adorable Mr Mira sitting at one of the tables laughing with Commander and Mrs Whitney. She probably had to go over there, say something. But she rarely saw her commander yucking it up, so she'd just wait on that.

'And there you are.'

She turned to Roarke. 'Yeah, right here. I guess you know Peabody liked the coat.'

'There's little more satisfying about giving than in seeing the receiver so genuinely happy.'

'Ha, that slides along with my quick talk with Charles about sex. Case-related sex.'

'Naturally.'

'Plus I wanted to give Louise her thing. I need to get Mira and Nadine and the others to give those things. Then I'll be done.'

'And if you take a few moments to brainstorm – case-related? I'm fine with it. As long as you dance with me.'

'But—'

The music had changed, turned slow, romantic, a little dreamy. Still, she always felt so damn awkward dancing in public. He gathered her in, circled with her, laughed into her eyes.

'You have such interesting areas of modesty. Couples routinely hold each other when they dance slow.'

'Yeah, maybe, but I bet not that many of them have their commanding officer watching.'

'A dance. I'm not taking off your clothes, Eve.'

'I bet you are in your mind.'

'Well, I am now, so thanks for the idea.'

When she laughed at that, he caught her for a quick, light kiss. She responded by linking her arms around his neck.

'What the hell. It's a Christmas party.'

16

Eve always felt strange and a little awkward socializing with Commander Whitney. Her strongest image of him would always be of him behind his big desk, New York City rising up in the window behind him. His dark, careworn face sober, his broad shoulders holding the weight of command.

So seeing him dancing (including the booty shake already mentioned by McNab) with his elegant and somewhat scary wife just threw her world out of kilter.

She didn't have the knack for mingling – not like Roarke, who apparently knew everyone on or off planet, or had the talent to act as though he did. Still she handled the small-talk thing, even with people she didn't know. Bigwigs from what she thought of as the Roarke Universe, their spouses or dates, research-and-development types, business colleagues.

Mostly they wanted to talk to each other, or dance or hit the bar and buffets so she could do the duty, and move on.

But it struck her odder yet to see her people mix with

his. To see Baxter leaning on one of the tables chatting up one of Roarke's R&D execs. Then again, the exec was female, single, and sexy, so it wasn't a shock.

And there was Caro, Roarke's efficient admin, dancing with the adorable Dennis Mira. Over there, Santiago engaged in an obviously animated discussion with a couple of Roarke engineers over tall glasses of brew.

'Here.' Nadine walked up, handed Eve a flute. 'Even in that amazing dress you look too much like a cop just standing over here.'

'The worlds have collided, I observe,' Eve said and sipped. 'And there doesn't seem to be any damage or destruction.'

Nadine scanned as Eve did. 'You've thrown parties including both worlds before.'

'Yeah, but they seem to get more heavily populated, and the natives from each have more crossover.'

'And still, the planet spins,' Nadine finished. 'I love your parties. First because I know there are going to be so many people here I know and like, and people I may not know who are interesting. And second, in a case like tonight, I get a fabulous gift. I really do love that bag.'

'Why do you haul around so much stuff? That's the question.'

'How do I know what I might need at any given time during the day? It's better to be prepared for anything. Oh, Morris is going to play with the band. I love when he plays the sax. He's better,' she said quietly, 'but still carrying a lot of sad. I've never lost anyone I've really loved. I don't know how anyone handles it.'

'Silver shirt, red tie, silver band through the braid.'

Nadine angled her head. 'What?'

'Color. He's been wearing more color again for a while. He's getting through it.'

'You know, I'm observant and fairly intuitive, too – reporter, writer – but I'd never have put that together. You're right. He's letting some color back into his life, and that's good to see. So. What's the story on him and DeWinter? Are they a thing?'

'No.'

'Well, you certainly sound sure, and, if I'm not mistaken, determined. Don't you like . . . speaking of which, I believe she's heading over here. And speaking of amazing dresses.'

DeWinter wore hot, slick red in a long sleek column that hugged every curve. A side slit ran nearly to her hip, revealing a long, long, toned leg and jeweled heels that sparkled like the Christmas lights with each stride.

'Dallas. I haven't had a chance to thank you for the hospitality. It's a fabulous party. Your home is beyond spectacular.'

'Thanks. Ah, Nadine Furst, Dr Garnet DeWinter.'

'We've met. The Sanctuary case.' Still DeWinter extended a hand. 'I very much enjoyed the last broadcast of *Now*, but I've become a serious fan of your work altogether.'

'Thanks. I'm a serious fan of your dress. Valencia?'

'Yes! What an eye you have. It turned out to be a fun choice when I saw Morris had chosen a red tie.' She sipped her own champagne, tossed back her hair – an explosion of caramel-and-gold curls. 'I love to hear him play.'

'So ... you and Morris are dating?'

Nadine's cheery smile didn't dim under Eve's baleful stare.

'Keeping each other company. Neither of us want, or are ready, I'd say, for dating. I have my daughter to consider. And he has Amaryllis. I think it's easier for him to talk about her with me as I didn't know her, or know them together. But he's certainly made my transition to New York smoother.'

'Oh?' Nadine broadened her smile. 'How so?'

'It can be challenging to be the new person, especially the new person in charge. Morris gives me a sounding board, and a good sense of the people I work with. One of the reasons I left D.C. was I felt I'd become complacent, and needed a change. It was a well-run machine – I insist on that – but the structure, and the individual personalities, didn't allow for much camaraderie or ... joy. I've found both here.'

She gestured to the ballroom. 'The work we do? All three of us. It's difficult and so often dark. Without this? Without the personal connections, the joy, the interest in each other, it can become more difficult, and darker. I want to be able to put on an amazing red dress now and again,

312

listen to a man I find smart and interesting play the saxophone. I want to eat and drink and talk about nothing particularly important – or about the vitally important – with people I like, respect, and admire. Doing so makes me better at my work. It makes me a better mother.'

She sipped her champagne as she studied Eve. 'You don't like me yet, but you will. I'll grow on you.'

'What? Like mold?'

DeWinter threw back her head and laughed, full and throaty. 'Possibly, and I suspect you might do the same on me because I don't like you yet, either. We'll see. What I do know, absolutely, is you're his friend. You're Li's good, strong friend. I can promise you I'm his friend. So that's a beginning.'

'I used to flirt with him now and then,' Nadine murmured. 'I stopped after Coltraine was killed.'

'You should start again. Normal keeps him steady. Dallas gives him that. Did you come stag?' DeWinter asked Nadine.

'Yeah. I thought about bringing a date, but I really wasn't in the mood. Dating over the holidays gets so damn sticky – too important, too symbolic.'

'I *know!* I swear it's the only time of the year I half wish I was married so people would stop asking if I have a date for Christmas, for New Year's Eve, for this party, for that event.'

'God, yes! And if you have a date New Year's Eve, some people are in your face with: So is it serious?'

'Exactly. Last year I was seeing someone, *very* casually, then because I — against my better judgment — asked him to a holiday event, people were all over me!'

'Tell me about it.'

They'd angled toward each other, Eve noted, drawn by the theme like magnets.

'I had to stop seeing someone because he started pressuring me about Christmas plans back in October,' Nadine said. 'It makes you crazy.'

'Domestic violence, suicide, and homicide percentages rise exponentially between Thanksgiving and New Year's,' Eve commented, and got baffled looks from both DeWinter and Nadine. 'Carry on,' she decided, and slipped away.

She considered ducking into the salon — ten minutes' quiet and solitude — but caught voices, laughter, so veered the other way. She could sneak downstairs to her office, she thought, grab those ten. But if she got caught in there — *Summerset* — there'd be hell to pay.

Plenty of other rooms up here, she thought, and headed away from the music, the voices, the lights, turned into what she recalled was a smallish sitting room.

Feeney was sprawled in one of the big, overstuffed chairs, his feet up, his tie loose. He looked half asleep, with the muted wall screen showing basketball.

He shot her a sheepish look. 'Just wanted to check on the game, take a break.'

'Great. You're now my excuse.' She dropped into another

chair, heaved out a breath. 'Jesus, Feeney, why do people like parties?'

'Like this one? Prime booze and eats, great space. And mostly girls – some of the guys, too – get a charge out of sprucing up fancy. Sheila's having the time of her life. When I ducked out, she was talking to Ana Whitney and some Roarke exec about knitting. The three of them were into it like it was their religion. I needed ten.'

'I just ducked out on Nadine and DeWinter talking about dating. About holiday dating.'

'Maybe you win this one, but knitting's pretty close. Music's solid, though. Roarke knows how to rock the house. How's the case going?'

'I've got some strong lines. I'm looking . . . ' She trailed off when she sensed movement, glanced over to see Santiago hesitate in the doorway.

'Private party?' he asked.

'No. Just taking a break from the crowd.'

'Then I'm in.' He brought in a brew with him, grabbed a chair. 'It's a hell of a party, LT. Hell of a party. I was talking to this guy Derrick, works for Roarke. He played minor league ball for a couple years – screwed up his arm, switched to programming and design. Anyway, he's got a local league plays ball. I'm going to check it out, see if I can get in on that.'

'What do you play?' Feeney asked him.

'High school and college? Shortstop. Got a partial ride in college on the sports scholarship. There's nothing like baseball.'

'You didn't stick with it?' Eve asked.

'I wanted the badge. Love to play, but it's play for me. Not the job. I wanted the job.'

They talked baseball, talked shop. Eve told herself to get up, go back, do her duty. Then Reineke strolled in.

'Hey. Anybody else got the weird seeing Whitney tear up the dance floor?'

'Yes!' Eve and Santiago said together, and Feeney shook his head.

'You think because somebody's got a few years on you, they don't have the moves? Me and Jack could dance and drink the lot of you into the ground.'

'I don't see you out there,' Reineke pointed out, flopped into a chair.

'You will.'

Carmichael came in, looking loose in a little black dress, bare feet, and sparkly red toenails. 'Is this the bullpen?'

She sat on the arm of Santiago's chair, copped his beer for a sip. 'Whew! Some party, boss. Some serious party. I just saw Dickhead doing the sexy dance with Dr DeWinter. I had to remove myself, save my eyes. She's pretty sexy. If I went for girls, I'd be pretty wound up. But Dickhead's just scary.'

'Christ. I better get back out there.'

'You could be next in the sexy-dance line.'

Eve started out, paused long enough to tap the tat at the base of her spine.

'What is that?' Reineke demanded.

'It stands for "kiss my ass",' she told him, and left the cop laughter behind her.

Mulling tactics, she took the long way, ducked outside, then started around toward the ballroom terrace. Anybody asked, she'd been doing her mingling out there.

The detour caused her to walk in on Trueheart in a lip-lock with his girlfriend, which caused all three parties a moment of deep embarrassment. Eve kept moving while the couple flushed scarlet behind her.

She ran into Baxter next, just inside the ballroom. 'Hey, Dallas, wanna dance?'

'Absolutely not. Don't you have a date or something?'

'A man can't bring a date to this kind of shindig. It's too symbolic of serious business this close to Christmas. And it prevents him from trolling the single females.'

'So that's actually true, on both sides of the line. Huh?'

'Since it's a party, and also true, I'm gonna tell you you look incendiary. Love the ass tat.'

'What are you doing looking at my ass, Detective?'

'Because it's there,' he said, unrepentant. 'All wrapped in pretty gold, and we're off duty and it's a safe ass to look at as it's married.'

'Oddly, I find those all reasonable answers, but stop it and look at someone else's ass.'

'Yes, sir. Want some of this?' He took a flute off a passing tray.

'Why the hell not?' As she sipped, she spotted Roarke, smiling as he leaned down to kiss Mavis.

'It's nice,' Baxter said with an easy, contented sigh, 'when the family gets together.'

She glanced up at him. A damn good cop, she thought, and not nearly as superficial as he liked to pretend.

'One dance,' she decided. 'And keep your hands off my ass.'

She did see Feeney dance, as promised. It amused her to see him hold his own with the ridiculously energetic Peabody and McNab. When he shed his suit coat for a second round, Eve picked it up, checked the size.

'I want to get him a magic coat,' she said to Roarke. 'I should've thought of it before. Maybe he's not in the field much like he used to be, but he should have one. Shit brown because he wears a lot of shit brown, so he must like it. Can we get him a magic coat?'

'Of course we can. Forty-two regular in shit brown.'

'Good.' She slipped an arm around his waist, let her head rest lightly against his shoulder. 'My feet are fucking killing me.'

'A number of the ladies have shed their shoes. You could do the same if you didn't have this naked-feet-in-public phobia.'

'Feet are personal. I don't know why nobody gets that.'

Amused, in love, he brushed his lips over her temple. 'The crowd's thinning a bit. We can find a table, sit for a while, till it thins more.'

'It's okay. They're past the if-I-can-just-sit-down stage.

318

It's like family, like Baxter said to me before. Some of them are your family, some mine, some ours, but luckily, for tonight, they're all getting along fine. Plus, they're inter-mixing, so we'll see how that goes. Santiago might end up playing ball with one of your guys. Baxter's going to end up sleeping with that blonde over there from your R&D. Caro and Mira had their heads together like sisters or whatever. Lots of that kind of thing going on tonight.'

'How do you feel about that intermixing?'

'I'm okay with it. Wasn't sure, but I'm okay with it. Still, after tonight, I don't want to talk to anybody but cops, sus-pects, wits, and you. Not in that order, but that's pretty much it for me. For as long as possible.'

'Understood. We could whittle that down considerably. Do I have to negotiate with you to convince you to take a post-New Year's break. You, me, an island.'

'I'm there. As long as—'

'Also understood. Cases cleared, no pursuit of some mad killer in progress.'

'Being married to a cop sucks.'

'You're entirely wrong.'

Because she knew he meant it, she smiled. 'Do you think McNab could be a genuine freak of nature? Nobody should be able to move or twist that way if they have actual bones and a spine. Maybe I should ask DeWinter. Who's not involved romantically with Morris, which is good, but is his friend, which is also good. Plus, I learned tonight you're not supposed to date over the holidays unless you're deadly serious because of the symbolism and madness, and Santiago played shortstop. And Trueheart and his girlfriend must be serious because they had their tongues down each other's throats during the holidays, and you have some guy, some exec, who considers knitting his religion.'

'My, my, Lieutenant. You've mingled.'

'Damn straight. It took considerable champagne consumption, but I held up my end.'

He gave her ass a light pat. 'Beautifully.'

She held up her end, if she said so herself, through the leave-taking where entirely too many people insisted on hugging her. Because they were slightly more than half lit, and it was simple, Summerset poured Peabody and McNab into one of the guest rooms he'd prepped, and that was fine with her.

As she expected, Baxter and the blonde left together, and with twin gleams in their eyes.

When the last straggler was out the door, Eve hobbled to the bedroom, pried her abused feet out of the shoes, winced her way into the bathroom to use the gunk Trina had left her to take off the gunk Trina put on her.

She stripped off the jewelry, remembered the hair thing, fought it out, dragged and raked her fingers through her hair until it felt normal. She stripped off the dress, the thong, grabbed a long, baggy T-shirt and fell into bed.

'What time is it? No, don't tell me. Yes, tell me.'

'It's about half three.'

'God.'

The cat walked up the bed, jingling, sniffed at her, climbed over her, and made himself a nest in the small of her back.

Roarke slid in, kissed her between the eyebrows.

'Did my part,' she said, words slurring. 'Not so bad.'

And dropped away to sleep like the dead.

She woke alone, which was no surprise – and even less of one when she checked the time. After ten? *Ten?*

She sat up, rubbed her hands over her face. Needed coffee, needed to move. After crawling out of bed, she hit the AutoChef, primed herself with caffeine.

She'd take a swim, she decided. A few hard laps would clear her head, shake out the post-party dregs. Then she could order Peabody out of bed – her own fault she drank too much to get out of range the night before – and they could work on the case for a couple hours.

She turned toward the elevator, then considered it was the middle of the damn morning. Somebody could just walk in on her down in the pool. She dug out a black, tank-style suit, pulled it on, pulled the sleep shirt over it.

She debated tagging Roarke, telling him to come join her. But he'd very likely get ideas once they were both wet – and there were people in the house, probably lots of people clearing out the party debris in the ballroom.

Best to keep the swim solo.

She stepped out of the elevator, into the lushness of

tropical plants. She heard the music, a low, quiet hum, and thought Roarke had beaten her to it.

So maybe she wouldn't mind if he got ideas as long as—

'God!'

She slapped her hands over her face, but the image of Peabody and McNab groping each other in the pool remained burned on her retinas. 'Why? Why aren't I blind? Why is there no mercy?'

'Sorry!' Peabody sang it out. 'We're not naked or anything. Roarke said we could use the pool, and there were suits in the dressing room. We're both wearing suits. Promise!'

Eve spread her fingers, risked peeking through them.

They were *half* naked, McNab standing in waist-high water, bony chest bare and gleaming wet, but standard black trunks below the waterline. Peabody wore bright blue that showed off plenty of cleavage. Hardly a wonder McNab's hands had been full of Peabody's girls.

She wasn't going to deny herself a swim, refused to give in to the cowardly urge to turn around and go back upstairs.

'This half is mine.' She cut a hand through the air. 'That half's yours. Stay on your side.'

'Thanks for letting us stay,' McNab said when she yanked off the shirt. 'Nothing like a good night's sleep after an aces party, and the bonus round of a swim.'

'Right. Your side, my side,' she repeated, and dived in.

She put them out of her mind, concentrated on the movement, on cutting through the water, pushing off, cutting through again. Her body loosened; her brain cleared.

Twenty-five laps later, she felt human – wanted more coffee. She let herself sink down, rise up.

And saw Peabody and McNab, still there, floating side by side. To her surprise, she saw Roarke, sitting at one of the little tables, drinking coffee.

She sank again, pushed off again, swam underwater to the far end. She got out, dripping, reached for his coffee first, then a towel.

'Good morning,' Roarke said.

'It's a better one now. I guess you've been dealing with the after-party breakdown.'

'Actually I had some other business. Summerset's on that. How about some breakfast? I could do with some. I waited for you.'

'Sure, yeah.' When he merely arched his eyebrows at her, she turned around. 'Breakfast, fifteen minutes, my office.'

Peabody flopped over, treading water. 'That'd be sweet. It's okay?'

'I just said so. Fifteen,' she repeated, and headed into the lush plants. 'I used up my limited supply of gracious last night.'

'I don't think Peabody or McNab require it. You'll want some time to work with her. There's no point in anyone going hungry while you do, is there?'

323

'I guess not. They were, you know — starting in on it when I came down. Her tits were half out of the suit.'

'Sorry I missed it.'

'You would be. Pervert.'

He grabbed her as they stepped out of the elevator, scrambled her brains with the kiss. 'If only you'd said thirty rather than fifteen minutes, I'd show you a bit of perversion.'

She laughed, but wiggled free. 'I didn't figure they'd be out of bed. I only bothered with a suit because I remembered there'd be people here, doing stuff, and better to be cautious. If I'd gotten up ten minutes later, they'd have been naked and humping like whales.'

'Do whales hump?'

'It sounds right.'

'Oddly enough. I'll see about breakfast while you get dressed.'

'I'll be quick.'

'Be that. And later? After whatever work both of us have to deal with today, I'd like a date.'

'A date for what?'

'A date for lounging with you. A vid, some popcorn, a fire crackling and absolutely nothing to do but lie there.'

The image made her smile. 'That sounds like a perfect date.'

Absolutely perfect, she decided as she dressed in black jeans, a dove-gray sweater, soft, flat boots. She dug out the teardrop diamond pendant, slipped it on under her sweater.

She started to reach for her weapon and harness – habit – remembered she'd secured it in her desk drawer.

She shoved her badge, her 'link, other daily paraphernalia in her pockets.

What else did people need to carry? she wondered as she headed out toward her office. Work stuff, maybe – so a file bag or a briefcase. But nobody could ever convince her one of those planet-sized purses was necessary for survival.

She caught the scent of food, of coffee, and followed her nose to her office where the table she and Roarke often shared had been extended to hold settings and chairs for four.

She watched Roarke come out of the little kitchen carrying a large, covered tray.

'You have droids to do that. I know you do.'

'Indeed we do, but it's fun to fuss a bit yourself for friends and family here and there. I went with full Irish, all around, as a Scot would recognize the similar tradition.'

'They eat enough for five people at breakfast, too?' Eve asked as she went to her desk, got her weapon.

'It's a fine meal that hits all the notes.' He walked to her, slung an arm around her shoulders, studied the board as she did. 'Have you a plan of action then?'

'Sort of. Working on it. I'm thinking, poke at the wife, get her to give away a little more on the husband. Copley's hands are dirty, and I think they're bloody. She's not stupid. I didn't get stupid from her. If I play it right, she'll wonder, and she may tell me something I can hook on to. Or the sister. Not stupid, either, but soft. I can probably find a spot or two on her to push. If she worries about the sister, I might get something out of her.'

'I've a feeling that family won't be having a happy Christmas.'

'Not if things go right on my end.'

Peabody and McNab came in, both wearing lounging pants, loose tops.

'Where'd you get those clothes?' Eve asked.

'Summerset had them for us. Soft.' Peabody rubbed her own sleeve. 'It'd be weird to eat breakfast in party clothes. Weirder to talk about the case wearing them.'

'Then we'll eat, and we'll talk.' Eve stepped back to the table, lifted the cover from the big platter.

'Wow! Look at all that. *Smell* all that.' Peabody sniffed the air, sighed.

'It's tattie scones.' McNab's face lit like a child's. 'You've had tattie scones. Remember, Peabody? We had some when we went to Scotland, to spend the holidays with my family there. My granny made them.'

'Potato scones? Oh yeah. Deadly and delicious. Good thing I danced like a maniac for hours.'

Roarke gestured them to sit. 'Summerset made them up, thinking you might enjoy a bit of home.'

'Fuel up,' Eve advised. 'After this, the party's over.'

'Tattie scones,' McNab said again, and dived in.

17

Tattie scones weren't half bad, Eve discovered. Nor was eating them the morning after a big party with Peabody and McNab. She let the postgame analysis – as she thought of it – run its course with discussion, comments, opinions on who wore what, who did what – and with whom – who said what.

It was an oddity, really, just how much gossip could be distilled over a full Irish.

'I'm still trying to process my reaction to seeing Dickhead doing the sexy dance,' Peabody commented.

'I never want to hear the words "Dickhead" and "sexy dance" in any sort of conjunction again. Seriously,' Eve added. 'That's an order. Moving forward.'

She gestured to the board. 'Copley remains top of the list. He fits the profile, his financial records demonstrate greed and deception, and indicate potential payoffs. His initials are listed on the vic's spreadsheet with amounts that correlate to said payoffs.'

'Giving him motive,' Peabody agreed. 'But then since

Ziegler was the man a whole lot of people loved to hate, a whole lot of people had motive.'

'Accurate. Now look at the method. Two hard, and we believe enraged, impulsive shots with a handy blunt instrument. That's where I bump down several of the whole lot of people. Rock could have pummeled him into paste – and if the vic showed any injuries from a fight, a beating, we'd be looking hard at him. Lance Schubert doesn't show up on the spreadsheet, but he might have learned about the vic having sex with his wife, confronted him. But my personal probability index says Schubert would've gotten in a punch or two, and straight off. Have it out straight off rather than heading back to the bedroom while the vic packed.'

She pushed away from the table before she ate more bacon just because it was there. 'McNab, what did you do when you thought – mistakenly – Charles had bounced on Peabody.'

'I punched him.' McNab danced his fingers up Peabody's arm. 'That's all five-by-five now.'

'Because he hadn't bounced on her, and because Charles is a reasonable sort of guy. But my point is, your first impulse was fist in the face. Schubert strikes me as the same, and I don't see him letting it rest with his wife, who just doesn't have the guile to lie to me about him knowing. Still, he's not off the hook.'

'Vic asks him to come by,' Peabody speculated. 'Tells him to try to extort money for keeping it quiet.'

'Exactly. Instant rage. Grab the handy blunt object. And

328

end it with the flourish. The flourish fits him, and it fits Copley. What Copley doesn't have is Schubert's sense of self-worth. Schubert doesn't have Copley's greed, or his pattern of going after wealthy women, cheating on them, cashing in on them.

'Copley's reaction, to my mind, would run like: Jesus, he took Ziegler to his club, treated him to golf and drinks and all that. Even though Ziegler's so obviously socially and financially inferior. He did him *favors*, and what does he get? Blackmailed. It's gone on long enough, time to take charge, time to show this asshole who's top dog. He loses his temper, which is also pattern, grabs the weapon, because he's not the type who goes into a fight fair. Now look what Ziegler made him do. But it's not enough. Ziegler humiliated him, so he'll return the favor.'

'Smarter, wouldn't it have been, to toss the place a bit?' Sitting back, Roarke lingered over coffee, as comfortable with cop and murder talk as he was with business and finance. 'Take some of the valuables, make it appear to have been a burglary or a confrontation with someone who'd take some profit from it.'

'He's not smart, that's the thing. Cagey maybe, but that's different. And he needed to get the knife in – literally, figuratively – to boost his own ego.'

She circled the board. 'Then again ... Charles mentioned something last night when I talked through this with him. Knife in the heart. Maybe it's a stretch, but it could mean a romantic connection.'

'Back to the girlfriends?' McNab speculated.

'I don't see it, just don't, but I'd like you to look a little closer there if Feeney can spare you. Sima's covered. She was with several people in a public place when Ziegler was killed, but you could pry the lid off Alla Coburn, and take a pass at some of the women who paid him for sex.'

'There's always time to take a pass at women,' McNab said and got Peabody's elbow in his side for his trouble.

'If it was sex – just sex – the symbolism would've been knife in the balls, so if we play that tune, it's romance, emotion, not just sex. Peabody, you and I are going to play both angles today. Enraged husband and/or blackmail vic, infatuated married female. And the third angle of undermining the married females enough to spill on the enraged husband. If it applies.'

'Natasha Quigley, Martella Schubert.'

'Yeah, we're going to split it, save time – and alter the approach. You take Schubert. She's softer, more vulnerable, more naive. She'll respond to your gentle, sympathetic approach. You tell her how you once had romantic feelings for an LC.'

'I didn't! Not exactly. Just … I just …'

'Play it,' Eve insisted, 'if playing it gets you in. You're going to talk to her on your day off, just to get a clear picture because your partner's pushing the angle her husband found out there'd been sex, and moved on Ziegler even before it came out the sex hadn't been consensual due to drugging. If that's not the approach, you'll find another.'

'Maybe, if it seems playable, I can hint around that I think Copley's more likely. The just-between-us bit, and it looks like Copley was paying Ziegler blackmail money. The sisters seemed pretty tight, so if she thinks her sister's husband could be a killer, she might open up more, to protect the sister.'

'That's not bad.' Eve paused, studied Martella Schubert's face on her board. 'That's not bad. If she has any dirt on Copley she's more likely to give it to you. Give it a try. Let's see if we can bring this to a head.'

'And you'll take Quigley.'

'She's not naive, not soft. I can go in harder, shove it at her. She used the illusion of romance as an excuse to pay Ziegler for sex, so I can hammer on that. And I can push how she's so worried Copley will find out. Maybe he has, what then? And I might be able to play the same angle as you – your sister's husband is on my short list. Like you, I'll play it so I get in, go from there.'

'Is it okay if I take McNab? We're a couple, and I can use that. I get what it's like to be in love, and all that. I have a sister, too, all the common-ground business.'

'Maybe I can talk her into letting me wire up the house 'link, her personal 'link,' McNab speculated. 'Put it out there like it's for her protection, her sister's protection.'

'If she bites on that she's more naive than I figured, but throw it in. If she bites, make damn sure you get her to officially sign off. I don't want it coming around to kick us in the ass later.'

'Solid,' McNab promised. 'I'll take some toys with me, in case she goes for it.'

'Full report when you're done. But first, for God's sake go home and put cop clothes on.'

'I get to wear my pink magic coat.' Peabody jumped up, did a quick dance. 'Hot dog! Thanks again for all of it, for every bit of it.'

'Send us a picture of your lady in her coat,' Roarke said to McNab.

'You got it. We'll totally rock it out with her coat, my boots. Ultimate thanks for all. Solid.'

'Then get out,' Eve said. 'Solid.'

When they'd gone, Eve turned to Roarke. 'What boots?'

'The custom airboots we gave him for Christmas. I'm sure I told you.'

'Maybe. Who can remember? Don't say they're pink.' Even the thought had her squeezing the bridge of her nose. 'Just don't.'

'They're the McNab tartan, a bold and rather attractive red and green plaid.'

'Red and green plaid airboots. Well, they're not pink, so that's something. I'm going to get going so I can get back and we can do that vid-and-popcorn thing.'

'I'm with you,' he said. 'And like McNab, I'll get a few toys in case she agrees to a tap.'

'She won't. You don't have to screw up your day on this.'

'How could it be screwed up? With you?'

'You could be handy,' she considered. 'Money, social

status – it's her language. And if he's there, you could lure him off to show you his golf clubs or something.'

'Now, that might screw up my day, but I'll risk it.'

'Get your toys. I'll meet you out front.'

By the time she got down, the vehicle was waiting. Not her deceptively bland-looking DLE, but a big, brawny, black SUV.

'Are we driving up a mountain?' she asked Roarke when he came out.

'Who can say? I did a little due diligence on Copley and Quigley when I poked into his finances, but I assume you took more time with that end. You can fill me in while we drive.'

'They're both cheaters,' she said flatly. 'Were both attached when they fooled around, then he fooled around some more, then took her off to Hawaii for an elopement he planned, using her family's facilities.'

'You don't like either of them.'

'Not a whole lot.'

'Which is why you sent Peabody off to the sister and brother-in-law, because you do like them.'

'I don't like or dislike. But they strike me as pretty straight. Not squeaky. Martella *thought* she'd screwed Ziegler voluntarily, and paid him off to keep it secret instead of sucking it up and dealing with it. And he struck me as a little too calm about the whole thing once it came out. Quigley, Copley? They're lying outright, but the other two hide things. Maybe they're hiding murder.'

'It may be both of them – the Schuberts are dealing, in their own way, with the trauma of it. It's a double blow for him. The first, learning his wife believed she'd betrayed him with another man. The second, knowing she didn't do as she'd believed but was drugged and raped. It's a great deal for any man to cope with.'

He'd know, Eve thought. He'd know what it was to cope.

'Maybe. Maybe they're both just trying to find their way through it. There's another player on their end. Catiana Dubois, the social secretary – which is a bullshit title in my world of titles.'

'For some, the social life is a kind of career or vocation, and having someone to keep order is helpful.'

'You don't have one.'

'I have Caro and Summerset. A man needs little more.'

She couldn't argue with that one. 'They seem cozy, the three of them. Not we-have-a-threesome-every-Tuesday cozy, but cozy enough. According to Catiana, Ziegler hit on her and she blocked. He then spread the word she was a lesbian, which she let pass because she didn't care. And he got pissed when the guy she's seeing came into the gym and it became apparent she liked men just fine.'

'Sorry, I'm a bit distracted by the threesome every Tuesday.'

'Wipe it out of your mind. The point is, Ziegler screwed with – on various levels – all five people in those two households. What are the odds?'

'Another reason you like one of them for the murder, particularly Copley as he appears the weakest in the moral sense, and somewhat of a dick.'

'That sums it up. Plus your basic motive, means, opportunity. Because he had time. He had enough time. Any of them did, really, if one of the others covered for them.'

'How did you get McNab's shoe size?'

'I have my ways.'

'You really do. Would you stab my dead body in the heart with a kitchen knife if I cheated on you?'

'Your mind is the most marvelous machine,' Roarke said, with a touch of wonder. 'Murder to threesomes to shoe sizes to speculative murder. No.'

'You wouldn't stab my dead body in the heart with a kitchen knife if I cheated on you?' She found herself oddly insulted.

'There wouldn't be enough left of it to stab. I expect I'd have already cut out your cheating heart and set it on fire. This, of course, after I'd – what was your phrase – "beaten your lover into paste", after which I'd have castrated him. But not with a kitchen knife, mind you. I'd have used a dull, rusty, and jagged blade, putting it to use again in the aforementioned cutting out of your heart. And I'd feed his cock and balls to a vicious rabid dog I'd acquired for that specific purpose.'

'That should cover everything.' Now, rather than insulted, she felt well loved. 'We're violent,' she said after a moment.

'Speak for yourself.' He negotiated around a pokey tourist triple tram loaded with shivering bodies, sparkling lights, and garland. 'If you hadn't cheated on me, I would never have laid a hand on you outside of love, passion, and tenderness.'

'You cleaned Webster's clock because he *wished* I'd cheat on you with him.'

'That should provide fair warning.'

'We're violent,' she repeated. 'We grew up that way. We know our own natures, mostly channel it. But our instinct would be to react with violence in this kind of situation. Or to threaten it in a way that should — and almost always would — have the opponent backing down. Then we'd own it. That's our nature, too. These people aren't violent — in the same way — by nature. This violence was of the moment, a control snap, and in every case if it was one of the four, a good lawyer would get them off on temp insanity, diminished capacity, extenuating circumstances. Except, that goes down the tubes with the flourish.

'The flourish was pure ego, was stupid, was very much bragging.'

'Which is why you like Copley.'

'Which is why.'

She rolled it around in her head while he parked.

'Follow my lead, okay?'

'Naturally. You know they may not be home on this bright and cold Sunday afternoon.'

'They're somewhere. I'll find them.'

Eve pressed the buzzer, did the scanning deal for the computer. The process moved quickly this time, and the house droid opened the door.

'Lieutenant. How can I help you?'

'I want to speak with Ms Quigley. Mr Copley, too.'

'I'm afraid Mr Copley isn't at home at this time. Ms Quigley has an appointment shortly.'

'Then I'll try not to keep her long.'

'Of course. Please come in. I'll let her know you're here. Make yourselves comfortable,' she added, leading them into the living area. 'May I serve you anything?'

'We're good.'

Eve waited until the droid left the room. 'You know she's already told Quigley who was at the door. Why do they always act like they haven't?'

'It's a procedure. It's a nice old building,' he observed. 'Very well rehabbed.'

'Taste and money?'

'It would take both, and an admirable respect for the character of the brownstone.'

He turned, as she did, at the quick click of heels. 'Lieutenant, I wasn't expecting ... Roarke.' Natasha's smile flashed out as she clicked over, extended a hand. 'We met, very fleetingly, several years ago, at an art show in London.'

'It's lovely to see you again.'

'Please, sit down. I didn't put it together when I spoke with you before,' she said to Eve. 'I suppose the upset over

337

everything fogged my focus. Eve Dallas, Roarke's wife – and the star of *The Icove Agenda*.'

'Marlo Durn's the star of that. I'm a cop.'

And you're a liar, Eve thought. She'd made the connection already. Why pretend otherwise?

'Of course. I heard Nadine Furst is working on a second book based on one of your cases. I'll look forward to reading it even more now that we've met. Even under the circumstances.'

'Where's your husband?'

Natasha blinked once at the flat tone, but kept her smile in place. 'JJ's golfing. He and Lance and two of their friends have a regular game every fourth Sunday, in Florida. They took the corporate shuttle this morning. He'll be back by six, if it's important.'

'You'll do. The last time we spoke you expressed considerable concern about your husband learning of your affair with Ziegler.'

'I . . . ' The faintest flush – embarrassment, anger, a combination, rose into her cheeks. 'I was forthright with you, Lieutenant. I'd prefer not to discuss it again.'

'If you know Nadine's book, the vid, you're aware Roarke often serves as an expert civilian consultant.'

'You can rely on my discretion, Natasha.' Roarke spoke smoothly, and with the lightest touch of sympathy.

'I appreciate that, of course. Still, it's very uncomfortable. It wasn't an affair, though I pretended it was to, well, sugar-coat it for myself. It was a business transaction, on both sides, which I engaged in during a difficult time in my marriage. I'm certainly not proud of it.'

'You were concerned if your husband knew, he'd end the marriage. Yet this wouldn't be the first time either of you engaged in affairs.'

The color deepened. 'I don't see what that has to do with Trey's death, or my current marital status.'

'It's harder for me to believe he'd toss it all out over . . . a business transaction, given the history.'

'The history is precisely why. We've made mistakes, we've both been unfaithful in the past. We promised each other we'd never do so again.'

'Felicity Prinze.'

She saw it, immediately. Natasha knew.

'You're not tossing it all out over your husband's . . . business transaction.'

'That business has been concluded.' She shoved to her feet. 'I won't have you come here and insult me, I won't have you pry into my personal life.'

'Your personal life is part of my investigation. Try telling me the truth, and I won't have to pry. You knew about Felicity Prinze.'

'Yes, I knew. It's over.'

'How long have you known?'

'Weeks.' She waved a hand in the air. 'I'm perfectly aware of JJ's pattern, and his weaknesses. The situation put a strain on our marriage.'

'The rough patch.'

'Yes. We discussed counseling, argued, discussed divorce. And I . . . I began my business with Trey. I was so hurt and angry. Then JJ promised to end it, asked for another chance. I needed to think about it, of course, to search my own heart, but under it all I wanted to save my marriage. I intended to end my association with Trey, as I told you. And when JJ asked if I'd go away with him after the holidays, just the two of us, I knew I had to give him, give us, a chance.'

'You caught him cheating. How do you resolve your frantic concern about him finding out about your relationship with Ziegler.'

Natasha closed her eyes a moment, then released a breath. 'One moment, please.' She stepped over to the house comm. 'Hester, please contact Brianne and tell her I'm going to be just a little late.'

She came back, sat. 'I'd lose my leverage. I'd lose any chance of patching this up, moving on. I was furious when I learned about this — this — *dancer*. I nearly tossed JJ out then and there, but . . . We argued, we said the usual horrible things to each other. But among those horrible things he had a point or two about my neglecting . . . some areas of our marriage, about expecting him to be present for my events and social needs while often not being available for his.'

She pushed at her hair, seemed to gather herself. 'You're married. There are ups and there are downs. I wanted time to think, to evaluate what I really wanted from JJ, for myself. And at a weak moment, I leaped into this business with Trey. It was stupid, it was emotional. By engaging with Trey I did precisely, or nearly, what JJ had done. I can hardly pretend to be outraged and list all the requirements for staying married to him if he learns I had sex with our personal trainer, can I? We're working toward making it all whole, and this would tear it apart again.'

'Not tit for tat?' Eve said.

'Like most men – at least in my experience – he has the mind-set that it's one matter for a man to dally, another for a woman. I can put aside what he did. He'd never do the same.'

'What would he do?' Eve asked.

'He'd slap me with it and walk away, or slap me with it and stay to slap me with it every time we had a problem. I can live with the secret. I can forget it. I can't live with him holding it over me.'

'You told me he wasn't violent, but you use a violent word to describe his reaction.'

'Verbally, of course. And . . . emotionally.'

But there was a hitch, a slight one.

'Has he ever hit you?'

'No! Absolutely no! Yes, he has a temper, it's foolish to deny it. But he takes his anger out on inanimate things. He might throw something, or slam doors. He's . . . it's a bit like a child really, a tantrum. One of the things we've discussed is anger management.'

She leaned forward, earnestly. 'He shouts, and it annoys

people, puts them off. We have house droids rather than human help as they don't become offended. I can promise you, if he knew about Trey, he'd make me pay, but he wouldn't physically harm me. Or anyone.'

She rubbed her hand up and down her throat. 'You can't think he had anything to do with what happened to Trey. I'd know. I would. He was here, getting dressed for our party that night. And he was calm and even cheerful. He'd have been enraged, but he wasn't. We even ... we were together that night, for the first time since I learned of that dancer. He could never have done what you're thinking then come home, and been so calm and cheerful, hosted a party, made love with me. He couldn't have.'

'A lot of "he couldn'ts" in there,' Eve observed when they walked back to the vehicle.

'You unsettled her.'

'I meant to.'

'Not enough for her to agree to any taps, which is a pity.'

'She was pretty unsettled about that, too. Lots of "absolutely nots." No spying on spouse. No more prying into personal lives.'

'She may have protested – and too much as the bard would say – but she showed some fear, plenty of doubt.'

'Yeah, she did. Still, the leverage makes more sense, rings truer to me than the "Oooh, don't tell JJ I did the nasty with the trainer." There's some truth rolled in there, it's just

342

rolled in with lies, half-truths, and bullshit. I need some time to sort it all out.'

'She doesn't love him.'

Pausing, Eve narrowed her eyes at him. 'Why do you say that?'

He opened the car door for her, walked around to slide behind the wheel. 'The bit about leverage? That's something you and I might joke about, as we do cutting out hearts or dancing tangos on battered bodies if unfaithful.'

'Who says I'm joking about dancing on your battered body?'

He leaned over, kissed her. 'That's love. She wants that leverage – as if she's to be believed he would hold a mistake over her head. Leverage, weight, payback. It's not love.'

'No. It's a power struggle with sex. Marriage is that, sort of – but it's only right with the love in there. She'd go on this trip with him, and they'd make love noises – I don't mean sex noises. Then, if he isn't the killer – in which case I'll have him in a cage – he'll cheat again. She expects it. Next time she'll boot him. They'll have a prenup so he'll get something, but she's too smart, the money's too old, for her to go into it without planning for this. Cheated with her, will cheat on her.'

'Logical enough,' Roarke agreed.

'Same with her. Cheated with him, and so on. Shit, when it comes down to it, they deserve each other.

'We've got a prenup, right?'

'We do, yes. You read it, had your lawyer go over it. We signed it and put it away where we never have to think of it again.'

'Yeah, right. I didn't read it or do the lawyer thing. I just signed it.'

He stopped the car, annoying several cars behind him. 'What? Christ Jesus, Eve.'

'Drive, before they get out the bats. What the fuck do I care? Your money was a big strike against you at the start anyway, pal. I never wanted it.'

'That's not the bloody point.'

She heard the temper – very real – edge his tone and just shrugged it off. 'It's exactly the bloody point. You've got billions of billions, organizations, corporations, enterprises on and off planet, and I don't even *want* to know all of it anyway. You have people depending on the income they earn from those organizations and the rest. All that needs to be protected, and if you didn't you're a moron. You're not a moron or I wouldn't have married you and we wouldn't be talking about this anyway.'

'The bloody point is, you have rights, expectations, rights to those expectations. And speaking of morons, who signs a shagging legal document without reading it first?'

'Roarke Industries needed the legal document. You and I never did.'

Just like that, she saw the temper dissolve. 'Ah, Christ, Eve.'

'You think I don't know the difference? That I didn't

344

always know? I signed it because I thought: Great, this takes what gives me the jitters out of it. Not all the jitters because getting married gave me plenty. But the main jitters, signed away, and it gave me some peace of mind on it. And if you think I'd take a penny with me if you boot me, you are a moron. I take what I came in with. Except this.' She tapped her wedding ring with her thumb. 'And this.' Lifted the diamond from under her shirt. 'They're mine, and if that's not in there, it's going to be amended.'

'You leave me speechless.'

'That'll be the day.'

'I love you beyond speech. Beyond reason.'

'That works for me. You work for me.' She leaned back, looked down. 'I might keep these boots, too, and the coat. Yeah, if you boot me, I'm definitely keeping the coat.'

He grinned at her, took her hand.

'You keep Summerset – that's firm.'

'I'm completely agreeable to all your terms.'

She glanced over as he drove through the gates. 'Can I get a lifetime supply of coffee tossed in? That should cover it all.'

Again he stopped the car. This time, he released his safety belt, hers, and pulled her into his arms. 'I adore you. But none of this matters as I'd only boot you if you cheated on me. Then there's the whole business of cutting out your heart and setting it on fire to follow.'

'Right. I forgot about that.' She held on a moment, content. 'I'd love to read the Quigley-Copley prenup.'

'Would you like me to arrange that?'

'Tempting, but no. There's no urgency on it, and I think I stirred up some dust. Maybe Peabody did the same.'

She leaned back. 'I'm going to check in with her, write all this up. Then let's pick a vid where lots of shit blows up, and eat ourselves sick with popcorn.'

'A fine plan, with one addition.'

'What?'

'Let's drink considerable wine with the popcorn, and have crazed sex after the vid – as a double feature.'

'A better plan. Let's get it done.'

18

It took some time, getting everything in place to the point she felt justified in taking another few hours off.

She talked to Peabody at length, briefly to McNab. Wrote her update, read Peabody's. Updated her board, her book.

The Quigley-Copley household was a mess, she mused. Then again in her experience a great many households ran on rocky, pitted, often ugly ground.

'Sometimes we do,' she told the cat, who seemed more interested in taking the next of his long series of naps in her office sleep chair. 'The rocky part. We've got the smooth running right now, but there are always going to be bumps ahead.'

Stepping back, she hooked her thumbs in her belt loops, studying the ID shots, the way they looked together. 'Both attractive − got a polished-up look about them that says money even just in the IDs. They even look like a couple, like two people who should fit. But they just don't.

'They just don't,' she repeated, leaned back on her desk. 'People could say that about us,' she said when Roarke moved from his office to hers. 'Probably a lot of them do.'

'What would that be?'

'That we don't fit.'

'I beg to differ.' He walked to her, leaned on the desk beside her. 'We fit as cleanly as a bespoke suit.'

'I'm saying what people outside it all might say. It's perception, pal. Look at them – Quigley, Copley. They look like a set – that's visual perception, and probable social perception. But when you crack the lid, it's a bad fit. She's never going to trust him, not down to the deep, and he's always going to look for the easy way to get more. Sex, money, prestige. When threatened, or maybe just bored, they lash out. Both of them used sex for that.'

'And possibly a blunt object.'

'Yeah, very possibly. Peabody said Martella was very cooperative, got a little overwrought here and there. The secretary, Catiana, kept her calm, as did Peabody's innate there-there approach. She agreed to the tap, with a little nudge on how it might help clear things up, might protect her sister. It meant she had to use the angle I'm looking at her spouse, but she's looking at Copley, and feels she's got the stronger case.'

'Essentially playing the couples against each other to see what breaks.'

'More or less. It's in there. My gut tells me it's in there. I had another round with Robbins, the blogger, and there's nothing there. It's not just because I get the rape angle, it's because I think I get her. And there's nothing there on this.'

'Then you're definitely shortening your list.'

'It looks that way. Peabody's going to take another pass at the girlfriend, but I don't see that, either. If we don't tie it up tomorrow . . .'

'Christmas Eve.'

'Yeah, that. If we don't, it could take days more, if we're lucky, with Peabody heading off to her family, and everything shutting down. Hell, half the city closes up between Christmas and New Year's, and if my prime suspect flies off to the tropics, I can't stop him. Not with what we have.'

'You'd like him to have his Christmas goose and pudding in a cage.'

'I think the best he'd get in a cage would be fake turkey, maybe a slice of pie, but yeah.'

'Does the idea that with you nipping at his heels he's unlikely to have happy holidays help?'

'I think anybody who could shove that knife into dead Ziegler, and according to the statement of witnesses, party directly thereafter, isn't going to sweat it. It's all about the right now. It's how he could set Felicity up in a swank condo, forget about his marriage while he was there, forget about her when he was with his wife.

'I'll tell you who fits,' she added. 'Ziegler and Copley. Two greedy, selfish, cheating assholes. And that's all of our time they get for today. Let's pop some corn.'

349

'I want my own,' he told her as they walked out of her office. 'I'd actually like to taste it rather than butter and salt.'

'I keep telling you, the corn's just the delivery system for the butter and salt. What's the vid?'

'We've an advance copy of *Unbidden*. It's being released Christmas Day – very hot property. Alien invasion, top-flight cast, strong FX.'

'But do things blow up?'

'Indeed they do if the trailer I previewed is any indication.'

'Sounds perfect.'

It was. Stretched out hip to hip on the sofa, plenty of popcorn and a nice, smooth red wine to wash it down. And the action on screen hit all the notes.

Alien invaders bent on conquering the planet, decimating or enslaving its human inhabitants. It offered a feisty yet emotionally scarred female lead, the reckless but charming male counterpart, and the motley and courageous band of resistance fighters who joined them. The story worked, the romance clicked, and lots of stuff blew up.

The effects worked so well she got mildly queasy during an air battle. And the characters resonated, causing a pang when the hero's feckless screwup of a brother sacrificed himself for the cause.

All in all, it provided an excellent excuse to laze around on a Sunday eating popcorn and getting a little buzzed on wine while Galahad sprawled over their legs.

'Good one. It was fun watching the guy who played Feeney in the *Icove* vid play the tough ex–Army vet. Figured he was going down, but he copped to the whiny redhead being an alien infiltrator in the nick. I don't get aliens.'

'Don't you?'

'They're always zipping down, wanting to take over the planet, and blowing up major cities on the way. It never works out for them.'

She tossed more butter-and-salt-saturated popcorn in her mouth. 'Smarter to start in the middle.'

He managed to reach around, snag the wine bottle, pour the very last of it into their glasses. 'The middle of what?'

'The country – since they're apparently all about the U.S. on top of it. Start in the middle, the less populated areas – like, say, Shipshewana, Indiana.'

'Of course it must be Shipshewana.'

'Then, work your way out to the cities as you gain ground, eliminate the populations.' She took a long, happy drink of wine. 'You'd think if they could get here from wherever the hell, they'd be smarter.'

'Lucky for us, for Shipshewana, and the planet, they aren't.'

'I'll say. Who wants an implant shoved into the base of your skull to control your thoughts and deeds?'

'Not I.'

'And what do the aliens accomplish?' Wound up, she drilled a finger in his chest. 'Sure they level some cities, kill a bunch of people – and there's always at least one of those people who tries to negotiate with them.'

'Fools.'

'You bet. After they destroy New York or New LA or East Washington, because those are usually prime targets, the survivors end up uniting the fractured world, creating heros out of the ordinary, and helping a couple of really pretty, bloodied, and sweaty people to find true love and hot sex.'

'Looking at it that way, we should hope for an alien invasion.'

She set her popcorn bowl aside, shifted over a little onto her hip. 'We don't need one. We found all that already without them.'

'And I didn't have to risk being vaporized to get you here.'

'True, but that's not a bad way to go, right? Getting vaporized is quick. You wouldn't even know it, just *ppsssht!* Gone. Better than getting run over by a maxibus or barely surviving an air crash, or getting bitten in half by a shark. Then there's—'

'Quiet.' He stopped her mouth with his, added a dance of his fingers along her ribs to make her laugh.

He rolled her over, then under him, pleased himself by ravishing her neck, her throat.

Galahad squawked, then hit the floor with a sharp ring of collar bells.

Sinking, she slid her bare foot up and down Roarke's leg,

angling her head to give him freer access before turning back again to offer her lips.

She twined and twisted her fingers in his hair, felt lazy and loose. Wine fogged her brain; pleasure misted it. She embraced both, embraced him.

The screen switched to its holding hum as the vid credits ended. Now she heard the quiet pop and crackle of the fire, the whisper of their movements in the nest of the sofa.

The tree's lights shimmered as the short day slipped into the long night.

He peeled off her sweater, slid down to possess her breasts with his mouth, his hands. As those mists thickened and swirled, she pressed up, stirring more heat. Moaning with it, she tugged at his shirt.

'Off, off. Too many clothes.'

She found his mouth with hers again as she fought off the shirt.

She had her teeth on his shoulder; he had her trousers halfway down her legs. Her communicator beeped.

'Ah, bloody hell' was his breathless and bitter response.

'I didn't hear anything. Don't stop—' It beeped again. 'Shit! Shit, shit, shit.'

She dragged herself from under him, stumbled toward the table as she struggled to yank up her trousers.

'Block video,' she ordered. 'Fuck. Fuck. Dallas.'

'Dispatch, Dallas, Lieutenant Eve.'

She muttered, 'Why?' Then with her trousers still unsecured, sat on the table.

'Report to 18 Vandam. One person dead, another injured. Possible homicide.'

'Who's dead?' she demanded, shoving up to hook her trousers.

'Data incomplete. See officers on scene.'

'Contact Peabody, Detective Delia. On my way.'

She shoved the comm in her pocket. 'That's the Quigley brownstone.'

'I know.' He was already up, putting on his shirt. 'I'll go with you.'

'I've got Peabody—'

'Christ, Eve, we just sat in that living room a few hours ago. I'm going with you.'

'God, I'm half drunk.' She reached for her weapon harness.

'Take some Sober-Up before you put that on. And I could use some myself.'

'What the hell time is it?' she muttered on her way to the bathroom.

'Twenty after seven.'

She paused, glanced back. 'She said Copley would be home by six.'

Grim, she dashed to the bathroom for the Sober-Up.

With that, and the coffee Roarke programmed in go-cups, the mists lifted, the fog parted. For the second time that day, she climbed into the muscular SUV.

'I planted it in her head. I did it deliberately, figuring she'd let something slip to me, or dig out something and come to me with it. I never figured he'd go at her, never figured he'd be that stupid. If he killed her—'

'You're jumping your fences, Eve. That's not like you.'

She closed her eyes, pulled herself back in. 'You're right. I know better. No preconceived notions. But you said it yourself. She seemed a little afraid of him. I didn't offer her protection, didn't drive that lane, because she could've been part of it and the fear was useful.'

No point, no point in speculating, she warned herself. For all she knew, Copley could be dead.

Her comm sounded again. 'Dallas.'

'Dallas, we're heading in,' Peabody talked fast, 'but it's probably going to take about twenty minutes. We were at the SkyMall and traffic's insane. We called in a black-and-white to speed it up, but we're probably twenty out.'

'Just get there.'

'Soon as we can. Do you know the DB?'

'Not yet. I'll get back to you.'

She shoved the comm in her pocket again.

The minute Roarke pulled behind a black-and-white, she jumped out, drew her badge out of her pocket.

Long strides took her to the door where a uniform scanned her badge, her face, skimmed a glance over Roarke. Nodded.

'What have you got, Officer . . . Kenseko?' she demanded, reading his nameplate.

'DB, female, head trauma. Another female, en route to the hospital, unconscious. Head and facial injuries. Male held on premises, ID'd as John Jake Copley, of this address. He ID'd the injured female as his wife, Natasha Copley. Wanted to go with her, but we held him here. He's a handful, LT.'

'I got it. Keep him out of my way for now. Are you first on scene?'

'No, sir, that would be Officer Shelby. She answered the nine-one-one. She and my partner have Copley secured.'

'Stay on the door, Kenseko. My partner will be here in about fifteen.'

As she moved in, she heard Copley shouting from another room, threatening to sue the officers, the entire department, the state of New York.

Ignoring him, Eve took the Seal-It out of the field kit Roarke offered, used it while she studied the scene.

She'd expected to find Martella, which proved the rule about no expectations.

A brunette lay with her head on the marble ledge of the hearth. Faceup, a deep, long gash scoring her forehead and right temple. Blood pooled, on the marble, on the floor, painted the hand flung out, stained the bright blue coat, the boldly patterned scarf.

'Catiana Dubois.'

'The social secretary?'

'Yeah, that's her. Somebody turned her over, somebody moved the body. Damn it. Kenseko!'

'Sir.' He hotfooted from the door.

'Did you or your partner turn the body over?'

'No, sir. Officer Shelby told us the scene had been compromised on her arrival.'

'All right. Had a struggle here, chair's shoved, table overturned, broken crockery and glass. And that.'

She lifted her chin to a large vase of thick, faceted crystal, stained now with blood. More blood on the floor, on the carpet by the cracked vase.

'What the hell were you doing here, Catiana?'

For procedure, she crossed to the body, used her kit to formally ID the vic. 'Victim is female, mixed race, age thirty-three. Catiana Dubois, employed by Martella Schubert, who is the sister of Natasha Quigley. The deep gash, the bruising on the forehead appear to be COD. Fell or was pushed, face-first, hit the ledge, the edge of it, and hit hard. Skinny-heeled boots,' she murmured. 'Not much traction. She loses her balance, falls, smashes face-first into the edge here.'

She took the gauges Roarke handed her. 'She hasn't been dead an hour.'

Gently, Eve lifted her hands, one at a time, by the wrist, examined them. 'No defensive wounds I can see, no sign of skin under the nails, but Morris will look closer.

'She's got her coat unbuttoned, her scarf unwrapped. Pretty cold out there, so it's likely she did that after she came in. Comes to the door, the house droid lets her in. We'll go over the droid. She comes in here . . .'

Sitting back on her heels, Eve looked around the room. 'I don't see any cups, any glasses, broken or unbroken. No drinks, no refreshments. Coat's still on, so maybe she planned to make it quick. An argument, a fight, a confrontation. With who? Copley or Quigley? Head and face trauma for Quigley, but Catiana here has delicate hands. No sign she hit anyone. If she fought with Quigley, it got physical and she knocked her unconscious with that vase, why is she dead over here and the vase lying over there? Doesn't work. If she fought with Quigley, and Quigley shoved her, killed her, who bashed Quigley with the vase and why? It's shaky.

'So.' She shoved up. 'We'll see what Copley and the droid have to say.'

Though Copley had stopped yelling, she followed the direction it had come from.

She found him sulking in a sitting room reflecting masculine decor. Deep colors, leather seating, hefty entertainment center, golfing art and memorabilia.

One of the uniforms – older, had vet written all over him – sat at his ease working on his PPC while a young female cop stood at parade rest.

She snapped to attention when Eve stepped in.

Copley lurched to his feet.

'For God's sake. My wife's been attacked. She may be dying, for all I know, and these – these – storm troopers are forcing me to stay here. I need to get to the hospital. I need to be with Tash.'

'Officer.' Eve looked toward the vet. 'Would you contact the hospital, get Ms Quigley's status and condition?'

'Yes, sir.' He stepped out.

'Sit down, Mr Copley. I'll be right with you. Officer Shelby, please step out with me.'

'Yes, sir, Lieutenant.'

'I demand to be taken to my wife! Immediately!'

'I said sit down.' Eve snapped it, cold and fast, had the shock of it jerking Copley back. 'And do us all a favor, simmer down while I do my job.'

She moved out of the room, took a few steps more, nodded to Shelby. 'Run it through for me.'

'Yes, sir, Lieutenant. I was walking my beat, about to go take my ten sit-down, when the nine-one-one came in. I was only three blocks north, so I responded. The Dispatch call came in at eighteen-fifty-nine. I was at this location by nineteen-oh-one.'

'You move fast, Officer.'

'Yes, sir, Lieutenant. There was no response to my knock or buzz for two minutes, twenty-three seconds. I was about to relay same to Dispatch when the man, identifying himself subsequently as John Jake Copley, answered. He appeared visibly disturbed, shouted incoherently, and rushed back into the residence. I followed him in, observed the female victim by the fireplace, the female victim beside an overturned table approximately ten feet away. Both victims were bleeding profusely from the head. I was forced to order Mr Copley to calm down, to no avail, while I checked the pulse on each victim. The woman he identified as his wife, Natasha Quigley, was alive. I called for medical assistance and for backup as Copley only became more agitated, and somewhat abusive in his language.'

'Is that a fact?'

'Yes, sir, Lieutenant. He called me a useless cunt, a moronic bitch, and at one point laid hands on my person. I was forced to restrain him.'

'He give you the bruise on your jaw?'

'During the restraining process, yes, sir.'

'I might have been forced to kick his ass. Restraining him was the better choice.'

Shelby's lips trembled into a quick smile. 'Yes, sir, Lieutenant. Officers Kenseko and O'Ryan arrived on scene, as did the medicals at nineteen-oh-eight and nine-teen-oh-nine respectively.'

She cleared her throat, blinked a bit when Roarke offered her a glass of water.

'Go ahead,' Eve told her. 'Hydrate, then finish your report.'

'Yes, sir, Lieutenant, thank you.' She gulped some down. 'After my fellow officers removed Mr Copley to another room, and the medicals began to work on Ms Copley, I again spoke with Dispatch, which informed me Copley was to be detained here until your arrival. The nine-one-one caller, who identified herself as Natasha Quigley, was attacked while calling nine-one-one, and at the end of the call shouted out.'

At this point Shelby swiped a fresh page on her notebook. "JJ! What are you doing? JJ, stop, stop! Don't!' before the call ended. There's a broken pocket 'link on the floor in the kill room.'

'Yeah, I saw it. Good work, Shelby. Stand by.' Eve glanced over at Roarke. 'Why don't you come in with me for this? You add an extra layer of fear and intimidation.'

'Always glad to lend a hand. Officer Shelby. You should get a cold pack for that jaw.'

'It's okay, sir, thank you. He just caught me with his shoulder when I restrained him.'

'No cold pack till we document,' Eve ordered. 'Resisting and assaulting an officer dribbles on some icing.'

Eve went back to the sitting room. Copley paced, drinking what looked like whiskey from a short glass. He'd obviously talked Shelby into removing the restraints, and just as well.

She nodded again when O'Ryan stepped up, murmured in her ear. 'Stand by,' she told him. 'Mr Copley.'

He whirled around, nearly slopping whiskey over the top of the glass. 'What the *hell* is going on here? Some maniac comes into my house and assaults – was that one of Tella's people? Was that Katherine?'

'Catiana.'

'Yes! Good God. She was dead. You could see she was dead. Her eyes staring. And the blood. But Tash. I ran in after I heard her scream. Ran downstairs, calling for her, and there she was lying there, bleeding. I ran to her, tried to lift her up. I couldn't tell if she was dead or alive. I couldn't tell. I thought she was dead. Why would that woman attack Tash?'

'I don't believe she did. The scene doesn't read that way.'

'But it had to be.'

'You've got blood on your shirt. Blood on your pants.'

'Tash – Tash's blood. I tried to pick her up. I heard Tash scream, and I ran down. It was only seconds. It couldn't have been more than a few seconds. No one was here. That bitch tried to kill my wife. Tash must have fought back, knocked her down.'

'After getting knocked unconscious?'

'Before, of course, then when they struggled or fought – about God knows what – she struck Tash. Tash must have fallen, maybe the women slipped and fell. How do I know?'

'What time did you get home from your golf outing?'

'I'm not sure, not exactly. About six, more or less.'

'And then?'

'What do you mean?'

'What did you do upon arriving home?'

'I went upstairs, spoke briefly to my wife. We talked about going out later for drinks, for dinner. I had a quick shower, changed, if you want specifics, stretched out, turned on the screen. I was just relaxing, as many do on a Sunday evening, when I heard Tash scream from downstairs.'

'Did you and your wife argue?'

'What? Of course not.'

'Did you argue with Catiana Dubois?'

'No! I barely know the woman. She's one of my sister-in-law's staff. I want to see my wife. I want to know what's happening with Tash.'

'She's in serious condition. She has some swelling of the brain, and is in surgery.'

He went sheet white as Eve spoke. 'The doctors are confident she'll recover.'

'Lieutenant, your partner's on her way back.'

'Thank you, Officer. Ask the detective with her to secure the house droid and question same.'

'Yes, sir.'

'Question the droid?' Copley shouted. 'Question me, question a fucking machine! My wife's having emergency brain surgery. You can't keep me here.'

'She can.' Roarke moved to block his exit. 'Yes, she can.'

'Just stay out of my way,' Copley warned, but backed up as he did so. 'I have rights! You can't keep me in this room. I'm not under arrest. I'm free to come and go as I damn well please.'

'We can fix that,' Eve decided, glanced over at an out-of-breath Peabody. 'Peabody, read Mr Copley his rights.'

'What are you talking about? You've all lost your minds. I'm leaving.'

He tried a charge across the room. Eve pivoted, but Roarke was faster, and merely shot out his foot. It sent Copley on a face-first dive.

'Oops,' Roarke said.

'Peabody, restrain the suspect, and read him his rights. John Jake Copley, you're under arrest for suspicion of murder, for attempted murder, for assault, for assault on an officer.'

'You have the right to remain silent,' Peabody began, then her voice was drowned out by Copley's raging.

'Give him to the female officer – Shelby. Have her and the other two officers transport him to Central. To a box. I'll be down to deal with him when we're done here.'

'Let me give you a hand with that, Peabody.' Roarke hauled Copley to his feet, and with Peabody taking the other side perp-walked him out, raging still.

'Whew.' McNab stepped in. 'And I thought the SkyMall was crazytown. The house droid's been shut down since sixteen-thirty, LT.'

'Shut down?'

'Yeah. Turned off. There's a secondary droid, but that one's been turned off since about noon. The main house droid reports Ms Quigley ordered her to shut down, as she routinely does on Sundays when they aren't expecting company or entertaining. She reports no one coming or going after you and Roarke earlier today. No help from that quarter.'

'Check the security cam, and let's make a copy of that.'

'On it.'

She pulled out her comm, contacted Dispatch.

'Dispatch, play back nine-one-one call from this location made by Quigley, Natasha, at eighteen-fifty-six.'

'Acknowledged, one moment. No video recorded. Audio only. Playback commenced.'

Nine-one-one, what is your emergency?
She's dead! I think she's dead! Oh my God, Cate.
It's . . . Wait, please. Oh God. This is Natasha Quigley at 18 Vandam. I need to report a – JJ! Oh, JJ, something terrible happened. JJ! What are you doing? JJ, stop, stop! Don't!

Eve heard a scream, a thud, pictured the 'link dropping to the ground. Then the recording stopped.

'Playback complete.'

'Okay, copy recording to my files. Dallas and Peabody, along with Detective McNab, currently on scene. Dallas and Peabody will transfer to Central to interview Copley, John Jake, now charged with suspicion of murder and related charges.'

'Acknowledged.'

'Dallas, out. Got ya,' she muttered.

'Your suspect's on his way to Central,' Roarke told her.

'And he'll stew in it for a while. When we finish up here, we need to go by the hospital, check on Quigley. If she's awake, we'll get her statement. You can go home.'

'Why do you want to punish me?'

She shook her head. 'Suit yourself.' She walked out with him, joined Peabody.

'I liked her,' Peabody said. 'There was something likeable about her.'

'Yeah, there was. Contact the sweepers, the morgue. Let's get started on getting her justice.'

'I was complaining, sort of, about working on a vic who was an asshole.' Peabody looked back toward Catiana. 'And now . . .'

'I know it.' Eve crouched to study the broken 'link. 'Looks like it's been stomped on. She drops it, he comes at her, stomps on it. The vase is right there. It sat on that table. He grabs it, comes at her, stomps the phone, smacks her with it.'

Before she could ask, Roarke handed her an evidence bag. She bagged and sealed the phone.

'He drops the vase, doesn't give her the second smack like Ziegler. Vase is big and heavy. It cracks, but it didn't break. Does he think smashing the phone erases the damn nine-one-one? Was he too wrought up, too far gone, to think about it? Just attack, just cover it all up. Then blame it all on a dead woman? He was upstairs, minding his own, heard his wife scream, ran down.'

'But there's no report, is there, that he called for help, for medicals, for the police.'

She looked at Roarke as she marked the vase. 'Nope. None. It took Shelby two minutes to get here, and took him another two to answer. Working on his story, getting himself under control. Not enough time to set up a fake break-in or burglary. He thinks he's got two dead women, until Shelby checks, gets a pulse. Now he's got to get to his wife, fix it somehow. Or run. But Shelby handled that, and then backup arrived. He can't push his way through three cops. He has to be outraged, the worried husband, the victim.'

She stood again. 'How it looks is, for some reason – and we'll need to talk to the sister – Catiana comes here. Copley lets her in. They come in here, argue. Maybe she knew something, maybe he thought she knew something. He loses his temper, pushes her. She falls way wrong, and that's it. He barely has time to think. Look what she made him do! And in comes his wife. Sees the body. Calls nine-one-one. He couldn't have been in the room.'

Frowning, she turned a circle. 'If he'd been in, he'd never have let her call through. So he ran out, to get something, to hide something, to get a damn drink, but he had to have come back in at that point in the call when she said his name. She's ruining *everything*. He has to make her stop. Snaps, or is still snapped, grabs the vase, charges in.'

She turned again, studied the body again, with guilt and regret clawing at her. 'What did you know? How do you fit in?'

'Dallas.' McNab came in, passed her a disc. 'Got it copied. You can see the vic come to the door. You can't see who let her in. You'll see for yourself, but to my eye she looked upset, worried. Rushed in, talking fast.'

'No audio?'

'No, no audio.'

Her eyes on Catiana, Eve slipped the disc into her pocket.

If you knew something, *anything* why did you come here? Why didn't you come to me?

But it was too late for that question, she thought.

19

The burly SUV proved a good choice since McNab and Peabody needed to pile in. Eve ignored McNab as he played with controls and options in the back while she worked on her PPC.

Catiana had parents – divorced, mother remarried, living in Brooklyn. Father also remarried, living in Phoenix, Arizona. One sibling, a sister, married, two children, in New Rochelle.

She'd need to go to Brooklyn, do the notification. But that misery would come after she'd checked on Quigley. She needed to . . . Was that chocolate she smelled?

She shifted around in her seat, narrowed her eyes at Peabody. 'What's that on your upper lip, Detective?'

Hastily Peabody swiped at it. 'Ah, um. A little whipped cream. It's hot chocolate. It's *real* hot chocolate. I couldn't help it. McNab did it.'

Unabashed, McNab grinned at her. 'Mini AutoChef back here has a full beverage menu. Peabody's been jonesing for hot chocolate. Want some?'

Yes, Eve thought, but said, 'No.'

'Iced squared accessories back here,' he said to Roarke. 'The total.'

'We do what we can,' Roarke responded.

'You got your entertainment with vid, straight screen, tunes, books, full D and C capabilities, mapping – solo, duet, or full vehicle modes. Then there's—'

'He probably knows what's loaded in this thing,' Eve interrupted.

'Add in the eats and drinks, we could motor to Utah.'

'Next time we plan to go to Utah, I'll let you know. Meanwhile, we're a little preoccupied here with murder.'

'Yeah, about that. Got the security disc from the crime scene on here.' His green eyes shifted from hers down to the screen while he took a contented glug of his own hot chocolate. 'We might be able to enhance and analyze the shadow of whoever opened the door for the vic. It's a long shot, but you gotta try it. Lipreading program's running on the vic. We've got a better chance at that, but her face angles away from the cam, and she puts her hand over her mouth once so it's going to be jumpy.'

Sometimes, Eve thought, she forgot he wasn't an idiot. 'Good. Stay on it. Here's the play,' she said to Peabody. 'We talk to Quigley, if possible, get the details. Odds are slim she'd try to protect Copley at this point, but if she tries, we could run the nine-one-one call for her, push it. DB, spouse in the hospital, no break-in, a fleet of lawyers isn't going to loosen the noose.'

She glanced at McNab. 'If we get lucky with the shadow ID, all the better. Confirm Copley opened the door to the vic, it throws out his claim of being upstairs when this went down. In addition, we tie him into Ziegler — that'll take more, but we're going to do it. With Quigley's statement, we can let him sweat. The victim's mother lives in Brooklyn. We have to go, notify her.'

'Man, two days — less — before Christmas. It's always hard, but this is just harder.'

'She has a husband and a stepson living at home, another daughter in New York. That'll help some. The vic may have talked to her about Ziegler, about Copley. We have to get whatever we can. We'll need to talk to the Schuberts again, asap, and I want to check in at the morgue, give an official COD, get Morris's — I've already requested him — take on her.'

'That's a long time sweating,' Peabody said as Roarke worked through the parking garage at the hospital. 'A long time for him to come up with a story, for the lawyers to shine it up.'

'It's not going to shine, not when his wife tells us he attacked her. Not when she gives us a statement from her hospital bed. I get in the box with him, he's going to break. I'm going to break him.'

She would damn well break him, Eve thought as they piled out, walked to the hospital's main entrance.

'Lipreading doesn't give us much, Dallas.' McNab held up his PPC. 'It has her saying: *Need to talk*. Break. *Come in.*

Break. *I remembered*. And that's it. Vic moved into the house, out of range.'

'The shadow?'

'Working it, but hell, Dallas, there isn't much there.'

'Play it out,' she told him.

She crossed the colorful lobby with its busy food court, passed a group of kids in school uniforms singing carols in front of a big tree, and arrowed in on a security guard.

'NYPSD.' She held up her badge. 'Here's what I need you to do, and fast. I need the floor, the room, and the doctor in charge of Quigley, Natasha, brought in earlier this evening via ambulance, with severe head trauma.'

'I'm not supposed to access patient information without my supervisor's authorization.'

'Right now, I'm your supervisor. Quigley, Natasha. Now. If she dies before I get to her, I'm coming back for you.'

'Yes, ma'am.'

He scrambled off.

'I hate that "ma'am" thing, but okay.'

'Between McNab and me,' Roarke commented, 'we could have hacked that data for you in about the same amount of time.'

'Would've been fun, too,' McNab said wistfully.

'Next time.' Eve met the security guard halfway.

'She's on six. I meant to say they'll bring her to six. She's still in surgery. Dr Campo's in charge.'

'Good. Thanks.'

She zipped straight for the elevators. 'Still in surgery, damn it. It's not likely we're going to be able to interview her anytime soon,' she said as the got on. 'We'll push on the nursing staff to give us a more detailed update, go from there.'

The sixth-floor elevator opened into yet another lobby – smaller, but all spruced up for the holidays. It held a waiting area, Vending, and a scattering of people sitting anxiously in miserable-looking chairs.

The woman at the desk beamed a bright smile that dimmed when Eve badged her. 'I need data on Quigley, Natasha. A Dr Campo's operating on her.'

'The Patient Privacy Act—'

'Is trumped.' Eve slapped her badge on the counter. 'Quigley is the victim of an assault. I have a suspect in custody who killed another woman and attempted to kill Quigley. I need her status, and I need it now.'

'I need to check your identification, and the identifications of those with you. Once verified, I can pass you through to the nursing station. The head nurse, Janis Vick, would be able to give you the information available to her.'

'Do it.'

While she did, Roarke wandered over to Vending. He knew the preferences, and offered Peabody and McNab fizzies, handed Eve a Pepsi.

Before she could crack it open, the woman at the desk shifted back. 'You're verified. Straight through the double doors.'

They buzzed, clicked, slowly swung open.

More decorations, brighter lights, and the sound of rubber soles padding on tile. Eve smelled hospital, a scent that always hit the center of her gut. Sickness, antiseptics, heavy cleaners – and a metallic underpinning she thought of as fear.

She moved to the wide semicircle of counter where some of the staff – all wearing a variation of a bright-colored tunic she supposed was meant to be cheerful – worked on 'links or comps.

'Janis Vick.'

A woman on a comp held up a finger. She had brutally short stone-gray hair with a snaking blue streak. Rising, she came around the counter.

'Lieutenant Dallas? You want the status of Natasha Quigley. She's still in surgery.'

'That much I know.'

'I can tell you there were some complications. Her BP dropped, and at one point her heart stopped. Dr Campo found a second, smaller bleed. They were able to stabilize the patient while Dr Campo closed the bleeds. While the patient has been downgraded to critical, the head surgical nurse reports the patient is, as I said, stabilized at this time.'

'How much longer will she be in there?'

'I can't tell you that, but from what I can gather, the surgery should be done within the hour. From there, the patient will be monitored in Recovery. It could be two hours, or several hours, before she's able to talk to you.'

'What are her chances? You're not head nurse on the surgical floor for nothing,' Eve pushed when Vick hesitated. 'You have a gauge.'

'I can tell you, the patient's lucky. Dr Campo, in my opinion, is the best neurosurgeon we have. With her performing the surgery, I'd give the patient strong odds. If you give me your contact information, I can see you're notified when she's in Recovery.'

The best she'd get, Eve determined. They couldn't wait hours to move on the rest.

'You want to start on Copley,' Peabody said as they rode down to the lobby again. 'I can do the notification. I can handle it,' she added when Eve glanced at her. 'You can be working on Copley while we – McNab and me – head to Brooklyn, take care of that.'

Eve cracked the soft drink tube, considered it. 'It'll save time. I'll take the first pass at him while you notify next of kin. If I don't crack him, first pass, we'll try for Quigley again, take him on together. You need to get the mother, and have her pull in the sister so you can work her. Get them to tell you anything, I mean anything, the vic might have said about Ziegler, about Copley, Quigley. Get a sense of the connections. Everything plays now.'

'I know.'

'Do you want transpo?'

'Be nice,' Peabody said, then sighed. 'But the subway's probably quicker.'

'Contact me once you have it done,' Eve ordered, and

parted ways. 'I don't like dumping the notification on her. She'll carry it longer than I would.'

'I doubt that,' Roarke said. 'You carry them all.'

Claiming otherwise would be a lie, she admitted, and why bother. 'I'll waste my time saying this again, but you could go home.'

'It's never less than entertaining, watching you interrogate a suspect.'

'Whatever floats.' She pulled out her 'link as he drove, contacted Mira. 'Sorry to disturb you at home,' she began, 'but you said you were interested in observing when I had Copley in the box.'

After making arrangements with Mira she contacted Central to make certain Copley was where she wanted him.

'Interview B,' she said when Roarke drove into Central's garage. 'Reo's heading in. He used his one contact for his lawyer. Didn't use it to check on his wife. The lawyer's with him, making lawyerly noises.'

'One expects no less.'

Eve eyed the elevator with distrust, but got on. 'The last time I was on this, Drunk Santa let loose a nuclear fart while showing me his grimy little dick.'

'You lead such a colorful life.'

'I'm pretty sure he puked right after I got off, because I heard they had to shut down this car for two hours.' She sniffed cautiously. 'You can still sort of smell the detox.'

'We can hope this ride proves less eventful.'

As it did, she peeled off straight to her office. 'I'm going to put a file together – DB, the first-on-scene's record of Quigley, the scene itself, the nine-one-one.'

'And Ziegler?'

'Second file. I may hold that back, depending. He doesn't know his wife's status, and I can use that. His lawyer can't access it – Patient Privacy Act – so they don't know I haven't interviewed her.'

'You'll lie.'

'Fortunately, I can lie my ass off.' She checked the time. 'He's had a good long sweat, the lawyer's told him to keep it zipped, but he won't.'

'He's . . . excitable.' Roarke looked over at her. 'You'll use that.'

'Damn straight. He doesn't know what the hell's going on regarding Quigley. He'll have a story though, and he'll want to tell it.'

'And lawyer or not, you'll make sure he does.'

'That's the plan.' She picked up the files. 'If you get bored in Observation, I'll find you. If you want to go home, just go.'

He put his hands on her shoulders, kissed her. 'I'll be here.'

Armed with her files, she walked to Interview B, and went in.

'Dallas, Lieutenant Eve, entering Interview with Copley, John Jake, regarding case files H–28901 and H–28902. Mr Copley has exercised his right to legal representation.'

'Edie McAllister with Silbert, Crosby, and McAllister, representing Mr Copley.'

'So noted.'

'As Mr Copley's legal counsel I demand his immediate release.' She clipped the words out, all confident, outraged lawyer. 'He's been held here for nearly three hours. He's been prevented from accompanying his injured wife to the hospital. He's been prevented from contacting the hospital to learn his wife's condition. This extreme hardship is—'

'You are aware evidence strongly indicates Mr Copley is responsible for his wife's injuries?'

'That's a *lie!*' Copley banged his fist on the table, rattling the chains that secured him.

'JJ.' The lawyer, a swirly-haired blonde in potent red, laid a hand on his. 'You have no tangible evidence, and, in fact, have Mr Copley's own account that he found his wife unconscious. *We* strongly believe, and evidence will show, that Catiana Dubois assaulted Ms Quigley, was killed during the struggle.'

'If you're thinking of that as your opening statement at the trial, it's not going to get you far. Catiana Dubois came to your residence – your own security disc clearly shows this, and shows she was upset at this time. You let her in, you argued. You've got an impressive temper, Copley, which I can testify to personally. You pushed her. She fell, striking her head on the edge of the marble hearth in your living area.'

'I never touched her. I barely know her. I never saw her.'

'You didn't see this?' Eve took the crime scene photo of Catiana from the file, tossed it on the table. 'In your living area?'

He glanced down at the file photo, quickly away again. 'I meant I didn't see her before. I didn't let her in. I was upstairs. Natasha must have let her in.'

'And, according to your fairy tale, Catiana subsequently attacked your wife. Why?'

'How the hell do I know?'

'Mr Copley is unaware of any friction between his wife and the deceased.' McAllister spoke firmly, working to focus Eve's attention on her and away from her client. 'However, in her capacity as social secretary for Ms Quigley's sister, the deceased often inserted herself in personal affairs.'

'How did she do that?' Ignoring the lawyer, Eve spoke to Copley directly. 'I thought you barely knew her? Which is it, Copley? You barely knew her or she stuck her nose in your business?'

'I didn't pay any attention to her. She dealt with Tella's social stuff, with women's business.'

'Define "women's business".'

'Parties, shopping, lunches.' He shrugged it off. 'Garden clubs and whatever women do.'

Eve smiled toothily at McAllister. 'Is that your business? Parties and lunches? Is that how you got your name on the letterhead? Going to garden clubs?'

'Obviously, my client means the victim handled his sister-in-law's social calendar.'

'I think we both know what he meant, and that he's a misogynistic asshole, but we'll let that slide for now. Were you aware of any tension between your wife and the deceased?'

'No. I don't get into that sort of thing. But she attacked Tash. It's obvious.'

'Contrarily, it's impossible.' Eve took out another photo. 'As you see, there are ten feet, four inches between the deceased's body and Ms Quigley's. Just how did Catiana DuBois manage to bash your wife over the head with this lead crystal vase while she was dead, ten feet, four inches away?'

'Don't be stupid,' Copley snapped even as his lawyer ordered him to stay quiet. 'That bitch attacked Tash, Tash fought back. The bitch fell, hit her head. Clear self-defense. Then Tash tried to get out, get to me, and only made it that far.'

'Let's have some fun with that. You're already seeing it,' she said conversationally to McAllister. 'Catiana attacks your wife, smacks her upside the head with this vase – the vase that's here, cracked and bloody on the floor right beside your wife's unconscious body. Then, somehow, with a fractured skull, with a brain bleed, your wife manages to struggle with the deceased, drive her across the room, where she conveniently falls and kills herself on the hearth. *Then*, in this miracle of physical determination, your wife gets back across the room, neatly hits the mark where she was attacked, and drops.'

'She's a strong woman.'

'Her neurosurgeon agrees with you. She also says your creative scenario is impossible. Our reconstruction will back that up.'

Eyes on him, Eve leaned back, kept her voice, her body language almost casual.

'You argued with Catiana, you shoved her – like you shoved your golf buddy, Van Sedgwick, at your country club.'

'That's ridiculous. That's a lie. He slipped. I never—'

'Only you don't have a handy water trap in your living area, so this shove resulted in Catiana Dubois's fall, in her death.'

Eve angled forward, just a little, hardened her tone, just a little. 'Where did you go after? Did you panic, run off, trying to figure out how to cover it up? An accident, it had to look like an accident.'

She built the edge – harder, stronger – tapping her fingers faster, faster, on the crime scene photo.

'But when you came back in the room, Natasha had come in, had seen. She's in the way, damn it! You had to get her out of the way. To shut her up, just shut her up, so you picked up the vase, charged at her.'

'I was upstairs!' He shoved up, shook the table. 'I heard Tash scream, and I ran down to help her. She's my wife, you ignorant cunt.'

'JJ, stop! Sit down, and stop. My client has nothing more to say at this time.'

'Fine, let's hear what Natasha Quigley has to say.'

Eve set the mini recorder with its copy of the nine-one-one call on the table, ordered on.

She's dead! I think she's dead! Oh my God, Cate. It's . . . Wait, please. Oh God. This is Natasha Quigley at 18 Vandam. I need to report a — JJ! Oh, JJ, something terrible happened. JJ! What are you doing? JJ, stop, stop! Don't!

Copley stared at the recorder, mouth agape.

'You were too enraged to hear her.' Eve tapped the recorder. 'Too caught up to think. It was act. Act now.'

'That's a fake. It's a fake! She was on the floor when I ran in. She . . . there must have been someone else there. Someone else must have been there. Maybe he looked like me. She was upset. She . . . she wasn't talking to me. She was . . . calling for me so I'd come help her.'

'Maybe you need to hear it again.' Eve replayed, letting it run under Copley's increasingly hysterical rants.

'You're doing this. It's you, it's you! You have it in for me. I knew it the minute you came into that meeting. You're trying to frame me. Someone else was there. I was upstairs.'

'JJ, we're done,' McAllister said, all but physically holding him down in the chair. 'Not another word. Do you hear me?'

'Maybe it was more than rage, more than panic. Maybe you saw your chance. Kill her, kill them both, make it seem like they fought. It clears the path for you and Felicity.'

'I didn't . . . How do you know? . . . It was you! You're the reason Felicity moved out, you're the reason she won't answer her 'link. You bitch! I could kill you!'

'No handy blunt object.' Like Copley, Eve surged to her feet. She leaned in, leaned hard. 'Ziegler knew, blackmailed you, and it's never enough. It would never stop. You *made* it stop. Taught that ungrateful bastard a lesson. Catiana knew, wouldn't listen to reason. You lost your temper, shoved her. Then it's Natasha. It's time to finish it. Just finish it. So you fractured her skull. You thought you'd finished it, would have finished it, but the cop's at the door so fast, too fast.'

She kept going, raising her voice over his rants, his lawyer's shouts. 'Girl cop at your door, stupid cunt, what the hell does she know? But she gets in your way, she won't do what you tell her to do. You have to make your best pitch, it's how you make your living. But it won't work, Copley. It's all right here.'

She slapped her hand on the file. 'It's all right here. Ziegler.' She dug out the crime scene photo. 'Catiana.' Slapped hers beside it. 'Natasha.' Added the last. 'But you left Natasha breathing. And she's going to bury you.'

His face glowed red. His eyes literally bulged. Eve half expected him to just explode, spewing flesh, brains, and fury all over the room.

Instead, he collapsed, wheezing, with sweat slicking those bright red cheeks.

'Get a medic!' McAllister ordered, and leaped to kneel beside him.

Eve glanced toward the two-way glass, turned to the door, wrenched it open. In seconds Mira rushed in.

'I'm a doctor. Lieutenant, some water?'

'Shit. Mira, Dr Charlotte, entering Interview to treat suspect. Dallas, exiting Interview for—'

She broke off, took the bottle of water Roarke offered from the doorway.

'Correction, Dallas remaining in Interview.'

She cracked the water open, offered it to Mira.

'Slow your breathing, Mr Copley. Look at me now, you're having an anxiety attack. Slow your breathing. Sip some of this.'

'Can't breathe.' He wheezed, staring out with eyes the size of moons. 'Can't.'

'Slowly. You need to take slow breaths. Lieutenant, send for a medic.'

'Already done,' Roarke told Eve when she reached for her comm.

'We're going to get you some oxygen, Mr Copley. That will help. We're going to help you, and take you to the Infirmary.'

'His heart,' McAllister began.

'We'll run all necessary tests, but this is a severe anxiety attack.'

'Dying. Chest . . .'

'You're not dying,' Mira said calmly. 'Look at me. Mr Copley, look at me. I'm Dr Mira. I want you to look at me, hear my voice.' She signaled for the med kit when the medic ran in. 'Get his BP,' she murmured as she took out the oxygen mask, activated it. 'I'm going to put this over your nose and mouth. Look at me, JJ. I want you to take slow breaths once I do. Slowly.'

'Two-ten over one-ten, Doc. Benzodiazepine in the kit.'

'Let's wait a minute. JJ, I know your chest hurts, it's difficult to get a breath. It will pass. Take those breaths, slow. That's good, very good. You're going to feel some relief in a moment. Breathe in. Let's transport him down to the Infirmary.'

'Will do. BP one-ninety over ninety. It's leveling down.'

'No one talks to him outside of my presence.'

'Get a grip, McAllister,' Eve advised.

'You badgered him into a heart attack! Don't tell me to get a grip.'

'Ms McAllister, is it?' In that same calm tone, Mira shut the lawyer down. 'Your client hasn't had a cardiac incident but an anxiety attack, which is passing. We will, of course, examine, test, and treat him.'

'I want him taken to the hospital immediately, and examined by his own physician.'

'Not going to happen,' Eve countered, 'unless Dr Mira deems it necessary. Out here,' she ordered when McAllister started to protest.

She stepped out, moved several feet away from the room. 'Look, you and I both know the record will show he worked himself up into a rage that turned into a panic attack. Fricking apoplectic. Medical assistance was speedy, and medical treatment will continue. But he gets it in my house.'

'I'll get a court order for his transfer to an outside medical facility.'

'Try it, go ahead. The record and Mira's rep will hold. I'm taking him down for two murders and an attempted. I've got him cold, and his own wife's adding the ice. He had a fucking panic attack. She's been on the table getting her brain put back together for the last few hours, so don't try to twist it.'

'You will *not* speak to him again without medical clearance.'

Eve shrugged. 'I'll wait.' Eve angled her head. 'The other two partners are men, right?'

'I don't see how that's relevant.'

'And out of town for the holidays, unavailable tonight in any case. Otherwise, he wouldn't have you as his legal rep on this. He doesn't respect you. You and I both know it. He'll use you, until one of the male types gets here, but you're a placeholder to him.'

'You're insulting.'

'Me?' Eve watched another medical hustle a gurney toward Interview B. 'You've got a strange way of defining insulting.'

Eve waited until they'd wheeled him out, with McAllister striding alongside the gurney like a guard dog.

Mira stepped to Eve. 'I'll go, oversee the tests, but I'm confident he suffered a panic attack. His BP is in the safe range now, and he's breathing normally.'

'Sorry to mess up your evening.'

'Not at all. It's part of the job, isn't it? You won't be able to continue the interview tonight. I couldn't approve it, medically, and his lawyer will certainly do what she can to block it in any case.'

'Figured.'

'It was real. The panic attack. And that's something to consider. His reaction to the extreme stress was both physical and emotional. Ziegler's killer didn't panic.'

'Killing doesn't upset him as much as being pinned for it does.' But it left a little hole she'd need to fill in. 'He was trapped in there, with me. With the evidence. With the truth. He couldn't handle it.'

'It's certainly possible. I'll review his medical history to determine if he's experienced these attacks before or been treated for them.' Mira let out a breath of her own. 'He's an ugly little man, isn't he? Still, I'll treat him to the best of my capabilities, and unless the tests prove me wrong, he'll be clear for you to interview tomorrow. I'll send you a report.'

'Thanks.' Eve stood where she was a moment as Mira walked toward the glide. 'Fuck. I want coffee.'

'I could do with some myself,' Roarke told her, went with her to her office.

'I had him. I would've had him.' She fisted her hand. 'He wasn't listening to the lawyer – the *girl* lawyer. Tripping himself up with this story, then another. Somebody else in there who looked like him? I mean, Jesus.'

She dropped down at her desk, drank coffee, scowled. 'Panic attack. His eyes actually bulged out of his head. More like a temper tantrum, all respect to Mira. He wanted to go at me. If he'd had a weapon, he'd have used it.' She pushed up, paced the small office, while Roarke sat with his coffee in her miserable visitor's chair.

'He couldn't get that release, so he had the attack. Maybe, maybe. He couldn't release the rage in any way, so his body went whack. I should've asked Mira about that, for the medical/psych terms for that.'

'I can only agree with Mira. He's an ugly little man.'

'How do ugly little men get laid the way he apparently did?' Eve wondered. 'I'm going to contact Felicity, who apparently had the good sense to break it off. And I want to talk to the Schuberts. And check in with Morris.'

'No point in reminding me I can go home. I have an excellent memory. I'm with you, for the fun and fascination.'

'Your choice. I'm going to call Peabody off then. No need for her to come in. We'll hit Copley together tomorrow. Maybe her soft-pedal will keep him from going purple and flopping on the floor like a fish.'

She pulled out her 'link. It signaled in her hand. 'Dallas.'

'Nurse Vick, Lieutenant. Dr Campo authorized me to

tell you Ms Quigley is out of surgery. Her condition has been upgraded to serious, but stable. The patient requires rest and quiet for the next several hours. If you check in the morning, after eight, Dr Campo will be available, and can let you know if Ms Quigley is up to speaking with you.'

'Fair enough. Thanks for letting me know. I'll be there tomorrow.'

Eve clicked off. 'There's good news. If I can get her statement, I can wrap Copley up in it. Well.' She drained her coffee. 'Let's go ruin the Schuberts' holidays. Whatever that asshole Copley thinks, Dubois was more to them than the one who handled Martella's woman business.'

'You'd do better, as would I, with something more than popcorn in the system.'

'Maybe.' She fell into step with him. 'We could grab a slice after the morgue.'

He took her hand. 'See what I meant about fun and fascination? How many people could say just that?'

'All the many people who are cops.'

He laughed a little. She had him there.

20

A giggling Martella opened the door before Eve buzzed. Both she and Lance Schubert wore coats and scarves, and both had sparkles in their eyes.

Eve recognized the sparkle. While obviously on their way out the door, the couple had enjoyed a little pre-departure sex.

'Oh, Lieutenant, you just caught us.' Martella slipped her hand into her husband's. 'We're ridiculously late.'

'I'm sorry. We need to speak with you.'

'Can it wait until tomorrow?' Schubert asked. 'We should have left nearly an hour ago.'

Martella didn't quite manage to stifle a fresh giggle as she sent her husband another sparkling look. 'So rude.'

'I'm afraid it can't wait. It would be best if we go inside, sit down.'

'Oh, well. Another few minutes can't matter that much.' As she stepped back to let them in, Martella's gaze shifted from Eve to Roarke. 'It's Roarke, isn't it? It's nice to meet you. Martella Schubert.' She offered a hand. 'My husband, Lance.'

'I suppose this is some sort of official business. We can't offer you a drink?' Lance led the way into the living area, where he turned up the lights.

'No, but thank you.'

Roarke waited as Eve did while Martella slipped out of a silvery fur coat, tossed it aside. Beneath she wore a hot blue cocktail dress with ice-white diamonds. Schubert didn't bother to remove his coat, but sat with his wife.

'If this is about Ziegler,' he began, 'I don't know what else we can tell you. I won't say I'm sorry he's dead.'

'Lance!'

'There's no point in pretense, Tella. As far as I'm concerned, he got what he deserved. You've got a job to do,' he said to Eve. 'But we have our lives to live.'

'We're not here about Trey Ziegler, not directly. I have difficult news.' The most difficult, and best done quickly. 'I regret to inform you that Catiana Dubois was killed earlier this evening. I'm very sorry for your loss.'

'What? No.' Martella grabbed her husband's hand. 'That's a terrible thing to say. Cate's on a date, with Steven.'

'She was killed, and your sister injured tonight at the Vandam residence. John Jake Copley is in custody, charged with her murder and the attack on your sister.'

'Tash is hurt? No, no.' Color high, breath quick, Martella pushed to her feet. 'You've got something horribly mixed up. I spoke with Tash this afternoon.'

'Tella.' Schubert rose, put an arm around her, but his eyes stayed on Eve's. 'What happened?'

'But she's *wrong*.'

'Tella,' Schubert said again, gently, as he drew his wife back down to the sofa. 'What happened? Please.'

'Ms Dubois went to the Quigley-Copley residence. We believe subsequently a confrontation between her and Copley ensued. During which she fell, struck her head on the marble hearth, and was killed.'

'No. No. No.'

'Could I get you some water, Mrs Schubert?'

Schubert looked at Roarke. 'We've given the staff the evening off. If you wouldn't mind – the kitchen . . . '

'I'll find it. I am sorry,' he said to Martella.

'JJ wouldn't hurt Cate,' Martella insisted, but tears streamed down her face. 'Why would he do that? And Tash – she's hurt? Where is she? I need to go to her.'

'She was taken to the hospital, is under medical care. I'll give you the details, but, at the moment, she's sedated.'

'Please, I have to go to her. She needs me.'

'When we're done here, I'll arrange your transportation. I've spoken to the medicals personally. She's stable.'

'JJ wouldn't hurt her. He'd never – Lance, tell her.'

'I don't understand it. I played golf with JJ today. We got back around six. He had an exceptional round, wasn't upset, wasn't angry. Why do you think he did this? It doesn't make sense.'

'Ms Quigley called nine-one-one. On the record she can be heard shouting your brother-in-law's name, pleading with him to stop, before the 'link was dropped and damaged. An officer arrived on scene within minutes. Copley was alone in the house.'

'Someone broke in—'

'There's no sign of break-in,' Eve interrupted Schubert as Roarke came back with a tall, clear glass of water. 'The security cam shows Ms Dubois's arrival. The time stamp of her entrance into the residence is approximately ten minutes before her time of death.'

'She can't be dead. Oh, Lance, not Cate. Not our Cate.'

'It still doesn't make sense. JJ and Cate rarely interacted. Why would anyone think he . . . ' Schubert stiffened. 'Ziegler. It all goes back to Ziegler.'

'I know this is hard, but there are questions I have to ask.'

'Is it my fault? Is this my fault because I let him come here? I had sex with him.'

'You didn't have sex with him, Mrs Schubert,' Eve corrected. 'Ziegler drugged you and he raped you. That's not sex. And the person who killed Catiana and attacked your sister is at fault. No one else. Did you know Catiana intended to go to your sister's home this evening?'

'No. No. I thought she was going home to get ready for her date. I don't know why she went there.'

'You said she and Copley rarely interacted. Was there friction?'

'Not friction.' Schubert rose to shrug out of his coat, laid it over his wife's. 'JJ can be a dick with women, especially those he views as subordinates, but that sort of thing rolls

393

off of Catiana's back. I apologized to her more than once, but she'd just laugh it off.'

'Apologized for what?'

'Oh, he'd tell her to get him a drink, as if she were wait-staff. It wasn't so much what he said, but the tone. Master to servant. I've spoken to him about it a number of times, and he feigns ignorance. Since Cate could laugh it off, I let it go rather than stir up family conflict.'

'She didn't like him. She never actually said so,' Martella said thickly. 'She never would, but she didn't. She's family, too, Lance.'

'I know, Tella. I know.'

'You don't like him, either,' Eve observed. 'Either of you.'

'He's family,' Schubert said simply as his wife wept quietly on his shoulder. 'You don't get to choose. Tella and Tash are close. He's Tash's husband. I might consider him a bit of a dick, as I said, but I can't conceive of him doing any of this. You think he killed Ziegler, too.'

Rather than answer, Eve changed tacks. 'You and Catiana must have talked about Ziegler. What he'd done, his murder. And now that it's come out your sister and he had an intimate arrangement, you must have talked about that.'

'We were surprised, all of us,' Schubert confirmed. 'But then ... he's her type.'

'Oh, Lance.'

'I'm sorry, sweetheart, but good-looking users seem to be Tash's type.'

'Did the three of you talk about that situation today?'

'Actually, I didn't really talk to Cate today, just in passing as she was getting ready to go as I got back from Florida.'

'We did. Cate and I did.' Struggling with tears, Martella burrowed closer to her husband. 'I was a little angry that Tash hadn't told me, even when she knew how horrible I felt when I thought I'd cheated on Lance. I told Cate, and she calmed me down. She does that. She did . . . Oh God.'

'I'm going to get you some brandy.' Schubert kissed her temple before he rose.

'You and Catiana talked about the situation,' Eve prompted.

'We did. It was all so . . . so sordid, really. What happened to me. Cate and Lance, they've both been so supportive. And Tash, too. So I was upset when Tash finally told me she'd had an affair with Trey, and that JJ was having one with some stripper. I can understand, really, I can, how Tash would turn to Trey. A kind of revenge, I guess.'

'So Catiana knew the details.'

'I told her. She was like my sister, too. She's family. Her poor mom. Oh, Lance, her mother.'

'We'll be there for her.' He handed Martella a snifter, swirled his own. 'Catiana would never insert herself in Tash's marital business. Never.'

'Was she invited to the party at the Quigley-Copley residence the night Ziegler was killed?'

'Yes. Well, more, really. Tash asked her to help out with

the prep. Cate's a whiz with party preparations. So she was over there a good part of the day. Family,' she repeated. 'Tash and Cate were good friends, were close. She must have gone there tonight to talk to Tash about something. I don't know. I can't imagine the rest. I just can't. It doesn't seem real.'

'You knew about your sister-in-law's relationship with Ziegler,' she said to Schubert.

'I just found out.'

'And Copley? To your knowledge when did he learn about it?'

'I don't know. I don't know if he knew or not. He certainly didn't tell me, or show any signs of it. But then, I didn't know he was having an affair himself. It's not the way we live, Tella and I. We don't live that way.'

'My sister. Please, I need to see my sister.'

'Give me a minute.' Rising, Eve pulled out her comm, stepped out of the room.

'Do you ... do you know where Catiana is?' Martella asked Roarke. 'Can we see her? Can we do something? Anything?'

'I know the person who's looking out for her now. He's kind. Lieutenant Dallas is looking out for her now as well. It's a terrible thing that's happened. When terrible things happen to those we love, we couldn't ask for anyone more capable and determined than Lieutenant Dallas.'

'How could he do this to Cate, to Tash? I didn't even ask. I'm so turned around, turned inside out. What did he do to Tash? Did he hit her?'

'Has he hit her before?' Roarke asked.

'No! Of course not. I . . . ' A mixture of horror and grief flashed into her eyes. 'I don't know anymore. An hour ago I'd have said absolutely not. I'd never have believed it of him, even though he had a temper. And I'd have sworn she'd have told me if he ever had. Now I don't know. I don't know anything. I don't know what happened to my family.'

Eve came back in. 'I've arranged for officers to take you to the hospital, escort you to your sister's room. It's the quickest way.'

'Thank you. I . . . I want to change. I don't want to go to Tash dressed for a party. It feels wrong. I want to go see Cate's mother as soon as I can. Am I allowed to do that?'

'Of course.'

'And Steven. Steven Dorchester, the man she's been seeing. Does he know what happened?'

'I can have that taken care of.'

'They were in love, just the lovely beginning of it. She was happy. And she was so worked up about their date tonight.'

'How? Worked up how?'

'Oh, just in a hurry to get home, get ready. She just seemed worked up about it all of a sudden. Distracted. Excuse me, please. I need to change. I need to get to Tash.'

When she hurried out, Eve turned to Schubert. 'Did you notice this distraction?'

'I did, now that you mention it. I wish I'd paid more attention. I suppose that's always the way. You always think, Oh, we'll talk about that tomorrow. And then . . . I don't want Tella to be alone.'

'We'll let ourselves out,' Roarke told him.

'Gotta get this down,' Eve said when they went back outside. 'Need to work it around, sort it out. *Sordid*. It's a good word. Also *convoluted*.'

'Do you still want to go by the morgue?'

'Yeah, I need to do that. And I need to get this down.'

'Do that. I'm driving.'

He left her to her notes, her muttering, her short periods of silence, eyes closed, then more notes and muttering.

'When I was a kid,' she said abruptly, 'in the whole foster/state school cycle, I sometimes wished I had a sibling. Did you ever?'

'I had my mates. That was family for me.'

'*Mates*. You think of that word first as lovers, that two-person connection. But it's a good word for friends when you mean it. My sense is Tella and Catiana were mates. She loves her sister, feels close to her, but for the deep and down, she'd turn to the mate. She'd have told Catiana about what happened with Ziegler before she told her sister. And here's what else. Neither of them much like Copley. They'd golf with him, hang out, go to parties, have family deals, but neither of them would have considered confiding in him. They wouldn't have trusted him to keep a confidence. And it irked them he treated Catiana like a servant – but they sucked it up, mostly for the sister's sake.

'And still,' she said when they arrived at the morgue. 'Both of them claim, with apparent sincerity, they can't conceive of Copley hurting anyone.'

'I think, speaking of general population and not cops, or me, most can't conceive of someone they know well, are family with, killing anyone.'

'A lot of the general population are wrong.'

Eve strode briskly through the tunnel, and through the double doors of Morris's room.

He wore a clear protective cape over a steel blue suit with steel-gray chalk stripes, a braided tie that twined the two tones. His dark hair slicked into three slim, stacked tails. He sat at a counter working at a comp while some sort of hymn soared through his music system like angel wings.

'Sorry to pull you in.'

'Don't be. The nights are long; work shortens them. And her nights?' He rose, walked to where Catiana lay on a slab. 'Are over. Filling in for Peabody?' he asked Roarke with a faint smile.

'I am.'

'I spoke with our favorite detective shortly ago. Catiana's family is coming in soon. They don't want to wait to see her until tomorrow. I've enough time to soften the worst.' He indicated the head gash. 'She has no other injuries to speak of. The fall broke her nose, and as you can see, there's some minor lacerations, contusions on her knees, forearms. They would have been incurred in the fall.'

'She went down hard.'

'The depth of the wound would indicate considerable force. The secondary wounds on her limbs? She didn't have time to brace for the fall, to try to catch herself. She fell face-first, striking a solid edge.'

'Marble hearth.'

'Yes.'

'Tripped or shoved?'

'Hmm. It can be both. A slip's unlikely, as unless she'd been impaired in some way – and I found no illegals or alcohol in the blood – she should have attempted to catch herself. Her palms would show some impact. Again the depth and width of the gash indicate force. I'd speculate she was shoved from behind, lost her footing—'

'She was wearing those high, skinny heels.'

'Harder to regain balance as heels, by construction, lean the body forward. She went down hard and fast, and had the very bad luck to have a marble ledge in the way of the fall. You won't get Murder One on her. I found no sign of offensive or defensive wounds other than what I've told you.'

'No, I know it. Murder Two's enough. Still. Are you sure about her being shoved from behind?'

'Highest probability given the angle of the wound, the lack of other injuries to the body.'

'She turned her back on him. Maybe walking away, except the fireplace is on the other side of the room from the doorway to the foyer. But she turned her back.'

'Pacing.'

Eve glanced at Roarke. 'What?'

'Pacing. You do that when you're thinking or upset. Stride away, back and away.'

'Huh. Yeah. She was upset, had gone there without telling her boss – and friend. Distracted. Got a date with the guy she's in love with, but upset and distracted enough to stop off there first. Talking, pacing, and telling him – speculatively – something she's figured out or knows that could implicate him with Ziegler. That's what plays for me. And, like with Ziegler, he goes with the raging impulse of the moment. In this case, he pushes her. She falls hard and fast, and she's dead. Blood coming fast, too. Head wound, you always get plenty of blood.'

Eve paced now, and the act of it made Roarke smile. 'He left the room, had to leave the room or the wife would never have gotten so far on the nine-one-one call. Does he hear her? Maybe she screamed. People do when they walk in on blood and a body. So he rushes back in, sees her. And that rage is still pumping, so he goes after her. It's what plays.'

'And fairly tidily,' Morris commented.

'Yeah, it's the fairly I have to eliminate.'

'It's going to be difficult for her family – the holidays. Difficult enough,' Morris continued, 'to get through holidays

401

after a loss, but when the loss is so closely connected to them, harder still.'

Hesitating, Eve slipped her hands into her pockets. 'If they have any questions, you can tell them to contact me.'

'I will, but I should be able to answer most.'

'Okay, well. Listen, if you don't have any plans for Christmas, you could hang with us.'

Morris looked at her. His eyes darkened a moment – a war of emotions. Then he crossed to her. 'You won't mind,' he said to Roarke, and laying his hands on Eve's shoulders, kissed her cheeks, one then the other. 'You don't need to worry about me.'

'It's not that. It's just . . . we're pretty loose that day. Depending. Right?' she said, appealing to Roarke.

'We are. And no,' he said to Morris. 'I don't mind at all.'

'I'm spending the day with my parents, and some other family. I plan to leave tomorrow, early afternoon, if possible.'

'Good. That's good.' Eve left her hands in her pockets, not sure what else to do with them. 'Have a good one, Morris.'

'And you. Both of you.' He looked back at Catiana. 'And we'll all do our best by her.'

She worked on the drive home. She'd forgotten about dinner, Roarke thought, but he'd see she got food – even if it was that slice of pizza – once they were home.

He found he wanted home – symbol and sanctuary. So much loss in one night, so much rage and grief. And all, from what he could see, generated from one man. Trey Ziegler's greed had spread ripples of betrayal, fear, blood, and murder.

Lost trust, lost love, lost joy, lost life.

So he wanted home, even though those losses would follow them.

'Mira reports severe anxiety attack as believed. No other issues, and no reason Copley can't be interviewed tomorrow.' She frowned as they wound up the drive. 'The lawyer will try to block. I may need to pull Reo in, block the block. I want to finish that fucker off. Check on Quigley, because I want to talk to her first thing in the morning, toss whatever she tells me at Copley.'

She got out of the car, looked up at the sky for a moment. No stars, she noted, no moon. A cold rain was coming.

'If they hadn't had sex, they'd have been gone when we got there, had another few hours without knowing they'd lost someone they loved. The Schuberts.'

'I'm aware. The grief would still come, Eve, inevitably. And the fact they'd been together shows they're not letting what happened with Ziegler divide them, mar their relationship. They'll get through this easier because they're together.'

'She's disappointed in her sister,' Eve added as they went inside, started up. 'She won't let it get in the way, or not for long, but she's disappointed not just because Quigley didn't tell her she'd paid Ziegler for sex, but because Quigley cheated on Copley. She doesn't have much respect for Copley under it all, but my sense is she has a lot for marriage – for the promises made.'

'And Quigley doesn't.'

'The second time – we know of – she's cheated. She doesn't deserve to get her head bashed in over it, but she doesn't earn a lot of respect, either.'

In her office, still wearing her coat, she walked around her board. 'If she'd been straight with me from the start, maybe things wouldn't be as bad as they are. Maybe I wouldn't be moving Catiana's photo to victim status, and she wouldn't be in the hospital. Martella might come to think that, and if she does, it's going to crack their relationship, too.'

'Fucking sex and money,' she muttered.

'Both of which can be enormous pluses as well as motives for murder. We need to eat.'

'What? Oh, we were going to stop for a slice. We forgot.'

'You may have, but I thought we'd have it here, at home.'

'Even better.' She'd hauled him all over the city, she thought, looking at death. 'I'll get it.'

'Deal with Reo, set up your block with our favorite APA. I'll take care of it.'

'Roarke? A whole shitload of things are better because we're together.'

'Truer words,' he said, and went into the kitchen.

She ate. She contacted Reo, talked to Peabody, checked

on Quigley's status – stable, still out, sister and brother-in-law by her side – checked on Copley. Sedated, in a cage.

After another review of her notes, she streamlined a report. She studied her board, ran probabilities. And to eliminate any possibilities, took a good look at Catiana Dubois's financials.

Pretty generous salary, to her mind, but probably not out of line, considering who she worked for, and their relationship. Lived within her means, saved up for rainy days.

Why did rainy days require more money than dry ones? she wondered. Really, how much did an umbrella cost?

When her mind wandered, she pulled it in again, rubbed the back of her aching neck.

She had Copley. She had him cold, but it all just nagged at her.

Ziegler to Quigley – sex for money. To Copley – money for silence. Then to Martella. Was that Ziegler's shot at Copley, or just another conquest? Why do the sister of a paying client? Had he just been that arrogant?

Not impossible.

He'd hit on Catiana, too – a close family connection.

She shut her eyes, tried to work through it.

The next thing she knew, Roarke was carrying her out of the office.

'I'm awake, I'm awake.'

'You weren't. Give it a rest.'

'I was working stuff out. He hit on all the women – the

Quigley-connection women. Was it to give Copley a jab? Sure you take me golfing at the club, but you make sure I know I'm the help. Guess what, fucker? I'm doing your wife. I did your sister-in-law. I'd do your sister-in-law's best pal, but she's a lesbian. Except not. Catiana's connected to both. I checked her financials, but maybe—'

'No other accounts, no secret money hidden away. I looked.'

'You did?'

'I did.' He set her on the bed. 'Anticipating you.'

'Oh.' She watched him, with sleepy affection, as he took off her boots. 'It didn't feel right anyway, but you've got to think about it.'

'Suspicious minds do, which equal yours and mine. Now, we're both going to turn off those suspicious minds so we can put them to work for us tomorrow.'

She peeled off her clothes, didn't bother with a night-shirt. That took too much energy.

'Do you need a suspicious one tomorrow?'

'I need one every day – yours and mine,' he repeated and slid in beside her.

'It's after midnight.'

'Well after.'

'So it's Christmas Eve.'

'It is indeed.'

'I'm going to wrap this up by tomorrow afternoon, then we'll have ours, right?'

'We'll have ours.' When she stroked his cheek he drew

her in and, knowing how to lull her, rubbed her back lightly until she dropped away.

They'd have theirs, he thought, but for a moment he saw Catiana lying in her own blood. Others, no matter the justice, would grieve.

He pressed his lips to Eve's hair, drew in her scent, and let it lull him to sleep as well.

21

In the morning, Eve got out early and still the traffic was vicious. The cold rain came, as predicted, and brought a bonus round of icy sleet that sizzled like frying meat when it hit the pavement and slicked the roads.

She watched a guy – she assumed male though he was wrapped up like an Arctic explorer in a hooded parka – make a dash for a glide-cart, slip and land solidly on his back, where he wobbled like an upturned turtle.

While the cart vendor – probably sensing a sale – clomped over to help him up, a skinny guy wearing a grimy cap with grimier earflaps reached into the cart and helped himself to some bags of chips and a soft pretzel he shoved into the pockets of his even grimier trench coat.

Spotting the thief, the vendor gave chase, dropping the Arctic guy so he once again wobbled and flopped.

The short vignette on street life entertained her during the red light.

She watched people slip and slide, cars fishtail as they took a turn too fast, listened to the harsh music of horns blasting when other vehicles didn't move fast enough to suit. Overhead, over all, an ad blimp blasted frantically through the dull gray sky, announcing THE LAST CHANCE! THE FINAL HOURS! so that Christmas Eve in New York took on the aura of the apocalypse.

Since the weather seriously sucked and Peabody's apartment was nearly on the way to the hospital, Eve arranged to pick up her partner. Five minutes out, she sent Peabody a text.

Pulling up in five. I wait, you walk.

When she did pull up, she glanced up at her old apartment windows – currently Mavis and family's windows – and found them outlined with festive green and red lights. They shined happily against the cold, gray rain.

She imagined them up there, maybe dealing with breakfast, the kid jabbering, Mavis laughing, Leonardo beaming at 'his girls'.

They'd carved out a good life, she mused. A colorful one, by anyone's standards, but a good, solid life. Who'd have thought, only a few Christmases ago, either of them would have a real home, and all that went with it?

Even as she thought it, she spotted Leonardo at one of the lighted windows – hard to miss with his big frame draped in a robe swirled with psychotic rainbow ribbons. On his hip Bella, all sunshine curls, bounced – and, yes, jabbered. Mavis slipped into view, and under Leonardo's free arm.

409

Nice, Eve thought, a nice little scene of home life in what had once been little more than a place to work and sleep.

Then she watched another scene as Peabody came out. Strutted out, Eve thought. Oh Jesus, what had they done?

Pink coat, pink boots, a multicolored cap – heavy on the pink – with a fuzzy pink ball on top.

Peabody got in the car with a *whoosh* of cold air and rain. 'It could snow! They're saying no way, but I think maybe. Wouldn't it be sweet if it snowed? Even though we're heading out tonight, it would be sweet.'

'You're not allowed to strut.'

'Huh?'

'You can walk,' Eve continued as she pulled away from the curb. 'You can stride or clomp. You can run in pursuit. You can hobble if wounded. In certain circumstances you can stroll. But you are not allowed to strut. Cops don't strut.'

'I was strutting?'

'You look like some sort of pink candy with a fuzzy ball on top. Strutting pink candy. The strutting ceases immediately.'

'Pink candy.' Instead of the insult Eve intended, Peabody appeared pleased. 'I love my coat. Love, love my pink magic coat. It makes me feel pretty. Sexy and strong and styling. Therefore I strut.'

'Well, stop it or . . . Crap, is that Drunk Santa currently mooning passing traffic?'

'Wow, that's some ugly ass he's got there. It *is* Drunk

Santa. Oh, please, do we have to stop? Think of the smell. Fear it.'

'We can't leave that ugly ass hanging out on Ninth Avenue.' Resigned, Eve started to pull over, then spotted two hustling beat cops. Pitying them, she kept going.

'It's a Christmas miracle,' Peabody said, reverently.

'Why do people do that? Why? Why dress up like an icon – which I don't get anyway. He's a fat guy with a big white beard in a strange red suit who wants kids sitting on his lap. Kids should be afraid, but instead we make him an icon. Then assholes dress up like him and wave their ugly asses at traffic. What do they get out of it?'

'On a morning like this? A cold, wet ass and a few hours in the drunk tank.'

'True, but somehow that's not enough. Maybe if they played those poppy, jingling Christmas songs on an endless loop in the tank it would be enough. Maybe.'

'That has to be against the Geneva Convention.'

'And still.'

After parking in the hospital's underground lot, they rode the elevator up to six. Eve wondered how many sick germs floated around like invisible gnats, just looking for someone to land on.

The woman in the sixth-floor lobby glanced at Eve, nodded in recognition, buzzed her through. Inside, Eve snagged the first nurse she found.

'NYPSD. Lieutenant Dallas, Detective Peabody. We need to talk to Natasha Quigley.'

'She's Dr Campo's. Let me page her, then—'

There was a dramatic crash from a nearby room, followed by wailing.

'I don't want that *slop!* I want to go home.'

'The fun never ends,' the nurse said wearily. 'Henry, it's Ms Gibbons again. And you got the short straw.' The nurse took a handheld out of her tunic pocket, keyed in the page.

'Can you give us Quigley's status?'

'I can tell you she had a quiet night, and was taken down for tests early this morning. It's better if you speak to Dr Campo – and there she is. Dr Campo, the cops are here about Suite 600.'

Eve shook hands with a short woman wearing a white tunic over black pants. Her hair sprang out in short, dark curls around a thin, long-jawed face. Her sharp green eyes assessed Eve, then Peabody.

'I knew the Icoves,' she said in a brisk, no-nonsense tone. 'Both of them.'

'Me, too. Briefly.'

'Didn't like them, never did. Like them less now. That said, our Ms Quigley is very lucky. Without quick medical intervention she'd be facing a much harder road – if she'd lived. I don't suppose you want all the medical jargon any more than I want a bunch of cop talk. Comes to a trial, I can give all of that. Now, I'll tell you she's lucky. No brain damage, and no reason she shouldn't make a full recovery. Her memory's a little spotty, and she's experiencing occasional double vision, but that's not uncommon in these cases. I'm going to tell you what I expect you already know I'm going to tell you. She's been through a physical and emotional ordeal, requires rest and as much calm as possible. You can talk to her, but keep it brief. If she becomes overly upset, that's it.'

'Good enough.'

'Word is, her husband whacked her.'

'He's in custody.'

'I had one of those once – a husband. Instead of whacking him, and it was tempting, I divorced him.'

'The simple reason you're not in custody.'

'Still wish he was. Okay, this way. We see too much domestic bullshit in here,' Campo said as she led them down a wide corridor. 'Not as much as you, I expect, but plenty. Makes me wonder why people don't need to take a psych test before they get a marriage license.'

Campo's demeanor changed from leaning toward irascible to gentle as she walked into 600.

The scent of roses from the huge bouquet across from the bed nearly overpowered the sticky scent of hospital.

Natasha lay in the bed, the head lifted to support her in an incline. Pristine white bandages covered the right side of her head and wrapped around her forehead, but didn't quite cover all the purpling bruising. Her hair lay over her left shoulder in a loose braid. Without enhancement, with the strain of the last hours, she looked older and more delicate.

Beside her, Martella sat in a roomy sleep chair, her sister's hand in hers, eyes exhausted.

'Doctor — oh, the police already. She's sleeping. She needs to sleep.' Moving slowly, Martella released her sister's hand, rose to walk quietly across the room that more closely resembled a good hotel suite than a hospital. 'Can you come back? She's just had all these tests. She's worn out. Lance ran out to get her some Greek yogurt, some berries. You said that was all right?'

'Yes, that's fine,' Campo told her, patted Martella's shoulder as she moved over to study the numbers on the machines. 'She's stable. Martella, you should get some rest yourself, and some food.'

'I will. I will. But I don't want to leave her until—'

'Tella.'

Natasha's voice, barely more than a whisper, had Martella rushing back to the bedside. 'I'm right here. Don't worry, I'm right here.'

'Ms Quigley.'

'Who is that?' Natasha turned her head. Her right eye showed more bruising and severe swelling from the blow. 'Oh. Yes. I know you.'

'Are you up to answering some questions?' Eve asked her.

'I can try.'

'You don't need to tire yourself, Tash,' Martella began.

'It's all right. I want to know what happened. It's all so confusing. Catiana? Is Cate really dead? It seems like a terrible dream.'

'What do you remember?'

414

'I was upstairs. I was upset, still a little upset from when you'd been there before. JJ was home. Yes, that's right, he'd come home. He'd been ... Where had he been?'

'Golfing,' Martella reminded her. 'With Lance.'

'That's right. Yes. What did we talk about? I'm not sure. I just can't quite remember. Then ... I was downstairs. Was I looking for him? I went into the living area, and – and I saw ... I saw Cate.'

Tears blurred her eyes, clogged her voice. 'I saw her by the fireplace. There was blood, so much blood. I ran over. Did I scream? I don't know. I ran over, I turned her over, but it was too late. So much blood, and her eyes ... Oh, Tella.'

'Ssh, ssh.' Martella pressed kisses to her sister's hand. 'Don't think about it anymore.'

'You turned her over?' Eve persisted.

'Yes. I think ... It's all so cloudy and in pieces. I think I did – trying to help her, but ... I think I screamed. In my head, my head was full of screams. I needed to get help. I think I tried to get help. Did I scream for JJ? I think ...'

'Do you remember calling nine-one-one?'

'I ... Yes!' She struggled up a little higher in the bed. 'Yes, yes. I called for help. Oh thank God, I called for help. I called for help, but ...'

Her eyes filled with more tears, more confusion. And fear. 'Something happened. Something ... someone.' Her free hand lifted to the bandages.

'Who struck you, Ms Quigley?'

415

'I . . .' The drenched eyes evaded. 'I can't remember. It's not clear. I can't say because it's not clear. I can't remember.'

'Ms Quigley, we have the nine-one-one recording.'

Her gaze darted to Eve, away again. 'I can't remember. I don't want to talk about this anymore. I'm tired. Tella, I'm tired.'

'You have to leave now,' Tella said. 'You have to leave her alone now.'

'Don't upset yourself, Ms Quigley.' Dr Campo moved in. 'You did very well. You get some more rest, and I'll be back to check on you later. Lieutenant, Detective, that's all for now.'

'You don't need to be afraid anymore,' Peabody said before they left the room. 'You're safe now.'

In response, Natasha choked out a sob, turned her head away.

Unsatisfied, Eve glanced back toward 600. 'Why not tell us? She's lying. She remembers. Why not just tell us?'

'Confused, conflicted, scared. Here you're trying to save your marriage – you know you've both screwed up, but you're trying to patch it back together. And in one big reveal, you find out your husband's a killer, and he tries to kill you. Add in scandal, embarrassment, media frenzy.'

Eve added annoyance to dissatisfaction. 'What kind of world does she live in where a woman's *embarrassed* her husband tried to kill her? Where scandal – which is inevitable considering Catiana's in the morgue – weighs over telling the cops. "Holy shit, my husband tried to kill me. Lock him up and protect me".'

'An old money world, I guess.' They rode back down to the garage. 'She's been through a big trauma, and maybe – yeah, she's lying – but maybe she's also convinced herself she's really not clear, not sure. She's going to come around when she's steadier.'

'Either way.' Eve shook her head. 'We keep tabs on her, regular updates on her status. If they even think about the possibility of releasing her, we know about it.'

'Pretty good bet she's going to spend Christmas in the hospital. At least it's a swank room.'

'Hospital's a hospital. We hit Copley, because if she doesn't come around, it's going to stick up the works. Let's pull Reo in, get the legal take on worst case, but we hit him and we work him, and we tie this up.'

But when she walked into the Homicide bullpen, Jenkinson hailed her. 'Yo, LT. There's a guy waiting in the lounge – Steven Dorchester. He wants to talk to you. Says he's Catiana Dubois's boyfriend.'

'Okay. I'll take him,' she said to Peabody. 'Set up the interview, contact Reo. Might as well give Mira the heads-up, too.'

She stood for a moment, studying a couple fake ears of corn now hanging on the pathetic tree.

'Isn't the corn thing Thanksgiving? Why is fake corn hanging on that tree?'

'For Kwanza,' Jenkinson told her. 'Trueheart said it's one

of the seven symbols. He looked it up. We're all-inclusive in Homicide, 'cause whatever your race, color, or creed, you can get dead.'

'We should write that up under a Merry Christmas sign.'

Eve made her way to the lounge with its scatter of tables, and vending machines. Somebody cursed at one, gave it a punch with the side of his fist. Knowing she wasn't the only one to war with those machines cheered her right up.

She scanned a few cops, a couple talking quietly with civilians. Then the man sitting alone, staring down at his own folded hands.

She crossed to him. 'Mr Dorchester.'

He looked up at her out of red-rimmed eyes. 'Yes. I'm Steven Dorchester. You're Lieutenant Dallas.'

'That's right. I'm very sorry for your loss, Mr Dorchester.'

'Steven. It's Steven. I ... keep thinking I'm going to wake up and it's all going to be a terrible dream. Or it's just some horrible mistake. But ... '

He went back to staring at his hands when Eve sat across from him.

Strong face, she thought, though the strain showed. Longish hair, a few reddish streaks through the dark brown, a single silver stud through his right earlobe, a trio of stars inked on the back of his right wrist.

Something artistic about him, she thought. Someone good with his hands. She speculated on it, considered he

418

and Catiana would have made an attractive couple, while she waited for him to compose himself and speak.

'There's nothing I can do. I'm going over to see her family this morning, be with them, but there's nothing any of us can do. She's gone.' He looked up again. 'I know there's probably not much you can tell me, but if there's anything . . . I'm going to be with her family.'

'I can tell you I'll do everything I can to see that the person responsible for taking her from you, from her family, who took her life, is punished to the full extent of the law. There may be something you can do to help.'

'Anything. I'll do anything.'

'When did you last see or speak with Catiana?'

'Yesterday morning, when she left for work. We went to a party Saturday night, and she stayed at my place. We were . . . we were going out last night, then going back to my place again. Sort of an early Christmas, just the two of us, because we were going to the parents' tonight. Mine, then hers. We were spending Christmas Eve at her mother's, the night, I mean. They have a big deal, so we were staying, and we were going to have our own little Christmas last night. But . . .'

'Can you tell me if she was upset about anything? Worried about anything?'

'No. She was great. We were great. I . . .' He reached in his pocket, took out a pretty little box. 'I made this for her. I do some silverwork, and I made this for her. I was going to give it to her last night.'

419

He opened the box. Inside a small, intricate key hung on a delicate chain.

'It's beautiful work.'

'It's the symbol – the key. I was going to ask her to move in with me. We said we were taking it slow, but I wanted her to move in with me. So, the key. For her.'

'How did this happen?'

'When I have all the details, I promise I'll tell you. Did she talk to you about Trey Ziegler?'

'Yeah. *Jerk*. That was her word for him. He put some moves on her. She gave him the brush-off, so he spread it around she went for girls. Like if she brushed him off she didn't go for men. Didn't bother her. Why would it? I went by the gym a couple times, just to give him the needle. Probably shouldn't have.'

'You talked about his murder.'

'Yeah. It shook her up some. She didn't like him, but still.' He stroked the key, still in its box, with his finger. 'She has a soft heart.'

'Did she talk to you about who she thought may have killed him?'

'We played that game, you can't help it, right? And after – when it came out what he did to Tella, and Cate said he did the same with other women, we figured one of them found out and did it. Or one of their husbands or friends, you know. It's why she went to work on Sunday, even though she could've taken the day off. She wanted to be around for Tella.'

'You didn't talk to her on Sunday after she left for work?'

'No. We were supposed to meet at eight for dinner, at this place we like, and she didn't show up. I tried to reach her, but she didn't answer her 'link. I went by her place, but she wasn't there. I even went to the Schuberts' place, but they weren't there, either. Then her sister … Her sister tagged me, and she told me. And everything just stopped. Everything stopped. I don't know if it'll ever start again.'

'Do you want some coffee?'

'No, thanks, no. I don't think I could swallow anything.'

'Steven, can you tell me how she felt about Natasha Quigley, JJ Copley?'

'She got along fine with them. She was really tight with Tella, and she and Tella's sister got along fine. She didn't much like the husband. She said he was a little bit of a prick.' He smiled a little. 'She had opinions. She'd help Ms Quigley out now and then.'

'Like for her holiday party.'

'Yeah, like that. I got to go, and it was okay. A little stiff for me, if you know what I mean. But she'd help out like that now and then. With parties, sending out invites, or thank-yous if Ms Quigley was slammed. She didn't mind. She liked the job.'

'Okay.'

'I didn't help any.'

'You did. You've given me a good picture of her. Who she was, how she was. I hope it helps you to know she matters to me. Getting justice for her matters.'

'Did you ever wish you could turn back the clock? Just one day.' His red-rimmed eyes, swimming with tears, bored into hers. 'Even just a few hours. If I'd said, "Please don't go to work today" – or "Hey, I'll go with you". Something. It wouldn't have happened. Did you ever wish you could do that, just turn the clock back?'

'All the time.'

When he left, Eve went into her office to shake off his grief. It wouldn't help in interview.

'Knock, knock.' Cher Reo walked in. The pretty blonde with Southern roots might have looked delicate, but Eve knew she could be an Amazon in court. 'I was in the building, keeping close in case. Give me coffee and we'll talk John Jake Copley.'

'Help yourself. You got the report. No sign of break-in, just him in the house with dead body and unconscious wife. Wife's nine-one-one call that clearly speaks his name.'

'I listened to it myself.' With her coffee, Reo walked over, sat in Eve's desk chair. 'I'm not sitting in that awful visitor's chair. You talked to the wife this morning?'

'She's awake, maybe a little confused yet.' Eve relayed the gist of the interview. 'She won't pull the trigger,' Eve finished. 'Won't confirm Copley struck her.'

'Could be a little problem.'

'The nine-one-one recording—'

'Oh, we'll use the hell out of it, but if I were his lawyer I'd use it, too. I'd claim the victim was in shock, in fear, was

422

calling *for* her husband, was then attacked, and this unknown assailant fled.'

'How – the cam clearly shows—'

'Out a window, into a hidey-hole until he or she could slip out undetected. It's weak, Dallas, and I can promise we'll tear it to shreds, but it could be a little problem. A confession eliminates that little problem. We'd deal the murder to Man One—'

'Bullshit!'

'Listen. Man One on Dubois, assault with intent on the wife. He does twenty-five – no parole. Another ten concurrent on the wife. Again, if I were his lawyer, I'd take it. Saves a trial, eliminates the possibility of life in a cage. Twenty-five years is a good long time.'

'Catiana Dubois won't get another twenty-five.'

'Nothing we do changes that. But consider how a man like Copley will deal with a quarter of a century in prison.'

He'd cry and wail and blubber like a little girl – but it wasn't enough. 'I'll get him on Ziegler, too.'

'If you get him on Ziegler, deal's out.' To illustrate, Reo flicked her fingers in the air. 'That's two murders and one attempted. Murder Two on both, but the addition of the knife in the heart? The jury will be appalled, I promise you. But you have to get him, and right now, you don't have him.'

'The day's young.'

'You can tag me until eight. After eight, I'm off the

clock and I mean it, until December twenty-sixth. Tie him up before that, we'll put a bow on it. Otherwise, have yourself a merry little Christmas. I mean that, too.' She rose, patted the bag Eve had given her. 'I love this.'

When she sauntered out, Eve kicked her desk. 'Man One, my ass!' She thought of Steven Dorchester and the key he'd made, put in a pretty little box. Fuck Man One.

She strode out. 'Peabody! With me. Let's do this,' she said as Peabody scrambled up from her desk.

'His lawyer's not here.'

'Then she better hustle.'

Eve pushed open the door of Interview B. 'Dallas, Lieutenant Eve, Peabody, Detective Delia, entering interview with Copley, John Jake.'

'I'm not talking to you without my lawyer.'

'Then don't talk.' Eve tossed down her files, played the nine-one-one call, hit replay, hit it again.

On the third play he broke, just a little. 'She was calling for me, calling for my help. Anybody who hears it will know that.'

'Really? I heard it, that's not what I know. Peabody?'

'Didn't sound like that to me. Just the opposite.'

'Of course, that's just the two of us. We could take a poll,' Eve suggested to Peabody. 'I'm betting people who hear it — like say a jury — hear what we hear. Just like they'll hear what we heard when we talked to Natasha this morning.'

'You talked to her? What did she say?'

Eve shook her head. 'He wants us to answer his questions, Peabody, but he won't answer ours. Doesn't strike me as what you'd call equitable.'

'I want to know what she said! Does she know I'm in here, in this place? Does she know what you're trying to pull?'

He banged both fists on the table. Working himself up to another tantrum, Eve thought, and turned casually to Peabody.

'So, when does your shuttle leave?'

Peabody smiled. 'We're catching one at six, if we can clear things. But we'll catch a later one if we have to. How about you and Roarke? Big dinner out? Quiet evening at home?'

'You tell me what she *said!*'

'Now, JJ, you want to watch that anxiety and blood pressure. My partner and I are just passing the time until your lawyer gets here.'

'Forget the lawyer. I want to know what Natasha said.'

'Are you waiving your right to have your legal representative present during interview?'

'Fine, yes. What did she say to you?'

'Let the record show Mr Copley has voluntarily waived said right. What did she say?' Eve turned straight around to face him, smiled. 'She said the son of a bitch tried to kill me. Lock him up and toss the key.'

'You're lying. You're a lying bitch.'

'Now, JJ, you've got to expect her to be a little upset

425

when you bash her in the head, when she's spending her Christmas in the hospital.'

'I never touched her. I never hit her. I was upstairs. I've already told you. I was upstairs. I had the game on. I fell asleep.'

'Fell asleep? That's a new one. Are you going to keep doing these add-ons? Because I can tell you, the story's not getting better.'

'Oh, I don't know, Dallas.' Peabody bopped her shoulders. 'You've got to give him a little credit for trying to add some texture to the overall bullshit.'

'I drifted off.' He set his jaw. 'I played eighteen holes, shot a sixty-eight. That's four under par.'

'Wow. Aren't you special?' Peabody commented.

'Just shut your mouth, you ignorant twat.'

'Aw, Dallas, he called me a twat. How come you get to be a bitch, but I only get to be a twat.'

'It's the rank,' Eve told her. 'You'll make bitch one day.'

'Thanks. That means a lot to me.'

'I'll make you both sorry. I'll make you both pay.'

'Blah, blah, blah.' Eve levered back, smirked at him. 'Do you want to brag about your golf game, exchange insults, or add more texture to your bullshit story? It's all the same to us.'

'Goddamn it, I was upstairs. I heard her scream. It took me a minute, maybe a couple minutes, because I thought maybe it was a dream. I was asleep, a little groggy. I got up, and I called for her, and I ran out. I ran downstairs.'

'Why downstairs?'

'Because that's where the scream came from.'

'If you were asleep, how do you know where it came from?'

'I just knew.' He slapped both fists on the table. 'I ran in, and I saw her on the floor, and I saw the other one – Tella's girl.'

'Tella's *girl*?'

'That's right. And I heard something.' His eyes flickered away. 'Like somebody running maybe. Maybe a door closing.'

'Seriously? Now there's running footsteps and closing doors?'

'That's some rich bullshit texture,' Peabody put in. 'You've got to admire it.'

Eve snorted out a laugh for form. 'Right. So, JJ, why didn't you mention these mysterious running footsteps and closing doors to the responding officer? To me in previous interview? Or, to any fucking body before this moment?'

He swiped beads of sweat from his forehead, more from his upper lip. 'I didn't think about it at the time because I could only think about my wife. I had to help Tash.'

'How? Not by calling for help.'

'I didn't have time! I was in shock, and then the police were at the door, and everything happened so fast. I was upstairs when somebody killed that woman and hurt Tash. I want to talk to my wife, goddamn it. She's confused and scared, and she has to be worried about me.'

'Her worry? That you'll try to kill her again. She's done with you, JJ. She's done, Felicity's done. You've got nothing and no one.'

'You leave Felicity out of it.' To Eve's shock, tears swam into his eyes. 'You told her lies about me, didn't you? She left me! You told her lies, and she left me. I love her!'

'Who? Your wife or Felicity.'

'I . . . ' He pulled himself in. 'Both. In different ways.'

'The different ways where you tell your wife you've broken it off, and you tell Felicity your wife doesn't understand you?'

'You don't know anything about it.'

'Christ, JJ, do you think we haven't had your type in here before? How many times, Peabody?'

'Couldn't count them.' Peabody cast her dark eyes to the ceiling, shook her head. 'But they all think they're originals.'

'They're so damn simple. Here's how it went. You bragged to Ziegler about the hot dancer you had on the side. He blackmailed you. You finally had enough, even though you'd been paying him off with money you extorted from your wife.'

'That's ridiculous.'

'We found the other accounts, JJ. Offshore, shell corporations. You're an amateur. Ziegler kept a book. Your name's in it. The money you paid him is on record.'

Eve pushed up. 'You went to his apartment to tell him you were done, to show him who was boss. He worked in

428

a gym, for God's sake. Who did he think he was? But he wouldn't let you off the hook. You lost your temper – you're good at it. You picked up the trophy and you struck him, struck him again.'

'No panic attack that time,' Peabody added. 'Not when you'd finally solved the problem. It felt good. It felt like something you should have done a lot sooner. Without him in the way, you were free and clear.'

'So you got creative. You're a creative guy. You dragged him onto the bed, got a knife out of his kitchen. You wrote a funny little message – you're good at that, too – and you pinned it on his chest with the knife.'

'I didn't do any of that.' His breathing shortened; sweat slicked his face. 'That's crazy. I was never there. I never went there. I want to talk to my lawyer. I demand to talk to my lawyer.'

'Peabody, get him some water. Take it down, JJ. Take it down before you end up in the Infirmary again. Believe me, I've got all the time in the world for this.'

'I don't have anything more to say until I've talked to my lawyer.'

'No problem.'

She waited while Peabody brought in a cup of water.

His hand shook as he drank.

Eve stepped over to Peabody, spoke quietly. 'Get a uniform to sit on him in case he has one of those fits again. Let's find out what's holding up the lawyer. We've got him on the ropes. We need to finish him off. I want to check something. Dallas, exiting Interview,' she said for the record.

Back in her office, she tried Felicity's 'link. Her stomach clutched when an older woman answered.

'Yes?'

'This is Lieutenant Dallas, NYPSD. I need to speak with Felicity Prinze.'

'This is her mother. She's not talking to you. You're that friend of that Copley person.'

The muscles in Eve's stomach loosened again at the use of present tense. 'No, ma'am, I am not his friend. I have Copley in custody.'

'For what?'

'For murder.'

'Oh my God. Oh my God! My little girl.'

'Has she been harmed, ma'am?'

'No, no – not that way. But he hurt my little girl's heart and soul. He killed his poor wife, didn't he?'

Not for lack of trying, Eve thought. 'Ma'am, I need to speak with your daughter. You're welcome to stay with her while I do.'

'You can be sure I will. Chantal! Get your sister. Right now! She came home,' the woman said to Eve. 'So I'm grateful for that. She came home because she found out he'd been lying to her, and using her. And I've been holding her 'link because he kept trying to reach her. Felicity, it's that policewoman you told us about. She arrested that awful man.'

430

'Arrested! Mom, let me have the 'link. Hello, hello. I forgot your name.'

'It's Dallas. Lieutenant Dallas. Felicity, did you see or speak to JJ Copley after we spoke?'

'I wouldn't. I got thinking when you left. I'm not as stupid as people think.'

'Nobody thinks you're stupid,' her mother said.

'He did. He thought I was stupid, and I was. But I started thinking, and I tagged up Sadie, and we talked.'

'That's good.'

'And after I talked with Sadie, I did what he told me not to. I called his house. I got the housekeeper thing, and she said how she'd take a message because he wasn't able to come to the 'link. So I said, Oh, he's out of town, and the housekeeper thing said, No, he was in residence – that's how she said it – but unable to come to the 'link, and she'd take the message. I just said never mind because I got upset. He lied to me. Did you know he lied to me?'

'Yes, I'm sorry, Felicity, I knew he lied to you.'

'It's why you said I should talk to Sadie, and she said how I needed to find out for sure. So I did. I even went over there, to his house, and I watched, and I saw him. I saw him and his wife come out together and get in a car, and he wasn't on a trip. They were laughing. She wasn't being mean to him. He – he *kissed* her before they got in the car, and I knew it was all a lie. I came home. Am I in trouble?'

'Why would you be in trouble?'

'I took some of the clothes he bought me, and I used the credit card he got me to pay for the trip home. I didn't have enough since I stopped working. I'll pay it back.'

'Did he give you the clothes?'

'Yeah, but—'

'Did he give you the card to use?'

'He did.'

'Then you're not in trouble.'

'I left him a memo cube. I said how I was leaving, and I wouldn't have anything to do with somebody who lied and cheated like that, and made me a liar and a cheater, too. I'm not coming back, I don't think. I think I don't belong in New York. Did he do something really bad? Worse than lying and cheating?'

'It looks that way.'

'He was so nice to me, so I loved him. But it wasn't real.'

'I may need to talk to you again, but I'm glad you went home. I'm glad you're with your family.'

'Me, too. Um, Merry Christmas, Dallas.'

'Same to you.'

Eve clicked off, sat back, sorted through.

'Lawyer's here,' Peabody said from the doorway.

'We'll give them some time, then start again.'

22

Eve gave them an hour, taking the time to fine-tune her approach, then walked through the bullpen to get Peabody.

She saw Jenkinson had taken her at her word.

A banner hung over the break-room door, facing out so any who came in would see the sentiment:

NO MATTER YOUR RACE, CREED, SEXUAL ORIENTATION,
OR POLITICAL AFFILIATION, WE PROTECT AND SERVE,
BECAUSE YOU COULD GET DEAD.

Obviously, there'd been some discussion, some teamwork on the wording, but Jenkinson's original sentiment remained. Her first reaction wasn't the amusement she'd expected, but a tug of pride. Because it was the righteous truth.

She took a quick scan of the men and women who served under her. Trueheart in his pristine uniform earnestly working on his comp. Baxter, kicked back, designer shoes propped on his desk, talking on his desk 'link. Jenkinson scowling at his screen as he chowed down on some questionable sandwich from Vending.

The room smelled of truly terrible coffee, someone's greasy lunch, the fake pine someone had sprayed on the silly tree. It smelled like cops at Christmas, she thought.

'Peabody, let's lock this up. The rest of you? That—' She pointed toward the banner. 'That stays up. Anybody from Maintenance or Standards or Legal tries to take it down, kick them to me.'

Peabody scurried after Eve. 'We're really leaving it up?'

'How did we start this investigation? Giving our time and effort to get justice for a worthless asshole. The sign stays. It speaks the truth.'

She walked into Interview, read the necessary data into the record, then sat across from Copley and his lawyer.

'So, here we are again.'

And let it hang.

McAllister broke the silence.

'My client is a victim of Trey Ziegler, a blackmailer, an extortionist, a man who – through evidence you yourself discovered – used illegal date-rape substances on a number of women.'

'I'll give you Ziegler was a lousy human being. It's still illegal to murder a human being, lousy or otherwise.'

'My client didn't murder anyone, and at the established time of death of Trey Ziegler was in his own home.'

'So he says, but he's got no one to back that up – including the wife he recently sent to the hospital.'

'I never touched Natasha.'

'She says different.'

'I don't believe that,' Copley continued, even as his lawyer tried to silence him. 'You're lying.'

'Do you want me to play the nine-one-one call again?'

'JJ.' With barbs in the name, the lawyer clamped a hand over Copley's. 'Ms Quigley was in fear for her life, and called out for her husband. Called out for him to help her.'

Eve smiled. 'You can try that one, but you know what the jury's going to hear. From the recording, from Natasha Quigley's own lips in court.'

'Ms Quigley suffered a severe head injury during an attack by an unknown assailant, one who very likely killed Ziegler, one who very likely was in league with him. Her recollection, and her testimony on the events, isn't trust-worthy.'

'And this "unknown assailant" mysteriously went poof?'

'My client believes that Catiana Dubois assaulted his wife, and in the struggle fell, was killed. My client believes the deceased was in league with Ziegler.'

Rage tickled the back of her throat. Eve let it show, let it come.

'So you want to try to hang Ziegler on her? Let me say this, so you both hear it. Try it. Just try it. Your client's a liar, a cheat, an adulterer, a fraud. Just who do you think a jury's going to sympathize with? A man who cheats on his wife with a naive young woman he lies to – one he's set up with money he's stolen from his wife? A man who paid a blackmailer to keep that arrangement quiet? Or an innocent woman, one who worked for a living, came from a nice family, had no smears on her record?'

'You leave Felicity out of this,' Copley demanded.

'I talked to her, too, just about an hour ago. Did you get her memo?'

He lurched up; Eve rose with him.

'You had no business talking to her. I'm going to explain everything to her. She'll come back to me. I *love* her. I'm going to marry her.'

'But you couldn't until you got rid of the wife you already have. Killing her clears the way.'

'I don't have to kill her! Why do you think I paid Ziegler to fuck her!'

'JJ, God! Shut up!'

'Don't tell me to shut up.' Color high, he rounded on McAllister. 'You useless bitch. Why haven't you gotten me out of here? I told you I wanted Silbert or Crosby.'

'You've got me.'

Eve sat again, looked at Peabody. 'Now, this is interesting. Don't you find this interesting, Peabody?'

'I'm riveted. Absolutely riveted. Did he say what I think he said – on record – that he paid Ziegler to sleep with his wife?' Peabody glanced at Copley. 'Did you get to watch?'

'Shut the hell up. You're disgusting.'

'He pays some sleaze to sleep with his wife, and I'm disgusting? Jeez. Okay, if you didn't do it for kinky watching, what did you do it for?'

436

'For Felicity!'

'She got to watch?'

More pride swelled in Eve's heart as Copley snarled at Peabody.

'I want to speak to my client in private.'

'You've had plenty of time for that,' Eve said. 'It sounds to me like JJ has things to say. Do you have things to say, JJ?'

'Damn right. And you shut up,' he told the lawyer, who just shook her head and sighed.

'It was love at first sight with Felicity. I wanted to give her what she needed, fulfill her dreams.'

'So you lied to her.'

'I didn't lie. I just needed time. I intended to divorce Natasha, but without certain stipulations and agreements, the divorce would have left me unable to fulfill Felicity's dreams.'

'You needed your wife's money to fulfill the dreams of the woman you were ditching your wife for.'

'There's no need to be crude. Love is its own reason. Natasha and I had grown apart, and—'

'Really, spare me all the old chestnuts. They're roasting fresh ones out on the street.'

'You're going to pay for your disrespect.'

'Name your price.' Eve pushed into his face again. 'Because I've got no respect for you. You've got something to say, say it. Clear, on the record. You made a deal with Trey Ziegler. Explain.'

The look he sent her burned with hate, but he spat out

the words. 'Simply put, I was aware Ziegler had sex with clients. He bragged about it to me. Claimed he could get any woman he wanted.'

Still trying, McAllister chimed in, 'My client wasn't aware Ziegler used illegal substances on those clients.'

After an eye flicker that told Eve Copley *had* known – Copley continued, 'Of course not. That's deplorable. As far as I knew all the women were willing. I told him I'd pay him if he could seduce Natasha. She had a choice.' Copley jabbed a finger at the table for emphasis. 'She *chose* to have sex with him, and more than once. It had to be more than once, there had to be a clear affair in order for me to pre-serve my . . . financial advantages.'

'Your prenup specified if your wife had a sexual affair, you got a divorce with a fat settlement?'

'It's fair.'

'So you hired Ziegler to draw her into a sexual affair, one I assume you documented.'

'That's right. It's not illegal.'

On the contrary, Eve thought, but the pimping charges weren't worth mentioning.

'I only needed them to do it a couple more times. By the first of the year, or right after, I could file.'

'But you suggested a trip with Natasha, to shore up your marriage, after the first of the year.'

'Okay, I did.' He shifted in his chair, leaned forward a bit as if explaining the perfectly reasonable. 'It would never have happened, but it was important I came off as trying to fix things up. It's marriage,' he said, obviously frustrated. 'It's personal business, not police business.'

'If you wanted it to stay that way, you shouldn't have killed Ziegler.'

'I didn't! I only needed him to screw her a couple more times. Now he's dead.'

'He couldn't finish the job because she broke it off, or was about to.'

'Maybe she did, maybe she didn't. But he'd have persuaded her.'

'One way or the other?' Eve said.

'He told me he'd persuade her.' Copley looked away. 'I told him he didn't get the money until he did. Just two more times, and I could take it to my divorce lawyer.'

'When did you tell him?'

'Just last week when I went . . . '

'To his apartment.'

'Look, fine. I went there. *One* time. Just that one time because he dropped it on me at our training session she'd made noises about working on the marriage, maybe stopping the sex with him the day before. And she was talking to me about fixing things, getting teary, getting flirty. I just needed a couple more times to seal the deal.'

'He couldn't do it, but he still wanted money. If you didn't pay it, he'd go to your wife, confess – and you'd lose. He'd tell her about Felicity. And you'd lose. The prick was hitting you from every angle. It was never going to stop. So you stopped it.'

'I didn't kill him. I wasn't there.'

'The same way you were upstairs when Catiana was killed, when your wife was attacked? What had Catiana figured out? What did she know? She'd tell Natasha, and you'd lose again. She had to be stopped. You stopped her. But your wife walks in, and that's not just losing your "financial advantage", that's losing everything. She had to be stopped.'

'He used me. They all used me. *I'm* the victim here. I'm the goddamn victim. I didn't do anything. I wasn't there. I want to talk to Natasha. I want to talk to Felicity.'

'They're done with you. What you've got now is me. So let's start again.'

He fumbled and stumbled, raged a time or two. He pleaded, and he insulted. But he didn't budge.

Eve decided spending Christmas in a cage might add the final incentive.

She sent him off, raging.

'He's talked himself into it,' Peabody commented. 'Didn't Mira say something like that? How he could make himself believe the lie so it's his truth.'

'Something like that. It may be harder for him to believe after another couple days behind bars. He keeps tripping up over things. Going to Ziegler's apartment, paying Ziegler to nail his wife. We'll keep piling up the stumbles until he falls flat.'

'There's more than enough to go to trial.'

'Without a confession, the PA's going to offer a deal. It's

440

not enough. Maybe I could swallow it on Ziegler, but not on Catiana. We'll hit him again after Christmas. Go, grab McNab's skinny ass, catch your shuttle, see your family.'

'Really? We have to write up the—'

'I've got it.'

'You always say that. I'll—'

'I say it because I'm the boss. Get the hell out of here.'

'Thanks. Merry Christmas, Dallas. Don't hit me.' Peabody flung her arms around Eve, squeezed. 'I hope you like your gift half as much as I love my coat.'

She dashed off, presumably to get said coat.

In her office, Eve wrote up the report, copied it to Reo, the commander, Mira, Peabody.

She could work on the twists and turns of it, she thought, maybe straighten some of them out, talk to Quigley one more time.

Then she thought: The hell with it.

She was going home.

Maybe it dogged her on the drive, the insane drive full of rain and revelers. It dogged her enough for her to use her in-dash comp, to ramble some thoughts and speculations into it to sort through later.

But when she walked in the house, she ordered herself to leave it outside.

It wasn't hard, not when she walked into warmth, light, laughter. Even if some of the laughter was Summerset's.

They were in the parlor, Roarke sprawled in a chair, a glass of wine in his hand. Summerset sat with perfect posture across from him. She didn't think Summerset could sprawl due to the stick up his ass.

Then she reminded herself it was Christmas and time for a moratorium on insults.

'What's the joke?' she asked.

Roarke smiled. 'Just a little stroll down memory lane.'

'How many pockets picked on the stroll?'

'Who's counting?' He rose to kiss her, take her coat, which he tossed onto the arm of a sofa. 'I'll get you some wine.'

'I'll take it. Party food.' She studied the tray of fancy finger food, chose one, popped it. She wasn't sure what it was except good.

'Everything tied up?' Roarke asked when he handed her the wine.

'Tied, but not pulled tight and bowed up. Still, Copley's getting stones in his Christmas stocking.'

'That's coal.'

'What's coal?'

'Never mind.' Roarke kissed her again, pulled her down into the chair with him.

Flustered – Summerset was right *there* – she started to push up. 'We have lots of chairs.'

'We're economizing.' Roarke held her fast. 'Summerset was telling me about a Christmas during the Urbans when he and some medics fashioned a Christmas tree out of rebar and rags among other things.'

'It was quite festive, considering,' Summerset added. 'We

442

lit it with mini, bat-powered torches, and some enterprising soul stole a case of MREs from the enemy camp so we had a feast.'

'That would be you.'

Summerset lifted an eyebrow at Eve. 'Perhaps it was. Making do can add to the sense of community.'

'My team hauled in a broken tree, a dented menorah, fake ears of corn.' She sipped her wine. 'It cheered the place right up.'

She relaxed, let the evening wash the day away. Maybe the cop in her couldn't approve of some of the tales they told – or the thievery often involved, but ... hell, the statute of limitations made them all just memories.

'I've friends waiting,' Summerset said at length, and rose.

Eve bit back the automatic retort involving ghouls and corpses and wait time. Moratorium, she reminded herself.

'Happy Christmas to you both. It's a happier one for me knowing this is a home fulfilling its promise and purpose.'

Glad she'd bitten back the barb, Eve cleared her throat. 'It helps having someone who knows what he's doing to handle the details.'

'Thank you. An unexpected gift. Good night.'

Roarke kissed Eve's cheek after Summerset left. 'Unexpected, and sweet.'

'I'm not sweet. It's truth. I'm big on truth tonight.'

'Difficult pieces to your day?'

'Yeah, and then some. We're not going to think about that because, hey, look. There are all these presents under the — Shit! Shit.' Now she did push up. 'I need twenty minutes.'

'All right.'

'Go ... do something,' she suggested and fled to wrap the gifts she'd neglected to wrap because there was plenty of time.

She hauled them down to the parlor, shoved them under the tree. Huffed out a breath, stepped back. And nearly yelped as she spotted Roarke lying on one of the sofas reading a book, the cat stretched out beside him.

'I didn't see you.'

'So I deduced when you reached for your weapon.'

'I didn't draw it. You're reading a book.'

'It's the Yeats you gave me our first Christmas together. I reread it every year at this time.'

'You're such a sap.' But she smiled when she said it because the idea filled her with pleasure. 'Do you want to see what you got this year?'

'I do.' He rose, set the book aside. The cat just turned over, stayed on the sofa. 'We could leave the gifts from friends for tomorrow,' he suggested, poured them both more wine. 'For Christmas Day.'

'Works for me. Then we could finish what we started last night. You know, drink a whole bunch of wine, have crazy sex.'

'That would absolutely work for me. Or.' He cupped a hand behind her neck, kissed her slow. 'We could start at the end of that, work back. Crazy sex, lots of wine, gifts.'

'It's a plan, but—' She pulled back, grabbed a large, clumsily wrapped box. 'Open this. I figured it would be the . . .' She threw her hands in the air, made a whooshing sound. 'What is it?'

'The explosion.'

'No, no, when the guy who—' With loosely fisted hands she waved her arms in the air. 'And the musicians all—'

'The crescendo?' He laughed, sat on the floor with the box. 'I do adore you. So, in this case, crescendo first.'

'Yeah. I want to see if I hit the mark. It's a crappy wrapping job.'

'It's charming.' He untied the ribbon, tore the paper. When he opened the box, she gauged surprise. But surprise didn't necessarily mean bull's-eye.

'You didn't get yourself a magic coat,' she pointed out.

'I hadn't gotten to it.'

He drew out the soft black leather, in classic style, and he noted – touched – the buttons held the symbol of Celtic trinity knots.

'You amaze me.'

'You can buy your own clothes – you can buy everybody's clothes, but this is . . . I want you safe, too.'

'Darling Eve.' When he leaned over, kissed her, she knew she'd hit the mark.

'It'll fit,' she told him. 'I went to your guys – the R&D guys on the lining, and that wasn't easy. I think I could get into the White House War Room easier. And your tailor.'

He stood to put it on. 'It's perfect. Absolutely perfect.'

And on him, the knee-length, supple black leather was ridiculously sexy. 'There's an add-on. Hidden interior pockets. I figure a guy like you can find them easy enough. For carrying things even an expert civilian consultant isn't suppose to carry.'

'Is that so?' He did, indeed find them, grinned like a boy.

Double bull's-eye, Eve thought. On a roll, she started to reach for another gift.

'No, your turn now.' He slipped out of the coat, laid it with hers. 'We'll just stick with the crescendo theme.' He chose a small box. 'This one.'

She expected jewelry. He couldn't help himself. So puzzlement came first when she opened it, found a simple business card. 'Master Wu? I don't get it.'

'You get him. He'll work with you, at his dojo, or here, in the one we're having put in beside the gym on the lower level.'

'The what? Dojo. Here?'

'The work starts next week. Master Wu will train you. If and when you're unable to connect in person, we've devised a holographic program.'

'Master Wu will work with me. *The* Master Wu?' She'd met the martial arts legend briefly on a case, had admired him for years. 'You bought me Master fucking Wu?'

'In a manner of speaking.'

'Holy shit, holy shit!' She jumped up, literally danced around the room, stopping to jab at an imaginary opponent, destroying them with a vicious side-kick. 'Master Wu!'

She leaped onto Roarke, bowling him back, kissing him hard when he laughed, and while the cat ran over to see what the hell was going on.

'This is the best. This is the most amazing gift ever in the history of gifts. You know I'm going to be able to seriously kick your ass now.'

'We'll see about that.'

'Master Wu.' She shoved up, pulled him up with her. 'You're putting in a dojo.'

'We are. It'll be fun, won't it, for both of us? I'll show you the design, the plans. Ah now,' he murmured when the insane joy in her eyes clouded with tears.

'You,' she said, and wrapped around him. 'You know me, and you love me anyway. I'll never get over it.'

'And you. My cop put stash pockets in my magic coat. I couldn't have dreamed you better.'

She sniffled, eased back, pulled another gift from under the tree. 'This one. This one needs to come next.'

'I could sit here, with you, under these happy lights, and need nothing else in the world. But since it's here,' he added, making her laugh as he opened the gift.

She'd framed a photo of them at the preview of *The Icove Agenda*. Not one of the glitzy red-carpet shots, but one taken after she'd squared off with a killer — after he'd bloodied the bastard's face.

They stood smiling at each other, his torn knuckles on her bruised cheek.

'It's us, that's what you said when you saw this.'

He looked up at her. 'So it is, and it's going straight onto my desk. Open this.'

Relieved the emotional jag had passed, she ripped in. And found the exact same photo. Different frame, but the same photo. Nothing could have struck her more.

'Look at us. We know each other.'

'And love each other anyway.'

'All glammed up, and your knuckles bleeding, my eye already going purple. To think of all that bullshit prepping for the cameras. The Trina treatment. Clothes, hair, face – and I end up with a black eye anyway.'

'You got your man. And it was a hell of an after party.'

'Bagging Frye was the best part, but, yeah, it was. If parties didn't take so much time and work, they'd ... Wait. Wait.'

'For what?'

'She helped with the party prep. That's what Tella told me today. Catiana was over there, helped out, got ready for the party there. Catiana.'

Roarke dangled a ribbon for Galahad to bat at. 'I suspect it's Christmas that'll have to wait.'

'I need to ... No, it can wait.' She started to reach for another gift, but he took her hand.

'We know each other.'

She turned her hand under his, gripped tight. 'Thank God. You can wear your new coat.'

So she ran those twists and turns as he drove, wondered if she indeed smoothed some of them out. It made a convoluted, nasty kind of sense. And considering those involved, it played right through to crescendo.

She didn't bother to have Copley brought up, but went down to the bowels of Central, logged in, badged through and walked up to where Copley paced his cell.

'What do you want? I don't have to talk to you. Fuck you, and you with her,' he said to Roarke.

'You can send for the lawyer you don't respect, or you can answer a couple of simple questions. On the night of your holiday party, what time did you see or speak to your wife for the first time?'

'How the hell do I know? I wasn't watching the damn clock.'

'Fine.' Eve turned away.

'Wait. Why does it matter? I told you when I got home, I told you I went up to dress. Tash came in later. She was running behind.'

'What about hair, makeup?'

'So what? Wait, wait. She had to deal with it herself. She was rushed, something about a screwup with catering. She was upset, said how she'd had to put out a dozen fires. I know she'd been running around dealing with things because Tella's girl called up, caught me just after I got out of the shower, looking for her.'

'Why not tag Natasha directly?'

'I don't *know*. I didn't ask. I had a party to get ready for. I don't get into the domestic stuff. Tash deals with that. She deals with the staff.'

'How long did it take you to get ready?'

'Jesus Christ. I don't know. I take my time. Maybe ninety minutes.'

'So Catiana was looking for your wife about six-thirty? Sometime around six-thirty?'

'About that. So what? The girl should've been able to handle whatever the problem was instead of bothering us. But I didn't kill her for it.'

'You're a complete dick, JJ,' Eve commented, and walked away with him shouting after her.

'He is, indeed, a complete dick,' Roarke agreed.

'Yeah, but he's not a murderer.'

Epilogue

A skeleton crew manned the hospital. That meant Eve had to go through more hoops for admittance to the surgical wing, but she found herself tolerant.

When she stepped into Natasha's room with Roarke, she noted they'd brought in a tree, gifts, strung some lights.

Natasha sat up in bed, flanked by her sister and brother-in-law. She looked more alert, and had added lip dye, other enhancements. She wore a lacy robe over a silky gown.

'Lieutenant.' Martella came over to greet her. 'Roarke. Oh, you work too hard to still be at it on Christmas Eve! Please, have some champagne. The doctor said Tash could have a half glass. She's doing so much better already.'

'So I see. You look better, Ms Quigley.'

'I feel more myself. A little weak and shaky, but much better. Tella and Lance brought me Christmas.'

'Nice. We'll have to skip the champagne, but this won't take long. I wanted to check in on you, and give you some updates.'

'So kind.'

'I'm going to have just a couple questions, to tie it all up. I'll keep it simple.'

'Of course – if you're sure it can't wait.'

'When we're this close to wrapping things up, we don't want any loose threads.'

'You know what happened?'

'I do. Mind?' Eve asked as she eased down at the foot of the bed.

'Of course not. I'm so grateful for your dedication.'

'Just doing my job. And doing it, I should remind you that you can have a legal rep present. I read you your rights the other day, but I can refresh you if you need it.'

'So formal. No need for that. Of course I remember. I don't want a lawyer.' She actually patted Eve's hand. 'Ask your questions so you can go home and enjoy your own Christmas.'

'Thanks. I did speak with your doctor before I came. She's very pleased with your progress, and expects you to make a full recovery, and hopes you can be released in just a few days.'

'It feels like a miracle.'

'I'm sure it does. I regret to inform you we have your husband in custody. He's been charged with Trey Ziegler's murder, with Catiana Dubois's murder, and with the attack on you.'

'Oh God.'

'You have to be strong, Tash.' Martella gripped her sister's hand as she turned to Eve. 'Lance and I talked about this.

We went over and over it because it just doesn't seem possible. But it is. It's the only possibility. He must have lost his mind.'

'He's a difficult man. I understand your loyalty, Ms Quigley – Natasha,' Eve said, and gently. 'But it's time for the truth.'

'He's my husband. How do I accept all this? How do I accept my husband is a murderer?'

'It's hard. It has to be really hard. But we've been able to put it all together. The events, the timelines, all of it.'

'JJ.' Natasha choked it out. 'I tried to tell myself I was confused. It couldn't have been … But why, why? Why would he hurt Catiana, why would he hurt me? Why would he kill Trey?'

'Tella's right. He lost his mind. I should have seen it, I should have gotten him help before it was too late.'

Martella slid onto the bed, drew her sister close. 'Don't blame yourself, Tash. Don't.'

'I don't understand it. I don't understand any of it.'

'He knew about you and Ziegler,' Eve told her.

'Oh God. God, I knew he'd be angry if he found out, but …'

'He didn't find out,' Eve corrected. 'He arranged it.'

'What—'

'He paid Ziegler to sleep with you.'

'He …' The tears in Natasha's eyes dried to hard embers. 'What are you saying?'

'I'm saying he paid Trey Ziegler to initiate an affair with

you, which, with Ziegler's help, he documented in order to retain a generous financial settlement when he filed for divorce.'

'Oh, Tash.' Tella leaned in to offer more comfort. Natasha pushed her aside.

'He's lying. JJ must be lying.'

'We have Ziegler's records, corroborating the transactions. It was just another job for him – really lucrative since both you and your husband were, essentially, paying him for the same service. Just another way to cash in. You didn't mean anything to him other than another body, another mark.'

'That's not true. That's absolutely not true.'

The flash in her eyes told Eve what she needed to know.

'He used you. Ziegler used you, and he and your husband laughed about it behind your back.'

'No. Trey cared about me.'

'He cared about the money you gave him, the money he got from your husband. He double-dipped, and it ended up killing him.'

'We had a relationship. Do you understand me?'

'I'm not sure I do.'

'Tash, don't upset yourself. The man was a bastard. He took advantage of you.'

'Of *you*,' Quigley tossed back at Martella. 'Not of me. No one takes advantage of me.'

'It's hard to take.' Eve patted Natasha's leg. 'Really hard for a smart, strong-willed woman to take when she's been

454

duped. Everything he said to you was a lie, and one your husband paid for – worse, paid for with your money. I know it's rough. It was bad enough when you found out Ziegler was seeing that idiot Alla Coburn again, bad enough when he lied to you about her, about others.

'He made you feel special, excited,' Eve continued. 'When you snuck out to see him that day – the day of your party – you just wanted to see him before he left for the seminar. But you saw he'd been with someone else. The cheap bra, the slutty shoes, right there, in your face.'

'What are you talking about?' Martella demanded. Eve ignored her.

'He brushed it off. He had a way, didn't he? She didn't mean anything to him. Just sex. Did he laugh at you when you told him you wouldn't tolerate it? Did he sneer when you said you loved him, wanted him to only be with you? Was he laughing when you picked up the trophy and swung it at his head?'

'You can't talk to her that way.' Martella tugged on Eve's arm. 'She's hurt. She's been victimized. Lance, make her stop.'

'Wait.' He stared at Eve, shifted his gaze slowly to Natasha's face. 'Just wait.'

'I don't want to talk to you.' Natasha plucked at the sheets, blinked tears into her eyes. 'You're saying horrible things.'

'You stuck the knife into his heart because he'd stuck one into yours. It was all lies, Natasha. Yours, your husband's,

455

Ziegler's. Everything you did: lies. You thought you'd gotten off clear, you told yourself you did what you had to do, and that was that. But the time it took? That tripped you up. You had to cancel your hair and face techs. I've checked with them, too.'

'I was busy preparing for the party.'

'You weren't home at the time Ziegler died. Catiana looked for you, couldn't find you.'

'I was home. Of *course* I was home. Dozens of people saw me.'

'And when I interview them, each and every one, none of them will be able to verify you were there between six and seven that evening because you were rushing over to Ziegler's apartment, killing him, and rushing back again.'

'I was home,' Natasha said coldly. 'You'll never prove otherwise.'

'Sure we will. And yesterday Catiana realized it. Talking with your sister, she started putting it together. Started wondering why she couldn't find you in the house, why you'd canceled your hair and face time. Six to seven-thirty, according to your hair and skin techs. But she was loyal, Natasha. She didn't run to me, to the police, she went to you. She went hoping you'd explain. But you couldn't explain.'

'Tella, please. Call the nurse. My head hurts.'

'Tash.' Slowly, Martella eased back from the bed. 'Oh my God, Tash. It can't be true. Not Cate. You couldn't.'

'But she did. She had to protect herself. Maybe you offered her money. She'd be shocked, insulted. You couldn't

456

trust her to keep her mouth shut, so you argued, you threatened. You shoved her. Did you mean to kill her or was it just a happy accident?'

Natasha shook her head, looked pleadingly at her sister. 'I didn't. I couldn't. Believe me.'

'I think it was violent impulse,' Eve continued. 'Like Ziegler. And like Ziegler, you couldn't leave it at that. After you turned her over, made sure she was dead, you knew just how to use it all to your advantage. You could get rid of JJ – have him locked away like he deserved for cheating on you with that little stripper with the big tits. It would take some guts, but you've got them. So you made the nine-one-one call. You could claim you blocked video in your rush, your shock. You faked an attack, using your husband's name. Then you dropped the phone, crushed it. You got your guts up, picked up that vase. You screamed – alerting JJ, boosting your adrenaline, then you struck yourself as hard as you could manage. Harder than you should have. It nearly killed you. You nearly died for pride and ego and payback to a cheating spouse.

'Was it worth it?'

'Every bit.'

When Martella began to weep, Roarke put an arm around her, looked at Lance. 'You should take her out. She shouldn't be here now.'

'Come on, darling. Come on now.'

'Go on! You always were the weak one,' Natasha called after her. 'Go crying to Daddy, like you used to.'

Martella stopped, looked back. 'You're my sister.' She straightened her shoulders, lifted her chin. 'But she was my best friend. Cate. I'll never forgive you for Cate.' And she walked away.

'Staff.' Natasha leaned back. 'Anyone who makes friends or family out of paid staff is a fool.' She looked at Eve. 'I was under duress. My husband's petty cruelties and neglect, a lover flaunting his flings. I had a breakdown.'

'You can play that tune.'

'A breakdown. What happened with Trey that day? It's as if someone else was inside my body. I couldn't control myself. Catiana? She slipped. We were talking. I was upset, of course, but she slipped, fell. I was in shock. Again, out of my mind. No one in their right mind would strike themselves that way.'

'You're going to learn the difference between legally sane and just being a cold, vicious, selfish bitch.'

'I'm in the hospital. I nearly died. I have a great deal of money to pay hard-hitting lawyers. No one mourns for Trey but me. And Catiana? She slipped.'

'You're a good liar, but with the evidence I'm going to have stacked up against you, even your lies will sink. Natasha Quigley, you're under arrest for the murder of Trey Ziegler, for the murder of Catiana Dubois, human beings. Additional charges will include but not be limited to obstruction of justice, lying to a police officer during an investigation. You will be held here, under guard until such time as you can safely be transported to prison to await trial.'

'I'll get out on bail.'

'I wouldn't bet on it.' Eve took out her restraints, stepped forward.

'Stay away from me. You can't use those on me.'

'Wouldn't bet on that, either.' Eve grabbed one of her wrists, managed to block the swipe of nails forearm to forearm. 'Add resisting arrest to the aforesaid charges.' She let the slap come, though the woman had some punch to her. 'And a little icing for me with assaulting a police officer. Which allows me to—'

She took out a second pair of restraints, cuffed Quigley's other wrist.

'I'll have your badge for this.'

'What you'll have is a crappy life in a cage. Your cheating putz of a husband is probably going to get a nice chunk of your money after all. Your name and face are going to be splashed all over the media, and the only social club you'll belong to is Big Nellie's Bitch-Slapping Circle. You'll be the mascot. Merry Christmas.'

'Big Nellie?' Roarke asked as they walked out.

'First thing that came to mind. Officer.' She signaled the uniform she'd ordered for the duty. 'Sit on her. I've got you on four-hour rotations, so you won't miss Christmas altogether.'

'I'm Jewish, sir.'

'Okay, Happy Hanukkah.'

She spoke to the head nurse on duty, relayed the status to Dr Campo via 'link.

'Her sister's going to suffer.'

'She's married to a steady guy – a fricking rock. But, yeah, she'll suffer. Murder doesn't stop at the vic, not most of the time. She set him up good, and he was such an ass-hole, it played. Little niggles here and there, but it played. They're so much alike – Copley, Quigley. He could've done it, for all the same reasons. Except, he doesn't have the balls to damn near kill himself to get away with it.'

'You closed it. You got both your victims justice.'

'Messy, but closed. Now I have to go spring Copley, that asshole.'

'You could do it in the morning, let him rot just a bit.'

'I could, but I won't.'

'It's what makes you not a bit like either of them.'

'It's a pisser right at the moment. It's going to take me a while.' She looked up at him as they stepped out of the ele-vator. 'Couple hours to deal with the paperwork, the lawyers. Screws up our Christmas Eve.'

'We've already had the crescendo, the rest can wait.'

'Yeah.' They stepped out into the night. The cold rain had stopped. She thought she caught the glimmer of a couple stars.

She took his hand, gave his arm a swing. 'Nice coat,' she said, made him laugh.

She'd do her duty, do her job. Then she and the man who knew her and loved her anyway would go home for Christmas.

EXCLUSIVE EXTRACT

Read an extract from

OBSESSION IN DEATH

The new J.D. Robb thriller

out February 2015

Prologue

Killing was easier than I thought it could be, and a lot more rewarding. I finally feel as if I've done something important, something that deserves real attention. All my life I've tried, done my best, but no one ever truly appreciated my efforts, really saw me for who and what I was.

I can say objectively, honestly, I did a good and efficient job on this new, important project, start to finish.

There were times during the weeks and weeks – months really – of planning, of selecting, of working out all the tiny details, I felt impatient, even annoyed with myself.

There were times I doubted, times I nearly lost my courage and my focus. It's too easy to become discouraged when no one values your skills and your efforts.

But I see now this time (and maybe it's been years in the developing really) was all worth it.

The time spent will be worth it again, as all that preparation and planning is done on all who come next.

Because I spent those weeks watching the target, learning her routine, made the effort to get into her building long before tonight, and made the investment in the very best equipment, practiced all the steps for hours, I have my first success.

My first weight on the scale toward balance. My first tribute, I suppose, in honor of my friend and partner.

That icy blonde bitch deserved to die.

Didn't Shakespeare say something about killing all the lawyers? I should look it up. In any case, I've taken care of one, and she won't be around to make any more money off the scum she represented, or most important of all, she'll never insult or demean the person I most admire. The person who deserved her RESPECT!

I'm honored to have played a part in righting the wrong, in bringing true justice to the woman who, due to the constraints of her job, is unable to mete out justice for herself.

I will be her avenger, her champion.

Soon, she'll know there is someone who will stand up for her, do what needs to be done. When she sees my message, she'll know she has someone behind her, who understands, admires, and respects her above all others. As no one ever did for me. Our connection is so strong, so intense, I can often read her thoughts. I wonder if she can read mine.

Sometimes, late at night, I sense she's with me, right here with me. How else could I have known where to start, and just what to do?

Ours is a spiritual bond I treasure, something deep and strong, and older than time. We are, in essence, the same person, two sides to one coin.

Death unites us.

I've proven myself now. There's still more to do, because the list is long. But tonight, I'm taking this time to write down my feelings, to have a small celebration. Tomorrow I'll go back to serving justice.

One day, when the time is right, we'll meet, and on that day, she will know she has the truest of friends.

It will be the happiest day of my life.

1

On a cold, crisp morning in the waning days of 2060, Lieutenant Eve Dallas stood in a sumptuous bedroom done in bold strokes of rich purple, deep metallic grays, and quick splashes of green. Outside the ad blimps manically touted the AFTER CHRISTMAS BLOW-OUT SALES! and street vendors hyped fake designer wrist units and knockoff handbags to throngs of tourists packed into the city for the holiday week.

Outside life went on. Inside the plush bedroom with all its color and style, it had stopped.

An enormous arrangement of white lilies and purple roses in a tall, mirrored vase on the pedestal centered in the wide window couldn't quite mask the smell of death. Instead the fragrance layered over it, sickly sweet.

On a bed big enough for six lay the body of a woman who'd once been a stunner. Even now her meticulous style showed in the perfect coordination of silver lounging pants, silky lavender top, the perfectly manicured nails – hands and feet – with polish of dark purple on all ten digits.

Her heavily lashed eyes stared straight up to the ceiling, as if mildly puzzled.

A razor-thin, bone-deep wound circled her throat. Blood, now congealed, had spilled from that ugly curve to soil and spoil the soft gray bedding and mat in the fall of pale blonde hair.

Her tongue sat in a faceted glass dish on the glossy night-stand beside the bed.

But the kicker, at least for Eve, was the message written on the wall above the thickly padded headboard, in precise block lettering, black against the gray.

FOR LIEUTENANT EVE DALLAS,
WITH GREAT ADMIRATION AND UNDERSTANDING.
HER LIFE WAS A LIE; HER DEATH OUR TRUTH.
SHE SHOWED YOU NO RESPECT, SPOKE ILL OF YOU,
SOUGHT TO PROFIT BY UNDERMINING ALL YOU WORK
   FOR.
IT WAS MY PLEASURE AND HONOR TO BALANCE THE
   SCALES.
JUSTICE HAS BEEN SERVED.
YOUR TRUE AND LOYAL FRIEND.

Beside Eve, her partner, Detective Peabody, blew out a long breath. 'Holy shit, Dallas.'

Whether or not Eve thought the same, she turned to the uniformed officer in the bedroom doorway. 'Who found her?'

'Her admin. The vic missed a dinner meeting last night, then didn't come in to work, where she had a morning meeting. So the admin, Cecil Haversham, came by. Nobody could reach her via 'link, she didn't answer the door. He had her codes and key pass – stated he waters her plants and whatnot when she's out of town. Let himself in at about nine-fifteen, heard the bedroom screen on like it is now, and walked through until he found her. We got the nine-one-one at nine-nineteen, so the timing works.'

'Where is he?'

'Place has a dining area you can close off. We're sitting on him there.'

'Keep sitting. I want the building's security discs, exterior, interior, and I want a canvass started, beginning with this floor.'

'Yes, sir.' He jutted his chin to the writing on the wall. 'You know the vic?'

'I've had some dealings with her.' To discourage any more questions, Eve turned away.

She and Peabody had sealed up on entering the apartment. She'd turned on her recorder before stepping into the bedroom. Now she stood a moment, a tall, slim woman with short, tousled brown hair, with long-lidded eyes of gilded brown cop-flat in her angular face.

Yeah, they'd had some dealings, she thought now, and she hadn't had a modicum of liking for the victim. But it appeared she and Peabody would be spending the last days of the year standing for the once high-powered defense attorney who'd had – to Eve's mind – the ethics of a rattle-snake.

'Let's verify ID, Peabody, and keep every step of this strict on procedure.'

With a nod, Peabody took off her pink leather coat – Eve's Christmas gift – set it carefully aside before she pulled her Identi-pad from her field kit. With her striped pink pom-pom hat still over her flip of dark hair, she approached the body. 'Victim is identified as Leanore Bastwick of this address.'

'Cause of death looks pretty straightforward. Strangulation, probably a wire garrote, but the ME will confirm. Get time of death.'

Again Peabody dug into her field kit. She worked the gauges, angled, as she read Eve's unspoken order, so the record would pick up everything.

'TOD eighteen-thirty-three.'

'No sign of struggle, no visible defensive wounds or other injuries. No sign, at a glance, of forced entry. The vic's fully dressed, and there's plenty of easily transported valuables sitting out. It doesn't read sexual assault or burglary. It reads straight murder.'

Peabody lifted her gaze to the message on the wall. 'Literally reads.'

'Yeah. Security discs may tell a different tale, but it looks like the vic opened the door – someone she knew or thought she knew. Her killer disabled her – note to ME to put priority on tox screens, check body for any marks from a stunner or pressure syringe – or forced her back here. Places like this have excellent soundproofing, so she could have shouted for help, screamed, and it's not likely anyone heard. Windows are privacy screened.'

'No sign on her wrists, her ankles that the killer used restraints.'

Eve approached the body now, examined the head, lifted it up, to check the back of the skull. 'No injuries that indicate blunt force trauma.'

She reached into her own field kit for microgoggles, took a closer look. 'Abrasion, small contusion. Fell back, hit her head maybe. Disabled, drugged or stunned, either when she opened the door, or if she knew the killer, after he was inside. Back here, carrying her or forcing her. The bedding's not even mussed, the pillows are still stacked up behind her.'

Lifting one of the hands, she examined the fingers, the nails, under the nails. 'Clean, no trace here, nothing to indicate she got a piece of her killer. You're going to struggle, if you can, when somebody garrotes you, so she couldn't struggle.'

With the microgoggles still in place, Eve leaned over the crystal dish to examine the severed tongue. 'It looks pretty clean – not jagged, not sawed. Probably a thin, sharp blade. Maybe a scalpel. Can't talk trash without your tongue,' she said half to herself. 'Can't defend criminals if you can't talk. This was a little something extra, a symbol, a . . . token.'

'For you.'

Eve studied the message, coated a layer of ice over that sick thought. 'Like I said, it reads that way. We butted heads over Jess Barrow a couple years back, and just before that when her partner was killed. She was a hard-ass, but she was mostly doing her job. Doing it as she saw it.'

Turning from the body now, Eve walked over into a large and perfectly appointed dressing room. 'She's got an outfit set out here. Black dress, fancy shoes, underwear, and jewelry to go with it that looks like the real deal. Nothing disturbed. She'd gotten out the wardrobe for her dinner meeting.'

She moved from there into an elaborate master bath, all white and silver. More purple flowers – must have been a favorite – in a square vase of clear glass on the long white counter.

'Towels on a warming rack, a robe on the hook by the shower, a glass of wine and some sort of face gunk set out on the counter.'

'It's a mask.'

'I don't see a mask.'

'A facial mask,' Peabody elaborated, patting her own cheeks. 'And that's a really high-end brand. Since there's nothing else set out, it looks like maybe she'd been about to give herself a facial, have some wine while it set, then take a shower, but she went to answer the door.'

'Okay, good. She's prepping for the meeting – we'll check her home office – going to get clean and shiny, but somebody comes to the door.'

Eve walked out as she continued. 'Nothing disturbed out here. Screen on in the bedroom – a little company or entertainment while she gets ready for dinner. She's back there, in the bath or the dressing room when she gets the buzz.'

'Security on the main door,' Peabody pointed out. 'Buzzed the killer in?'

'The security feed should tell us. However he got inside the building, she answers the door.'

She imagined it, Bastwick in her swanky at-home wear, going to the door. Look through the security peep first, check the monitor?

Why have good security if you didn't use it? Used it, Eve concluded, felt no threat. Opened the door.

'He takes her down,' she continued. 'Drags or carries her.'

'Or she took him back?' Peabody suggested. 'A lover maybe?'

'She's got a meeting. She doesn't have time for sex. Not wearing sex clothes, no face enhancements. Could've forced her back, but it doesn't feel like it. Nothing disturbed. Nothing out of place.'

Eve paused there, went back in, studied Bastwick's feet, still cased in silvery slippers. 'No scuffs on the heels. She wasn't dragged.'

'Carried her, then.' Peabody, lips pursed in her square face, gauged the distance from living area to bedroom. 'If he did take her down in here, it's a good distance to cart her. Why?'

'Yeah, why? No overt signs of sexual assault. Maybe he re-dressed her after, but … Morris will tell us. Killer gets her onto the bed. No sign she was gagged, but the ME will check that, too. He kills her while she's still out or stunned. Quick, cuts out her tongue to prove a point, writes the message so I'll know what a favor he did for me, then gets out.

'Let's talk to the admin, then review the discs. I want to go over this place before we call in the sweepers.'

Cecil Haversham looked like his name. Formal with a side of dapper. He wore his hair white, short, and Caesarean, which suited the natty, perfectly trimmed goatee. The center leg pleats on his stone-gray three-piece suit looked sharp enough to draw blood.

Distress emanated from him in apologetic waves as he sat on a curved-back chair at the side of the lipstick-red dining table with his hands neatly folded.

Eve nodded to the uniform to dismiss her, then rounded to the head of the table with Peabody taking the chair opposite their witness.

'Mr Haversham, I'm Lieutenant Dallas, and this is Detective Peabody. I understand this is a difficult time for you.'

'It's very disturbing.' His voice carried the faintest whiff of British upper class, though Eve's quick run on him gave his birthplace as Toledo, Ohio.

'How long have you worked for Ms Bastwick?'

'Nearly two years as her administrative assistant. Prior I served as Mr Vance Collier's – of Swan, Colbreck, Collier and Ives – admin.'

'And how did you come into her employ?'

'She offered me the position, at a considerable increase in salary and benefits. And I felt moving into criminal law from corporate and tax law would be . . . more stimulating.'

'As her admin, you'd be privy to her case files, her clients, and her social engagements.'

'Yes, of course. Ms Bastwick is . . . was a very busy woman, professionally and personally. Part of my duties is to arrange her schedule, keep her calendar, make certain her time was well managed.'

'Do you know of anyone who'd wish Ms Bastwick harm?'

'As a criminal defense attorney, she made enemies, of course. Prosecuting attorneys, clients who felt she hadn't performed adequately – which would be nonsense, of course – and those individuals represented by the prosecution. Even some police.'

He gave Eve a steady if slightly distressed look. 'It would be the nature of her work, you see.'

'Yeah. Does anyone stand out?'

'I've been asking myself that as I sat here, digesting it all. There have been threats, of course. We keep a file, which I'd be happy to have copied for you if the firm clears it. But nothing stands out in this way. In this tragic way. Ms Bastwick always said that if nobody threatened her or called her . . . unattractive names, she wasn't doing her job. I must say, Lieutenant, Detective, you must often find yourself in that same position. The work you do creates enemies, particularly, one would think, if you do it well.'

'Can't argue there.' Eve sat back. 'Take me through it. When did you become concerned about Ms Bastwick, and what did you do?'

'I became concerned, very concerned, this morning. I arrive at the offices at eight-fifteen, routinely. This provides me time to check any messages, the daily schedule, prepare any necessary notes or documents for the morning appointments. Unless Ms Bastwick is in court or has an early outside appointment, she arrives between eight-thirty and eight-forty. When I arrived this morning, there was a message from Misters Chance Warren and Zane Quirk. Ms Bastwick had a dinner meeting with them last night, eight o'clock at Monique's on Park. The message came in at nine-oh-three last evening. The clients were somewhat irritated that Ms Bastwick hadn't arrived.'

'They contacted the office – after hours?'

'Yes, exactly. In the message, Mr Warren stated that they'd tried to reach Ms Bastwick on her pocket 'link – the business number she'd given them as she does all clients. Failing to reach her, they tried the office, left a message.'

He paused, cleared his throat. 'As this is not at all characteristic, I was concerned enough to try to contact Ms Bastwick via 'link, but was only able to leave a voice mail, which I did on both of her numbers. I then contacted Mr

Warren, and discovered Ms Bastwick had never arrived at the restaurant, and he and Mr Quirk had dinner, remained there until after ten.'

When he paused, cleared his throat again, Peabody interrupted. 'Can I get you some water, Mr Haversham?'

'Oh, I don't want to be any trouble.'

'It's no trouble. We appreciate your cooperation,' she said as she rose.

'Very kind.' He brushed his finger over the knot of his tie. 'I had expected Ms Bastwick's arrival at eight-twenty this morning as, per her request, I had scheduled an early meeting at the offices. She didn't arrive, and I rescheduled with the client, again tried her 'link. I confess, Lieutenant – Oh, thank you, Detective,' he said when Peabody brought him a tall glass of water. He sipped delicately, let out a long breath.

'As I was saying, I confess I was deeply concerned at this point. I worried Ms Bastwick had taken ill or met with an accident. I made the decision to come here, in case she was ill and unable to reach the 'link. As I explained to the officer, I have her codes as I tend to her plants and other business whenever she's out of town. When she didn't answer the buzzer, I took it upon myself to use the codes and enter the apartment. I understand that might seem forward, an invasion of privacy, but I was genuinely worried.'

'It seems sensible to me.'

'Thank you.' He took another delicate sip. 'I called out for her, and as I heard voices – I realized after a moment it was the entertainment screen in the bedroom – I called out again. Very concerned now as she didn't respond, I went directly to her bedroom. I called out once again, in case she was indisposed, then I went to the door.'

'Was it open or closed?'

'Oh, open. I saw her immediately. I saw . . . I started in, somehow thinking I could help. Then I stopped myself, just before I reached the foot of the bed, as it was all too clear I could be of no help to her. I was very shaken. I . . . I might have shouted, I'm not sure. I got out my 'link. My hands trembled so I nearly dropped it. I contacted nine-one-one. The operator, who was very calming and kind, I'd like to add, instructed me not to touch anything, and to wait for the police. I did touch the front door upon entering, and again when I admitted the officers. And I may have touched the doorjamb of the bedroom. I can't quite remember.'

'It's okay.'

'I saw what was written on the wall. I couldn't not see it. But I don't understand it.'

'In the file of threats you have, do you remember any that involved me? Anyone threatening her in connection with the Jess Barrow matter?'

'I don't. I came on after the Barrow case, though I'm familiar with it.'

'As a matter of procedure, can you tell us where you were last night, between five and eight p.m.?'

'Oh my.' Now he took a deeper drink of water. 'Well,

yes, of course. I left the office at five-oh-five. My wife had plans to have dinner with her sister as it was my turn to host my chess club. Marion isn't particularly interested in chess. I arrived home about five-twenty, and began preparations for dinner. Marion left about five-forty-five, to meet her sister for drinks, and the first of the club arrived at six, precisely. We had a light meal, and played until . . . I believe it was about nine-thirty. The last of our club would have left just before ten, shortly after Marion returned home. There are eight of us. I can provide you with their names.'

'We'd appreciate that. It's routine.'

'I understand. Ms Bastwick was an exacting employer. I prefer that as I do my best when I have tasks and goals, and challenges. I believe we suited each other very well. I also understand some found her difficult. I did not.'

For the first time he looked away, his eyes moist. Eve said nothing as he visibly struggled to compose himself again.

'I'm sorry. I'm very distressed.'

'Take your time.'

'Yes, thank you. I didn't find Ms Bastwick difficult. Even if I had I would say what I say to you now: anything I can do to assist you in finding who took her life, you have only to ask.'

'You've been really helpful,' Peabody told him. 'Maybe you could give us a sense of how Ms Bastwick got along with her partners, her colleagues, the people at your firm.'

'Oh, well, there would be some friction now and then, as you'd expect. A great deal of competition. But I will say she was valued, and respected. I . . . my own assistant has tried to contact me several times. The officer asked I not answer my 'link, so I've switched it off. But I should go back to the offices when it's permitted. There are so many things that need to be done, need to be seen to.'

'Just one more thing,' Eve said. 'Was she working on anything big right now, anything hot?'

'I suppose Misters Warren and Quirk would qualify. They are accused of embezzlement and fraud, from their own financial consulting firm. The matter will go to the courts next week. Ms Bastwick was very confident she would get a not-guilty verdict on all charges. She was a fierce litigator, as you know.'

'Yeah. Is there anyone we can contact for you, Mr Haversham?'

'For me?' He looked blank for a moment. 'No, no, but thank you. I'll go back to the office, do what needs to be done.'

'We'd appreciate copies of those threats.'

'Yes, I'll speak to Mr Stern right away.'

'We can arrange for one of the officers to drive you back to the office,' Peabody offered.

'So kind. But it's not far, and I believe I'd like to walk. I believe it would help if I could walk and sort through my thoughts.'

He rose as Eve did. 'Her family. I just thought. She has parents and a sister. Her parents live in Palm Beach, and her sister . . .' He paused a moment, rubbed at his temple. 'She lives with her family in East Washington. Should I contact them?'

'We'll take care of it,' Eve told him. 'If you think of anything else, let us know.'

'I will, of course. I want to ask, for my own peace of mind. Would it have been quick?'

'I think it would have.'

'I hope she didn't suffer.'

While Peabody guided him out, Eve returned to the dressing room.

'He was sweet under the stuffy,' Peabody commented when she came in. 'And I think he really liked her.'

'He'd be one,' Eve said. 'She was a hard-ass, cold-blooded and snotty with it. I don't think she'll have a long list of actual friends, but there'll be plenty of acquaintances, clients, associates. There's a safe here, as I figured. It doesn't look like it's been tampered with, but we'll want EDD in here to get it open, check it out. We'll want to talk to her insurance people, cross-check valuables. Just cover the bets, Peabody, on the very slim chance the message is a herring.'

'A red herring?'

'Why are they red, and what the hell does that expression really mean anyway? It's annoying.'

Eve took a moment, pressed her fingers to her eyes.

Your true and loyal friend.

The last words of the message played around and around in her head. She had to push them out. For now.

'Okay, this is going to be a freaking shitstorm. We need

to do the family notifications right away as this is going to leak fast. We need to get the PA to cover us on getting copies of whatever we can get. The threats, her client list, case files. Her firm's going to make the usual noises, and maybe louder than usual. The media's going to start salivating as soon as this message crap gets out, and it will.'

'Who'd kill for you?' Peabody waited until Eve lowered her hands. 'I mean who'd kill because somebody was rude to you, or, well, snotty?'

'Nobody leaps to mind. I tend to avoid relationships with the homicidal.'

'I don't mean a specific name, Dallas. A type, a category even. Like someone you helped, someone you maybe saved from harm. Or someone close to someone you helped or saved. That's a possibility. Someone who's followed your career is another. A wannabe. You get a lot of media, Dallas, whether you like it or not. And it's "or not," I get that. But you get a lot of media. You've closed a lot of big cases.'

'We've closed.'

'Yeah, but I'm not married to the kick-your-ass-sideways gorgeous Irish guy with more money than God. Who gets plenty of media, too. Add in all the buzz from the Icove case, Nadine's book on it, the major success of the vid.'

'Fuck.' Frustrated, a little headachy, Eve shoved her fingers through her hair. 'That's going to hound me forever. But you've got some clear thinking here, and it's the sort of direction we need to pursue. Someone who feels like they owe me, and twist. A wannabe who figures they'll *defend* me by doing what I can't. Kill off enemies, or someone perceived to be. Because screw it, Peabody, I haven't given Bastwick a thought since Barrow lost his appeal, more than a year ago.'

She stepped back into the bedroom, read the message again. 'She didn't show me respect,' Eve murmured. 'Let's hope that's not the thrust of the motive, because there's a list that could circle the damn planet of people who haven't shown me respect. I'm a goddamn cop. "Her life was a lie; her death our truth". Our? Does he have a partner? Is he talking about me – him and me?'

'It follows a theme, doesn't it? It's for you, and for jus- tice. Bastwick, criminal defense attorney, you the cop. Plus, somebody knows grammar and so on. The semicolon. How many killers do we know who'd use a semicolon?'

'Huh. That's a point. Okay, we're going to have to look at the cop, justice, disrespect deal, at the big, wide picture, but right now, let's focus in on the vic, and why her, specif- ically. High-profile, rich, attractive, with plenty of enemies.'

'Sounds like you,' Peabody said quietly. The concern that pressed on her chest showed in her dark eyes. 'Maybe that's another connection.'

'I'm not rich. Roarke's rich, and I don't deck myself out like she did every day.'

'You look good.'

'Gee, thanks, Peabody.'

'Look, you're tall, skinny, got the cheekbones and the

dent in the chin going. You look good, and you look good on camera. Tough, and okay, you come off as a cop even if you're decked out for one of Roarke's deals. Maybe it's a guy with some lust going, and this is his way of, you know, wooing you.'

'Screw it again.' Because that idea made her a little bit sick. 'Let's review the discs instead of speculating. And let's go ahead and call in the sweepers and the morgue.' Eve glanced back at the body. 'She needs to be taken care of.'

'The killer?' Peabody jutted a chin toward the note before she picked up her coat. 'He doesn't get that. Doesn't get that at all.'

The Eve Dallas series

Eve and Roarke are back in
Obsession in Death
out February 2015

Next in the Eve Dallas series

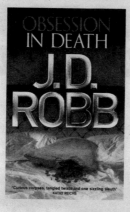

OBSESSION
IN DEATH
J. D.
ROBB

'Curious corpses, tangled twists and one sizzling sleuth'
KATHY REICHS

A crisp winter morning in New York. In a luxury apartment, the body of a woman lies stretched out on a huge bed. On the wall above, the killer has left a message in bold black ink: FOR LIEUTENANT EVE DALLAS, WITH GREAT ADMIRATION AND UNDERSTANDING.

Eve Dallas is used to unwanted attention. Famous for her high-profile cases and her marriage to billionaire businessman Roarke, she has learned to deal with intense public scrutiny and media gossip. But now Eve has become the object of a singular and deadly obsession. She has an 'admirer', who just can't stop thinking about her. Who is convinced they have a special bond. Who is planning to kill for her – again and again . . .

With time against her, Eve is forced to play a delicate – and dangerous – psychological dance. Because the killer is desperate for something Eve can never provide – approval. And once that becomes clear, Eve knows her own life will be at risk – along with those she cares about the most.

'This series gets better with every book' *Publishers Weekly*